For Laura,
I hope you enjoy
this as much as I did!
Mom

THE
BAG LADY
WAR

CAROL LEONARD SECOY

iUniverse, Inc.
New York   Bloomington

THE BAG LADY WAR

iUniverse books may be ordered through booksellers or by contacting:

iUniverse
1663 Liberty Drive
Bloomington, IN 47403
www.iuniverse.com
1-800-Authors (1-800-288-4677)

ISBN: 978-1-4502-2055-2 (pbk)
ISBN: 978-1-4502-2056-9 (ebk)

Library of Congress Control Number: 2010906381

Printed in the United States of America
iUniverse rev. date: 5/17/10

Special thanks to the staff of the California Institute for Women (Frontera) at Corona, California, and to the officers of the Santa Ana Police Department, none of whom may recognize the flight of fancy their information has taken.

Loving thanks to my family. The heavens are bright with the stars their tireless support and good humor have earned them.

This book may never have seen the light of day if not for my treasured friends of the Haywire critique group, who helped to comb the troublesome knots from it.

Well-behaved women seldom make history.

Laurel Thatcher Ulrich, 1975

Women are like tea bags.
You never know how strong they are until they get in hot water.

Anonymous

In profound gratitude to the real life
Josie and Theodore, Mil and Bliss, and Mabel and Gertie.
You made the world a brighter place.

INTRODUCTION

America was awash in crime. Scientists studied it, statisticians charted it, social workers theorized about it, the government bemoaned it, courts waffled over it, police grew jaded by it, citizens decried it, the church sermonized about it, and lawyers proliferated from it. Schools blamed parents for the delinquency that produced criminals, and parents blamed the schools. Gun control advocates blamed crime on guns, and the NRA blamed it on irresponsible people. But no one knew what to do about it.

By the 1990's, Santa Ana, California, population 210,000, was just another city in crisis, in a state whose over-generous welfare programs and easy access to drugs continued to seduce a growing number of down-and-outers. It was also home to gentle octogenarians Josie, Mabel, and Mil, who, despairing for their nation and for themselves, found the courage to turn things around.

PART ONE

ONE

They won't be there. Not in this deluge. Josie Winkworth struggled into her coat and rain hat, ready to grab her little wire cart and run for it the minute the rain let up. Minutes went by as she waited, knowing how risky it was to walk through the park. She looked at the clock again. *Mabel will be here for lunch at noon. I can do it if the rain will just stop. At least they won't be there to yell and throw things at me. It's my only chance until Sunday—they probably have to go to mass and behave on the Sabbath.*

Sudden shafts of dazzling sunlight pierced the sky, and Josie was out the door. Going as fast as an eighty-two-year-old can go, she made a dash across the park to George's market, carrying her folded-up cart.

The small neighborhood park was deserted. Gang activity discouraged use of it even in the best of weather, and today it was all the more uninviting. Its well-worn paths were slimy with mud and the soggy grass and benches left nowhere to sit. Few cars splashed by. Only the hum of traffic escaping the noise barrier along the freeway and the drone of a plane's descent into John Wayne Airport marred the serenity of this bright, freshly scrubbed morning.

With the letup in the rain, four teenage Latinos sauntered into the park. They wore stocking caps and oversized shirts that flapped,

3

untucked, over long, baggy pants that engulfed their shoes. They stood talking, hands in their pockets, when Josie's bright blue coat caught their attention. She had started back across the park, carefully picking her way along the muddy path, pulling her cart full of groceries. Like junkyard dogs, the boys sprang into action.

"Hey, ol' lady!" one of them called. They ran to intercept her, kicking up muddy water and drenching the ragged bottoms of their pants legs. Josie looked up to see them coming and made a feeble attempt to run. But she was no match for them. She froze in her tracks when they fanned out to cut off her escape. Turtle-like, she seemed to shrink into her heavy coat, leaving only wisps of white hair and a pair of terrified blue eyes staring out from beneath her floppy rain hat.

"Hey, *pendeja*, I was talkin' a' you!" came the voice again as the four youths moved in to surround her. Her mouth worked as if to speak but she made no sound. Again she tried to flee, but upon finding nowhere to turn she simply stood there, a cornered mouse awaiting her fate.

Locking her pleading eyes in the grip of his piercing black ones, the shortest one danced like a determined gnat in her face. If she tried to avert her eyes, he darted around to make sure his were there, too. His acne-scarred face boasted the shadow of dark adolescent fuzz, and the silver rings that pierced his nostril and lip announced that he was not to be messed with.

"Whatta we hafta do to get'cher attention? Huh? You got no respect for the First Street Boys? Wha-at?" His pubescent voice betrayed him in several octaves, but he made up for it by spitting a frothy glob of phlegm on the toe of her shoe.

"Stupid ol' bag," he muttered, wiping his mouth on the sleeve of his shirt. "We warned you enough times. You didn' git nobody's say-so t'be here." Again he thrust his face within inches of hers, bugging his eyes out at her as he did so. Terrified, she lurched backward, stumbling over her little cart and nearly falling.

The tallest of the boys, his black hair now bound pirate-style in a red and black bandana, eyed the little cart the little grocery cart she clung to for support.

"Whatcha got there, ol' lady?" he drawled. "Geritol and prunes?" He lazily twirled a toothpick between his teeth while his friends laughed and high-fived each other at his joke.

Feeding on Josie's terror, the fat, simple-looking one hiked up his sagging trousers and kicked her cart with his imitation Air Jordans. The cart caved in as though it were made of matchsticks. Encouraged by the group's laughter, he yanked the grocery bags from the cart and whirled them around, sending their contents flying in every direction. At the same time, the fourth one of the group, a skulking youth with a tattooed scorpion clinging to his neck, snatched the worn leather purse that hung from her shoulder and danced off with it into the park.

"No!" she cried, reaching into the empty air between them. She staggered after him, calling out, "Please, no! That's all I have!"

It became a boisterous game of Monkey in the Middle as they threw the purse back and forth over her head, luring her ever farther off the path. They laughed at her vain attempts to catch it each time it sailed by. The fat one had a hard time keeping up, encumbered by the drooping pants that shackled his stride. Stumbling over his trailing shoestrings and blowing like a harpooned whale, he was of little help to the others. They paused at the approaching wail of a police siren, but it went on by and left them to their fun.

Gasping for breath and rain hat askew, Josie looked around desperately for help. But at this hour, on this day that threatened more rain to follow, the park was still deserted. If anyone in the few cars that passed had seen through the trees and shrubs that screened the shortcut to the market they would have seen only boys at play.

Tiring of the game, the pirate intercepted the flying purse and deftly removed the wallet before upending it and dumping the contents onto the muddy ground. While the others scrabbled to pick through what they might want, he helped himself to the few bills in the wallet. Outraged at its meager contents, he threw the empty wallet back at her, where it bounced off her chest and joined the rest of her things in the mud.

"Thirty-two bucks!" he shouted for the others to hear. "Thirty-two fuckin' bucks! That's all you have? Jeezuz Christ, ol' lady, if *that's* all you have you ain't worth *shit!* You ain't even worth messin' with."

He held up the few bills for the others to see, prompting a chorus of jeers.

"Thirty-two fuckin' bucks!" he repeated, waving the money around in disgust. "Barely enough for four Fat Charlies and some cigarettes. Well, thank you very much for nothin'." He looked up to curse the tree that dripped on him from overhead, threatening to make him look uncool.

"Thinkin' you could dis us an' keep walkin' in this park?" he went on, brushing at his rain-spotted shirt. "How many times we tol' you to stay outta here, anyhow? The First Street Boys says who does what aroun' here. An' it takes more'n these thirty-two fuckin' bucks t'get our permission t'be here." Again he waved the money around as proof of her deceit.

The short one crowded in on the panicked woman once more, adding in a syrupy voice that broke now and then in spite of his attempt to control it, "You go to the police an' you be sorry, lady. Maybe you die. We been watchin' you. We know where you live, an' nobody'll miss your dried up ol' *concha*." He pointed to the fat one, who stood panting beside him. "You tell on us, an' we sic Gordo here on you."

The fat one's dull expression took on a doltish gleam.

"Yeah," he said, his words wallowing thickly in his throat. "Gordo getchoo!"

The others laughed with him, cheering him on as he stroked the growing bulge in his pants. He had begun to drool, little trickles of saliva quivering at the edges of his meaty lips. He took a tentative step toward the woman, looking to the others for permission. But the pirate, who seemed to be in charge, had lost interest now that he had a little money.

"She's not worth messin' with," he growled, cramming the money into his pants pocket. "Too stupid and too old." He turned to go, waving her away in disgust. "Lucky fer you we have better things to do than mess with ol' bags like you. Git'cher stupid shit and git the hell outta here before we turn Gordo loose on ya. He likes teachin' people a little respect. You come aroun' here again, there won't be no stoppin' 'im."

He waited for her to move. But Josie still stood there, frozen in place.

"Are ya *deaf*, ya stupid ol' bitch?" he shouted, snatching the rain hat from her head, leaving her rumpled white hair to poke out in all directions. "Git your damn shit and git the fuck outta here, *now!*"

She dropped to her knees in the muddy grass and began scooping up her belongings. The fat one they called Gordo found it amusing to torment her at her work. A few shoves of his muddy shoe nearly sent her sprawling. When she was unable to get back up on her feet without crawling to a tree for support, they howled with laughter.

Tired of toying with her, and with enough money for the Hamburger Den up the street, they set off across the park, laughing and bantering in Spanish. They sailed her hat back and forth among themselves, unconcerned that their demand for respect had flown in the face of their disrespect for her.

Nylons ripped and knees bleeding, Josie dragged her lopsided grocery cart back to the security of her gated apartment complex. She met no one on the way who might have helped her, or who might have remarked on the storm or the sparkling beauty of this morning. Grateful she hadn't wet her pants and too much of a lady to cause a scene, she wouldn't give in to her hysteria until she got home.

Mabel Rockwell freely came and went with her gate pass to Josie's. She wrestled her old green Buick to the curb beneath Josie's kitchen window and, with a light step that belied the weight of eighty years of unbridled appetite, quickly made her way up the walk. The rising wind caught her graying black hair, threatening to loosen it from where it was anchored in a bun at the nape of her neck. She leaned into the wind to protect the carefully wrapped lemon meringue pie she held cradled in one arm, while with her free arm she tried to shield her flying hair. The tantalizing aroma of freshly baked bread lured her like a beacon to Josie's door.

No one could bake like Josie, she always said, even though Mabel and her husband, Earl, had spent almost forty years running their own bakery—before the robber had shot Earl dead, right there in the bakery, right under her nose. But she had promised herself not to dwell on that today and ruin this special occasion. Earl would have understood.

She paused to pet the golden tabby that ran to meet her. He didn't seem to belong to anyone in particular, but bestowed the honor of his company upon those who would feed him. One of the residents of the apartment complex had dubbed him Captain Beefheart, after a cat in a book he had read. But Josie wouldn't be tricked into saying *fart* and instead called him Buzzy, which made him seem more like her own.

Mabel knew how Josie loved the cat and that she spent many a lonely evening with him draped over her lap, talking to him and petting him while he filled her apartment with the raucous purring that had inspired his name. Even if he were just a cat, he was the comforting presence of another warm body.

When no one answered her knock, Mabel produced the key Josie had entrusted to her and let herself in, shooing away the disappointed cat. "Yoo-hoo! Josie, it's me, Mabel!" she called out, dropping her handbag onto the spindly-legged entry table and attempting to straighten her hair in the wavery mirror that hung above it.

Josie's studio apartment was really just one large room with a closet and a bathroom; clearly, she was not home. Mabel hoped Josie hadn't forgotten inviting her for lunch. She took her pie to the kitchen alcove, following the fragrance of the Parker House rolls that lay cooling under a tea towel on the counter. They were still warm, which meant Josie hadn't been gone long. Knowing her dear friend would urge her to help herself, she did—but not until she had filled the teakettle and started it heating, to be ready for their celebration.

She downed two of the delicate rolls while inspecting Josie's profusion of houseplants, vigorous specimens slipped from greenery in the building's common area, and settled in on the daybed to greet Josie's family. A framed photo of a golden-haired little girl, enveloped in a fluffy party dress, sat on the maple end table next to one of a clean-cut, smiling young man in army fatigues.

"Well, Jennie and Bobby, don't you look spiffy today. Where'd your mother go?" It seemed natural to talk to them, for their mother always did. She could never look at them without feeling pity for poor little Jennie, dead of leukemia at the tender age of eight, and for Bobby, his parents' bright hope for the future, killed in the steaming jungles of Vietnam before he was even old enough to vote.

Her mind turned to the thought of her own tiny babies, who had, each in turn, died on the day of its birth. Each an unbearable loss. But, she thought, looking at the sweet faces in the photos, if it's possible to suffer even more, it would be from losing a precious, pink-cheeked child or an energetic young adult, full of promise—children you had grown to love with all your heart.

At an angle, above a plaque emblazoned with the Pledge of Allegiance and sprouting an American flag, sat a picture of another soldier. Solemn with the weight of authority, he wore the full dress uniform of World War II.

Theodore. The love of Josie's life. Shot and killed by a prowler as he lay beside her in their own bed.

For what seemed the millionth time, Mabel wondered at the strength of her friend, who could endure all this loss and still be the sweetest, kindest person in the world. In fact, she thought, if the world just had more Josies in it, what a wonderful place it would be.

At that moment the door burst open, and there stood a disheveled Josie. Her beautiful blue coat was splotched with mud, and blood seeped through the mud on her knees. "Oh, Mabel!" was all she could say before dissolving into tears in the warmth of her friend's quickly-offered arms.

"Josie! What happened! Oh, my dear. Here, sit down and tell me what happened to you! Oh, poor thing, your knees are bleeding."

Flustered, she guided Josie to the little armchair that time had molded to every curve of her body, and hovered over her, at a loss for what to do next. Josie's wailing completely unnerved her, and something awful had happened to her grocery cart.

Outside, the cat yowled to get in out of the wind and rain that had begun again.

"Let me get a washcloth for those knees, Josie," she called, careening off to the bathroom. She returned a moment later, with a glassful of water, as well.

"What in the world happened to you? Should I call the doctor … or the police?"

Josie only sat with her hands over her face, sobbing, so Mabel carefully rolled down her knee-high nylons and dabbed at her injured knees with the wet cloth. Luckily, Josie's lovely print challis dress, reserved for special occasions, had escaped unharmed. But Mabel winced at the mud and grass stains on her coat, a recent purchase from the Salvation Army thrift store. She knew how lucky Josie had been to find such a beautiful coat in her tiny size, in a color that enhanced her soft blue eyes and delicate fair skin. And now look at it.

"Oh, Mabel!" Josie cried. "Those awful kids in the park! I just needed a few things at the market … thought they wouldn't be there in the rain." She pulled a tissue from her pocket and loudly blew her nose.

"You know those kids who hang out in the park. Usually they don't bother me much. They just holler mean things or throw things at me. But this time … this time…" She resumed sobbing and blowing her nose.

"What in the world did they do?" asked a wide-eyed Mabel. She pulled Josie to her feet and gently eased her out of the soiled coat, looking her over for injuries before helping her back into her chair.

By now the cat had given up and found shelter elsewhere. His cries were replaced by a fresh bout of wind-whipped rain rattling its way through the downspout and slashing at the storm-darkened windows.

"Oh, Mabel, it's so embarrassing! Pushing and shoving me, saying I can't walk in the park..." She closed her eyes tightly to blot out the memory, reaching to the small table beside her chair for another tissue.

"They took my purse and said if I ever came by there again, or called the police, they'd hurt me ... or maybe kill me!" She covered her face and struggled to contain a fresh bout of hysteria.

"Why, those hoodlums!" Mabel replied. "The very idea!"

She carefully laid Josie's coat on the daybed and encompassed her friend in ample arms, bending to rock and soothe her with little murmurs of, "It's okay now, love. It's okay, Josie honey. Oh, my poor dear."

But her eyes, too, brimmed with tears. "They took your purse? Right off your arm? Oh, Josie, whatever will you do?"

Josie told what the boys had done, humiliating and robbing her.

"I got my purse back, though," she said. "But it was so embarrassing, being shoved around and made fun of ..." She paused to wipe the tears from her glasses.

"Everyone around here is scared of them," she continued, "and most of the homes over by the park have bars on the windows now. You never see children playing there anymore."

She fought back more tears, nervously twisting a fresh tissue until it was shredded beyond use. "Why do they want to be mean? I wasn't bothering them."

Not knowing what to say or do, Mabel just stood patting and soothing her.

"Here I am, using up my savings to pay for this high-security apartment," she went on. "Gates, guards, fences. But I'm only safe if I never *leave* it. Now what's the sense of *that*." Not trusting the strength of her trembling hands, she allowed Mabel to help her take a few sips of water.

"I know what you mean," replied Mabel with a roll of her eyes. "My house is a booby trap of alarms and locks and bars, but for it to be any good, you have to stay locked up inside. We might as well be in jail."

She put the glass back on the table beside Josie and sat down heavily on the daybed, careful to avoid Josie's coat. The screech of the kettle reminded her that a cup of tea was just what they needed. Helping Josie to the bathroom, she assured her she'd feel better if she freshened up and tried to relax while Mabel fixed tea.

Josie returned to find that Mabel had produced two steaming cups and a crystal sugar bowl and creamer on a small lacquered tray. When the tea had worked its magic and they found Josie's wounds to be only superficial, they knew they had to get on with their day and put this ugly incident behind them. They made an event of setting out lunch on the chrome dinette in the alcove, lighting the candles that stretched Josie's budget, and doing their best to talk of cheerful things. Josie had lost her appetite and only picked at her food, but Mabel thoroughly enjoyed the tangy four-bean salad, meatloaf and gravy, homemade rolls, and lemon meringue pie.

It was a feast for them. Their slender budgets seldom let them splurge like this. Today they would even steep their tea bags only once, for they were celebrating the third anniversary of their meeting, the only senior citizens in a support group for people who had lost a loved one to violence.

The group met every Tuesday evening at the Santa Ana Library. It had been a hardship for them, because Mabel hated to drive after dark, and Josie had to take a cab. But their case workers urged them to attend. It was a frightening experience, being exposed to the aimless groups of homeless, drunk, or demented people who hung out in the sprawling complex that the library shared with the police station and the courthouse. Mabel braved it alone, but Josie was lucky to find an earnest young Ethiopian cabdriver named Hali, who made it his weekly responsibility to escort her from the door of his cab to the door of the library and back. He assured her that these people weren't dangerous but just wanted to be near the food-handout station that a local group set up every day on the courthouse lawn. Josie wasn't so sure, and swore she would never go there if Hali couldn't take her. She was fascinated with Hali's tales of Ethiopia and loved his gentle manner.

Mabel had attended sporadically for almost a year before Josie's circumstances brought her to the meetings. Being the only senior citizens in the group they had immediately clung together. However, they found it most unbecoming to tell their troubles to all these strangers, and soon left the group to commiserate in the privacy of their own homes. But they took with them the slogan recited at the opening of each meeting: "I have a life to live. I will honor my loved ones by living it." Repeating it every morning, or anytime they felt alone and blue, usually made them feel better—for awhile.

But that was all in the past. It was the present they had to deal with now. They had come a long way in adjusting to their tenuous existence without husbands or family, and Mabel was determined not to let Josie's experience in the park ruin their celebration. However, today's lunch—which had promised if not a festive atmosphere, at least a bittersweet one—was subdued and occasionally interrupted by Josie's tears.

"I'd go to the police if I thought it would do any good," she snuffled, lifting her glasses to dry her eyes with her napkin. "But what if that bunch really does come after me? I'll just have to wait for someone to take me shopping, I guess. And forget my walks in the park. But those poor squirrels—they wait for my old bread ..."

Hoping to divert her attention to something else, Mabel broke in with, "It's nearly time for *All Our Tomorrows*, dear," and, with effort, rose to clear the table. "Maybe it'll take our minds off those hoodlums in the park. Besides, we might find out whose baby Sabrina is carrying and whether Todd is really Amy's missing twin brother."

"And old Aunt Clara, lost in a snowstorm in Alaska," Josie added, glad for something else to think about. She picked up the rest of the dishes and followed Mabel to the sink. "Imagine! A sixty-year-old woman dyeing her hair and changing her name to *Brandy*. Thinking she can pass for forty, and answering that ad for a wife in *Alaska*, of all places! How many times has she been married, anyway?"

They washed and dried the dishes, recounting Aunt Clara's many husbands and the unbelievable dramas surrounding each one, clucking over the problems the soap opera's characters always seemed to bring upon themselves. Then they took their usual places in the cozy living room, which also served as Josie's bedroom; Josie in her little armchair and Mabel settled in among the piles of pillows on the daybed.

Conversation ceased when, with a great swooping of the familiar theme song, their program began. They watched in silence, each relieved of trying to be cheerful for the other. Their minds tumbled from the shock of Josie's attack. For the first time they noticed the program's endless commercials aimed at the elderly: adult diapers, denture stickum, and cemetery lots. It was impossible not to think of their own mortality.

They hardly heard a word of today's episode as horrid images paraded through their heads. They envisioned being trapped in their homes and found dead by strangeres—or mugged by punks, left disabled, and then dumped in a cheap nursing home with no one to look in on them.

At the same moment they looked at each other. The horror each saw reflected on the other's face sent a heart-pounding panic rushing through them. They were through with the pretense of watching this soap opera.

"Josie, what will happen when we can't take care of ourselves anymore?" quavered Mabel. "When I can't drive anymore?" She couldn't believe she was saying these things. She had always feared the mere voicing of her scary thoughts could make them come true.

"I know, Mabel," Josie answered in a tiny voice. "I never dreamed I'd be in such a predicament. I mean, I thought since I was a teacher, and we had the hardware store …" She began to cry again. "We really did try to do everything right, Theodore and I. Whoever dreamed I'd end up like this, alone and scared, barely making ends meet? But here I am, just taking up space, with nothing to do but worry." Chin trembling, she sat locked in the debilitating fear only the desperate can know.

"How much worse can it get?" she continued. "I thought it was terrible when the bank took our hardware store, when we couldn't keep up with those big building centers that popped up all over. But they took our house, too, that we'd mortgaged to save the hardware store … And then I lost Theodore to some … some …" She stopped, unable to speak a word bad enough to describe the prowler who had come halfway through the open window that night. "And now a nasty bunch of juvenile delinquents has me trapped inside this little apartment. What in the world is next?"

Mabel sighed. "If we could just live in one of those senior developments, where they take care of you and feed you and bus you around. Where we'd be with other people. It seems most of our old friends are dead or too feeble to get around, like Esther and Marlene. Or dying by inches in a nursing home, like Harry Epps and Emma Johnson. And it's only a matter of time till we're in the same fix."

She shuddered, chilled at the thought. They sat in silence for a time, oblivious to the drama unfolding on TV.

"Well, I guess we have to look for a bright side," Josie said, reaching to rap her knuckles superstitiously on the small wooden table beside her. "We're lucky to have our health, you know. Just a little high blood pressure and a bout of arthritis now and then. Well, you do have your trick knee, and I have these hearing aids … and we're both a bit forgetful. But, at our ages, our health could be a lot worse. And we have dear Mil and Bliss. They're *definitely* a blessing. Of course, with Bliss pushing ninety it's just a matter of time until *he* won't be able to drive and cart us around."

This dreadful thought left them speechless. They could only stare dumbly at the TV, blind to the drama's twists and turns of intrigue and the titillating glimpses of what was promised for tomorrow. It dawned on them in a rush that their lives were no different from those of the characters in the soap opera; there was always worse to come.

Before Josie could turn off the TV, a news clip followed of Senator Edmund Farley, ranting about his war on crime. Portly and officious as ever, he was determined to convince the nation that Social Security and Medicare were luxuries the nation could no longer afford.

"People are living longer and in greater numbers," he cried, his pudgy forefinger stabbing at the camera while his jowls shook in oratorical zeal, "using up these dwindling funds at an alarming rate! And unnecessarily, as we have shown you! Why, many of our senior citizens don't even *need* that extra income from Social Security. It's just gravy on the meatloaf, you might say, for which the working stiffs of America must pay!"

A dramatic pause.

"What better use of that money," he asked, grabbing the podium as though it were an escaping hoodlum, "than to build more prisons! With your help we can lock up the criminals who hold us hostage and remove them from our streets!" He emphasized his foolproof idea with a slam of his fist on the villainous podium, and waited triumphantly for applause, his arms folded over his imposing belly and his head bobbing up and down in a way that reminded Josie and Mabel of the old Italian dictator, Benito Mussolini.

"Heroic!" he resumed, again pounding his fist in appreciation of the nation's martyred elders. "This generation of elders would go down in history as downright *heroic!* Remember, it was they who gave their lives for us in the Great War. And now their surviving brethren can have the honor of returning safe passage, so to speak, to their crime-plagued fellow Americans. Why, they'd be the equals of our cherished Founding Fathers! No other generation in the history of the nation will have contributed so much. Their sacrifice will make the country a safer place for *everyone.*"

They'd heard his spiel before, but, added to the despair this day had brought, the threat of losing their pensions had the women on the edges of their seats. An explosive mixture of emotions, fueled and fanned by fear, brewed darkly in the air between them.

"Don't tell me *he* thinks it's okay to rob us, too!" cried Mabel when she could find her tongue, her dark eyes flashing. "Good grief, he's no better than those thugs in the park. Little as it is, we need that money to survive!"

Josie clutched the arms of her chair, flushed with anger. "He's a fine one to talk about using up the nation's money," she sputtered. "Look at him. You can see he's never had to miss a meal. Living at public expense in a fine house, with a fine car, junkets all over the place …"

Mabel interrupted, outraged that a raid on the Social Security fund could even be an issue. "Josie, he's *determined* to get his hands on that money. And what do you suppose those congressmen would do with it if they got it? Ha! That's no mystery. They'd give themselves big, fat raises, like they gave themselves last year, when they cut all kinds of things out of the federal budget. And we're powerless against them. I'd like to see someone tell him he doesn't need his *Senate* pension," she went on angrily, "and that it was simply going to be taken away. Boy, he'd squawk to high heaven! And how come he can take away *our* pensions, that we've paid for, and no one can touch *his*, that we've also paid for?"

By now the newscasters were covering the weather, which was in the process of clearing, but neither of them was listening.

Josie wavered between bewilderment and fury. "We paid into Social Security for over forty years," she said emphatically, as though Senator Farley might have forgotten that fact. "Whether we wanted to or not. It was *required* of us. So why shouldn't we have it? Just because we don't sit out there begging with all those street people doesn't mean we're rich. Besides, we're too old to start over, and who would hire us, anyway?"

Mabel was lost in her own thoughts. She was about to lose her house, as well, if she didn't start making payments on her delinquent property taxes. She'd been too embarrassed to talk about it to anyone, but now realized she had no choice but to sell it and maybe take an apartment here, in the same building with Josie. Her house was too old and had too many problems, anyway. Sort of like herself, she thought wryly. Without Earl to see about things it had become a never-ending burden, always needing something she didn't know what to do about.

On top of that, it was stuffed from basement to rafters with a lifetime of accumulation. She felt weak every time she thought about the enormity of a move.

"I guess they can just have target practice on all of us old people," she offered, emphasizing one outrage with yet another. "That would be the quickest way to get rid of the whole useless bunch of us and save the country the expense of keeping us alive."

Josie snorted, "Well, now, that's a silly thing to say, Mabel. That's no answer."

She thought for a moment and added, "But if I knew how to use a gun, I'd wage my *own* war on crime, starting with that bunch of bullies in the park. I'd have open season on all the crooks and spare the country *their* cost and *their* nuisance. That seems a better idea to me than pulling the rug out from under law-abiding old people. And I bet it would save a lot more money, too. You heard what Senator Farley said it costs to keep one man in jail for a year. Forty thousand dollars! For one man! And they're more useless than we are!"

Mabel had to laugh in spite of her anger. "Oh, Josie, what a thing for you to say. Your own war on crime. It might save money, all right, but … what a picture! You on a shooting spree! Then *you'd* be the one in prison!"

She continued to chuckle until Josie asked, "Well, would it be so bad to live in prison? That's not the worst thing that could happen to me, Mabel. At least I'd be safe, and my financial problems would be over. And you said, yourself, if we have to stay locked up in our homes to be safe, we may as well be in prison."

That was when it hit her: the plan that would solve everything. She bolted out of her chair, electrified with insight.

"Mabel!" she gasped. "That's the answer! Imagine life in a totally secure place, where you're fed three meals a day and probably even snacks in between. You could watch TV, play cards, and read all you want." She stared, unseeing, over Mabel's head, entranced by the images playing in her head.

"It wouldn't be much different from those senior developments you were talking about, except you wouldn't get bused anywhere. If you became ill, you'd be taken care of. Your laundry is done for you, and your clothing provided …"

She grew more animated by the moment as a bewildered Mabel looked on.

"On top of that," she continued, shaking her finger in Mabel's startled face, "we could do our country the favor of getting rid of a bunch of costly crooks. We have nowhere to go, anyway, so being locked up wouldn't be so bad, now, would it? Just think—we'd have no worries and could finally relax!" Cheeks flushed and eyes dancing, she held her breath, waiting for Mabel's response.

The TV chattered on in the momentary silence. Mabel was aghast, her face grown comically slack. "Josie," she said slowly, hardly trusting herself to speak, "are you talking about living in jail? With all those murderers and thieves? You must be joking!"

But, shocked as she was, a seed had been planted. And, of its own accord, the seed began to germinate as she sat gaping at her friend.

Josie threw herself into her chair, her look of resolve scattering Mabel's unspoken protestations. A sudden bright shaft of sunshine flooded the room, highlighting Josie's small figure like a well-placed spotlight. She hurried on.

"Don't you remember the program we saw about prisons on TV? How, with the ACLU monitoring them they've become more like country clubs? Old folks aren't asked to do anything too hard, and if their needs aren't met, why, lawyers jump right on it. That's where we should be, Mabel! At least there are young people there. It wouldn't be like a nursing home, where everyone is old and sick and just waiting to die."

Josie could almost see the wheels and gears cranking in Mabel's head. Earl had usually done the thinking for both of them, and now Mabel's mouth worked wordlessly as she struggled to process this information all by herself. Somehow, she accomplished what was, for her, a quantum leap of imagination. They looked at each other in stunned silence, their thoughts welded into a single, revolutionary concept.

"But ... but ... how? But ... what would people say? I don't know ... I don't want to do anything bad, Josie," stuttered Mabel. Her fleshy chins wobbled in rhythm as she vigorously patted at her face with a handful of tissues. She had stretched her mind well beyond its rational limits, and it now slogged along, lost in uncharted gray matter.

Josie took Mabel's hands firmly in hers.

"Mabel, I don't want to do anything bad, either," she said, still aglow in the late-afternoon sun, her face only inches from her distraught friend's. "But, don't you see, if we get rid of *bad guys*, that's *good!* If we eliminate enough criminals, at forty thousand dollars apiece for every year they're in prison, the government can use the money we've saved them to take care of *us!* And we'll be helping to make the country a safer place! What do we have to lose, Mabel? Either we can die wards of the state in some depressing nursing home, or we can die having done something useful for our country. Like ... yes! Like one of George H. Bush's 'Thousand Points of Light'!"

Josie's eyes gleamed with insight. She'd never seen anything so clearly.

"We've both done things we never dreamed we could do. If we plan this right, it could be easier than we think." She arose, trancelike, with one hand upraised to the heavens and the other over her heart, an evangelist locked in the throes of a spiritual breakthrough. "Remember the words of John F. Kennedy," she exclaimed, gazing proudly over Mabel's head at unseen throngs of fellow patriots. "Ask not what your country can do for *you*; ask what *you* can do for your *country!*"

Mabel had become a leaden lump among the sofa pillows, watching her friend in astonishment. This couldn't be the mousy Josie she knew.

"But Josie, you know what fraidy cats we are. We both hate guns and scary things. I don't see how ..."

Josie-turned-evangelist beamed an all-knowing smile. "Mabel, with everything else we've had to do, we can learn to use a gun. Then we won't be charity cases when we run out of money. We'll have *earned* our keep."

They talked on into the early evening over many cups of tea, nibbling on leftovers from lunch, until the unique plan made sense even to Mabel. There was a job for them! And the promise of a secure future! Like the young men in the park to whom they owed their inspiration, and to whom they would forever be bound in history, they couldn't have imagined the magnitude of their simple plan.

TWO

It was happening again. The rustling at the window. Theodore pushing to an upright position beside her in bed. The deafening roar of the gun, echoing endlessly in her head. Unable to move ... or scream. The shattering stillness that followed. And blood ... oh, yes, the blood! The waves of shock that washed over her, carrying her away on fuzzy, throbbing clouds of nothingness. The need to do something—but what? The fear—that unholy fear... Gordo! Was it Gordo there at the window? Struggling, numbing fear ...

Josie found herself balancing on the edge of her bed, desperately fumbling for the phone that wasn't there. Slowly it came to her; this was another time, another place. This was not the home she had shared with Theodore. Her bed was now in the living room of a small apartment, her phone on the counter in the kitchen.

Trembling and exhausted from the adrenaline rush of her dream, she let herself fall back onto the narrow daybed that was a lonely substitute for her marriage bed of over fifty years, in the cramped apartment that had replaced her comfortable home of thirty-five years. Relief that she wasn't reliving Theodore's murder was broadsided by her bottomless rage that the whole, senseless thing had ever happened at all.

Still shaking, she began to cry softly. Like all the other times, her nightmare had been a cruel replay of Theodore's death. There would be no more sleep tonight.

She stepped into the fuzzy blue scuffs that sat in their usual place beneath the bed and shuffled to the tiny closet for her robe, reaching to turn up the thermostat on the way. Her gaze lingered where Theodore looked down at her from the two gold-framed portraits that hung, side by side, over her daybed. One was of the shy young couple on their wedding day, and the other, two smiling best friends celebrating fifty years of marriage. She desperately missed his reassuring pats on the rump and his impish voice calling her "Bitsy" or "Tuffy." She felt certain no man could have been more honorable or more appreciative of the slightest thing she ever did for him. With a sigh she turned and made the rounds of the windows, checking again that they were locked, and then padded over to her well-worn armchair.

Once more she was thankful for old, middle-of-the-night movies. They took her mind back to happier days; the days of her youth, the days of Theodore's love. Lost in the song and dance of Ginger Rogers and Fred Astaire, the antics of Laurel and Hardy, or the drama of Charles Boyer and Ingrid Bergman, her mind could heal again. Until the next time.

At dawn, still sitting in her chair, Josie awakened in a sweat, thinking she'd really seen Gordo at the window during the night. But her morning talk with Theodore had set her straight.

She feared the neighbors would think her crazy if they heard her talking to him. They knew he was dead. But it was the only thing that kept her sane. She had always depended on his counsel. All she had to do when she needed to talk with Theodore was to call in the willing cat, so anyone within earshot would think she was talking to him.

Buzzy now lay curled up snoozing on the daybed, his rumbling purr filling the room while Josie ate her breakfast of oatmeal and toast. She didn't seem to mind that Buzzy's ever-kneading claws had left a trail of snags on the floral upholstery of her new daybed. It was a price she willingly paid for his company.

All she had been able to think about this morning was their plan. No matter how she looked at it in the light of day, it seemed ridiculous. What had they been thinking when they talked of killing people! Two old women who could barely stand to swat a fly, let alone shoot someone. But it had seemed so *real* last night. So *possible.*

Her mind churned as she went through the motions of tidying her already spotless apartment. She scrubbed out a few garments in the sink and draped the newly washed clothes on the short, retractable line mounted in the kitchen. Thinking of all the quarters she saved never failed to give her pleasure. Sheets and towels were now the only things she paid to wash in the laundry room.

Even while berating herself for thinking she and Mabel could pull off such an outlandish plan, the theme from last night's talk continued to haunt her. *Freedom doesn't mean people have the right to do bad things. And people who do bad things shouldn't be granted the same rights that good people have earned.* What if the men who shot Theodore and Earl had clearly understood this and had not murdered or robbed anyone? How different Mabel's and Josie's lives would be!

Mabel was supposed to be looking for the gun Earl kept somewhere in their basement. She had dreaded the task, for she hadn't been down there in years, and didn't know where to start. But their plan couldn't proceed without the gun. She had no choice but to find it.

Meanwhile, Josie tried to stay busy, nervously keeping her eye on the clock over the TV. What if Mabel couldn't find the gun? What if she'd had second thoughts, too, and decided to forget the whole thing? Why didn't she call with a progress report?

She contemplated another cup of tea to soothe her nerves. And, she thought, maybe her budget could spare a few sugar cookies to go with it. Why not? If things went according to their plan, it wouldn't be long before she'd never again have to worry about making ends meet.

With her teacup rattling in its cookie-laden saucer, she made her way to the armchair. Nestling the cup and saucer on the table beside it, she settled in to occupy her mind with one of her soaps, *Inheritors of the Wind*. But she couldn't concentrate, and today's episode became a blur of drama mixed with commercials. When the phone rang, she jumped up to answer it, stiffly dodging the clothesline.

It was Mabel, and she was crying.

"Oh, Josie, "she sobbed. "My poor, dear Earl. How I *loved* that man." For a moment she couldn't speak and only sobbed into the phone. "Going through his things … it was like being with him again. I don't want to be alone, Josie. I found the gun. And bullets … lots of bullets. I hope you're not busy, 'cause I'm coming right over." With that, she hung up.

Josie sat with the receiver in her hand, stung with shame. Why hadn't she thought to help Mabel? She should have remembered from her own experience how difficult it might be for Mabel to sort through Earl's things.

Damn! she thought, allowing herself to use that forbidden word. *Damn* those people who just live to cause other people grief! Hanging up the phone, she could only sit there, her anger rekindling the logic of their novel plan. *In a civilized society, bad people shouldn't be rewarded with the freedoms good people enjoy.*

She was still sitting there when the doorbell rang. It couldn't be Mabel already, could it? She pulled herself together, hoping she didn't look as disoriented as she felt. Again avoiding the clothesline, she hurried to the door.

The peephole revealed her helpful friend and neighbor, Herb Watson. He and his wife, Pearl, had moved into their apartment shortly after Josie had moved into hers. Pearl was mostly confined to a wheelchair because of advancing multiple sclerosis, and Herb doted on her. It was a May-December marriage; Pearl was considerably younger than Herb, a handsome man of about Josie's age.

As much as she loved Herb and Pearl, she didn't want to get sidetracked right now. But she couldn't pretend not to be home, with the TV blaring away. She hoped it wasn't an emergency with Pearl.

Fortunately, Herb's visit was brief, and he gave her a few magazines they had finished and invited her and Mabel for Laurel and Hardy videos on Saturday afternoon. She was delighted to accept and sent him happily on his way. Not only did she love Laurel and Hardy, but Herb made the best popcorn in town. He was also wonderful at helping her with little things that baffled her, like adjusting the clocks between standard and daylight saving time, and often invited her to ride along with them to the market.

Back in the kitchen her mind returned to Mabel. Probably she'd been too upset to think about lunch, so Josie busied herself making up a bowl of Mabel's favorite tuna salad, with chopped onions and celery and pickle relish. She was just putting it into the refrigerator when she heard the unmistakable roaring and lurching and scrunching of tires that announced Mabel's attempt to park along the curb outside her kitchen window. She gathered up the sleeping cat, put him out into the cool, thin sunshine, and waited in the doorway for Mabel as she came puffing up the sidewalk.

"Oh, Mabel!" she said, reaching for Mabel's arm and tenderly assisting her into the room, "I've been so worried about you. I never thought about what we were asking you to do …"

Mabel took Josie's face between her soft hands and patted it gently, saying, "Josie, honey, I'm okay now. Really."

She took a moment to compose herself.

"I'm sorry, dear. I didn't know … I guess I didn't expect such a reaction from handling Earl's things." Her eyes misted as she struggled for words. She did her best to stifle another outburst.

Josie threw her arms around her and they cried and laughed and rocked in the comfort of each other's arms. Then they made their way to their customary places in the living room, Josie in her armchair and Mabel nestled among the pillows on the daybed.

"Well, here we are," said Mabel, straining forward to remove several boxes of bullets and a small silver handgun from the pockets of her raincoat. She studied the gun suspiciously before handing it to Josie, whose immediate reaction was to recoil from it. Cautiously reaching out her hand, she asked Mabel to promise it had no bullets in it.

"Bullets?" Mabel replied. "Gee, I don't know. How do you tell if a gun has bullets in it?"

"Mabel!" Josie gasped, feet scrabbling, nearly tipping her chair over backward in her frenzy to get away from the gun. "Put that thing down and don't aim it! Here," she pointed, "on the coffee table!" She looked as though someone had struck her. "We could kill ourselves! Or each other!"

Reality washed over their bright idea like a rogue wave over a child's sandcastle. Neither of them had a clue as to how to handle this gun, let alone use it, or even protect themselves from it. Treating it like a time bomb, Mabel warily placed it on the table between them, where they stared at it, and each other, dumbfounded.

Eyes glued to the gun, Josie finally said, "We're going to have to find someone to teach us how to handle that thing if we're really going to … you know, use it."

Mabel nodded, afraid to move.

"Boy," she said, "I'm lucky I didn't shoot myself, or someone else, with that thing bouncing around in my pocket."

The enormity of that thought, and the absurdity of their total naiveté, started them to laughing. Soon they were shrieking and holding their sides, sagging in their chairs with tears running down their cheeks. Each time one caught the other's eye it provoked more shrieks of laughter. It was some time before they could compose themselves between splutters of laughter and groans of pain at their aching sides.

"Let's have a tuna sandwich and think this over," Josie said, wiping tears from her eyes. "Have you had lunch yet?"

Mabel shook her head, amazed she hadn't even thought about it, for little came between Mabel and a meal.

As they sat eating and sipping their tea in her snug alcove, Josie got up the nerve to broach the subject that hung in the air between them.

"What do you think, Mabel? Any second thoughts?"

Mabel thought Josie must be reading her mind. Unable to meet Josie's eyes, she started fussing with her napkin.

"Oh, honey, I just can't do it. What were we thinking! I can't just walk up to someone ... and shoot him!" She continued folding and refolding her napkin, creasing it neatly with her thumbnail, still not looking up. "My job was to find the gun, and I did. But we both must have been crazy last night."

The *click-click* of the gardener's clippers beneath Josie's window was the only sound in the room. Mabel finally dared to meet Josie's eyes.

"Those darn kids in the park just made us crazy, that's all there is to it," she explained, her eyes asking forgiveness. "I'm not saying living in prison is a bad idea, Josie, but, for heaven's sake, whatever made us think we could go around killing people!" She looked so apologetic it made Josie laugh.

Still smiling, Josie rose to reheat the teakettle, reckoning this could be at least a three-cup session. Her stooped figure was hardly taller than the chair on which she had been sitting.

"We might be crazy, Mabel, but don't doubt that we're on to something. An idea as different as this *would* give you reason to scoff. But just because it's never been done doesn't make it wrong. Don't forget how grateful we would have been if someone had done this for us, so those creeps would never have lived to murder our husbands! Think about it, Mabel. We have an important job to do. People we don't even know are counting on us."

As usual, Mabel was wavering. Decision making had never been easy for her. She sat woodenly holding her sandwich, eyes looking for an escape, and beginning to sweat.

"But Josie," she began, picking what looked like a cat hair from her sandwich, "this is going to be hard. I lay awake all night wondering how we'd know the bad guys from the good ones, and how I'd get the courage to really pull the trigger, and what we'd do if we got caught ..."

"Mabel, Mabel!" cried Josie. "One thing at a time. We don't even know how to use the gun yet, so our plan may be going nowhere, anyway. Let's just start by learning to use it. That can't hurt anything. We can make the decision about our plan later, when we've had more time to think."

Mabel was visibly eased.

"But how are we going to learn?" she asked.

"We're going to have to call Bliss," Josie replied. "He's been in the army and should know all about it. I'm sure he'll teach us. I know we didn't want to involve anyone else, but, you know, we really have no choice. We can't do anything until we learn to use this gun."

She paused, her eyes troubled. "But," she went on, "involving him means involving Mil, too, and, well, you know poor Mil's problem with telling things she doesn't mean to. But we couldn't keep it a secret from her if Bliss is in on it. And what if ..." Elbows on the table, she clasped her head in her hands. "Oh, Mabel, it's like the old story of the mice trying to bell the cat. It's a great idea ... but how do you do it?"

Bliss and Mil Steinberger were their dearest friends. The two couples, Josie and Theodore and Mil and Bliss, had been like family for many years. Their sons, Bobby and Keith and Jimmy, just a few years apart in age, were inseparable. When news came of Bobby's death in Vietnam, both families had been inconsolable. And when Theodore was later killed in his own bed, both families had again been devastated. Bliss had assumed responsibility for Josie from that day forward, and when he later met Mabel, he'd tucked her under his wing, as well. His wife, lovely, lighthearted Mil, was a gifted pianist and the life of every party. But it was true: her spontaneity often got her in trouble.

Mabel was no help. She resumed folding and refolding her napkin, trying to remember if the mice had actually managed to hang a warning bell around the cat's neck.

"Well, there's no other way," Josie declared at last. "Every journey starts with the first step. If we're really going to learn to use that thing, involving Bliss and Mil is a chance we'll have to take. But we won't announce our war plans right off. We'll just tell them you've heard prowlers and about my run-in with those mean kids in the park. The worst that can happen is they'll think we've lost our minds. If only Mil didn't have to hear about it. The poor thing can't keep from telling everything she knows."

"Well, we can't get in trouble just for taking gun lessons, can we?" asked Mabel, still a bit nervous.

"Of course not," replied Josie. "But we must arrange a card game right away with Mil and Bliss, to see if he'll help us. The sooner the quicker, as Theodore used to say. I don't think gun practice is something we can ask him about over the phone!"

She pointed Mabel to the phone. "You call them," she said, "since we'll be meeting at your house."

No one answered at the Steinbergers'.

Josie's thoughts returned to the specter of the gun.

"But what are we going to do with it?" she cried, staring at it as though it might sneak up on her when she wasn't looking.

Neither of them wanted to touch it, so they left it right where it was, and Josie covered it with a lace doily taken from the back of her chair. But, even out of sight, it loomed like a big, dark presence, overshadowing everything in the room.

"We've got to do something fast." Josie pleaded. "I'm going to have to *live* with this thing until we figure out what to do. Oh, Mabel, my commitment is being seriously tested here!"

Mabel hastily grabbed her things and left, promising to coordinate a card game and potluck with Mil and Bliss as soon as possible, leaving Josie to let in the ever-hovering cat. Not only did she need the warm comfort of the cat's presence, but she was left the task of explaining the whole thing to Theodore.

THREE

Luckily, traffic was light returning from Josie's, because Mabel's mind was everywhere but on her driving. Her thoughts spun with the abrupt changes their plan would require: learning to use a gun; clandestine missions; leaving the old house that had been her home since Earl's return from the war in 1954.

Thinking of her house, she realized how silly she had once been to think the warmth of her home had been generated by its vast array of trinkets and doodads. Only after Earl's death had she realized it had been, instead, his good-hearted presence that filled the house with joy. And now she was stuck with over fifty years of useless clutter. How could she ever sort through three stories of junk to move anywhere! The attic, where she stored most of her mother's things, would be next to impossible. But the worst would be the basement. Earl's realm. She couldn't even *think* about that.

Two things she wouldn't miss, she thought, slowing for a red light after having daydreamed through two stop signs, were that dreadful alarm system she'd had installed in the house and the bars on all the windows. Her blood pressure rose just thinking about the shrieking siren she'd sometimes set off when opening a window or a door without first remembering to turn off the system. She was certain no burglar could be as scared of all that racket as she was. But with Earl gone, and her home the only one left on the block, she hadn't been able to think of any other way to protect herself.

Her mind returned to the horror of foreclosure. And overdue taxes. There seemed no way out of this dilemma. The only way she could get her hands on enough money to pay the taxes would be to sell the house. If she didn't, she'd lose it anyway, to the tax man. It was a real catch-22. No matter what, she had to leave her home. Her insides roiled. She couldn't think about it.

Rounding the corner to her broad, once tree-lined street, she let her mind return to the memory of the huge fichus and acacia trees that used to welcome her home in their sheltering bower and, scattered among them, the towering palms Earl had said looked like oversized and frayed artist's brushes. Lush and gracious against the ever-blue sky, the trees had exuded the distinctive flair of Southern California. She was certain there couldn't have been a lovelier street in all of Santa Ana. But they were gone now, replaced by the crisp, architecturally perfect landscapes better suiting the office buildings that had replaced every house on the street but hers.

Pulling into the narrow, grassy driveway that led along the right side of the house to the dilapidated one-car garage in the rear, she forced herself to look at her old house through new eyes. She hadn't realized how tiny and shabby it looked, wedged between modern office buildings on both sides and a massive concrete parking structure on the lot behind it. When had the paint begun to blister and peel? And the porch to sag so badly? Earl had suspected termites, but … Her eyes swept over the yard. Front and back, it languished in Earl's absence. The weeds had grown knee-high and turned to seed. Time for that nice Mr. Gonzalez to come and mow them down again, she thought, even while admitting to herself that the problems ran much deeper than weeds. The roof leaked. The plumbing and electrical systems were archaic and unreliable. Everything squeaked and creaked. Her house was simply used up.

She parked in the driveway, for the lopsided entrance to the garage was too great a challenge for her driving skills. Handbag in hand, she clambered out of the car to become instantly aware of the flash of something—a person?—crossing between the back of her house and the garage. She stopped, her mind struggling to process the image she had just seen. The person appeared to be wearing a black robe. A nun or priest from the church down the street? But what could they be doing in her backyard? Was she just spooked by Josie's experience and seeing things? Her knees grew weak. Whatever it was, she instinctively knew it was bad.

Hurrying up the front porch stairs, fumbling with her keys and managing to open the front door were only parts of the gauntlet she had to run. With shaking hands she now had to open the closet door and fit the little key into the alarm panel mounted there in less than the fifteen seconds for which it had been programmed. Her dread of dropping the key and having to scramble for it before the earsplitting alarm went off had her heart pounding.

"Oh, Earl," she wailed, "this would have been so easy for you! Why did you leave me?"

Safely inside, she drank in its comforting old-house smell, a musty blend of moldering wood and perennially rain-dampened plaster and wallpaper, combined with the faint, earthy remnants of Earl's pipe tobacco. Gripped with fear, she dropped onto the bench of an elaborately carved and mirrored hat rack, still draped with a collection of Earl's hats, and allowed herself to be lulled by the familiar ticking of a houseful of clocks.

Her mind was awhirl. Had she really seen someone, or were her eyes playing tricks on her? And if she had really seen someone, was that someone a threat or just passing through her yard for some reason? She balked at the idea of calling the police, certain they had more important things to do than listen to the ravings of an old woman. She couldn't think of what to do, and the longer she sat there, the more convinced she became that she'd been seeing things. Like her back taxes, she decided not to deal with it. She could imagine Mil's and Bliss's reactions to being told that not only was she going to wage war on crime, but she had seen a ghost in her backyard as well.

Around dinnertime she called the Steinbergers again. They had just returned from the market and were putting away groceries.

"How about a card game and potluck with Josie and me?" she asked, trying to sound as normal as possible. "We're overdue, you know."

Bliss had taken the call, and she could hear him talking over his shoulder to Mil. When he came back on the line, he said, "Yeah, how about tomorrow? We're leaving Friday for Phoenix to visit the kids."

It was understood that their potluck card games would always be at Mabel's, for Josie's place was too small, and Mil and Bliss lived too far out in the country, on a few acres in Modjeska Canyon. The canyon had taken its name from one of its earliest settlers, the famed Polish-born stage actress, Madame Modjeska. In the late nineteenth century she had developed her own compound there, complete with servants' quarters and stables, and brought to the area a lingering aura of mystery. Carpenters working on the project brought out word of the exotic embellishments she had imported, such as the rose-tinted window glass for her boudoir that flattered her delicate complexion.

The compound had since fallen into disrepair and been passed on to others. But the area remained a rural and affordable community of small, often ramshackle cottages where one could live almost any way he liked, in the tradition of canyon people. It was, however, only a half-hour commute to the cities of Orange and Santa Ana. Bliss's pension from the highway department allowed them to live there quite comfortably. He enjoyed the lack of hovering city government, and Mil was content wherever she was, as long as she had a piano, TV, her cigarettes, plenty to read, and friends with whom to share cocktails and cards.

Mabel reported back to Josie that their card game was a go for tomorrow. She asked her to bring a dessert and told her that Bliss, who also had a gate pass, would pick her up just before two. She had to fight with herself to say nothing about seeing someone in her yard. She knew Josie had enough to worry about with the gun in her apartment.

But she did add, "Let's not say anything about your experience in the park until we're through playing cards, Josie. No sense in ruining the fun. There'll be plenty of time to talk about it later."

Josie agreed. "But I just *hate* being locked up with this ... weapon. I know I won't sleep a wink tonight with the darned thing right here beside my bed, staring me in the face. Oh, Mabel, I hope the rest of our plan won't be as nerve-wracking as this part!"

Mabel somehow survived a sleepless night, fraught with dreams of eyes peering through her windows and eerie shapes flitting through the yard. Rather than lie in bed and stew, she got up early and busied herself setting up the card table in the living room, covering it with one of the many intricate, cutwork linens she'd been making since she became a bride. The idea of being safely in prison had a greater appeal than ever. She knew she'd never again be at ease in this house by herself. Not really wanting to know what might be in her backyard, she stifled the urge to peek out of the back windows, where the blinds had been closed since Earl's death. But while she prepared for the party, she had the creepy sensation that unseen eyes followed her.

Wearing her lovely print challis dress, Josie was ready with a freshly baked apple pie when Mil and Bliss came for her that afternoon. She was more than happy to get away from the gun. The bags under her eyes told of her exhaustion from keeping an eye on the doily beside her bed all night.

Mil, in a rust pantsuit that accented her long, slender legs, brought four large potatoes and a pork loin she'd seasoned but not yet cooked. She planned to let it all bake while the foursome played cards, knowing the tantalizing aroma wafting from the kitchen would make their meal all the more enjoyable.

They exchanged warm greetings, put the food away in the kitchen with Mabel's many salads, and gathered, chattering, around the card table. Mabel felt immeasurably safer surrounded by her friends and convinced herself that her scary experience had just been part of her fretful dreams.

This time they voted to play contract rummy. Mabel, flushed with excitement and glowing in her plus-sized jacket-dress of green and gold polyester, had placed little bowls of nuts and candy on the table and provided lemonade made from the fruit of the hardy old lemon tree in her yard. Bliss usually set up a howl about the clutter of glasses and candy dishes on the table, but his protestations always fell on deaf ears. He also grumbled about the dozens of clocks that ticked away, blaming his bad plays on their distraction. Every fifteen minutes they would begin their chiming or cuckooing, and it seemed to take forever from the time the first one began until the last one ended. While Josie dealt with it by simply adjusting her hearing aids, there seemed to be nothing that bothered Mil when she was having a good time. When she was alone, Mabel loved the clocks' reassuring clamor, but she had to admit the noise interrupted their card playing from time to time.

The room resounded with laughter and righteous indignation. Bliss held his own against the women, who talked so much that it wasn't hard for him to put one over on them. He delighted in catching them without a meld, slamming down his own runs and groups and yelling things like, "R-r-r-*ipp* went my new dress!" or "D-ow-w-wn-n with hot pants!" It was all good fun, and the afternoon went quickly.

Dinner was dished up in the cramped little kitchen and eaten in the dining room, which, like the rest of Mabel's house, could have passed for an antique shop with its hodgepodge of china and glass and porcelain collectibles. It was a banquet for Josie, and she wished she could have eaten more. No one had saved room for pie, so they took a break in the comfort of Mabel's living room, stretching out to visit among the piles of hand worked pillows on her dated, overstuffed furniture.

Josie and Mabel gave each other the nod. It was time to bring up the subject that had brought them here. It was now or never.

Josie started by asking Bliss if he didn't feel a little nervous about living so far out in the country, considering all the robberies going on. "I've heard you complain that it takes too long for the sheriff's department to respond out there," she said.

"Well," he admitted, "it certainly isn't as safe as where you live, Josie, but I don't expect a person is safe much of anywhere anymore." He turned his attention to Mabel. "You're the one I'm concerned about. You don't even have a neighbor. I haven't wanted to scare you, but I worry about all those creeps who hang around town at night."

Mabel agreed that, even with the security system she'd installed after Earl's death, she'd had some anxious moments. She was bursting to tell them about the apparition in her yard but bit her tongue. Surely she had been seeing things.

Surprisingly, it was Mil, who seldom had a serious thought in her head, who got the ball rolling. Her usually dancing green eyes were grave with concern.

"It seems darned unfair that we decent people practically have to live behind bars to be safe," she said, "and the crooks and criminals have all the freedom. They can go wherever they want, doing whatever they want, and we're scared to stick our noses out at night. What's happened to this country, anyway?"

Everyone seemed surprised at her outburst. Unruffled, she went on.

"Don't you remember when we used to feel safe wherever we were, and people were respectful of each other? Even during the Depression, back in the thirties, folks who had lost their homes felt safe sleeping out in parks and on the streets. And no one locked their doors against them. People helped each other, instead of taking advantage of each other. Did any of you even own a house key then, let alone use it?"

To a chorus of noes, she continued.

"Well, today's children will never know that kind of trust. In fact, we go out of our way to teach them to be suspicious of everything and everyone. They don't have the freedom we had as kids to roam around and learn to cope on their own. Our kids in Phoenix are afraid to let our grandchildren out of their sight and have 'em scared to death of anyone they don't know. What kind of life have we accepted, anyway, just to accommodate the rights of people who don't understand the responsibilities that go along with those rights?"

There was a momentary pause while all the clocks, led by the sonorous old grandfather clock in the living room, began a frenzied chiming of the half hour. Then they all began to talk at once.

Bliss reminded Mil she was referring to the "olden days," when mental patients were kept in institutions, not turned out on the streets to fend for themselves. Josie swore it was the advent of drugs that turned even normal people into dangerous criminals. Mabel added her opinion that the new mind-set of "nothing is anyone's fault" had a lot to do with it. And they all agreed that too many people weren't adequately parenting their children anymore, so what could you expect of such children when they grew up?

Mil reclaimed the floor, raising her voice to get their attention. "You're all right. Every one of you. Every point you make is part of the whole picture. But why do we allow it? What's the matter with everyone?"

Josie was mystified. "Why, what can we do about the government's turning those poor mental patients loose? Remember, the ACLU warned there would be lawsuits if they didn't. They said if someone hadn't committed a crime, it was unlawful to hold them against their will. But it really is pathetic how they only get into trouble with drugs and alcohol and end up dead or in jail. And there's no help for them there."

Mabel added, "But the worst part of giving all those mental patients and drug users *their* freedom is that it deprives *us* of *ours*. I'd like to know whose idea *that* was.

Bliss had mostly been taking it all in, but now he nodded in agreement. "That's the rub. We seem to value the weakest members of our society so highly that we jeopardize the whole of the system for 'em. Makes it kinda hard to feel patriotic anymore. I was proud to serve in Korea and would've been honored to give my life for my country. But now, with bureaucrats skimming off the top and indigents sucking off the bottom … and crooks taking their chunk out of the middle …

there's less and less of the American pie to put your life on the line for." The irony showed plainly on his face; this was a difficult thing for a proud old soldier to say.

Josie and Mabel looked at each other. They hadn't expected so much support from Mil and Bliss. Maybe their idea of a war on crime wasn't so crazy after all.

Emboldened, Josie blurted out, "Well, we haven't given up. Mabel and I are going to do our part to turn things around and provide for our own futures at the same time."

The room echoed in silence against the ticking of Mabel's clocks.

Mabel couldn't help but laugh at the blank look on Mil's face, knowing it took a lot to silence her. "I think we should have pie while we unveil our fabulous plan," she declared. "It's really so exciting!" She struggled up out of her sagging goose-down chair to usher them back into the dining room.

Josie was virtually dancing with enthusiasm, scooting ahead of them into the kitchen to begin dishing up pie onto Mabel's white china plates. Mabel put on a pot of decaf and started the kettle boiling for tea. Mil and Bliss took their places at the dining room table, with Mil calling to them to hurry up because she couldn't stand the suspense. Only when everything had been served did the two women begin to speak.

"To start at the beginning," said Mabel, "it isn't news to either of you that Josie and I are barely hanging on, financially. What you don't know is that my house is about to be foreclosed on for back taxes."

This produced a gasp from Mil, and Bliss just stared back at her in stunned silence.

"Anyway," she continued, "it probably won't be too long before we are put out on the street if Senator Farley has his way. If he succeeds in reducing or doing away with Social Security, we're going to be up a creek." She left them to think about that while washing down a forkful of pie with a sip of tea.

Josie jumped in. "It's nearly made us crazy," she said, her cheeks flushing with anger. "He says his war on crime needs our pension money to build more prisons, and we should feel good about it. Can you believe that? We're supposed to think it's just fine to give away the only money we have. You really *can't* trust a politician with a name like Bart Farley!"

They allowed her the little joke, which had been part of his opponent's campaign material. The idea was for folks to find him ridiculous and irreverently think of him as Fart Barley. However, the public loved the oblique slur, and the strategy backfired. Edmond "Bart" Farley won the election by a huge margin.

Neither Bliss nor Mil could tell where this conversation was going, so they just picked at their pie in silence.

Mabel resumed, picking up steam as she went.

"Josie and I feel it's the crooks and criminals who need to have the tables turned on them, not the old folks who are doing their best to take care of themselves. So we developed the most exciting plan." Her eyes lingered on her friends, praying she had read their moods correctly.

"We've decided to wage our own war on crime," she cried, and quickly raised her hands against the protests she knew would be coming. "Now, give us a chance to explain, 'cause I know it might sound kinda crazy at first. But once it sinks in, you'll be surprised at how logical it is."

Bliss and Mil gave up on their pie and just sat staring from Mabel to Josie. Josie took this as her cue to tell about her attack in the park.

"And that was when the plan came to us," she said, after filling them in. "We can go on with our useless little lives, scared to leave our homes, and die wards of the state in some depressing nursing home, or we could die having done something for our country. Like one of George H. Bush's 'thousand points of light'. Our plan is to do away with enough criminals to pay for our own incarceration and make the streets a little safer while we're at it."

Mabel broke in with, "Now, being in prison may sound like punishment to some people, but not at our ages and with our needs. You see," she went on, "Josie and I need all the things that are freely provided in prison: food, clothing, security, things to do, *and* people to do things *with*. According to the program we saw on TV, prison accommodations for people our ages are better than what many folks have *ever* had. And think of all the problems it would solve for us! So we thought of the most helpful thing we could do for our country to earn a retirement there."

Bliss and Mil still sat staring. After a moment, not knowing what else to say, Bliss said, "I believe I'd like a cup of coffee," followed by Mil with, "Me, too. And make it a double." She reached for her cigarettes; this was clearly more than they had bargained for.

No one spoke during the pouring of coffee and the serving of the rest of the pie. Mil and Bliss were too shocked to know what to say. When they were all settled in again, Mabel continued. Waving her fork for emphasis, she said, "Senator Farley's right about one thing, though. Criminals *are* steadily destroying the country. Why, they're doing more to undermine us than the Germans or Japanese ever did in the Great War. We were able to unite against them. But we stand by and let criminals and deadbeats jerk us around by the nose."

She elaborated on their earlier discussion about the social disintegration that bred criminals. No one argued with her, so she went on. "We don't know how much longer the government can afford to cater to them. Who is going to pay for all this nonsense when that element of society has bankrupted and demoralized the whole country?"

Then Josie took over. "We would decline a trial and all that expense and just let them put us in prison and take care of us in our declining years. And, of course, we'd be model prisoners. They wouldn't have to guard us very much, because we wouldn't want out ... we'd have nowhere to go, anyway. And you could visit us almost any time you want. Besides, we don't eat as much as men do, so it seems as though everyone would benefit." She thought for a moment, and added, "Well, maybe the guys we have to kill wouldn't benefit very much. But we really shouldn't allow *any* benefits to bad people."

Bliss choked on his coffee, and Mil gave a shriek of surprise. The unimaginable had been revealed. Josie and Mabel actually intended to *kill* people!

Unrelenting, Mabel picked up where Josie left off, summarizing their plan.

"When we realized there was something almost patriotic about this, we were much better able to come to terms with our situation. After all, running out of money and becoming wards of the state is such an inglorious way to end your life. But if we can offset our keep by saving the government some of the expense of housing criminals, we wouldn't just be charity cases; we'd be like the other war veterans and have *earned* our reward."

With that she stopped, knowing they'd already given Bliss and Mil too much to ponder. After all, she and Josie had had an entire evening to develop their plan. They couldn't expect Bliss and Mil to get it in fifteen minutes. Remembering how excited they had been when the fully formed plan presented itself, Mabel was sure that, given a little time, it would make perfect sense to others, too. They just had to get past the killing part. She smiled to remember their almost electric experience, like the flash of a lightbulb over a character's head in the comics. She waited to see Mil's and Bliss's faces light up with insight. But neither of them said a word.

Mil was bursting with a thousand questions. But she waited to let Bliss speak first.

At that moment, he sat imagining life in prison. In his eighties, Bliss was far from feeble, but he didn't think he was strong enough to survive the bullying of cocky, younger men.

At last he spoke, focusing on the stirring of cream into his coffee. "First things first," he said, while Josie and Mabel whisked away the empty plates and silverware. "I think we need to address the problem of your back taxes, Mabel, before you lose your house. If we can save it, maybe you could forget this whole … this whole business."

He looked up at her over the top of his glasses, squinting against the light that flashed from the crystals of Mabel's ornate chandelier and gleamed like a halo from the top of his utterly bald head. He didn't want to offend her, but he had to talk some sense into her.

"How far behind are you?" he asked, groping in his shirt pocket for a pen. "This is going to take some figuring."

Flustered at speaking of this delicate issue, Mabel meekly responded that she didn't think she'd paid property taxes since Earl's death.

Bliss's eyebrows shot up. "Good God, Mabel! Where's your paperwork? It looks like we need to do something, and do it fast."

Mabel nodded and went to her little cherrywood desk in the living room. She rustled around, gathering up papers.

While she was out of the room, Mil could contain herself no longer. "I want to know more about this plan of yours," she breathed conspiratorially to Josie. "You aren't really going to kill people, are you? How will you decide who's bad … and how are you going to do it?" She rushed on without giving Josie a chance to answer. "Aren't you afraid of getting yourself killed? And those guys in the park …"

Mabel's return silenced her. She laid out the paperwork in front of Bliss, saying, "Please don't worry about finding a way to save the house, Bliss. I've thought it through, and I'm going to let the government have it. They can figure out what to do with it while I'm relaxing in jail."

Mabel shuffled through the pile of papers, found the Tax Postponement and the Tax Assistance documents that had been sent to her, and brought them to his attention. "You might find these interesting, in case you ever need to apply for help. But as for me, help is on the way."

The first of the clocks began to announce the hour with a raucous dinging, followed by the others in a rapid succession of cuckooing, bonging, and chiming: soldiers on parade, cuckoos springing out of birdhouses, children swinging from tree boughs—every kind of wall clock that had caught Earl's eye. Mabel's contribution had been the more mellow shelf clocks competing for space on every surface and the stately grandfather clock in the living room. She spent part of every day talking to them and winding them. Set a few moments apart so each could be heard, the clocks had become her family.

Bliss waited impatiently to speak until all the clocks had finished. Actually, it gave him a moment to think. He couldn't imagine why she would just let her house be taken away from her.

"But Mabel," he insisted, "how about that new thing, I think it's called a reverse mortgage or something? You know, where you kinda give your house to the bank and they sorta pay you to live there, till you kick the bucket or somethin'? Now, that might be your answer."

"Why, Bliss," she retorted. "Why in the world would I want to give my house to the bank? I'd rather give it to you! You'd let me live here free, I know. But, you see, that's only part of the problem."

She reminded him that as soon as she and Josie had conceived their plan, they found release from the grinding worry about taxes, repairs, security, and all the other problems concerning her house.

"And frankly, Bliss, I'm tired of living alone, scared all the time. Can't you see how easy this would be for me? Besides, this is really the fair and responsible thing to do, letting the government have my house in exchange for room and board in prison. You see, we're going to be asking them to take care of us for the next ten, maybe fifteen, years or so. So we want to make it a good deal for the government, too. We'll save them money by eliminating a few crooks and throw in my house as a bonus. Is there anything more valuable we could do for our country, at our ages? I don't think so."

Josie hung on her every word and applauded her speech, saying she wished she had something to give the government, too, because it was such an honorable thing to do. But she guessed there was nothing she could do about it except do away with a few extra criminals.

By this time, Bliss realized they were deadly serious. He'd humored them long enough.

"What is this craziness!" he yelled, face red and eyes blazing. "Have you been into Betty Jean's weed patch?" He was referring to his neighbor in the canyon, a middle-age flower child who still cultivated a little marijuana for her own use, hidden among rows of corn and tomatoes.

They all knew the story of Betty Jean's marijuana-laced brownies, and how she had served them to Mil and Bliss at a party at her home. They had awakened in their own beds the next morning with no memory of how they'd gotten there or of having been helped home the night before by more experienced partygoers. After Bliss got over being mad, they'd had many a good laugh over it.

"What makes you think you have to kill people!" he continued, still shouting. "This is the craziest thing I ever heard of! If you want to go to jail, go rob a bank!"

Both Mabel and Josie looked crestfallen. He didn't get it.

"Bliss," Mabel began, addressing him as though he were an impossible child, "robbing banks is bad. We don't want to do something bad. We want to help our community by getting rid of bad *people*. And we don't want a short term for robbery. We want to stay where it's safe, in prison, forever."

"Besides," Josie continued, looking every bit the schoolteacher she had once been, "the people we're going to get rid of never learn. If Mabel and I could reclaim them, that would be a worthwhile project. But the whole U.S. government hasn't been able to. These same people get in trouble again and again. Believe me, if just one person is safer because of us, it will have been worth it."

Bliss opened his mouth to argue, but Mil interrupted him, shouting, "Bliss! Let them talk. It may not be as crazy as you think." She asked the two women how they figured to "execute" their plan, making sure they noticed her clever pun.

"Well, that's where Bliss comes in," Josie said. "We were sure he knows about guns, since he was in the war. So, we hoped he'd teach us how to use Earl's." She went on to tell them about Mabel's retrieving the handgun from the basement, and that it now rested in her living room, scaring the wits out of her.

"And just where do you plan to do that?" an incredulous Bliss asked. "It's against the law to shoot a handgun at my place, even if it is out in the country. You can't go out on a firing range without a permit for it, and they'd know you're crazy, for sure, if you try to get one." He turned his head away, muttering things not meant for their ears.

The mental image of the two women waving a gun around, endangering everyone at the firing range, threatened to give him another round of heartburn. His hand went protectively to his chest. It didn't take much to bring it on anymore. But he felt it was up to him to dash this preposterous war thing, and hope the rest of their harebrained scheme would collapse with it. However, he had an eerie feeling this notion wasn't going to go away and that, as when they played cards, his words fell on deaf ears.

Mabel brightened and said, "Why, right here, Bliss. Right here in the basement. If we practice during traffic hours, no one will hear us. Whoever gets the house will just tear it down anyway, so it won't make any difference, now, will it?"

"Aren't we lucky," cried Josie. "It shouldn't take us long to get the hang of it, and it will feel so good not to be afraid of Earl's gun anymore. But till then," she said, her hand fluttering to her temple, "*please* get it out of my house."

So there it was. He was embroiled in the middle of their scheme whether or not he wanted to be. They already had a role for him to play.

"We want you and Mil to have any of our things you want," continued Mabel. "The tax man will get my house, of course, but we won't be needing any of our other things, and it seems only fair that you should have whatever you want in exchange for our gun lessons. Whatever you can't use you can give to charity."

Josie nodded in agreement. She knew she had little to give, but it made her feel magnanimous, nevertheless.

Mil sat wreathed in a sweet smile. She had simplistically bought into their plan as they unfolded it, already planning her visits to them in prison. As always, they were so considerate. She could think of a few of their things she would like to have if they wouldn't be needing them anymore.

Bliss felt himself crumble. He needed time to think. He guessed it would be alright to teach them to handle the gun before they hurt themselves with it. He'd have to make it clear, however, that he wanted to hear no more about this ridiculous plan of theirs.

But he knew those two. They'd scare themselves out of this crazy war when it got right down to it. They might enjoy talking about it, but *doing* it was completely beyond them. Yet, he couldn't deny the intrigue of their novel idea.

Finally Josie spoke. "Of course, we hope we won't be killed before we can make a difference. But at least we will have died from *living* instead of waiting for the infirmities of age to do the job. It will be a small, two-woman war, I admit, but that doesn't make it any less important."

Bliss wasn't listening. He was thinking about Mabel's house. If he could get her to think about the money she'd get for it, maybe she'd change her mind.

"But Mabel, you must know your piece of property is worth a lot of money. Not the house, of course. It will be torn down. But the land it sits on. You could sell it to me for the amount of the taxes," he said, "and *I* could sell it to some builder. I'd put the money in trust for the both of us, and if you change your mind about this cockeyed war, you could have the money back. But if you're so gol-darned determined to spend the rest of your life in the clink, Mil and I'd have a pile of money. Don't be so darned anxious to give the house away!"

Mabel smiled at his perplexity. "I did think of that, Bliss. You know I'd give you and Mil the sun and the moon if I could. But this thing we're doing goes beyond anything I ever dreamed of. It's almost … I don't know … like we've been *called*." She shook her head firmly. "I have to be fair, Bliss. The house goes to the government. I'm sure I could also sell it to a builder for enough money to get by on, if I don't live too long. But who'd take care of me when I'm old and feeble?"

Josie summed it up, the smile on her face lighting up the room.

"We don't want to think about taxes, housecleaning, getting to the doctor, and all the rest of it. Paying the bills, figuring out what to cook, and getting to the market—just think of it! All of that will be taken care of! And with the ACLU keeping an eye on things, we'll be more closely monitored than we would be in a nursing home. And we'll have the company of healthy young women. That alone is worth something."

Mabel nodded vigorously, patting at the nervous perspiration on her nose with one of her delicate lace handkerchiefs.

"I don't know if I could take being in a nursing home," she said, "where *everyone* is old and just 'waiting for the last bell to ring,' as my sister, Dora, used to say. And she found that staying in your own home isn't always the answer, either. Remember what happened to her, in Kansas? By the time she died, nearly deaf and blind, the help had walked off with everything of value, including most of her bank account."

Just the memory of it made Mabel angry all over again. Dora's children had been deprived of many priceless heirlooms, as well as the money to settle their mother's estate.

They knew from the way she was fidgeting and grinning that Mil was taken with their idea. Like them, she would be lost without a husband to see about things. They could also tell they had worn Bliss down with their odd logic. He was at a loss for words.

Mabel scooped up the tax papers from the table and scrunched them into a ball.

"Let's let somebody else worry over this whole tax matter," she said. "We need to get on to the matter of learning to use the gun."

Bliss seemed almost glad to change the subject back to gun lessons. By now it seemed rational compared to the idea of Mabel giving her home, free and clear, to the government.

"Mil and I are spending a few days with the kids in Phoenix," he said wearily, "so this whole thing will have to wait till we get back. Promise you won't do anything or talk to anyone about it. We all need to think it over. And Mil, for God's sake, you can't mention it, either. The kids'd think we've all gone nuts."

The three women beamed at him. They had a deal.

FOUR

The next few days flew by. Josie was in high spirits, catching up on her reading and taking short walks. Careful to avoid the park, she greeted the neighborhood's profusion of spring flowers that flourished from the recent rainstorm. She chatted on the phone with Mabel, telling her the gun, which Bliss said was a model 60 snub-nosed Smith and Wesson revolver, had not been loaded. They had another laugh at their ignorance and were eager to get on with their plan, thrilled to think their all-consuming worries about finances and safety were nearly over. They had a purpose! A whole new chapter was unfolding for them, right when they had given up hope.

"It's like we're government agents," Josie said, tingling with excitement. "We have a mission vital to our country that we don't dare tell anyone about!"

Mabel professed that she could think of nothing else. "Sometimes I feel as giddy as I did on my first date with Earl. Oh, boy, that was something. I nearly passed out the first time he held my hand."

As the days went by, Josie found herself becoming frivolous with her budget. She sometimes used a tea bag only once, and often helped herself to a handful of sugar cookies at a time. It felt so good to be alive! She slept soundly, free from the wrenching nightmares that had left her afraid of going to bed at night. Her daily soaps even lost their allure. She had lost patience with the characters, who seemed bent on creating their own problems and then wallowing in self-pity. Remembering her mother's remedy for everything, she decided that what they all needed was a good dose of salts—whatever that meant.

Saturday afternoon came quickly. Josie dressed for the Watsons' in a light blue linen suit and the good shoes she'd bought for Theodore's funeral. Her old ones, which sat beside the bed the night Theodore was killed, had been gruesomely splattered with his blood, and she disposed of them immediately. She never wore these new ones without remembering the trauma of having to buy shoes at a time when she couldn't even think straight. This explained the little plastic bows permanently affixed on the toes. Josie had always worn simple, sensible shoes. Every time she wore these fancy shoes she asked herself why in the world she had chosen them. But she couldn't think of spending the money for new ones. Certainly, the prison-issue ones would be an improvement.

Buttoning up her trim jacket, she wondered what color uniform she would wear in prison, and hoped it would be blue, for she had always loved blue. The thought suddenly struck her that she might have to wear pants. She stopped, flustered. She had never worn pants in her life. Probably there would be many more things she'd have to get used to in prison—things she couldn't yet imagine.

"But I have a new life to live," she said to her smiling image in the mirror, enlarging on the slogan from her old support-group days. "And I will honor my loved ones by living it … without complaining!"

The Watsons lived across the common area, also in a downstairs unit, but a larger one designed for the handicapped. Herb, neatly groomed and delighted to see Josie, met her at the door. Giving her a hug, he ushered her into the book-and-curio- filled apartment where Pearl sat waiting in her wheelchair. Arms outstretched, she greeted Josie with a big, "Hi, neighbor! It was good of you to make the long journey!"

Pearl was considerably younger than Josie, with the innate composure and warm, dark eyes that instantly put everyone at ease. She motioned for Josie to sit near her so they could chat before starting the movies.

They had a lot in common. Pearl and Josie had been teachers, and Herbert and Theodore had both been in heavy artillery units duringthe Korean War. Upon discharge, however, Herb had taken advantage of the GI Bill to go on to college and make a career in banking, whereas Theodore had returned to help run his father's hardware store, a landmark in Santa Ana that eventually became his. But Herb had two grown and married sons, whereas Theodore and Josie had tragically lost both of their children.

It was a second marriage for Herb and Pearl; they had been married only fifteen years. Herb's first wife had died of breast cancer, and, like Josie's son, Pearl's first husband had given his life in the Vietnam War. By the time Herb and Pearl met, Pearl was in her forties and Herb well into his sixties. They had teased each other that she was marrying a meal ticket and he was marrying a nurse.

It wasn't long, however, before Pearl began evidencing symptoms of what turned out to be multiple sclerosis. It came as a dreadful shock to them. Their plan had been to tour the world, country by country, but her condition worsened until it was Herb who was playing nursemaid to her. To make matters worse, Herb began having heart problems of some sort, which left him almost as fragile as she was.

They continued to travel until the effort became too much, when they sold their home and moved to the security of the Glendon Arms apartments. Josie was always touched by the way they enjoyed life in spite of their hardships. Clearly, they were still very much in love.

Today the Laurel and Hardy movies seemed funnier than ever to Josie. They talked and laughed their way through the afternoon and ate all the popcorn they could hold. After visiting them, Josie always felt certain she had the best friends in the world.

Mabel had declined the invitation for movies and popcorn in order to have some time alone in the basement with Earl's things, before she and Josie began preparing it for target practice. The basement had been Earl's world. She had never wanted to know what he did down there. For years they worked side by side all day in the bakery, and she knew it was good for him to have a place of his own to disappear to in the evenings. She always envisioned it as a big rat's nest. Well, she had been right—it was. But what fun Earl must have had!

She had to brace herself for it, because searching for the gun had proven so devastating. But now she was having quite an adventure, discovering piles of dust-covered and long-forgotten treasures amid the clutter of paint cans, tools of one kind or another, old furniture, plumbing parts, and odd pieces of building materials. She laughed aloud when she came across such things as the beekeepers outfit he'd found at a garage sale, the dried two-headed snake he'd bought at the county fair, and countless other funny things he had dragged home from somewhere.

When she found one of Earl's old denim shirts thrown over a section of water pipe that hung from the ceiling, she had pressed her face into it, inhaling deeply of his precious blend of tobacco and aftershave. She carried it around over her shoulder, using it to swat cobwebs and to mop up her tears. By the end of the day she had cried and laughed and lovingly handled each item she could reach, until her heart felt at peace. With a final look around, she knew she was ready. Bliss could cart it all away.

On Sunday evening, Bliss called Josie to say that they were home from Phoenix.

"Got that war thing outta your system yet?" he asked.

She promised him that they were as determined as ever and assured him that nothing and no one was going to stand in the way of this final, unique, and glorious chapter of their lives.

He took a few moments to absorb the finality of her response and replied, "Well, it's against my better judgment to turn you two loose with a gun. But I'm afraid you'll hurt yourselves with it if you try to figure it out on your own. I guess a few lessons can't hurt. Might help you get over your big idea. So, we'd better clear Mabel's basement for target practice."

At that moment, Josie loved him, her steadfast and loyal friend, more than she had words to say.

<u>FIVE</u>

Bliss stood in awe of Mabel's basement. A lifetime of squirreling away broken or worn-out things had produced a junkman's dream. Earl had intended to fix or use some of it one day, and there were things he had saved as a precaution against the next depression. The rest of it was just there.

Bliss had never been in Mabel's basement and, of course, had never met Earl. His pack rat's heart was wild with anticipation as he stood viewing it for the first time. From the looks of it, he and Earl would have been soul mates. He felt cheated that he never got to know this fellow pack rat, this lover of the earthy and unusual.

Mabel gave him a brief tour, showing him a stack of things she'd set aside for some of Earl's buddies. She assured him that he could have whatever he wanted, insisting it was small payment for the lessons she and Josie were about to receive.

After pointing out the short rear wall that seemed the logical area for their lessons, she left him to assess whatever he might want. He spent almost an hour going through the things he could get to, and then climbed back up the steep wooden stairs leading to the kitchen, where Mabel stood ironing. The sharp odor of a hot iron on starched cotton hung heavy in the air. He interrupted only long enough to get permission to return when he could get Betty Jean's son, Hap, to help him.

"You know, Hap's kinda simple," Bliss reminded her, baseball cap respectfully in hand. "He's been on marijuana since before he was born. Nursed it from Betty Jean, too. I guess she liked 'im mellow an' easy to handle. You know how she still cooks it up in stuff. But he's a good worker if you can get him motivated. And I think promising him those pretty rocks in the basement will be just the ticket."

Mabel was effusive with her gratitude. "Bliss, It's so good to have a man in charge again. You and Hap can do it any old way you want. Heavens knows I can't deal with all that stuff myself, and it would be too embarrassing to let anyone else see it. Why, there's hardly room to move around down there, let alone have target practice!"

Bliss nodded, chuckling. "You're sure right about that. Your old man might'a been a worse junk collector than I am, and that's goin' some!"

Josie stayed to help Mabel for the next few days. They spent many hours in the basement, shifting things around and dragging bulky objects away from the intended practice wall. Doing so had exposed the rusty-hinged door to the outside, hidden behind piles of gritty boxes draped in bug and debris-laden cobwebs. They were thrilled with their find, for this door would provide Bliss wider passage and fewer, more graduated steps up to the driveway and his truck. Mabel had invited Earl's friends to come and take the things she'd set aside for them, and the only one who hadn't responded turned out to have died.

Within the week Bliss returned with his pickup truck and big, strapping Hap, whose idea of work was doing only what it took to survive. He was the result of Betty Jean's brief sojourn in a commune near Lompoc, where she had run away as a teenager. He and his mother had never been separated for longer than a day and couldn't imagine a reason for being so. They mostly tended the garden that surrounded their rustic canyon home, scrounged for odds and ends, and celebrated life in their own quiet way. He loved Bliss, who took the place of the father he'd never known, and Mil, who responded to his love of music by patiently teaching him to play the harmonica.

Bliss and Hap got right to work, carrying lumber, plumbing parts, rock and woodworking equipment, old furniture, rugs, and other odds and ends to Bliss's truck. By the end of the third day, they had carried away nine truckloads: six to Bliss's and three to the dump.

Meanwhile, Mabel and Josie spent their time lining the walls of the target area with an insulation of boxes containing old photographs, worn-out clothing and linens, magazines, files from the bakery, and similar things that Mabel deemed useless to anyone else. Bliss had explained the danger of bullets ricocheting off the hard concrete walls, so with that in mind they not only built a cushioning stack of these densely packed cartons, but also fashioned a bull's-eye with a felt pen on a large piece of cardboard. They planned to place it right in the center of the buffer, attaching it with duct tape when the buffer was complete.

It was a hard three days for the four of them. They hadn't run up and down so many stairs or exerted so much energy in years. As for Hap, he never complained while doing the work of two men, for Bliss had been right: the glittering amethyst and quartz and pyrite specimens excited him more than the wages he was earning.

When Bliss returned without Hap on the morning of the fourth day, the women showed him where their cushioned practice area needed only the final, top row of boxes. With his help, they hoisted the last of the cartons into place. Bliss used the duct tape to attach their cardboard bull's-eye but hauled over an old army footlocker to steady the base of it, just in case.

Satisfied with their effort, they were exhausted. Mabel's knee had acted up on the first day and had her limping, and Bliss admitted that the strain had given him a "hitch in his git-along." But tomorrow they would begin. Bliss figured that starting the lesson in mid-afternoon would give Mabel and Josie time to become acquainted with the gun before shooting it under cover of late-afternoon traffic. He would also bring Mil, who pleaded to be in on this new adventure. She hated to have missed the fun of the basement preparation but had been committed to a four-day bridge tournament and couldn't let the group down.

It was both sobering and intensely exciting for them to realize they were finally ready for their lessons. But their aching, arthritic bodies betrayed them. All they wanted now was a soothing hot bath, dinner, and bed.

It was only their enthusiasm that got Josie and Mabel out of bed the next morning. Every muscle in their bodies ached. It took another warm bath and breakfast to put them back on their feet, but they were as charged up as they could ever remember having been. Mabel's knee seemed a little better, but Josie kept running to the bathroom, afraid of wetting her pants in her excitement.

Bliss and Mil arrived around two, and although Bliss tried to appear calm, Mil was as antsy as the other women. This was the big day, and it seemed they'd waited for it forever.

They gathered around Mabel's dining room table, chattering nervously while tying on the aprons Mabel provided. A respectful hush fell over them as Bliss patiently began to explain the weapon. For the next hour, they took turns learning the proper way to handle it, how to load and unload it, and how to hold their arms straight out in front of them to shoot it. By the end of the hour, Josie's and Mabel's arthritic hands and shoulders were worn out. But their enthusiasm was still strong. They felt ready for anything.

Bliss consulted his watch, and at four o'clock he led the women down the stairs into the basement. Their excitement had given way to determination, and they moved with the purposefulness of a small army. The dust they had kicked up in the last few days had settled, and in the dim light the nearly empty basement looked quite tidy. Bliss pointed out the weight-bearing post that stood about fifteen feet from the target wall.

"You're gonna be surprised at the recoil from that gun," he said. "Till you get used to it, you'd better brace yourself against this post."

Josie, Mabel, and Mil took turns following his instructions with the empty gun while waiting for traffic noise to pick up. Leaning against the post, they pretended to load the chamber, steadied the weapon with both hands, took aim, and pulled the trigger. On one of Mil's turns, Bliss surprised them by handing out earplugs left over from his road working days. He also gave each of them a handful of rounds for the pockets of their aprons and announced that dress rehearsal was over.

"Do your stuff, ladies," he said. "Just remember the danger of ricocheting bullets if you miss the padded wall." From then on he mostly stayed on the sidelines, calling out instructions only when necessary.

Shrieks and laughter accompanied the passing of the gun from Mil to Mabel to Josie. They cheered and applauded each other, all of them surprised at the smooth transition from their earlier dry run session. Before long they became brave enough to step away from the post to experience the recoil of the gun and quickly learned to brace themselves for it. They continually thanked Bliss for being such a good instructor.

By six thirty the heavy smell of gunpowder filled the air, and their ears were ringing in spite of the earplugs. Bliss declared the session over and commended them on exceeding his expectations.

"You won't be needin' me anymore," he told his enthusiastic students. "You're a darn sight better'n I thought you'd be."

The women began noisily congratulating each other but hushed when he added, "Just remember what I told you about droppin' your mark at close range. You've got to hit his sweet spot, between the upper lip and nose. A bullet to the heart, or anywhere else, can still leave him able to lunge at you. And trust me, you don't want that."

Josie and Mabel gave each other a disbelieving glance. They had expected him to discourage them in some way, but he referred only to self-defense, never mentioning their war. Neither of them responded, obviously relieved that he hadn't brought it up.

They were ready for the refuge of Mabel's kitchen and a refreshing glass of cold lemonade. Trembling with fatigue, they were exhilarated beyond description. Bliss gave them a brief demonstration of how to clean and oil the gun, explaining that if it became encrusted with gunpowder it could blow up on you. This was a sobering thought. The women silently hoped their war would be over before they needed to worry about that.

Mil felt slighted when Josie decided to stay another night at Mabel's so they could have an early-morning practice. Making them promise to invite her to another session soon, she consoled herself with one more cigarette and then headed for home with Bliss.

The morning practice began at seven forty-five, along with traffic noise. The two women, sharing Mabel's bed, had talked and laughed far into the night, feeling like a couple of kids again. If it hadn't been for the insistent ringing of the alarm clock they might have slept right through the beginning of another workday in Santa Ana.

They were dressed and ready, earplugs in hand, apron pockets filled with ammunition, when they decided traffic noise was just about right. They agreed that filling the chamber three times, or firing fifteen rounds, constituted a turn.

Their aim was much better than they could have hoped for, and the smoke and noise added to their excitement. Soon the cardboard target, which had been nearly shredded the previous night, was in tatters. They needed a new target.

"Are you ever going to use all those preserves you put up years ago?" Josie asked, pointing to the shelves of ancient, dust-covered canning jars. "They'd make great targets."

Mabel replied that she planned to empty them and keep the jars, which were probably collector's items by now. Then she caught herself. "Why in the world should I save them? I won't be canning anymore."

Gleefully, Mabel lined up five dusty peach jars on the footlocker in front of the cardboard target. Josie shrieked with delight when she hit four of the five.

Then she lined up jars for Mabel, and they took turns until the sweet smell of fruit and jam, mingled with the sharp odor of dill pickles and gunpowder, was overpowering. Gooey contents of the jars were splattered everywhere, along with sticky shards of exploded glass. They were racing the clock when Mabel, gun in both hands and arms straight out in front of her, slowly turned, seeking a new target. She shot at a nail on a ceiling joist and hit it. Emboldened, she shot at the juncture of two joists and hit that, too.

"Remember, 'We have lives to live!'" she cried, prancing over to give Josie her turn. The prancing set off her knee again, but even though she squealed in pain, she wasn't going to give up as long as she could hobble.

"Yes," Josie cried, between blasts at knotholes on the wooden stair risers.

"We *really do* have lives to live! And we *really will* honor our loved ones by living them!" Their pace picked up to a frenzy. Catching each other's eye, they screeched in unison, "I have a life to live!" They shot the knobs off the cabinets, riddled the shelving, and attacked the large weight-bearing posts, howling like banshees but careful to avoid the hard cement. Josie was turning to aim at the water heater when Mabel came to her senses.

"Oh no," she shrieked. "I'm going to need that for awhile."

Josie dropped her arms in surprise, slipping the gun into the pocket of her apron. Only then did they become aware of the carnage they had created. Choking on the smell, they looked at each other in dismay and erupted in a fit of laughter. Throwing their arms around each other, they sank to the floor in hysterics.

"I have a life to live!" one of them would howl when she could get her breath, which further fueled their hysteria. They laughed until they cried, kicking their feet and writhing on the cement floor. Neither one could imagine doing what they had just done. The lunacy of it brought on fresh fits of laughter every time they looked at each other. Sitting up, they pulled the plugs out of their ears and attempted to regain control. But they collapsed in laughter again when, holding her sides and hardly able to speak, Josie spluttered that she had wet her pants. Struggling to her feet, she stood holding the sodden dress away from her body. Still laughing helplessly, she found even this assault on her dignity to be riotously funny. Leaving the mess and the stench of the fray behind, they were still laughing as they stumbled their way up the bullet-scarred stairway to the kitchen.

They were ravenous. Josie showered and washed her hair while Mabel fixed breakfast. She came to the breakfast table lost in Mabel's bathrobe, with a pair of Mabel's panties pinned around her tiny waist. Her freshly washed clothing tumbled in the dryer off the kitchen. A bit more sedate now, they ate their breakfast of toast and soft-boiled eggs to the accompaniment of the radio.

"Time to get civilized again," Mabel had said, tuning in to her favorite oldies station. Their earlier hysteria had been replaced by the heavy question of each other's commitment to their plan. Once started, there could be no undoing it.

"Will you miss your home a lot?" Josie asked, motioning with a sweep of her arm to include its contents as well. She knew from experience the jolt of abruptly leaving a home in which you'd spent virtually your entire adult life.

Mabel responded philosophically, saying "Josie, it's only a matter of time before I couldn't stay here alone anyway." She gazed wistfully around at her treasures. "We both know we're on the downhill slide. If we don't begin planning for the future someone else will have to do it for us."

Josie nodded her agreement. "It's a funny thing, isn't it," she said quietly. "As you get older, the glow seems to go out of things you once prized so highly. I was in such a state of shock when I had to leave my home that it took months to remember the things I'd left behind— things that Theodore had been willing to defend with his life."

She looked ready to cry. "I can tell you, my arms still ache for little Jennie, after all these years, and for Bobby and Theodore. All the 'stuff' in the world couldn't equal hearing their voices again ..." She hugged her precious memories to her heart, unaware that she had begun rocking gently, her arms cradling one of her sweet babies. Her memories were the dearest things in her life.

"I feel so bad for mothers of young people gone wrong," she continued, talking more to herself than to Mabel. "Just imagine the pain they suffer when their children keep getting in trouble. If we really do this—this war thing—we must remember that behind every hoodlum is a brokenhearted mother."

Mabel knew she had to head off Josie's ramblings before she had them both in tears.

"We can't get sentimental now, Josie, and lose our courage. And we can't spend more time worrying about the criminals than we do their poor victims. We have to think of the peace of mind we'll have in prison. And the free time to do all the things we haven't been able to do in years. This old house and all its 'stuff' have consumed me way too long!"

They clasped aged hands across the table and looked into each other's eyes.

"Are we going to do it? Our plan?" Josie asked softly.

"Is the Pope Catholic?" Mabel replied. "We're ready. We just need to get started."

As if programmed for that cue, the radio newscaster began a litany of local murders, carjackings, and robberies. Amazed at the irony of it, the women gave each other a high five the way they'd seen done on TV and, with Mabel limping along, carried the dishes to the sink.

Mabel's shower could wait until she had taken Josie home. They needed fresh air, for the pungent smell of the mess in the basement was beginning to seep into the kitchen.

SIX

All the way to Josie's they formed their battle plans. They saw no use in waiting; they were as ready as they were going to be. The trick, they agreed, was to avoid getting themselves killed or imprisoned too soon. They didn't object to putting their lives on the line for their country, but they hoped to see a little action first. The big decisions were where, when, who, and how many.

"Personally, I'd like to put a scare into that bunch of thugs in the park," said Josie, with a look as close to menacing as she was capable. "I'd love to see their faces when I tell them this is *war*. Boy, it feels good not to be afraid of *them* anymore."

She pictured herself boldly walking up to them and imagined the shock on their faces when they saw her gun. She relished their terror as they danced from the carefully aimed slugs churning up the earth at their feet. The image of the fat one attempting fancy footwork in his sagging pants made her laugh aloud. All their attempts to be so cool! She'd cool them off, all right!

Thinking and driving at the same time proved quite a challenge for Mabel. By the time they arrived at Josie's, they had run through the usual two stop signs and a red light as well, leaving a chorus of angry horns and squealing brakes in their wake. But because neither woman could see much above the dashboard of Mabel's car, they remained oblivious to their near disasters as they concentrated on their plans.

They discussed looking for purse snatchers, carjackers, and burglars, but had to disqualify burglars because they couldn't think of how to catch one. And it didn't take long to realize they'd never tempt a carjacker with Mabel's old car. This seemed to leave purse snatchers, and they were certain they could be found anywhere. Besides, they agreed, anyone who would stoop to stealing a purse from an old lady would do worse things, as well. That took care of the "who" part.

The "how many" part was more difficult. Josie realized there was some figuring to do and produced a pen and a folded-up grocery bag from her purse. She always tried to keep a paper bag or two handy, in case someone should offer her a ride to the market. George's market allowed her a nickel's credit for each bag she returned to use again, which helped stretch her tiny budget.

"Okay, now," she said with a flourish. "Where do we start?"

"Well, let me see," said Mabel, obviously stumped. "Maybe we should start by figuring out what it's going to cost the government to keep us for the next ten or fifteen years. At Senator Farley's estimate of $40,000 a year, that makes it ... uh ... $400,000 for ten years. Then, if we figure out what it would be for fifteen years ..."

Math was never one of Mabel's best subjects. When Earl had finally managed to teach her to use a calculator at the bakery, all the factors and equations she'd labored to memorize in school had immediately and joyously evaporated from her head.

Josie scribbled on the bag, struggling to write as the car bounded along on its sprung suspension system.

"$600,000," she announced incredulously. "But does that include medical care?" Neither of them knew the answer to that, so they agreed to a figure of $800,000 for each of them, to be sure they wouldn't be shortchanging the government.

"Just think of that," Josie said in amazement, tapping her pen accusingly at the figures on the bag. "Senator Farley accepts the idea of paying that much to support people who contribute nothing and only cause trouble. But he begrudges us seniors, who've *paid* for our Social Security pensions, the little pittances we've *earned*. Something is wrong here. *Really* wrong." She gazed, unseeing, out of the window, wishing she'd had the chance to live on $40,000 a year.

Mabel could see by Josie's flushed face that she was ready to take off on another one of her tangents. "You're right, Josie," she quickly agreed, unaware that driving at fifteen miles an hour had produced a line of impatient drivers behind her. "But that isn't the issue here. We have to figure out how many bad guys we need to get rid of."

They had only hypotheticals to deal with. Twenty men behind bars for one year? One man for twenty years? Two men for life? If two men for life, how long is that?

After many calculations that led nowhere they decided to assign $100,000 to each criminal, on the premise that a criminal must drain the system of at least that much in his lifetime, considering court costs, prison time and all. So, each of them needed to remove at least eight— or, to be safe, nine—criminals before turning herself in. Then, with Mabel's house thrown in as a bonus, they wouldn't feel beholden to anyone. As far as they could figure, it was more than a fair bargain, and they could hold up their heads with pride in prison.

Making it strictly a business deal helped sanitize the acts they were about to commit. After all, they reminded each other, they had declared war, and no one could deny that war involved things getting broken and people getting killed.

"One thing concerns me, though," said Mabel, slowing for a hugely pregnant woman crossing the street ahead of her pulling a wagon carrying three small children and a pile of groceries. "It's risky carrying the gun around. What if someone sees it? We'd sure have some explaining to do."

It didn't take long for the solution to pop into Mabel's head. "I know! Earl's old socks—a whole drawer full of them! We can just slip the gun into a sock and no one will know."

Josie beamed at her friend, clapping her hands in appreciation of a brilliant idea. That left only the decisions of where and when. The verdict: Fifth and Flower, a run-down area of pawnshops, scruffy bars, and bail bondsmen, late that very afternoon.

Jonas watched the two old women across the street. They appeared to be awaiting their ride. Hands in his pockets, he casually leaned against one of the graffiti-covered buildings. His plaid shirt and khaki trousers blended seamlessly into the artwork that brought a bit of color to this dreary part of the city.

He had been on the lookout for just such a hit. The fat woman seemed a bit feeble, leaning against the building with her arms folded. The little one, in the blue coat, carried a grocery bag and paced back and forth, checking her watch every few minutes.

Old people. Next to cats, they're the most useless things goin'. At least you can have fun with a cat … cram an empty can on its head and watch it go crazy. But the law's fussy about old people. So far no one's fingered me for dumpin' those ol' drunks down by the tracks. But I was too easy on that ol' lady. She got away an' told on me. Well, these ol' bags won't be gettin' away. I'll stick 'em good. If they just got fifty bucks between 'em … He ticked off the things that were in his favor. Old women carried more cash than young ones, and their attention seemed to be on looking for their ride. With a new storm threatening, the street was virtually empty, and he knew the good alleys where he could hide. Trembling and sweaty in spite of the cold, he was in bad need of a fix.

He waited to cross with the light, hoping not to be noticed. Once he reached their side of the street, switchblade palmed, he pulled his baseball cap low over his forehead and began to jog in their direction, hoping to look like someone trying to get where he was going before the rain began. What he didn't know was that the women had their eyes on him, too.

By the time he had Josie's purse in one hand, knife at work in the other, he was swinging around to grab for Mabel's. She was ready for him, with the gun nestled in the crook of her folded arms. The last thing he saw as he lunged for her was a stiff white athletic sock aimed right up his nose. One shot did it, and it was over. The women stared in horror at what was left of the man's shattered face. They couldn't take their eyes off the gory sight for the eternity it seemed to take him to sag to the sidewalk. On an impulse, Josie quickly covered the ghastly sight with her grocery bag.

Rattled by the frightful scene and the scuffle, they fled in panic. They were saved by the sad fact that gunfire in this part of town simply sent people running for cover. No one even came to determine whether they'd heard a gunshot or a car backfiring. And if anyone had come to see, all they would have noticed was two old women, probably too deaf to have heard anything, getting into a big old Buick parked around the corner.

The drive back to Josie's was the most perilous part of their mission. By now the rain had begun, and gusts of wind streaked it across the windshield. Mabel, at the wheel, was hyperventilating and hardly aware of her surroundings. Josie alternately grabbed the wheel and shouted directions. Somehow they made their way back to Josie's and parked at the curb beneath her window.

On rubbery legs they made their way into the apartment, where they dropped unceremoniously into their usual seats. Eyes closed and body limp with relief, Josie breathed, "Mabel, what have we done?"

Splayed out like a plump rag doll on the daybed, Mabel looked dazed. "I don't know—it all happened so fast!" After she caught her breath and calmed her racing heart, she added, "If he just hadn't grabbed our purses..."

For a moment they were quiet, shocked by the impact of what had seemed so impersonal, so clean, in the planning stages. They had talked this through many times, agreeing there could be no turning back once they actually killed someone—no second thoughts and no recriminations, for they were at war. And it had been so easy! He had stepped right up to assault them, just *asking* to be their first victim.

"Well," grunted Mabel, restrained by the weight of her body on her raincoat and struggling to sit up on the daybed, "it was his choice. He attacked us of his own free will. If he hadn't chosen to be bad, he'd still be alive. We can't forget that, Josie. Remember, someone out there will be thanking us." She found enormous consolation in thinking he'd brought it upon himself.

Josie hadn't said a word since collapsing into her chair. The sight of so much blood had overwhelmed her. It was all she could do to shake off those dreadful images and focus on the situation at hand. Their war was now officially under way. They had expected their first foray to be the hardest and their first casualty to be the most upsetting. They had promised each other to be good soldiers, but still …

Mabel had a sudden recollection. "Josie, I just remembered. You covered his head with your grocery bag. That was so sweet of you!" She wrinkled her nose as though smelling something bad. "He did look awful, and he wouldn't have wanted anyone to see him … well, looking like that."

Josie grimaced, squinting her eyes to shut out the sight. "Oh, Mabel, covering him seemed the only decent thing to do …" She trailed off, struck by the pity of a young life ending like this, when there were many better choices he could have made.

"I guess no one ever taught that poor man about being nice," she went on. "To think, he was once just an innocent little boy, with a whole life ahead of him."

"Well, he'll never be bad again, Josie," said Mabel. "I think we've prevented a lot of misery, both for him and for everyone else he'd surely have hurt. Heaven knows how much he's cost the government already, but he won't be costing them any more."

Again they sat in silence, until Josie realized they hadn't checked to see whether he had also been carrying a gun. They could use another one, she said, so they'd each have one. Next time, they agreed, they wouldn't overlook that.

Emotionally and physically exhausted, Mabel rose to go home. "Tomorrow afternoon, if the storm blows over?" she asked.

Josie nodded. "But this time maybe we should take the bus someplace else, like Los Angeles or San Diego. It might not be a good idea to conduct another mission so soon in the same town."

"Los Angeles!" Mabel perked up. "What a good idea. I haven't been there in years and haven't been on a bus since I don't know when. That could be fun! Besides, the smell from the basement is beginning to get to me. I need to get out of there. It means I'll have to drive home after dark, I suppose … but after doing what we just did, I guess I can do anything."

Mabel gave the gun to Josie, who wanted another practice without shells. She promised to check the bus schedule and be back for Josie tomorrow afternoon, weather permitting. She also promised to bring a supply of Earl's socks.

Josie congratulated Mabel on her first $100,000, saying, "Well, nasty as it is, I guess we've proved we can do it."

They sealed their first mission with a mark on the wall by the thermostat, and Mabel wrote the initial *M* over it. A few inches away, Josie placed her *J*.

"Okay, all you creeps out there," she threatened with her newfound bravado. "Next time it's my turn!"

Long after Mabel had gone home, Josie lay alone in the darkness, gripped by the dramatic thunderstorm that shattered the night sky with stabs of lightning and reverberating crashes of thunder. Her talk with Theodore had left her comforted, free of the remorse she was afraid would set in. Snug from the rain that pelted her window, she pondered this new twist in her life. Whoever would have thought it! Certainly not she, who had in high school been voted "Most Likely to Prove the Existence of the Boogeyman."

Later she would find and mend the six-inch slash in her coat that stretched from beneath her right shoulder blade to her waist. Only then would she know that Mabel's bullet had interrupted the deadly thrust of a switchblade knife.

Mabel hadn't heard a thunderstorm like this since she left Kansas as a child. Tired as she was, she got out of bed and rolled up the yellowed old window shade to enjoy the storm's magnificent display. The howling wind, crashing thunder and brilliant slashes of lightning made her feel like a girl again. She had been terrified of thunderstorms then, certain that God was punishing her for her misdeeds—especially the misdeed of trying to avoid going to Sunday school, which scared her just as badly as the thunderstorms.

Her mind wrenched back to those days and Mrs. Foster, the teacher who continually reminded her that God was listening to her every thought, ready to condemn her to eternal damnation for any wickedness He detected. Vivid images skittered through her head: pictures around the Sunday school room of sinful souls trapped forever in steaming pits of putrid glop, and, many years later, the pitiful succession of what her doctor had called "blue babies," who lived only long enough to give Mabel hope before quietly taking their last breath. The doctor had blamed incompatible Rh blood factors, a relatively new discovery at the time, but Mabel wasn't so sure. God had to have known she sometimes had mean thoughts and that she hadn't always turned the other cheek.

The memories nudged at her now. Had they brought down God's wrath with this storm? She forced herself to be rational, reminding herself that Earl had helped her get over all that superstitious stuff long ago. But she gasped in disbelief, skin tingling and hair rising on the back of her neck, when, through the rain-fogged window she saw a faint glimmer of light glowing from beneath the door of Earl's tool shed, next to the garage.

Oh no! I'm seeing things again! There can't *be light coming from there. It has to be a reflection of something else … maybe wind rippling the rainwater...* She scrubbed at the glass to clear the misty window, unable to tear herself away until a huge crash of thunder rocked the house. She jumped, fumbling in disarray, and then groped her way to the kitchen and the phone. She took one last look over her shoulder. Yes, there was definitely light coming from under the door.

But wait! She stopped in the dark hallway. *I can't have the police out here. They'll see what Josie and I have been doing. They'll surely smell the gunpowder and the rest of the mess in the basement. Oh, dear! What do I do?*

Back in the bedroom, she risked another peek out of the window. The glimmer from the shed was gone. In dismay, she plopped down on the bed, her mind a scramble. *Is seeing things how Alzheimer's starts? Flitting black robes and lights in the shed?* Her imagination produced images of herself, drooling and demented, locked away in some dreadful nursing home. It was too awful to think about. *Could this be it, the beginning of senility?* Another gust of wind shuddered the old house, and a sudden clap of thunder caused her to jump and cry out for Earl.

She wrung her hands and argued with herself until the storm moved on, rumbling in the distance. By now she was more angry than frightened.

She *wasn't* crazy. Although she had managed to put the image of the flitting black robe out of her mind, the light in the shed was going too far. Someone was out there. She certainly wasn't going to go snooping around by herself, so there was only one course of action. Because she was too agitated to sleep, she'd do her best to clean up the basement during the night and call the police in the morning.

SEVEN

Daylight found a haggard Mabel in the basement, broom in hand, exhausted. She had filled six trash bags with debris from their target practice and spread piles of newspapers to soak up the liquid remains. She had also lugged a dozen or more cardboard boxes up the stairs to burn in the fireplace. This seemed a good way to destroy the bullet-riddled evidence, and at the same time diffuse the smell from the basement.

But she'd never built a fire by herself. Her fire quickly became a roaring blaze with a staggering stench of its own, belching thick, black clouds of smoke and filling the air with a sooty haze. Aghast, she realized the damper must be shut—or at least not fully open. Without thinking, she hunched over the fire to look up at the flue. She was instantly repelled by the searing heat and unmistakable odor of singed hair.

"Oh, Earl," she wailed, clutching at her hair with both hands, surprised to find it still intact. "Oh, Earl—what do I do now?"

As if in answer, her eyes fell upon the fireplace tools. She grabbed the heavy iron poker and struggled with it over the open flame, finally ramming the damper open with several glancing blows. After accomplishing this, she gathered her courage and threw open what windows she could to let the smoke escape. She was certain whoever was in her shed would seize the opportunity to climb right into her house, regardless of the bars on the windows. But there was no time to waste. She couldn't call the police with her house in such shambles. How could she ever explain all this mess?

Throughout the night she fearfully checked on the open windows with every trip up the stairs, armed with the fireplace poker. Now and then she peeked out at the shed from behind her bedroom shade, dreading what she might see. But all was still.

By early morning the sun was out brightly, as though apologizing for the rough treatment of the night before. But Mabel was too tired to care. And her bad knee was swollen and throbbing. On the stove boiled a pan of water with sticks of cinnamon and cloves, which she hoped would overcome the horrid smell that must have saturated every pore of her house.

In spite of her woes, she smiled as she prepared that concoction. Earl used to call it her aphrodisiac. Warm memories of their intimate moments flooded over her. He had been such a gentle, considerate man. As old and sagging of flesh as she had become, he still professed to find her beautiful. Her love for him flooded over her in waves of remorse.

Oh, Earl, I never knew how much I loved you. I just took you for granted and got mad at you for the silliest things.

Overcome with fatigue, pain, and sorrow, she allowed herself a good cry before showering and dressing in the soft green pantsuit that had been Earl's favorite. Then she headed for the phone.

Her first call was to Bliss, who was dumbfounded with what she had to tell him. A flitting robe and a light glowing from under the door of the shed? He wanted to come right over, but she convinced him to wait until she'd talked to the police. They may not want anybody else on the place, she said. Over his protestations, she promised to call him as soon as she could.

Then she called Josie, who was just getting up and couldn't believe her ears. Black robes and unexplained lights, Mabel alone and frightened, tackling the mess in the basement—it was too much for her sleep-fogged brain.

"Mabel, you should have come and got me! I'd have helped you. Poor thing—you must be exhausted."

"Josie, it was too stormy … and I was too scared to walk out to the car, anyway. But I sure wish I'd a'had that gun. Although it's probably just as well. I might have shot someone by mistake."

Talking with her friends helped to calm her. Maybe she'd made a mountain out of a molehill. But, just to be sure, she would still call the police.

"I'll catch a cab and be right over, Mabel," Josie was saying. "I'll bring the gun and spend the night with you."

Mabel hastily told Josie the same thing she'd told Bliss.

"You're a sweetheart to offer, and I'll call you as soon as I can."

Two policemen in a squad car responded within half an hour of her call. They looked so formidable in their uniforms that Mabel was instantly sorry she'd called them. However, they listened respectfully while she told them about the black-robed person and the light in the shed. She could see their eyes scrutinizing her while taking in every detail of her living room behind the mask of their dark glasses. Telling her to wait in the house, they said they would make a cursory pass through the yard to see what they could see.

It wasn't long before they were back, asking her to accompany them. They helped her down the front stairs and through the weed-choked yard to the sturdy shed Earl had built one long-ago summer to house his gardening equipment. Pointing to the door, they invited her to look inside. Her heart was pounding. Their grim manner made it clear that something wasn't right. Fresh oil stains were obvious in the paint-peeled wood by the hinges. *Who had oiled the door?*

Morning sun flooded the small, dusty room. *Where were Earl's tools? And what was all that other stuff?* It took her a moment to realize someone was living there.

Cans, candles, blankets, tumbled clothing, and the rancid odor of unwashed bodies all struck her senses head-on. She felt her legs buckle. As if that weren't enough, the policemen helped her through the damp weeds to the rear of the house and showed her where a tool, probably Earl's crowbar, had been used in an attempt to pry apart the security bars on the windows.

Afraid she was going to faint, they held her sagging body between them, prepared to offer first aid. The white officer, who seemed to be in charge, ordered the tall, black one to call an ambulance.

"No," she cried, leaning on them heavily. "No ambulance. Just help me into the house ... oh my God ... Oh my God!"

They half-dragged her, whimpering, back into the house and propped her up on the sofa in the living room. The tall, black officer hurried into the kitchen to get a glass of water, and then they both hovered over her where she sprawled, eyes closed, moaning in shock.

"Just let me lie here a minute. Oh, dear. I'll be all right ... I'm sure I'll be all right. But ... but what should I do? Oh, dear ... oh, dear!" She fanned desperately at her face with a small lavender pillow that, with the impact of her body, had tumbled from the mound of pillows on the sofa. Her initial fear of the officers' take-charge presence had now changed to a quavering reassurance. They'd know what to do. Policemen always knew what to do.

They calmly gave her time to rest, taking down what information she could give them over the dinging and clanging and bonging of the clocks. Then they called the station. The sound of one of them speaking on the phone washed in and out of her consciousness like the gentle swooshing of the surf.

But one thought refused to be cloaked by the swirling mists that clouded her mind: they *mustn't* drag her off to the hospital. She *couldn't* leave and let them snoop through her house and figure out what she and Josie had been up to.

She wondered what they made of the concoction of smells in the house. Undoubtedly, her own nose had grown accustomed to the odor, making it impossible for her to discern anything at all. From the comfort of the fuzzy, drifting fog that dulled her senses, she reasoned there was nothing she could do about it now but pretend not to notice.

The officer whose badge read "McClung" returned frequently to where she lay, making sure she was okay. She professed to feeling much better than she really did—she didn't want them calling a doctor or taking her to the hospital. But there was that singed hair …

"One thing is certain," McClung was saying. "Whoever is living in the shed will be back. But not if he sees a police car on the premises. We're going to have to get it out of here. Can you arrange to be gone for a few days? We'll set up a surveillance, and it may not be safe for you to stay here."

She panicked, knowing Josie had no extra bed and that Mil and Bliss's house was too remote for conducting missions. Besides, Mil would insist on going with her if she went into town. How could she explain wanting to go by herself?

"But I'm *always* home at night," she cried. "If I turn up gone they'd know something was wrong for sure."

Her main concern was their war. They had just got the hang of it, and now *this*.

"I'll spend most of my time with friends and give you a lot of latitude, but please don't make me leave." Her eyes were tearful with her pleading.

McClung couldn't believe she wanted to stay. He called the station for further instructions and found they really couldn't force her to leave. And he had to agree that what she said was true; her being there might lead the squatter to think he hadn't been seen and that he could carry on as usual.

"Do you think you can keep from telling anyone about this?" asked McClung, folding his notebook and pushing his sunglasses up on his forehead to reveal startling blue eyes. "The fewer people roaming around over here, the better. The squatter won't come back if he thinks anyone will see him. Now, both times you've seen evidence of him is when we've had bad weather. That's when our drifters seek shelter. If the weather clears, he may not be back anyway, so your problems may be about over."

He got up to go. "Stay out of the backyard and away from the windows. We can operate a stakeout from that parking structure on the street behind you. If your squatter thinks the coast is clear, he could still return. And we'll get 'im. The main thing right now," he said as he and his partner headed for the door, "is to get that police car out of here. Are you sure you're going to be all right? Do you want me to send someone to stay with you?"

Mabel hastily assured him that she would be fine and that friends had already volunteered to stay with her. To prove she was all right, she willed her trembling body up from the sofa and ushered the men to the door. They promised to keep in touch.

Once in the police car, McClung turned to his partner, a huge man fondly called Squirt, and said, "What's your take on it? Seems like a nice old lady. Great old house. She's got a regular clock shop there. But, whew," he said with a wince, hurrying to back the car out of Mabel's driveway, "whatta you make of that god-awful smell?"

Squirt was picking his teeth with a matchbook cover. "She's usin' her fireplace as an incinerator," he said, speaking between jabs of the thin cardboard imprinted with 'Carl's Garage.' "She was so upset I didn' wanna nail her on it just yet, but from the looks and the smell of it, she's had one nasty blaze in there, and recently. Hair's been singed. Lucky she didn't burn the whole place down."

He reached for a tissue from the box they carried in the car and loudly blew his nose. "Wonder if she knows incinerating has been against the law for over forty years." He shook his head as though to clear the pungent odor from it. "She might be used to it, but man, that stink put a major hurt on my nose."

Mabel was snoring loudly when Josie let herself in. She finally awakened in the late afternoon to find Josie keeping watch over her from the armchair beside her bed. They had little appetite for dinner, so they spent a quiet evening nibbling cheese and crackers while watching television, trying not to think about what might be going on in the yard behind them. Mabel's peril had strengthened their resolve tenfold; they were more committed than ever to their war on crime.

Josie managed to convince Bliss, who felt duty-bound to help his damsel in distress, that all Mabel needed was sleep and that because the police were watching the house, she wasn't afraid to stay with her.

"They don't want anyone snooping around out there and scaring the man off," she said. "But believe me, Bliss, we'll call for you as soon as we can."

Neither Josie nor Mabel slept well. By morning they were worn out from listening for things that weren't there. They knew they had to get out of the house and away from its eerie noises. So, early in the afternoon, they set out for the Santa Ana bus station, ready to try a mission in Los Angeles.

After receiving directions from attendants at two different gas stations, they found, on Santa Ana Boulevard, the beautiful new Spanish-style station that now combined both train and bus service. They couldn't believe the difference between this thoroughly modern structure and the quaint little bus and train stations it had replaced. A gracious fountain splashed a bubbly welcome into the station's airy lobby, and, unlike the old stations, the new one provided acres of parking.

"What a transformation." exclaimed Mabel. "They really went all-out here."

Josie, too, was amazed. "That grubby old bus station used to give me the creeps. But this one's lovely."

It was a clear but chilly day, and they were eager for the adventure of their bus ride. After a quick look around they had bought their tickets and were boarding the bus like field trip-bound schoolchildren. They peered out of the windows all the way, marveling at the changes that had taken place since they had last been to Los Angeles. Modern buildings sketched across the skyline kept them poking each other in awe. They thought they had never seen anything as beautiful as the City of Angels under a clear afternoon sky, tucked beneath the towering San Gabriel, San Bernardino, and San Jacinto mountains that formed an impressive barrier to the north and east.

But by the time they arrived at the station the sense of majesty had been shattered by the crush of blighted buildings. Clutching each other's hands, they stepped off the bus into what seemed like a sea of lost souls. The noise and confusion overwhelmed them. They looked around for signs to get their bearings and, among the bewildering array, noticed large posters warning of crimes taking place aboard buses.

"My goodness," clucked Josie over the din of loudspeakers echoing endless, indecipherable information. "Aren't we lucky *we* didn't encounter any such shenanigans."

Neither of them knew her way around Los Angeles, so they decided not to stray too far from the bus station. They'd have to find a less crowded area, however, because they couldn't use the gun around all these people.

Before leaving the building they visited the restroom and were appalled. They couldn't believe women could be so slovenly. What they didn't know was that the bus station had become a home of sorts to a constant stream of transients. Overwhelmed, they left the noise and confusion and made their way out to the crowded sidewalk.

"Doesn't anyone ever go home?" Josie asked, astonished at the number of unkempt, dazed-looking people loitering about who, in her estimation, should be home getting ready for dinner or at least getting in out of the chill air. This was worse than what she'd encountered when Hali took her to the support-group meetings in Santa Ana, and she had thought *that* was bad.

Still clinging together, they arbitrarily turned and walked as quickly as the press of people permitted, assaulted by the stares of idle men and mumbled pleas for money. After a few blocks they stopped at a corner to rest, leaning against the cold concrete of a once-stately but now dingy, boarded-up hotel.

"Wasn't this the old Belmont?" Mabel asked, looking for something familiar on its weathered facade.

A baffled Josie didn't know. "It's nothing like *anything* I remember."

The clamor of traffic and the stink of diesel exhaust overloaded their senses as they continued to walk. It was all they could do to keep from fleeing back to the safety of the bus station.

Finding a side street that was a bit less trafficked, they turned again and walked through a blur of grimy shops, each offering a mix of shopworn goods behind burglar-proof steel bars.

"I'm sure these used to be the fancy boutiques that served the hotel trade," said Mabel. "What's happened to Los Angeles?"

Josie could only shake her head.

Cars and taxis went by with well-dressed people in them, but the women were painfully aware that they were the only respectable people on foot. They clung to their purses and each other, feeling more like a target than a threat to any evildoer they might encounter.

After walking another few blocks they turned onto a somewhat quieter street, where Mabel said the empty buildings had once been ritzy department stores. If they could have peeked inside them, they would have seen that scores of enterprising homeless people had found a way through the various barricades to claim bedroll space among the nooks and crannies of the mazelike interiors. During the day the occupants sat around on the sidewalk, bumming cigarettes and change from passersby and measuring time by the daily food service provided at a nearby rescue mission.

The women endured the gauntlet of eyes and catcalls for another block before they paused again, uncertain which way to go. Mabel, whose knee was still sore, wanted only to sit down.

"But there's no place we *can* sit down," she wailed. "We have to get out of here before we get lost … or robbed! Oh, Josie, this was a really bad idea."

Josie tried to be the strength for both of them.

"If we turn here, Mabel, we can get back to the bus station without retracing our steps. I've been keeping track of our turns. If we go left and then left again, we'll come up behind the bus station, and we won't have to walk by those rude men again."

They had gone only half a block, near a darkening alley, when they heard the unmistakable sounds of muffled screaming. Their hearts stopped as one. They looked to each other in confusion, not knowing which way to go. Sure of her shortcut back to the bus station, Josie pulled Mabel forward to the edge of the alleyway, where they risked a quick glance down its gloomy depths before starting across. A foul odor accosted them. Trash from overflowing dumpsters lay scattered everywhere. Just as they started to cross, a furtive movement caught their eyes.

Two men stood over the body of a third. In the moment it took their feet to obey their brain's command to turn and flee, the men had seen them. The women were stopped short by a deep voice yelling, "Hey!" Panicked, they instinctively huddled together, forgetting everything they had rehearsed.

Josie and Mabel stood rooted in the entrance of the alley as the two men approached them, the taller, huskier one covering the ground with long, confident strides and the frail, scruffy-looking one scurrying along behind. The men's eyes scanned the street, making sure the coast was clear.

"Git lost on yer way t'church or somethin'?" asked the nattily dressed black man, his voice a rich baritone. His darting black eyes seemed to have the ability to look in all directions at once, but Josie and Mabel could only stare at the gun he held. "You all dressed up so nice. Maybe you hookers, cuttin' in on my territory."

His scruffy friend laughed at the joke and tried to make one of his own.

"My, my! Well-aged white meat," he lisped, his tongue flapping through gaping holes where teeth used to be. "Gettin' a little old for the night shift, ain't ya?" Thinking himself ever so clever, he began to laugh until he was enveloped in a fit of helpless, consumptive coughing.

The third man lay still on the littered asphalt between two dumpsters.

"Well, you picked a bad time t'strut yer stuff aroun' here," hissed the larger man. "Yes, ma'am, a ba-a-d time. Caught us collectin' from a ver-ry un-appreci-ative client. So I guess you know you ain't never leavin' this alley. But I don' guess our client gonna mind havin' two ladies fer comp'ny. Fact," he sniggered in the direction of the lifeless body, "I don't guess he gonna mind much'a nothin'."

"Step on into my office, ladies," he said, gesturing with his gun to usher them farther into the alley. He looked them up and down in mock admiration. "Hookers, huh? Well, now, as pretty as you two are, you musta worked up more money'n you can carry, and it ain't even dark yet."

He loomed like a bad dream in front of Mabel, who stood transfixed with Josie plastered to her arm.

"Bein' as you workin' my territory wit'out axin' me, and you ain't gonna live t'spend it anyways, you won' be mindin' if we take these here han'bags."

He had stooped, his hand firmly on Mabel's purse, when the shot rang out. The frail man jumped, straightening up abruptly from his coughing.

"Shit, man," he spat. "You didn't have to shoot her. Makin' all that damn racket. Just grab their fuckin' purses and let's get the fuck outta here!"

He stepped up, grabbed Josie's purse, and had turned to run when he saw the look of shock on his companion's face. His gaze lowered to the gaping hole where bright red blood pumped from the big man's chest. In disbelief, he looked back at the women, giving Josie a clear shot.

Leaning against Mabel for support, Josie had now taken the gun out of her pocket. The man was mesmerized by the stiff white gym sock she held out in front of her; his puzzled face was a perfect target. One more shot rang out only seconds after the first, and the alley was quiet again.

They later remembered they had covered the men, as planned, with hastily placed shopping bags and that they had been hustled out of the way by the first men to arrive on the scene.

"This ain't no place for ladies," one of the men had shouted, and gallantly sent them on their way before a knot of spectators began to converge in the alleyway.

Witless in their panic, Josie and Mabel had little recollection of finding their way back to the bus station. They were fortunate to find two seats together on a bench in the middle of the waiting room. It was an incredibly noisy place, with constant announcements echoing from its cavernous walls. People dozed, read, and argued all around them. No one seemed to notice the two old women who came rushing in. They sat as still as they could, out of breath, their pulses banging like jungle drums in their ears. Finally they dared to look at each other and then risked speaking a few words.

"Are you okay, Mabel?" Josie whispered, barely making herself heard.

"I guess so," Mabel responded in a thin voice. "But that was a close one."

"I know," replied Josie. "And those men were so rude. They called us hookers!" She almost blushed at the word. "And now I have a hole in my coat. Darn those guys, anyway."

She couldn't bear that her beautiful coat had taken all this abuse. The cleaners had managed to get the mud stains out, and she was able to mend the knife gash, but now it had a perfectly round, singed hole in the pocket from the shot she'd fired at the first man. She examined it and decided it could be patched with a little piece from the hem. But her beautiful coat would never again seem as nice.

"Darn those guys," she repeated. "They came before we were ready, and I had to shoot the first one right through my coat pocket."

Mabel nodded, still in shock.

Josie nudged her with her elbow and whispered, "You'll never guess what I have in *my* pocket."

Mabel was absorbed in fingering the outline of the big man's gun in her own pocket. She'd picked it up from where it had fallen on the sidewalk.

"A big wad of money," whispered Josie, unable to hide her excitement. She looked around warily to make sure no one was listening.

"The big man had a wad of money in his pocket. And the other man had a gun, too." She started to reach into her pockets to provide proof when Mabel grabbed her arm.

"Not here," she gasped. "Not till we get home."

Josie shrank in her seat, realizing the confusion had left her addled.

"We've got to find out about the next bus to Santa Ana," she mumbled. Struggling to her feet, she made her way to the ticket counter. After studying the arrivals and departures and consulting her watch, she hurried back to where Mabel still sat in a daze.

"We're in luck," she announced. "Next bus leaves in fifty-five minutes. We're going home, Mabel."

Grateful for the refuge of the bus, Josie and Mabel settled in seats near the front, relieved to be off the clangorous streets and away from the teeming bus station. They had hoped to doze most of the way home but soon discovered that this bus was not an express, as the afternoon one had been. Instead, the bus wended its way through the City of Commerce, Santa Fe Springs, Norwalk, Buena Park and Anaheim, picking up and letting off passengers. It seemed to take forever to make the slightest progress, with the door opening and closing, people jostling on and off, and the lights turning on at every stop.

Josie and Mabel spoke very little but commended each other on having had the presence of mind to cover the men, as planned, with shopping bags. After Josie had so thoughtfully covered their first man in Santa Ana, they'd decided to make shopping bags standard equipment on their missions. Killing had proved to be an ugly business, and covering the men did seem a bit more humane. Besides, they thought there might be a requirement in the Articles of War about protecting the dignity accorded to fallen foe.

Josie was elated. She'd done away with *two* men, each worth $100,000 toward her keep in prison, in one night's mission.

"It's such a shame those men chose to be bad," she said sadly. "They could just as well have been nice, you know, instead of hanging out in alleys, killing and robbing people. Their poor mothers …"

Josie rode along quietly for a time, and then she sighed, saying, "Well, the choice was theirs. They had to know better. We really did them—and everyone else—a favor by stopping them in their tracks. Sooner or later they'd have been caught, anyway, so we just saved the government the bother."

Mabel was deep in thought, reliving Earl's death at the hands of a person such as those two. During his trial, the killer had had the nerve to say that it wasn't his fault; society had failed him. She nodded her agreement with Josie and added, "And you know what else? I think if society failed those men, it was in letting them get away with stuff like this too many times. I think the truth is, Josie, those men failed society."

It was after nine o'clock when they arrived at the Santa Ana station. They hadn't been able to nap a bit and were thoroughly exhausted. But at least Mabel hadn't thought about the person in her shed all afternoon. Knowing her house was being watched by McClung's men eased her fear of returning to it after dark.

This time, Mabel's Buick provided a subdued ride home. They were too tired to think about the money or the guns they'd found. Even Mabel forgot they hadn't eaten dinner.

McClung's men were on the job. The women hadn't been home five minutes when the phone rang. Officer McClung said he'd begun to worry about them and wished them a good night.

EIGHT

They were up early, chenille robes over flannel nighties, eager to check out the money and the guns. Josie was beside herself to find that the wad of money on Mabel's kitchen counter consisted of nothing but hundred-dollar bills—three neat stacks of ten bills each.

"Three thousand dollars!" she said to Mabel, who hovered over her shoulder.

"I bet they took it from the dead man in the alley," said Mabel. "This proves those men were bad, Josie. But what should we do? We can't return it to that poor man."

Mabel's mother had always said "find the owner" whenever Mabel had been lucky enough to find some little treasure. When Mabel was in the third grade, she found a dollar bill on her way home from the school bus stop. She ran with it all the way down the dusty gravel road, even taking a shortcut under the barbed wire fence and through the wheat field, bursting with visions of things she could buy. But after she gleefully showed it to her mother, her mother called around to all the neighboring farms until, sure enough, that crabby old Mr. Ohlsen was certain the money was his. And that was the end of her dollar bill—and the end of her ever expecting something for nothing.

"We can't give it to *anyone* without giving ourselves away, Mabel," Josie reminded her. "But we could use it for bus tickets and things. And we can give whatever's left to the government, as part of *my* bonus."

Mabel applauded her generosity.

"You're right, Josie," she said, looking askance at the piles on the counter. "It's dirty money. Drugs or something. And in that neighborhood, whoever found those bodies would have robbed them anyway. We can put it to much better use." She decided not to waste any more thought on the possibility of suffering eternal damnation for keeping this money.

They examined the guns and discovered that both of them used the same bullets as Earl's. They practiced with them, chambers empty, the way Bliss had shown them. As long as McClung's men were out there, they couldn't really shoot. But they felt confident about using the guns on further missions, because they planned to fire at close range, where they couldn't miss.

With the matters of the money and the guns settled, they enjoyed their breakfast of French toast and bacon to the accompaniment of the radio. It was a beautiful morning. The recent rainstorm seemed to suffuse the whole world with an uncommon brilliance, and ecstatic birds soared from tree to tree, celebrating earth's splendor in song.

"It is Sunday, you know," said Josie, smothering her French toast with a big blob of grape jelly. "And while I'm not a churchgoer, I really don't think we ought to kill anyone on Sunday."

Mabel agreed. War on Sunday would definitely be a sacrilege.

"But you know," Josie continued, "while you have me here to help, we should start sorting out your closets. We shouldn't inflict that on Mil and Bliss after we're gone."

Mabel hesitated. "Oh, Josie, I don't know if I'm ready for *that*." She laughed, both perplexed and embarrassed. "I've managed to avoid that for years. I'm not sure I even *want* to know what's in them."

Nevertheless, after cleaning up the kitchen and getting dressed, they took a box of large trash bags into the guest room and started with the bulging closet that Josie was using. Her few things were squeezed between years of accumulated clothing, as well as piles of books, baskets, and boxes stuffed with who knew what.

"Ooh," moaned Mabel, holding her head. "This is going to be hard. I hate decision making, 'specially early in the morning. Promise me we don't have to do the attic, too?"

Josie didn't give up. "No, we won't touch the attic. But come on; it'll be easier with two of us. If it's stained or torn, out it goes," she said, inspecting some of Earl's workpants. "Or if it wouldn't fit Bliss—and I'd say Earl was shorter than Bliss. Your things would never fit Mil, as tall as she is, so that makes it simple."

They began filling trash bags with clothing and shoes, uncovering an old RCA Radiola with vacuum tubes still in place, sitting atop its embroidered, fabric-fronted speaker cabinet. Buried at the back of the closet, behind the clothes and under a lamp shade, was an antique Marchant hand-crank calculator with its cracked and faded oilcloth dustcover.

"Some of these things ought to be in a museum," said Josie, moving on to pull the sheet off an old dress form.

"That was my mother's," said Mabel, gazing reverently at the dress form and running her hands over its worn, sawdust-filled body. "It's been a long time since I was *that* size. My goodness, that brings back memories. And the radio! I remember lying on the floor in front of it, listening to *Amos and Andy*, *Fibber McGee and Molly*, *Jack Benny*— remember, with Dennis Day and Rochester ..."

Josie could see why Mabel had never wanted to tackle this job.

"We can put them back in the closet when we're through, Mabel," she said gently, "and leave it to Mil and Bliss to do the right thing with them. We'll just take care of all the other stuff and get it out of the way."

She continued ferreting out clothing and things, separating the worn-out items from what could be passed along to someone else. "The Salvation Army can use this good stuff," she said. "We can stack it up here, in the guest room, can't we?"

Mabel halfheartedly joined her in the effort, but by mid-morning she insisted they stop for a rest and a cup of tea.

"Don't you wonder what's going on in the backyard?" whispered Josie, looking over her shoulder apprehensively. It was the first time that day they had spoken of the spooky goings-on at Mabel's.

Mabel cringed. "I don't want to know if someone is out there, Josie. That's for McClung's men. Having you here and staying busy has been such a help. I don't know what I'd have done without you and Officer McClung."

"McClung's men are a comfort," agreed Josie. "But I'm still going to worry about you, Mabel. They could miss seeing someone break in after dark."

She looked around, skin tingling at the thought.

Mabel, who had been reaching for a piece of leftover bacon, stopped in midair, wincing at Josie's suggestion.

"But if they look in the windows and see both of us they'll know I'm not alone. Don't you think that would stop them?" Unnerved, she arose from the table, dabbing at her mouth with a napkin, and went to check the windows for the umpteenth time. She wasn't sure whether she had locked them again after airing out the house following the blaze in the fireplace.

"Well, it sure didn't stop the burglar who shot Theodore," exclaimed Josie. "He knew we were home, with our bedroom window wide open. He just took the screen off and started right on through ... and shot poor Theodore for protesting! No, I'm afraid seeing two old women might not scare off *anybody*, especially if he really wants in. He won't know we're armed, or that McClung's men are out there." She took a deep breath. "If our husbands were alive, we wouldn't be dealing with any of this."

She got up, needing something to do with her frustration, and busied herself with refilling their teacups. "There must be something we could do. If they just *thought* we had a man ..."

"I've got it," Mabel cried. "The dress form—and a jacket and hat Oh, Josie, I have a wonderful idea!"

She began talking so fast Josie could hardly keep up with her.

"Remember that little boy in the movie who made dummies to fool the burglars who kept trying to break into his house while his parents were away? He even put them on a train track to keep them moving…"

She had Josie by the hand, pulling her down the hall to the bedroom.

"Look here, Josie. My sixties wig on its holder."

She pushed a stool over to where she had earlier seen the wig, on a shelf between a brightly striped hat box and a huge jar filled with every shape, size, and color of button. "The holder can be his head."

Josie squealed with glee and began rummaging through one of the trash bags for some of Earl's clothing.

"A shirt," she cried, triumphantly pulling one out of the bag. "And a jacket. I think I put some neckties in this other bag…" She began rifling through another bag while Mabel worked to affix the Styrofoam wig holder, shaped like a head with faintly defined facial features, to the rusty metal rod protruding from the neck of the dress form.

"It works," Mabel cried. "Now for the wig … and a hat!"

In no time, they had the dress form looking like a rather respectable gentleman, complete with a pipe stuck into its Styrofoam face. They had to take him apart and put him back together several times, discovering at once that the jacket hung wrong on him; he was still clearly a woman. Wrapping a blanket around his midsection had remedied that, filling him out with a generous belly. For pants, they took the backside out of a pair of trousers and secured the front part in place with a pair of Earl's colorful suspenders.

They tried many of Earl's hats before settling on the red and gold baseball cap. They thought it went well with the suspenders, as well as the red clip-on bow tie, their only choice. Neither of them knew how to tie any of the others. Earl's straw hats had made their dummy look too much like a scarecrow, whereas the felt Homburgs had given him the villainous air of a gangster from an old movie.

"He's wonderful," said Josie, standing back in appreciation. "At night, with the sheer curtains drawn and the lights shining behind him, he'll just be a shadowy image from outside. He's *bound* to look real."

She threw her arms around Mabel. "This is such fun! Now we just need a name for him."

Mabel was way ahead of her. Smiling impishly, she announced, "Mr. Moonbeam." She started to giggle, embarrassed to be revealing her intimate moments with Earl. She and Josie had never talked about such things.

"Earl would have been so proud of him, taking care of his women," she cried, unable to keep from laughing.

"Mr. Moonbeam?" Josie asked, puzzled. "How did you come up with *that?* I have a hunch there's something here I should know."

Blushing and fidgeting, unable to meet Josie's eyes, Mabel said, "Well, that's what Earl called his ... well, you know, his ... thing. He said it only got to come out and shine at night, so he called it ..."

Josie exploded in laughter. "*Mr. Moonbeam.* Oh, Mabel, I love it!"

They hugged each other, dancing around until they fell backward onto the piles of clothing strewn on the bed, and then lay laughing, crying out such things as, "Mr. Moonbeam to the rescue! Mr. Moonbeam, the answer to every maiden's prayer!" They carried on until they had exhausted themselves of Mr. Moonbeam jokes, and then lay there, eyes tracing the water-stained patterns on the ceiling. Like tree rings, the stains recorded storms of many a season past. It gave them time to reflect.

"Oh, Josie, what have we got ourselves into," said Mabel. "These are supposed to be our golden years—you know, rocking chair and loved ones and all. No one ever said anything about being lonely and afraid."

"Well," said Josie, "I guess it's sort of like finding out there's no Santa Claus ... and no Easter Bunny and no Tooth Fairy, all at once. But we have to get over it. We were lucky to find a solution. Most folks never find a way out of the morass of their final years. Who would have imagined people our ages could do what we're doing? We're pioneers. And our rocking chairs are just waiting for us in prison." She struggled off the bed and turned to help Mabel. "Come on, now. We have work to do."

Their dummy was ceremoniously placed in the living room window, where he could keep an eye on anyone approaching from the front. They fussed around, arranging him until they agreed he was just right.

"Better move him once in a while," suggested Josie, patting the stuffed sleeve that rested in his jacket pocket. "If he's always in the same place, people might catch on."

"I feel safer already," replied Mabel. "This was the best idea, Josie."

They returned to their work, peeking now and then into the living room to exclaim anew over their creation. They attacked one closet after another, and then moved on to dressers and cabinets, with Mabel detailing the history of each item she handled.

In the middle of the afternoon Officer McClung called to reassure Mabel his men were still out there and to ask whether she had noticed any activity in her backyard. Pleased to hear from him, she reported that she hadn't, and told him Josie was still with her, helping to clean out closets. Between his assurances and their fancied protection by Mr. Moonbeam, they felt an amazing peace of mind for the first time in days.

At five o'clock they stopped for a sandwich and another cup of tea, glad for a chance to sit down. Then they returned to their work with a vengeance.

"This is much easier than I thought it would be," Mabel confessed, stacking a pile of books in the front closet for Mil and Bliss. "It's not like moving, where you have to figure out what to take, or organizing, where you have to decide where to put things. We just have to separate the junk from the good stuff. Josie, this was such a good idea."

They worked on into the evening, when they ran out of trash bags and boxes. The guest room and dining room were piled high with their efforts.

"If you feel safe enough, Mabel, I'd like to go home now," said Josie. "I really do have a lot of catching up to do. And we need more trash bags, paid for with our war fund, of course," she said, patting her purse. "That is, if you think you'll be okay alone."

Mabel laughingly responded, "Josie, if Mr. Moonbeam is half the man he used to be, I'm in very good hands!"

NINE

"What the hell is this all about?" Detective Investigator Paige Turner asked no one in particular as she scanned the memo at the top of the pile. She had just arrived at her cluttered desk in the Santa Ana police station, the only female homicide investigator on the force. "A hit with a paper bag over his head? Get outta here!"

She was the last one in her hectic office to see the memo, as usual. Her male counterparts respected her and worked well with her, but in their good-old-boy way, they always reserved for themselves a head start on anything new or interesting. Blond and lithe, she often intimidated her coworkers with her looks and her "woman's intuition." It drove some of the officers crazy when she beat them to the heart of things in her quiet, unassuming way.

Mark Wisneski, who had worked at the equally cluttered desk next to hers for the past three years, gave her a preoccupied glance. "Had two more of 'em in L.A. Saturday night. Same kind of thing: shot at close range, bag over the head. There was a third stiff nearby, but he was beat-up. Head busted. No bag."

"Oh, brother," she muttered. "What will they think of next. Any ideas? Witnesses? Anything at all?" She scanned the memo while eating the apple that was her breakfast.

Two other investigators shared their austere office, where the only decor was an array of haphazardly hung memos and notices lining the walls, along with a framed photograph of Orange County District Attorney Rupert T. Bennings III, upon which someone had used a felt pen to draw a goatee and mustache. But the other two officers were engaged on the telephone, yelling over the noise of messages blurting from overhead speakers, each other, and the general din echoing down the halls. She wouldn't get any answers there.

"I see our local hit, Jonas Something-or-other-ski, wasn't your ordinary upstanding citizen. Gang stuff?" She continued to chew on her apple.

Wisneski shook his head. "Jonas Szajkowski, another dumb Polack like me. Small potato. Habitual. Petty theft, drugs, animal abuse, that sort of thing. Remember? He's the one who cut that old lady's phone line a few years ago, and nailed her doors and windows shut. It was a couple of days before anyone found her. She had a heart attack and died right after that. His lawyers called it a youthful prank, no intent of bodily harm. Look at his sheet. He was either locked up or working his way through the revolving door for the past, let's see … eleven years. The guy was only twenty-eight."

"And the ones in L.A.?" Turner asked. "How about them?"

Wisneski stretched and yawned. He'd come in early, trying to tie up loose ends so he could leave for Hawaii late this afternoon with his wife and teenage kids. He was finding, as usual, too many ends with nothing to tie up to. But his mind had already made the transition to his wife's parents' condo in Maui. He knew he was wasting his time here.

"The ones in L.A. Now you're talkin'," he said, leaning back to cradle his head in his hands. "Big Ben and his stooge, Alphonso. Some real slimeballs. We're talkin' big-time drugs, prostitution and pimping, fencing stolen stuff, battery, suspected murder—you name it. Rap sheets as long as your arm." He smiled. "The civilized world won't miss those two. Or the other one, without the bag, Johnny What's-'is-name. A loser from the git-go."

Always restless, he hunched forward to lean his elbows on the desk while absently stroking the ends of his mustache. "I'd like to know who finally got Big Ben in that alley," he added. "Had to be someone he knew and trusted, to get that close to 'em. No guns on 'em, no sign of a struggle. But the paper bag thing, I can't figure. We're guessing drugs, from the scribbling on the bag of the Santa Ana hit. Big numbers, probably outstanding debts."

"Yeah, why the paper bags?" Paige asked. "And what's the connection between our small potato and the hits in L.A.?"

Wisneski shrugged. "If it wasn't drugs, maybe they all got on the bad side of the same bag lady. Who the hell knows why the bags. Maybe someone thought the poor bastards were just too ugly. Well, they're only a drop in the bucket of shit that stinks up this whole country. Someone oughta bag 'em and shoot 'em all."

Paige was accustomed to Wisneski's jaded humor. It was a policeman's first line of defense. Dealing with the down and dirty every day, every month, every year, would drive him crazy if he couldn't make light of it.

"So what are we supposed to do about this memo?" she asked. "It has no directives."

"Well, honey, we just sit on it, like L. A. is gonna do, and see what happens next." Wisneski, already decked out in a brightly flowered Hawaiian shirt, scooped all his papers and scraps of notes into a pile in the middle of his desk and then swept them off into a waiting folder in his file drawer. He was notorious for his hit-or-miss filing system, as well as his disdain of computers. He freely admitted to being roadkill on the information superhighway, and could usually get Paige to help him if he had to do more than retrieve routine information. However, no one matched his unerring ability to read the criminal mind.

He and Paige worked well together. Her natural intuition matched his deadly instinct, and they both had a willingness to go to any length in the line of duty. Although they would have made a handsome couple—two trim, athletic forty-somethings—they shared a strong professional respect neither wanted to risk losing. Paige knew well the pain of a philandering husband and wouldn't inflict that misery on Alison, Mark's wife, under any circumstances.

Paige's ex-husband, also an investigator, had considered himself God's Gift to Women and hadn't been able to keep his pants on around worshipping females. Handsome in a craggy sort of way, his ego was at its best when he was servicing his fawning admirers. Paige refused to admit what everyone else already knew until she could deny it no longer. She'd gone home after lunch one day to change the slacks she'd dribbled spaghetti sauce on. There he was with one of their young dispatch trainees. He'd simply zipped up his pants, professing to think it was no big deal. She turned on her heel and went straight to the courthouse to retain a divorce lawyer before returning to her office in the adjoining police station.

"So much for loose ends," Mark said, closing his bulging file drawer and reaching for the latest "wanted" poster on Paige's desk. He stretched back in his chair, studying the poster, trying to get into the minds of the two young men pictured there. Looking back at him were the sullen faces of the two cousins from Missouri who were killing their way across the country, seemingly headed for Southern California.

"It'll just be my luck these two will show up while I'm gone," he said. "Damn! I'd like to be the one who outsmarts 'em."

He sat staring at the memo. "Turner, give me your fix on serial killers. Is it a genetic thing or what? Like, do these cousins share a bad gene?" He thought for a moment. "If it's genetic, it must be sex-linked, 'cause these repeaters always seem to be men."

Paige, who was going over notes in preparation for a court appearance, looked up at him as he slouched in his chair. She mulled over his premise for a moment.

"I don't know, Wisneski. Maybe you're just talking about the natural differences between men and women. Hormones. You know, estrogen that works to gentle a women, make her motherly and all, and estrogen's evil twin, testosterone, that turns guys into raging beasts. The reason we have wars. But I don't think anyone knows why some murderers get off on killing over and over again. Maybe it's more of a 'power and control' thing. Men seem to need that more than women. You know the kind," she said, in a transparent jab at her ex-husband. "They have to prove their manhood by screwing or fighting with anything that crosses their path." Her expressive blue eyes sparkled as she baited him. "But you are right about the genetic sex-link thing, Wisneski. Men do seem to have a haywire gene that makes them prone to do really dumb things."

With a growl, he snapped forward in his chair and threw his pen at her. She adroitly caught it, smiled, and blew him a kiss from her fingertips.

"Well," he grumped, settling back, "more likely it's because women have that PMS thing every month and get rid of a lot of their aggression. Without that release, just think how ornery they'd get. They'd be dangerous as hell by the time they were sixteen."

Paige closed her notebook and checked the time. She didn't want to be late for court.

"This discussion will have to wait till you're back from Hawaii," she said, groping under her desk for her purse. "I'm going to miss you, Mark. And you did bring up an interesting premise: PMS as it relates to crime and aggression in women. There might be more to it than meets the eye. But what do you suppose happens after menopause? No more aggression release. Scary thought, huh?"

He laughed, his hands framing a headline in midair, and in the urgent voice of a newscaster with a breaking story cried, "KILLER GRANNY STALKS CITY!" Amused at her off-the-wall notion, he chuckled and added, "I'm afraid not, Turner. The old gals have had a long time to get it out of their systems. By menopause they've tormented their husbands into early graves and are content to live off the old man's estate. Playing bridge, taking cruises. It's definitely the men you have to look out for. Especially psycho men like these cousins from Missouri."

Halfway out the door, she turned and said teasingly, "Well, you never know ..."

TEN

The first thing on Josie's agenda today was to do her laundry, before all the machines in the laundry room were taken. She'd soiled almost every dress she owned in Mabel's basement. Although she begrudged the coins for the Laundromat, her laundry had become too much to do in the sink.

She was glad to be home, for she missed her morning talks with Theodore—and the cat. This morning, she reveled with him at the irony of being overlooked with age, the very thing that had increasingly rankled both of them. But now it was paying off. She and Mabel were able to move about freely, with no one seeming to notice them.

Loading her laundry and soap into the wire cart that Bliss had repaired for her, Josie set out for one of the two laundry rooms that served the complex. They were tidy places, and well equipped with the necessary amenities. Tenants often visited and left their newspapers and magazines there for others to enjoy. Spiced with the tangy aroma of soap and bleach, the laundry rooms had come to function as social centers.

Luckily, there were a few empty machines. Once she had them loaded and filling, she gathered up her things to leave—but not before another tenant, Molly Flannery, came in to check on her laundry.

Josie blanched. *Oh no—not her, of all people!*

Molly Flannery was the undisputed busybody of the complex. Josie was seldom able to extricate herself from the woman's incessant chatter.

What if she sees something different about me? She may see right through me and know what Mabel and I have done. Certainly, she seems to know everything about everyone else... For a moment Josie thought she was going to be sick.

"Josie Winkworth," gushed Molly. "I haven't seen you in weeks. I've been so busy fighting the manager about the leak under my kitchen sink, and you know how *that* goes. You know, I wanted my bathroom painted while she had the handyman out about the leak, but she says she has 'priorities to consider,' you know, in that funny way of hers, and she '*may* do it in the fall.' Well, it isn't as though we don't pay good rent, you know, and it seems to me that handyman just stands around talking most of the time, anyway ..."

About twenty years younger than Josie, Molly looked almost youthful in her jeans and sweatshirt. Today she wore her graying brown hair pulled back in a ponytail, and flitted about with the effusiveness of a teenager. Without seeming to take a breath, she continued on with her chatter.

"How have you been? Have you heard about the romance between Mr. Tweedy and Ms. Atkinson?" She exaggerated "Ms." with a roll of her eyes.

Mr. Tweedy, a quiet, bookish man, lived above Josie. He reminded her of a shy, obedient child. In the three years Josie had lived there he had never looked directly into her eyes or spoken to her; a nod of his head seemed to take care of his communication needs. Ms. Atkinson, who lived across the courtyard from Molly, might have been a little older than Mr. Tweedy and seemed a bit addled. But that was all Josie knew about her.

"They met right here in this very washroom, you know," babbled Molly, thrilled to share her gossip. "She needed to borrow some soap, you see, and he was standing right there with his box of soap in his hand. They're both kind of shy, you know, and I think she let the machine go almost halfway through the cycle before she got up the nerve to ask him for half a cup or so. Actually"—she paused, thinking it over—"it was probably closer to three-quarters of a cup, you know, because it looked like he filled his half-cup measure twice." She paused, shaking her head as she argued with herself, and decided that maybe it had been only half a cup after all, because he was so careful not to spill that he'd probably filled it only halfway each time.

"Anyway, I was standing right over there, folding my towels," she said, pointing to a long table. "I'd already folded up the sheets and stuff, and I saw it all myself ..."

Josie was frantic. Even if she'd had something to say, she knew she'd never get it in edgewise. And she really didn't care about Mr. Tweedy and Ms. Atkinson. She was sure they were nice people, but didn't want to hear about them. She wanted to get away from Molly.

She'd often pitied Mr. Flannery. She seldom saw him, and when she did, he just quietly came and went, much like Mr. Tweedy. All Josie really knew about him was that he and Molly had met through their work at the marine base in Tustin. They'd been married for about five years, enabling Molly to retire. Josie was certain Molly's endless chatter had driven away her first husband, as well as her son and daughter, who, she complained, seldom called her. She wondered how long it would be before Mr. Flannery also fled.

". . . and the next thing I knew, he was over there, knocking at her door one evening," she was saying, unaware that Josie's face had taken on the glazed look of a wounded sparrow.

Josie inched backward, closer and closer to the door, with Molly following behind, still prattling away. She suddenly shifted gears to complain about the possible base closure her husband was facing.

"It'll put him out of work, you know, before we can afford for him to retire. What does the government expect us to do? It will be like shutting down a small city, you know," she went on, still oblivious to Josie's discomfort. "All those facilities just boarded up and the civilian employees left without jobs. Why, you know that whole base will just go to wrack and ruin, and us with it, if my husband can't find another job."

She again shifted gears to inform Josie about the couple in building C who had been assaulted in front of the pawnshop on Fourth Street. "Why, they just dumped that poor lady right out of her wheelchair, grabbed her shopping bag, and took off running. She was lucky, you know …"

Josie felt the blood drain from her head. *Wheelchair. Building C. Oh no!* Shock gave her the courage to interject, "The Watsons? Was it the Watsons? Tell me—what happened?"

Molly, surprised at Josie's interruption, looked at her quizzically. "Yes … I forgot you knew them. Well, I think it happened just a day or so ago. What in the *world* they were doing at a *pawnshop* I can't imagine. It just goes to show, you never know about some people. Putting on those proper airs around here, you know, and hanging out around *pawnshops*. Now, I'd never go near that part of town, myself," she added in her officious manner. "You're just asking to get hit over the head or worse. If you want my opinion …"

Josie never heard her opinion. She was out the door, leaving her cart behind, on her way to the Watsons'. The handyman, hosing off the sidewalks after some sprinkler repair, turned the hose aside to let Josie pass. He tipped his cap and said, "Mornin', ma'am," hoping to strike up a little conversation. But Josie hardly saw or heard him. She gave him one of Mr. Tweedy's little nods and was gone.

The Watsons were not in. She wished she'd had a scrap of paper so she could leave a note on their door, but resigned herself to reaching them by phone from her apartment.

Please let them be okay, she prayed, heading for home as fast as she could go. *The rotten so-and-sos who did this! I'd shoot them—and everyone like them—if I could.*

With each ring of their telephone, she begged, *Please pick up the phone … please pick up the phone …*

No one answered at the Watson's. This was ominous. They were almost always home and usually told her when they would be away. If they were at the market or drugstore, they surely would have invited her to go along. While she sat deciding what to do, her phone rang.

It was her eighty-five-year-old friend, Gertie Scheidler, who lived out in the canyon near Bliss and Mil, with her eighty-four-year-old husband, Waldo. Gertie was distraught with the news that she'd just put Waldo in a nursing home.

"He fought like a damn mule," she shouted, because she was nearly deaf. "But, Josie, I jis' didn' know what else t'do. That ol' fart still smokes like a chimney, an' I cain't keep very good track a' him no more. He gits to wanderin' off without tellin' me, and I never know what damn fool thing he's gonna do next. The last straw was settin' his paper diapers afire, right through his overhauls."

"Gertie! How in the world did he do that," cried Josie, shocked at the image of old Waldo with his pants on fire.

"Well, he was settin' out on the back porch last week, smokin' a' course, droppin' them damn sparks all over hell, and just set hisself afire. You know, I don't hear so good no more, and by the time I heard all the commotion he'd about beat hisself to death tryin' to put out the fire. Lucky fer him it was mostly just smolderin', so he didn't get hurt too bad."

Josie knew Gertie could hear very little of what she had to say. In frustration, she could only listen as Gertie talked on.

"But it didn' scare that man enough to stop smokin' or even to look out about his damn embers flyin' all over the place. I tell ya, he's burnt holes in ever'thing aroun' here, ever'where you look. 'Specially that broke-down ol' chair he likes so much. Why, it wouldn'a been more'n a matter a'time till he'da set the whole damn place a'fire, with us in it."

Josie tried to console Gertie, but knew there was really nothing she could say that would make either of them feel better.

"But what will you do?" she asked. "Are you going to try to stay there alone?"

"Well, that remains t' be seen," shouted Gertie. "The big question is how he's gonna git along in that home. They don' allow smokin', ya know, and no one's ever tol' that man what he kin an' cain't do. Why, he ain't even good crowbait no more, an' still thinkin' I'm gonna waller with 'im any time he wants. Still b'lieves he's a USDA prime stud, paper diapers and all. Don't know why he cain't do whatever the hell he damn pleases …"

Josie was emotionally drained when she hung up. Poor Gertie. As tough as Gertie talked, Josie knew she loved Waldo dearly. At least Gertie had been proud to say that her son Orvul, in Michigan, was going to take care of all the expenses.

Small compensation, Josie thought. Gertie was a brave, resourceful old woman. She'd never go to live with her son as long as Waldo was alive, and it would be impossible to transplant Waldo to anyone else's home, especially their son's fine home in Michigan. But what would Gertie do when she couldn't drive in from the canyon anymore? When her eyesight and health failed?

Josie sat by the phone, her thoughts tumbling. Thank God she and Mabel were taking care of those worries for themselves. If there were just some way to help Gertie.

Gertie and Waldo—no matter how odd they seemed, they were as genuinely good as folks could be. They minded their own business and asked for nothing, but would turn heaven and earth for their neighbors. Subtle as the mindless ticking of a clock, four decades had passed since she'd first met them at a card party at Mil and Bliss's.

Like many Oklahomans of the thirties and forties, Gertie and Waldo had been blown out west by the relentless, earth-scouring dust storms. But they never got over their funny ways. Josie could still see Gertie, hitched to the plow when Waldo deemed the patch he wanted to plow to be too small to bother catching and hitching the mule. And work-gnarled old Waldo in his best overalls, coming to visit Mil and Bliss on a Sunday afternoon, hair slicked down and fragranced with vanilla extract. There couldn't have been two more like them anywhere—or another topsy-turvy house like theirs, which had started as a one-room shack and grown, in fits and starts, in several off-kilter directions.

Nor could there have been another group of such rambunctious children as the ones they had raised. But they had all been respectful, hardworking youngsters in spite of their rough-and-tumble upbringing. How they turned out a stodgy one like Orvul, who made it big in the world of insurance, was a mystery.

Josie smiled to herself, remembering the time Bliss had teasingly asked Gertie how she'd managed to have such a lovely daughter as Velma, fathered by that ugly old buzzard, Waldo. Gertie had cackled in delight, responding, "Well, Bliss, we don't make babies with our *faces*, you know!"

She shook herself out of her reverie. She must call Mabel immediately and tell her about the Watsons and the Scheidlers. She and Mabel would have to postpone any further missions until they figured out how they could help.

Mabel was slow to get to her phone, and Josie had about given up when Mabel came puffing to answer it. She'd been in the basement, she said, fine-tuning her cleanup job. The smell had pretty much subsided, but it had occurred to her that she might be invaded by ants if she left all that sticky stuff around. It took the rest of the wind out of her to hear about the Watsons and Scheidlers.

"Well, for crying out loud! What do we do now?" she cried. "Every time we get started, something else happens."

"I won't know till I get hold of the Watsons," Josie replied. "But I'm thanking my lucky stars for the money we found. I know it'll help. But Mabel, I'm just furious. Poor Pearl, attacked by some stupid old … stupid old …" She was unable to utter a word bad enough to describe someone who would pick on a woman in a wheelchair.

Josie had barely hung up when the phone rang again. This time it was Mil. She had also talked with Gertie. They lamented the Scheidlers' predicament, and then Josie added the sad story about the Watsons.

A sober Mil replied, "We need to get together again soon, Josie. There's too much trouble going around. We'd better make hay while we can. Besides, we've missed you."

Josie felt a twinge of guilt for keeping secrets from Mil. She and Mabel had hardly spoken to her since their war began, afraid of letting something slip. Knowing Mil's propensity to speak without thinking, she could give the whole thing away without meaning to. Actually, the subject hadn't come up again. Mil and Bliss probably hoped Josie and Mabel had forgotten their crazy idea. However, a return to their comfortable potluck and cards routine sounded heavenly.

"Good idea," Josie replied. "That's just what we need. How about next Wednesday? At Mabel's, of course. You can bring the vegetable dish this time."

Mil had called to tell Josie how worried she was about Bliss. She wanted to confide the obvious discomfort he was hiding and that he just hadn't been himself since cleaning out Mabel's basement and organizing all his loot in the barn. He refused to speak of it and forbade her to bring it up. On top of that, she'd seen him cleaning and loading his shotgun one night. Something was going on. But she realized there was already too much bad news. She'd have to find a better time to talk about it.

Josie's next call was to the apartment managers. Surely they would have some information about the Watsons. The manager's wife informed her that the Watsons were at St. Joseph's Hospital in Orange, but she knew nothing about their condition.

"*Their* condition?" Josie blurted. "Is something wrong with Herb, too?"

The manager's wife didn't know, but gave Josie the number.

Josie's call to that number produced, to her surprise, the muffled voice of Pearl Watson.

"Pearl! I can't believe I got right through to you. I'm so relieved to hear your voice. This is Josie, and I've been *so worried* about you."

The line was silent for a moment, and then Pearl's hushed voice returned. Her speech was so thick Josie could barely understand her.

"Oh, Josie … Can't speak now … I'm okay. It's Herb … his heart. Could you … come over?"

Josie hung on her every word, shocked at how strange she sounded and that Herb was worse off than she was. "I'll be there, Pearl. Give me your room number."

She called Mabel again, telling her they needed to get to the hospital, and gave her what little information she had about the Watsons.

"We could have dinner in the hospital cafeteria," she added as an incentive, knowing Mabel's love of many choices of food. She insisted she would pick up the tab from their war fund. They agreed on a short visit around four o'clock, after Pearl had rested and before her dinner was served.

Josie hung up and sat quietly for a moment. This day had produced so much trauma, and it was only a little past noon. She knew she had to finish in the laundry room, but couldn't bear the thought of running into Molly Flannery again. Maybe she'd just watch the midday news for a while and give Molly a chance to get her things and go.

She prepared a cup of tea and turned on the TV. Balancing a handful of cookies on a napkin, she settled into her little side chair, but fell asleep, head lolling to one side, before she'd even warmed up the chair.

Even though it wasn't a happy occasion, Josie and Mabel enjoyed the ride to the hospital. It gave them a chance to be together without the intention of killing anyone. Mabel had cleaned and oiled Earl's gun and brought it along, hidden under the seat in a black sock, for Josie to take home with her.

"I felt you'd be more comfortable with this gun, Josie, since you're used to it. It's loaded, so you'll want to take the bullets out to practice. But once you put them back in, you'll be ready to go. I'll sneak in a basement practice with the new guns when it's safe."

"You are such a love, Mabel." Josie reached over to squeeze her friend's arm. "When McClung and his men go, we can *both* practice." An impish gleam came into her eye. "Theodore and Earl would never believe we're talking like this. You and me, the two fraidy cats." Their gaiety ended when they pulled up to the hospital. They were here on serious business.

Pearl's room was closely guarded by nurses. The cute young Filipina one agreed to take their greetings to Pearl and see if she felt up to a visit. Herb, who shared her room and benefited from her presence, was under doctor's orders to receive no one.

They didn't have to wait long. Out came the young nurse, pushing Pearl in a wheelchair. Pearl's left arm hung in a sling, and although she looked drawn and uncomfortable, she produced a smile for them. The nurse suggested they visit in the Family Room. She accompanied them down the hall, pushing the chair to a cozy den furnished with a scattering of muted sofas and chairs. Making sure Pearl was comfortable; the nurse said she would be back for her in time for dinner.

The moment the nurse left, they all started talking at once. Pearl's strength was obviously limited so Josie and Mabel hushed, giving Pearl a chance to speak. Both women were shocked at the slurring of Pearl's speech and the limpness of her body. The trauma had visibly aggravated her condition. They had to listen carefully to make out what she was saying.

"Took some things to be pawned … were leaving the shop … Some creep … saw me put … purse in my shop-ping bag." She had to rest before she could continue. "Picked up … front of my chair … dumped me over back … back-ward." She took another rest, and by now she was crying. "Grabbed my bag … and ran."

Josie and Mabel could see that talking was too much for her, and Josie motioned, finger to her lips, for her to rest.

"All this heals," Pearl labored, showing them the big goose egg on the back of her head. "It's Herb … his heart … No idea it … was so bad. He never said …" She cried softly, turning her head aside to shield them from her grief.

Hands clasped and in tears, the three of them huddled together, sharing pain too heavy for one person to bear alone. All had known devastating sorrow, and they communed, without words, from the depths of their souls.

Pearl didn't know what she was going to do. She couldn't stay in the hospital much longer, but didn't think she could take care of herself at home, either. Heaven only knew when Herb would be released. *And then what?* her eyes seemed to ask.

Pearl told them that her sister could come from Chicago for a week, and the hospital would send a nurse every morning for a while. But there was so much she didn't know how to do by herself, things that Herb had taken care of; laundry, shopping, cooking. She reminded them she would never really be well. She would always have multiple sclerosis.

Josie could only hold Pearl's good hand and gently stroke her tear-streaked face. *Dear God, could that rotten creep have any idea of the misery he had caused? All for a handbag that might have contained only a few dollars?* She thought she would burst with anger.

Pearl confided that they had pawned the gold jewelry bought in Turkey, as well as a small marble statue from a gallery in Greece. Their plan was to reclaim them when Herb's pension check arrived. She was mortified at having to reveal this information, but neither Josie nor Mabel asked any questions.

When the nurse returned, Josie and Mabel tearfully counseled Pearl not to let this thing get her down. They'd think of something. Kissing her good-bye, they exchanged glances that said some nasty crook—or maybe a lot of nasty crooks—would pay for this.

Dinner in the hospital cafeteria was subdued, although Josie and Mabel managed to eat heartily. Dining out was a treat. They took their time, savoring the food, and enjoyed watching the parade of people. Each person, whether staff or visitor, had the potential of a whole new drama. This was far more fascinating than dinner in an ordinary restaurant.

The middle-aged couple who sat gravely in the corner—were they here for parent or child? The young woman who breezed in, heavily made-up and scantily dressed—was she trying to catch the eye of a doctor? Certainly she didn't look worried about anyone, and she didn't appear to be a staff member. The man with no feet, sitting at a table in his wheelchair—what had happened to him? Was he here for treatment, or was he visiting someone? They watched with fascination, sipping tea and commenting. It was growing dark when they finally left.

"This may sound callous," said Mabel, settling into the driver's seat, "but we mustn't let everyone's problems sidetrack our war for too long. We should be able to squeeze in a mission now and then, don't you think?"

She suggested hanging around pawnshops, waiting for thugs like the one who attacked Pearl, or maybe taking another bus ride. There was a chance that robbers might be on board, according to the signs at the station. At least they'd see new places while waiting for some action.

As they neared George's market, Mabel slowed and asked Josie if she wanted to stop in for anything.

"Oh, yes, thanks, Mabel," said Josie. "It won't take me long. I just need a loaf of bread and some chicken for our potluck. Luckily, I brought along my shopping bags just in case."

Mabel always parked a distance from the entrance to the store, where the spaces seemed larger and there were fewer cars. This way she wouldn't have to risk backing out. She pulled up to the right of a dark pickup truck with a camper shell and vaguely noticed two men in the cab of the truck. She didn't think much of it until, from the corners of her eyes, she caught them craning their necks to look at her. Josie had just opened her door when the men jumped out of the truck.

It all happened so fast that both women acted on instinct. They heard the one on the passenger side call out to the driver, "I'll take care a'this one," pointing to Josie with a jerk of his thumb. "You get her," meaning Mabel.

Josie struggled to shut and lock her door. In spite of her shock, Mabel managed to reach under the seat, grab the gun, and work her hand into the sock. By the time the driver came around the back of the truck and yanked open her unlocked door, she was ready, with an unobstructed view of his torso in the open doorway. The explosion of the gun was deafening in the close confines of the car.

"What the hell," spluttered the one on Josie's side. "Watch where the hell you're shootin', man! Goddamn …" When he couldn't open Josie's door, he started around the front of the car for Mabel's side. Then he said, "Hey, man, where are you?"

By this time, Mabel had rolled down the window of her door, which was held ajar by the body of the dead man. It gave her a wide view of the other man as he came, cursing, around her front fender. Her left arm on the open window supported both her leaning body and the stocking-encased gun. The gun went off with a roar the moment the still-muttering man came into view.

Deafened by the blasts, the women sat stunned. No one moved outside. Finally Josie risked opening her door and sneaking to where the men lay, between the two vehicles. She couldn't tell, in the gloomy light, whether the men were dead or just stunned, but neither of them moved. She called in a hushed voice for Mabel to toss out the grocery bags.

The next thing they knew, Mabel had lurched out of the parking lot and they were on their precarious way home. They were aware of a passing police car, slowly cruising on its rounds, but the policemen inside didn't seem to notice them.

Neither of them spoke until they pulled up at the curb under Josie's window, where Mabel offered a shaky little prayer of thanks. They sat blankly, letting their minds catch up with their bodies.

"Well, for heaven's sake," Josie said in a rush of relief. "What do you suppose *that* was all about? And what if you hadn't had the gun!"

Mabel just shook her head. The irony was too much for her. Without speaking, she handed the stocking-encased gun to Josie.

Still struggling to make sense of it, Josie asked, "Do you suppose they wanted our purses? Your car? They had to be crazy, to come after us like that. Well, anyway, Mabel, your quick thinking just saved the government another $200,000 toward our retirement."

Again, Mabel shook her head. She declined Josie's offer to come in for a minute, saying she wanted only to go home to the security of McClung's men. With mock enthusiasm, she thanked Josie for a splendid evening and drove away.

Before going to bed, Josie added two more marks on the wall under the *M* for Mabel.

<u>ELEVEN</u>

Paige drove to work through what was probably the last of the spring rains. She was always sorry to see the season end. Southern California needed all the rain it could get. Wet weather also cleared the plaza, shared by the police station, courthouse, and library, of the clumps of homeless who were lured there by an on-site feeding program. Bad weather, rare in Southern California, was the only thing that sent some of them to the shelters provided for them.

However, shelters cramped many homeless people's style. They were not allowed to use drugs or alcohol there or to have indiscriminate sex. They were also expected to behave and respect the curfew. For many of them, this seemed too much to ask in exchange for their care.

"Speed bumps on the road of life," Wisneski called them. He swore their only purpose was to ensure slow going for the rest of mankind. And these "speed bumps" came in all colors. His definition helped Paige realize she was not a racist, as police officers are often accused of being. She'd met too many fine people of all races through her work. But she would readily admit to being a *culturist*, for she had little patience for the cultures of laziness, insolence, or violence. Color made no difference.

Clearly, some of these people were incapable of making it on their own and should be receiving care in an institution. For the rest she had no sympathy. Too many of them seemed homeless of their own volition, content to loll around and wait for the next meal. If it hadn't been for the underground parking structure, she would have to confront them every day on the way to and from her office. She found it unnerving to walk among the sleeping or glassy-eyed men who found the plaza a sanctuary from the world they had turned their backs on. Not only did they take up all the benches, leaving users of the complex nowhere to sit, but the scarier ones often walked around talking to themselves or shouting at unseen adversaries.

At lunch she'd have to run the gauntlet through them to return a stack of books, each dealing with serial killers, to the library. The regulars knew she was a police officer, so they wouldn't ask for money. She didn't have the answer but knew there must be a better way to care for these people, who either couldn't or wouldn't take care of themselves.

The station was abuzz when she arrived at seven thirty. She could feel the excitement in the air.

"What's going on?" she asked the desk sergeant as she walked by, motioning with her head to the clusters of officers in animated conversation. She dropped the heavy book bag to the floor and took off her raincoat, hanging it on a hook in the hallway.

"What's going on," he echoed. "Big-time is what's going on! You know about these guys, I'm sure," he said, pointing to the bulletin on his desk featuring the cousins from Missouri, the ones who had fascinated Wisneski.

Staring back from the bulletin were Darryl Nickerson and Raef Rivera, wanted by law enforcement officers from the Mississippi River to the Pacific Ocean. Robbers, rapists, and killers; young men undaunted by the constraints of society. They'd left a trail of crimes and broken bodies from Hannibal, Missouri, to Bishop, California, stealing cars as they needed them. There was a one hundred thousand dollar reward offered for them, dead or alive.

"Well, word's just in. We got 'em!"

"No kidding," cried Paige. "Gee, Wisneski's going to be sorry he missed out. He wanted to be in on this. Tell me ... who did get 'em, and where, and when?"

"Well," said the sergeant, "that's where the mystery begins. We don't know who got 'em, but last night a patrol car found 'em lyin' in the parking lot of George's grocery over on Santiago Street. Their camper turned out to be the one stolen from those fishermen found shot near Bishop."

Incredulous, Paige repeated, "They were just lying there?"

"Not hardly. Each one was dropped with one shot to the heart. No sign of a struggle."

The sergeant looked almost apologetic.

"But there was one funny thing," he said. "They were each covered with one of those paper grocery bags."

TWELVE

Mabel awakened Josie with a phone call just before nine. They had both collapsed from fatigue the night before, numb from the accumulation of events. Josie was sleeping soundly when the phone rang.

For a moment she didn't know where she was. Fumbling with her hearing aids, she stumbled to the kitchen, where the phone sat on the kitchen counter. Fortunately, there was no laundry to duck. Her muffled hello was barely audible.

"Josie, turn on the news! You aren't going to believe this…we could have been killed last night!"

Josie did not respond at first, and then she said, "Mabel? What are you talking about?"

Mabel could hardly contain herself and regaled Josie with all ends of the story at once.

"Those men in the news! Killers … truck stolen … fishermen shot near Bishop! Josie, can you believe it?" The sound of a houseful of clocks announcing the hour filled the phone line between them.

Josie plopped down onto a kitchen chair, her groggy mind unable to catch up. "Wait a minute … wait a minute. Mabel, start over. Your clocks … I can't hear you."

Mabel told the story more coherently now, and Josie's eyes grew wider and wider. What she was hearing jerked her out of her sleepy fog and left her reeling.

"You don't mean to tell me those were the guys we got last night!" Her body sagged with the impact of it. "Why, Mabel, without your gun *we'd* have been the ones lying in the parking lot. Let me turn on the news. I'll call you back."

While dressing and eating breakfast, Josie kept her ear to the local TV channel. By noon she'd heard the story three times, with the camera panning in on the men's truck in the shopping center and mug shots taken of them earlier.

The faces meant nothing to her. She hadn't really seen them clearly in the gloom of the parking lot. They had looked like any other young, unkempt men she'd ever seen. The thought of what might have been washed over her in a wave of nausea. What if Mabel hadn't had the gun or hadn't reacted so quickly! It was beyond her to understand why these young men would have done the heinous things they were accused of. They had to be crazy or on drugs. As with their other fallen foe, she felt an intense pity that they'd chosen to waste the only lives they'd ever have.

She had to think about something else. Pearl's and Gertie's plights were still heavy on her heart, and far more urgent than the two cousins from Missouri. Their final chapters had been written; both Pearl and Gertie were about to begin new, formidable ones.

A sudden inspiration sent her looking for pen and paper. Sign-up sheets in the laundry rooms might be the answer for Pearl. And Molly Flannery could be counted on to spread the word.

She quickly composed two notes, one for each washroom, to alert the other tenants that sign-up sheets would be appearing for laundry, shopping, and meals when Pearl returned home from the hospital. Again thankful for her windfall of money, she added that these services would be paid for. She didn't know how much of a response could be expected but felt she should at least try.

Then she called Molly Flannery and trusted her to take it from there.

Mabel and Josie both needed a quiet afternoon. They had to regroup, and Josie desperately needed to talk to Theodore. But they knew they must have a strategy session soon: war doesn't have time-outs. When Mabel called to suggest a bus ride the next day, Josie thought it was a splendid idea. Mabel would pick her up at nine.

Tuesday's bus ride became nothing more. They rode from Santa Ana to Los Angeles and back before having the good idea of transferring to a city bus on the afternoon return to Los Angeles, for more sightseeing. They took their lunches along to save money and to avoid hunting for a restaurant in an unfamiliar area. It made the outing seem more like a picnic than a mission, especially when they became brave enough to chat with the passengers seated around them and offer tidbits of their lunch.

They were intrigued by an old black woman on one of the city buses. She told of the gang that virtually held her neighborhood hostage. They had spray-painted their gang name, Simbas, on everything in sight: buildings, lampposts, sidewalks, fences, and traffic signs. When they couldn't find anyone to fight with they threw rocks and bottles at people's homes, sometimes even firing random shots into houses and cars.

The old woman told how the Simbas trained their gang members young, often sending kids to do their dirty work. The gangbangers knew the law did little to offending children. And drug sales took place openly from a crack house across from her home. Her front windows had been broken out twice with flying bricks and bottles, and now she lived with plywood in place of the glass. She vowed she would give anything if she could afford to move. Mabel took down her name, Mrs. Ophelia Jackson, and her address, in case she and Josie could work out a mission there.

Then there was the funny old drunk who sat near the middle of the bus on their return to Santa Ana. He was the perfect caricature of an old-time hobo, looking as though he had just crawled out from under a packing crate. He amused everyone by wrapping one leg around his scrawny neck and singing hillbilly songs while accompanying himself on the harmonica. One of the songs, "Grab your partner by the craw and swing her, down in Arkansas," had everyone laughing and clapping in rhythm.

When he ran out of songs and out of steam, he unwrapped his leg from around his neck and informed the man across the aisle that he was on his way to pick up his welfare check. And none too soon, he cackled, for he'd about run out of booze. He fell asleep, hiccupping and snoring, just as they reached Santa Ana.

While riding around, Mabel and Josie had time to think about Gertie. They decided the best way to help her was to pay Hali to take her to visit Waldo three times a week. With that resolved, they planned tomorrow's potluck with Bliss and Mil, hoping they'd know how to act if the subject came up of the men slain in the George's parking lot. It was still too soon to tell anyone of their complicity.

Mil awakened to the realization that Bliss was not beside her in bed. What had awakened her? She usually slept like the dead.

She scrambled to put on her slippers, impelled by a dreadful sense that something was wrong. Calling out Bliss's name, she headed for the bathroom. He was not there. Nightlights along the way guided her into the kitchen. She had just flipped on the light when she heard the blast of his shotgun. She froze in her tracks.

What was that—skunks? Coyotes? For goodness sake, what is that man up to now?

Then she heard the crunch of gravel and his voice yelling, "Call 911! Call 911!" as he came running across the side yard. He appeared headed for the mud room off the kitchen. She wheeled around to the living room, grabbed the phone, and placed the call. At that hour the call went right through. As she was trying to explain a situation she knew nothing about, two more shots rang out in the still night air, and then Bliss came stumbling through the door. He was red-faced and breathless, his shotgun slung over one pajama-clad shoulder.

The roar of a truck and the scrunching of tires on gravel drowned out what he was shouting to Mil. He sank onto a kitchen chair, panting and clutching the table for support, letting the shotgun fall with a thud to the tabletop.

"Mil! Did you get 'em? Are they coming?" he gasped.

"They heard those last shots," she said. "They're coming. But what in the name of heaven is going on?" She slammed down the phone that sat on the end table between their easy chairs and scrambled to join him at the kitchen table.

"Damn thieves," he shouted. "Damn thieves!"

She leaned over his chair, enfolding him in her arms. Wheezing and breathless, he told her he'd heard them prowling around a couple of nights ago, whoever they were.

"It's the stuff from Mabel's basement they're after. Damn thieves! I hope I got at least one of 'em."

Mil was speechless. Finally it occurred to her to get their robes, if the sheriff was coming. It must have been half an hour before they heard the wail of sirens in the distance. By this time they had calmed down somewhat and were sitting at the kitchen table, warming themselves with a pot of fresh coffee.

This area was serviced by the sheriff's department since it was in an unincorporated part of Orange County. They could never figure out the difference between the sheriff's department and the police, but they'd never had to call for help before. Maybe tonight they'd find out.

The two young sheriffs who responded were all business, refusing fresh coffee and a slice of coffee cake left over from breakfast. They sat stiffly in the living room taking notes as Bliss spoke. Bliss then led them around outside in a search for possible bodies, as well as evidence of the intruders. After about fifteen minutes they decided to return in the daylight, when they would be able to see better. They'd turned up no bodies, however.

Bliss was miffed, saying he'd hoped to have shot at least one of them. The sheriff whose badge said "Davini" looked shocked.

"Sir, I don't think you know what you're saying. If we'd found a body, we'd be taking *you* off to jail."

Bliss couldn't believe his ears. "You mean if someone is trespassing on my property, breaking into my barn, stealing from me, I can't defend my property?"

"No, sir," replied Davini. "Not with a gun. Only if he's in your house, threatening someone's life. And then we'd still have to take you away until we made sure it was self-defense."

Bliss was stunned. "But if he's clearly where he's not supposed to be, clearly attempting to rob me, and possibly armed and willing to shoot me …"

"Nope. No way."

For a moment, no one spoke.

"Do they know that, the crooks?"

"Most of them, sure. They know they can be apprehended only by officers of the law. They don't have to listen to you."

"You mean, I can't even order them off my property with my shotgun?"

"You can order them to leave, but they don't have to go. And they can have you arrested for threatening them with a gun. You can't do much about it but call us."

By now, Mil had found her tongue. "They can rob us and scare us to death, and we can't defend ourselves? Sneaking around in the middle of the night, driving their truck right onto our property? You know they were up to no good. What's the point of letting everyone have all these guns if only crooks can use them?"

"Sorry, folks. It's lucky no one got hurt. You scared them off, and that's all you can do. They could sue for everything you have if you hurt them or even if they hurt themselves on your property while robbing you."

It was too much for Bliss to comprehend. It seemed they were completely at the mercy of the dregs of society.

"Well, then, how can I detain 'em till you get here if I can't nick 'em a little? It takes a long time for you boys to get out here."

Davini shook his head. "No answer to that one. We don't like it any better than you, but the law is the law. We're lucky to get as many as we do, and a lot of them get off on a technicality. The rest of them get away with it. You only put yourselves at risk by playing vigilante."

When the sheriffs left, Bliss and Mil returned to bed, to lie talking until dawn. It was all Mil could do to keep Bliss from working himself into a state of apoplexy. They'd have to postpone their card game and potluck tomorrow. This thing had taken a lot out of them, and they would have to deal with the sheriffs again tomorrow morning. Josie and Mabel had been correct: all the rights seemed to belong to the bad guys.

The only answer for Mabel and Josie's anger at their friends' experience was another mission. They talked about lying in wait at Bliss's to catch the would-be thieves: he was sure they'd be back. But who knew when that would be? Instead, they decided on another bus day, even though the previous one hadn't produced a thing for them. There was always the chance the next one would, and they both enjoyed the outing.

"Besides, it's good for me to get out of the house, Josie," said Mabel. "It's become so depressing here, and it makes me so mad. I used to love my home and all the memories. But," she said sadly, "everything's different now." Then, brightening, she added, "Mr. Moonbeam sure does a good job of protecting me, though. He really fooled McClung and his men the other day. They thought I was entertaining a gentleman and felt uncomfortable spying on me."

Since Josie had already fried the chicken intended for their potluck and Mabel had baked chocolate chip cookies, they had only to throw in a peeled, sectioned orange and a quartered apple to complete a picnic lunch for their outing. Toting their weapons in their picnic basket, they boarded the 12:35 bus for Los Angeles.

This time, they spent a full day on the bus, going back and forth from Santa Ana to Los Angeles. By the time the bus was making its final trip back to Santa Ana, they decided this bus idea was fruitless. Although it had been an enjoyable day, the trip hadn't produced a thing.

The bus was rolling along at a fairly good clip, only minutes from the station in Santa Ana, when Josie and Mabel became aware of angry shouting in the rear, followed by screaming and what sounded like a gunshot. From where they sat near the front, they couldn't see a thing. Josie, who had a right aisle seat, clutched the back of the seat in front of her and twisted around to get a better look.

"Mabel," she gasped. "There's a man with a nylon or something on his head, waving a gun!"

By this time, the gunman was running up and down the aisle, screaming orders, demanding that all heads be down and money and jewelry passed to the center.

"Now! Now," he screamed. "Heads down! Pass it over! Bills and jewelry. Now! Now!"

The terrified passengers complied, doing their best to extricate money from wallets and purses while bent over their laps. Jewelry was a little harder to remove in such a position, but if a head came up too high, the gunman screamed in anger and fired another round through the roof of the bus to show that he was serious.

"Don't stop the bus," he yelled to the driver. "Go into the station, open the door, and keep the engine running!"

He saw the driver looking at him in the rearview mirror and responded with one well-aimed shot that shattered the mirror into a million flying pieces. Each shot he fired caused more screaming and crying.

The bus rolled on in the gathering darkness, interior lights off at the gunman's request. No one on the outside would have known that anything unusual was going on inside. The shaken driver struggled to maneuver the off-ramp from Interstate 5, while the gunman kept up his screaming to confuse and intimidate the passengers. Starting at the back of the bus, he now demanded that everyone drop their valuables into an open duffel bag.

"All of it! Now!" He made his way to the front of the bus, still screaming and shouting. Heads stayed down, and sobs were drowned out by the roar of the engine and the hysterical voice of the gunman. The bus arrived at the station in a shrill blast of airbrakes and came shuddering to a stop in its assigned place, the motor idling and the door wide open.

The bandit had timed it well. He was accepting money and jewelry near the front of the bus just as the bus arrived at the station. In less than a minute he would be out the door and gone, lost in the crowd, just another commuter running to make a connection.

Josie did her best to keep from getting flustered. Head down, she was poised as he made his way down the aisle, still yelling, and thrust the duffel bag in her face. He must have been certain he had nothing to fear from the two old women seated up front, because he took a moment to turn and crack the driver over the head with the butt of his pistol. All he saw when he turned around again was a stiff white gym sock aimed up his nose. The explosion of Josie's gun set off another burst of screaming from the passengers. Heads and arms hugged knees even tighter. They would stay that way until rescued.

When the curious stationmaster finally approached the idling bus, with the now open door from which no one seemed to be emerging, he was appalled at what he saw. The sound of sobbing passengers, cowering in their seats, was almost as shocking as the sight of the unconscious, bleeding driver but not as grim as what was under Mabel's hastily thrown paper bag. Already distorted by the tight nylon stocking of his disguise, the face of the dead man sprawled in the aisle was now grotesque.

None of the passengers could tell the police exactly what had happened. They'd heard gunshots, they'd been robbed by a screaming gunman, the bus had stopped, there had been another gunshot, and then they had heard only the sound of the bus's engine. No one remembered who, if anyone, had been sitting in any of the empty seats. And with their heads in their laps, no one noticed the two little old ladies who had slipped out the open door.

Pearl was discharged from the hospital on Wednesday. Her sister, Peggy, was there to bring her home. Josie walked over to Pearl's to welcome them and found that Peggy not only looked a lot like Pearl, but was just as gracious.

Pearl's condition was not good, and her already failing vision was worse. Yet, her main concern was getting back to the hospital every day to see Herb, even though it was an effort for Peggy to get her into and out of the car. As it turned out, the problem was short-lived. Herb died quietly on Sunday.

They all tried their best to keep up Pearl's spirits. The sign-up sheets in the laundry rooms had been remarkably successful in rallying her neighbors. The visiting nurse worked with her, and friends brought food and flowers. But her decline was precipitous. Her only wish was to die.

Laboriously, Pearl made her case to the two women. She would never be well. There was no future whatever for her. She was unable to care for herself and would rather Herb's sons have his small estate than to squander it on maintaining what could only be a marginal and lonely existence.

She confided that one of Herb's sons could use whatever cash would be left of their estate, because his teenage son had a serious drug problem. Herb's grandson had been in one rehab center after another, and Herb had been selling and pawning things right along to lend him money. Still, no one in the family had been willing to give up on him. Much as Pearl hated the possibility of all that money going down a rat hole, she still hoped for the best. Unlike her, he at least had a chance of recovery.

Shocked as she was to hear Pearl speak of death, Josie understood. After thinking about it for a while, so did Mabel. Pearl deserved to choose her own destiny just as much as they deserved to choose theirs. They prayed they'd never have to face such a thing as Pearl faced. And, if such adversity should ever befall them, they further prayed for friends who would do for them what they knew Pearl wanted done for her.

They decided Pearl would have a grand farewell party. It was the least they could do for their dear friend, who feared the lonely and limited life that lay ahead of her more than she feared death.

A week later, both Josie and Mabel left their doctors' offices with prescriptions for sleeping pills.

THIRTEEN

Paige found herself obsessing over what the newspapers called the Bagman Case—but not because she felt sorry for the victims. From the looks of their rap sheets, each one had already made his own deal with the devil. It was those grocery bags. No matter how or where they fell, the victims were easily identified by those damn grocery bags. If she could figure out the reason for the bags, she would be closer to solving the mystery.

She'd never before had a case where the murderer purposely left an identifying clue, the way killers often did in the murder mysteries she read as a child. She thought back to one of her favorites, *Keys to Murder*, in which the crafty killer left a different antique house key at the scene of each crime. It nearly drove the amateur sleuth, a lady librarian, crazy. It was just this kind of intrigue that had lured Paige into the profession.

As a child, Paige had read nothing but murder mysteries, living every drama, thrilled when she correctly waded through the morass of clues and distractions to solve the case herself. It was to her mother's horror that she wanted to become a detective. Her mother had hoped it was just a phase she would outgrow. Surely she would pursue a career more befitting a girl who'd grown up with every advantage. It was bad enough that she really did become a police detective, but when she married and divorced one, too, her mother gave up. Paige had to do what Paige had to do.

Paige sat at her desk, shuffling through papers relating to the Bagmen, reading them again and again, trying to squeeze out a clue. They were working on the premise that the murders were drug-related, because all the hits were known users or dealers. Another funny thing was that no one had claimed the reward money for the cousins from Missouri, Nickerson and Rivera, which in itself was suspicious. This last one, on the bus, had blown the premise that the victims knew their killer. Unless … unless there had been a co-conspirator on the bus who decided to grab the take and blow away his friend. But, no, that wouldn't work. The duffel bag of money and jewelry had been in the dead man's hand. His gun, however, was missing.

But if the murders were drug-related, why were the hits such small players on the grand stage of drug trade? It couldn't be a racial thing, because the hits were a random mix of colors. Could it be jealousy over a woman? That was a possibility. All but the consumptive and whacked-out Alphonso were virile young men, and all but the two from Missouri lived within driving distance of each other or the same woman. Could those two from Missouri have met up with her and been killed as a result? She'd have to be some kind of woman! No, that seemed unlikely. But still, it was a possibility.

They'd ruled out robbery because, except for the bus incident, each victim's wallet had been intact, no money or jewelry missing—which led them back to drug-related murders. Maybe the bus incident was an execution, with the killer tailing the bus bandit, riding along and shooting him before he left the bus. Of course, the killer would have planned it for when he could best make his escape into the milling passengers at the station.

But why had no one seen who he was? Even the bus driver, when he regained consciousness, couldn't remember seeing anyone who might have been an accomplice or an executioner. In fact, why had no one *ever* seen a Bagman killed? How could so many people be shot, seemingly in plain sight of others, without the killer being seen?

The lab had isolated fingerprints on the grocery bags. There were smears of several patterns that led nowhere and two different sets of small, clear prints that weren't on file. California driver's license applicants had been routinely fingerprinted since July of 1982, so the suspects had to be too young to drive, too old to drive, foreigners, or nonresidents. Excluding children and the elderly, the detectives were back to foreigners and nonresidents, typical for a drug connection— small people, probably Asian or South American.

Dejected, Paige sat hunched over her desk defying the clues to elude her. Without the grocery bags they would have been just an unrelated string of killings, the kind detectives saw every day—no mystery. *But those damn grocery bags!* She could hardly wait till Wisneski got back from Hawaii.

At least we know how they get back and forth between Los Angeles and Santa Ana, she thought. The bus. Although they probably had to have a car to get to that George's grocery on Santiago, where Nickerson and Rivera were found.

Something else about the case niggled at the corners of her mind. If there were just time to concentrate, time to think this through. Glancing at her watch, she tucked the latest memo, on which she had scrawled "Bus Bagman," into the file.

The growing knot in her stomach reminded her that she was on call for a one-thirty court appearance and again having her credibility impugned by that crass, belligerent defense attorney, Lebanoff. His ego could never take a standoff with a woman, especially a woman lawyer, and the female deputy district attorney assigned to the case was giving him a run for his money. He made quite a show in court but was a genuine pain in the ass. Paige knew she'd have to fight to keep her cool. But, she reminded herself, this was part of the job.

She pulled out her notes for one last, quick overview. The case had been dragging on for weeks now, with motions and countermotions, charges and countercharges. The accused was a Newport Beach bimbo who had married an elderly—and wealthy—Santa Ana widower just a year and a half before his untimely death. She convinced the court that thieves had broken in and riddled him with bullets, but had spared her life because she had opened the bedroom safe for them. She wasn't able to identify the assailants, for they'd worn ski masks and dark clothing.

When she disappeared some months later with the insurance money and the contents of the safe, her jilted lover had gone to the police. He admitted to helping plan the entire thing, even confessing that he had offed the husband. He now realized she'd only used and dumped him. It had taken time to extradite her from Brazil, but the law is patient.

Paige was tired of the whole thing. A case as open-and-shut as this should have taken no time at all. Lebanoff had the jury so confused with his histrionics and outrageous aspersions on the police department that they seemed to forget who was on trial.

Impatiently flipping her calendar ahead, the knot in Paige's stomach tightened. The homosexual serial killer case was slated for trial next. She'd love to find a way out of that one. It was going to be gruesome. And there would be no winners, no matter how it was resolved.

Sighing, her mind returned to the Bagman case. She was anxious for Wisneski's input on this one. And somehow she thought Wisneski was connected to the vague thought struggling to escape her unconscious mind. It was something they had talked about—a clue to the grocery bags.

FOURTEEN

Bliss called Betty Jean and Hap and invited them over to discuss their prowlers. If people were snooping around in the neighborhood, Betty Jean and Hap should know about it.

Bliss and Mil's early-morning ponderings, when sleep would not come, had brought them face-to-face with their own mortality. It outraged them that the decisions they were being forced to make were being dictated by no-good punks. Bliss reluctantly suggested that his searing bouts of what he thought were indigestion might be his heart acting up. His constant rage since the first time their property had been violated certainly hadn't helped.

They had never talked much about the infirmities of age. Mil wondered what she would do if Bliss really *did* have a heart attack or something, and she was stung with guilt when her first thought had been that she might be stuck at home caring for him. She turned shock at herself into anger at the prowlers. This whole thing could ruin *her* health, as well.

She was up early, working off her anger by getting ready for her guests. When Betty Jean and Hap arrived, she was ready with a freshly baked cinnamon-and-walnut coffee cake and a pot of her special French roast coffee. The four of them gathered around the oak table in the kitchen, savoring the warm cake along with the steaming coffee, upon which floated big blobs of whipped cream. Hap was content to eat quietly and listen to the others.

After hearing Bliss's story, Betty Jean reminded him that she'd had prowlers before—someone helping himself to marijuana from time to time. She was just glad whoever it was hadn't turned her in.

"Nah," scoffed Bliss. "Punks like that are too lazy to grow their own. They'd like to keep you in business. Could even be that my prowlers are the same ones that visit you, scouting around and getting bolder. Well, I don't want to deal with 'em, since it seems there's nothing I can do to defend myself. Legally, anyway."

In impotent rage he slammed his fist on the table, rattling the dishes and sending the sugar spoon flying out of the bowl and skittering across the floor. Red-faced and eyes bulging, he yelled, "God*damn* I'd like to wring their necks!"

Mil tried to soothe him, stroking his arm and reminding him of his heart. He pushed her away, angrily announcing that because of these fools, he and Mil would have to make some changes.

"First thing we have to do," he said, "is have a yard sale and get rid of all the stuff that would attract thieves. I'd give it to you, Betty Jean, but then I'd have to worry about them stealing it from you. The only way out of this damn mess is to sell all that stuff and put the money in the bank, where it's safe. Then," he continued, "we're going to have to find a place to live, closer to town. It's just a matter of time till we'll be too old to make the move by ourselves, anyway. And we sure don't want our kids to make these decisions for us."

Mil winced at hearing Bliss admit he was growing old. She felt terrible for him. Looking at him now, it did seem he'd aged since this basement cleaning and prowler business began.

Hap looked as though he would cry. "You mean you're going away?"

He looked to his mother for an explanation. He loved Bliss, who would let him putter in the barn with him and challenged him at checkers when Betty Jean was busy and Mil was off playing bridge.

And he adored Mil, who had patiently accompanied him at the piano while teaching him to play his harmonica. He couldn't imagine life without them.

"Hap, they aren't going far," Betty Jean said. "We can go visit whenever we want, and you can still play checkers with Bliss and play your harmonica with Mil. And we can take them canned tomatoes and green beans …" Betty Jean knew how to soothe him.

Mil tried to make it sound like fun. "You'd be a big help with our yard sale, Hap. You can make the signs, so all we have to do is put an ad in the *PennySaver*. Then," she continued, encouraged by their nods of approval, "I think we should have a sheriff out here on the day of the sale. Since we found we have no right to stop anyone from taking whatever he wants, it seems foolish to invite that kind of trouble."

Bliss agreed to check with the sheriff's deputies, who were due to return at any moment to finish their search. "Might be a good idea, if they could do it," he said, helping himself to a third piece of cake.

Betty Jean and Hap quickly finished their coffee and left, not wanting to be there when the deputies arrived. They might offer to search her place, as well—and find her marijuana. Forever a flower child, Betty Jean would always think of lawmen as pigs.

Tire tracks, a cigarette butt, and marks where a metal cutter had scored the lock to the barn were all the deputies found. Although they didn't have the manpower to assign a deputy to Mil and Bliss's yard sale, they would try to have a man in the area patrol off and on because the house had been the scene of an attempted crime.

For the next few days Mil and Bliss priced and tagged the conglomeration in the barn. The unmarked stuff would have to be set out on a what-will-you-give-me-for-it basis. In anticipation of a move they threw in all kinds of odds and ends from the house, as well. Hap came to help and became infatuated with Earl's beekeeper outfit. Bliss generously gave it to him, and he and Mil had a good laugh as Hap, performing his impression of a moon-man, lumbered around in it like a mummy from an old horror movie. But they found themselves on guard at night and grumpy from lack of sleep by day. More than ever, they understood how Josie and Mabel felt.

Their son, Keith, had flown in from Phoenix to help with their Memorial Day sale, which produced hordes of people. They had decided to have a one-day sale, on Sunday, and extend it to Monday only if it were necessary. Contractors and handymen arrived early, while Bliss was hanging out their big American flag and Mil was posting Hap's laboriously lettered signs. Next came antique dealers and collectors of all sorts. After that came the families, whose children had a lively time playing among the rows of sale items.

Betty Jean and Hap were there bright and early, for she was to be cashier and Hap was excited about being Bliss's helper. Keith and Hap got right to work, carrying things out of the barn and onto the front lawn in some semblance of order. Bliss was to do the bargaining.

The weather was so beautiful that Josie, Mabel, and Gertie, who had brought Waldo home for the weekend, decided to join the fun. They offered to set out a picnic under the grape arbor in the side yard, to make a party of it. Josie arranged to have Hali transport them both ways, to make it easier for everyone. She was waiting at her window with bags of freshly baked bread, cold cuts, and a big bowl of coleslaw when he arrived in his dilapidated taxi. Dented and rusted through, the cab nevertheless seemed to get him where he had to go. With a flourish, he escorted her to the worn front seat beside him, and together they set off for Mabel's.

"I been drivin' cab aroun' here for almos' five years now," he confessed to Josie, "but I don' know about this Modjeska Canyon. How you git there?"

Josie assured him she knew the way very well, and that she was sure he'd love the drive.

Mabel stood waiting for them under her big lemon tree with a tub of fried chicken and another tub of chocolate chip cookies. She looked forward to the adventure of riding in Hali's taxi. Every time he brought

Josie to her house, Mabel always marveled that the vehicle still ran. Acting as though it were a princely carriage, he ceremoniously settled Mabel on the shredded backseat, and off they rattled for the long drive to the canyon to pick up Gertie and Waldo.

As they rode along chatting, Mabel commented on the American flag pin Hali wore on his lapel. He proudly told her he was waiting for the results of his citizenship exam. She loved his accent and long, wavy black hair. He seemed almost feminine with his prominent, high cheekbones and delicate bone structure. They found that he had never been married and that he shared a room with three other immigrants. Mabel was full of questions about Ethiopia and kept him busy answering them as he followed Josie's directions out of the city and onto Chapman Avenue. The aroma of Mabel's fried chicken and Josie's freshly baked dill bread permeated the cab. Josie caught his sidelong glances at her still-warm bag of bread.

"Uh, Hali, would you ... would you like a piece of my bread?" she asked, not sure whether she should suggest it. Maybe he wasn't allowed to accept anything but money from his passengers.

"Oh, yes, thank you, ma'am," he said with a shy grin. His soft accent made "ma'am" sound more like "mom." He hoped she hadn't heard his growling stomach. "I like dat 'merican food," he said. "Dose doughnuts, Big Macs, 'tucky Fried Chicken ..."

"Big Macs and doughnuts," called out Mabel from the backseat. "My goodness, Hali, is that what you live on? How about home-cooked food? What do you eat at home?"

"I don' have a kitchen, ma'am. But I have a bery good can opener." He laughed over his shoulder at her, exposing perfect white teeth. Josie interrupted to tell him to turn right on Santiago Canyon Road and to follow it past the county dump. He was amazed at the beauty of the drive, and marveled aloud at the winding roads with their split-rail fences and canopies of gnarled old trees. "Bery different where I come from, for sure. Nothin' to look at dere, jis' dirt an' more dirt. An' so many peoples."

He enthusiastically devoured Josie's dill bread. "I never have dis before," he said, licking the flour from his fingers. "Where you git somethin' like dis?"

Josie told him she had made it herself, which greatly impressed him. "Have you ever been invited for a home-cooked meal here in America?" she asked.

"No, ma'am," he murmured. "I jis be in one house, one time, and I didn' like it. Dey said I hadda marry dere daughter. Oooh, big fat t'ing wit' four mean litto kids." He took both hands off the wheel to show them how fat she was. "Dos kids, callin' me a dumb nigger, and dey was black as me. So I run away. But I seen 'merican houses on TV, so many diffren' kinds! When I git 'nuff money, boy, I sure gonna buy me one. Jis a litto one, for me an' my can opener." He chuckled at the idea. "But maybe I buy some pans and learn to cook injira an' wat, like my mama." He smacked his lips and patted his stomach at the memory. "No, maybe is better I get a woman do the cooking." Again he laughed, and finished another slab of bread that Josie offered him.

"Pull in here," said Josie, pointing to the winding gravel lane leading to Gertie's house. Hali's brakes squealed and jerked in protest as he made the sharp turn onto the narrow road. He barely missed one of the rotting posts positioned at each side of the entry, meant to keep cars from falling into the drainage ditch below. The waterway now ran quietly but could run full and treacherous in the winter.

"Boy, dis some road," he said, smiling with the spirit of adventure.

The two women nodded at each other. They both had the same idea. There would be enough food today for another person, and they had plenty of money in their war fund to pay Hali to stay all day and take them home later. Mabel leaned forward, holding on to the back of Josie's seat as the cab bounced along the rutted lane. Long, thorny branches of wild blackberries screeched like fingernails along the sides of the cab as they passed.

"Hali," she said. "Why don't you just stay and have lunch with us? We'll pay you to wait, and you can have some home-cooked food."

Josie chimed in, refuting his timid protests, and by the time they had maneuvered around the muddy wash at the bottom of a gentle slope and driven along the fence by a mostly dead lemon grove, Hali had agreed.

Gertie stood in the doorway shouting greetings, with Waldo peering over her shoulder. With some effort Hali got both of them and their food basket loaded into his cab, nearly swooning at the delicious aroma of Gertie's baked beans and warm apple cobbler. Then they were off to join the others at Bliss and Mil's.

Cars lined the road for the yard sale, which was in full swing, leaving Hali to park out back by the barn. Mabel and Josie introduced him to their friends, who were curious to meet this Hali, of whom Josie had spoken so highly. Hap, giddy to have a friend more his own age, showed him around the sea of sale items. Shy at first, Hali stayed by Hap's side but soon warmed up to this exuberant gathering of good friends. He delighted Mabel by asking if he could buy the worn braided-rag rug, tagged for ten dollars, to put on the bare floor of his apartment. She was so happy to know the rug, made of her and Earl's old clothes, wouldn't be going to a stranger that she threw in a bent brass floor lamp and a few mismatched knives, forks, and spoons to boot.

The congenial commotion in the out of doors reminded them of bygone Decoration Day festivities, held in the parks of their small towns when they were young. They reminisced about how everyone would decorate the graves of loved ones early in the morning and then gather for the big parade down Main Street after lunch.

"I loved the prancing horses," said Mabel, "and the homemade floats. People didn't have all those fancy materials they use now. We thought it was fun to use whatever we had in some new way and get a laugh from the crowd."

"And the kids got into it, too," added Josie, "decorating their bikes with crepe paper and flags and riding along to the park. In my town, anyone who had been in the parade got free ice cream and soda pop at the end. Boy, they looked forward to that."

Bliss liked the high school band and how it split the air with exhilarating military marches that made him want to march, too. Then he coyly added that the best part was the high-stepping drum majorettes, twirling their batons and treating everyone to the flash of silky shorts under fluttering little skirts. The women hooted him down.

They missed those days, when patriotism moved men and women to tears. People solemnly held hats or hands over their hearts when Old Glory passed by, carried by proudly marching veterans of several wars. Some of the older, disabled vets left their beds to ride in horse-drawn carriages of Civil War vintage, stiffly waving or saluting along the way. Some of the adults got into it, too, bedecking their jalopies and tootling their way down the parade route. Now it was called Memorial Day and held on the last Monday of May instead of the thirtieth of May. No one made much of it anymore. It had become just another three-day weekend.

The women helped by rolling coins and keeping the busy workers supplied with sandwiches and lemonade. When Hap wasn't strutting around in his beekeeper's outfit to impress startled youngsters, who thought they were seeing a robot, he was delighting the crowd with his harmonica. He had everyone singing and clapping to old-time favorites like "Battle Hymn of the Republic" and "This Land Is Your Land." Some folks were disappointed to find the food they saw being served wasn't for sale: they wanted to stay and make a day of it.

Hali was carrying his new acquisitions to his car when he heard Gertie and Waldo scuffling at the picnic table under the grape arbor. They were shouting in their struggle to get Waldo into his chair. The women came running to see what the commotion was about, although they were accustomed to such antics from Gertie and Waldo. Hali dropped his things in the driveway to come to the rescue. Nodding his head toward Waldo, Hali silently asked permission of the others to seat him.

"So much food," Hali soothed, sniffing the tantalizing aromas that floated from the table. "And this nice day," he added, gently easing the tottery Waldo into his chair. He tried not to stare at the shocking tufts of gray hair that erupted not only from Waldo's eyebrows, but from his nose and ears, as well. He caught the scent of vanilla wafting from Waldo's hair. "Umm, even *you* smell good enough to eat," he offered enthusiastically, spreading a napkin over Waldo's lap. "Dis gonna be a feast, for sure."

Waldo stiffened and glared over his shoulder at Hali. "What the hell are you, a damned cannibal?" he growled. "Where the hell you from? Somewheres in Africa? They eat people there, don't they?"

They all laughed as Gertie shouted Waldo down, assuring him that Hali was no cannibal and that he had no intention of eating anyone. Hali slunk off like a chastised puppy to finish putting his new purchases into the trunk of his car. He had to be coaxed back to the table, but he was so hungry that once he picked up his fork, he needed no further urging.

Waldo kept a wary eye on him and stuck to his own eating, slurping and grunting, "yup ... yup." When he was through, he struggled up from the table, trailing his napkin and bits of food, and went to sit in the porch swing to have a smoke. He'd had enough chatter for a while. But he sat where he could keep an eye on that cannibal, Hali, still muttering, "yup ... yup" between puffs on his cigarette.

Hali ate until he could eat no more, and the women enjoyed watching him relish every crumb. "I mus' find a wife who can cook like dis," he said, rubbing his groaning belly. He leaned back in his chair. "Den, when I buy my litto house, I can t'row away my can opener. But maybe den I gittin' too fat." He grinned with pleasure at the possibility.

"Tell us why you never married, Hali" said Mil. "A nice-looking man like you, with a good job ..." The women all settled into their chairs, sated with food and ready for some good conversation. The yard sale seemed to be going along well without them.

"Why I never marry?" asked Hali, surprised that they were interested. "Well, mos' everyone I know was kill in my country, in

Et'iopia. My family, my frien's. You know da war dey had dere." He looked uneasy; these were painful memories for him. "So my father's frien' in Los Angeles says come here. He from Et'iopia, too. He call de embassy, what you say, sponsor me. Says he fin' me work an' maybe a wife. So, I come, an' I stay in a litto room behin' he's house. An' he fin's me work, good work, sweepin' an' washin': floors, windows, ever'ting. He finds out I such a good worker, den he say de law say I have to marry he's daughter. Oh, boy, dat's da bad part." He screwed up his face at the memory. "Dat woman, wit' dos mean litto kids—better I never come to America." He shook his head sadly. "So, I run away. Maybe da law still lookin' for me, I dunno."

"Hali," cried Josie. "That man was just trying to trick you into taking his daughter and those kids off his hands. The law doesn't make people get married. The law doesn't care if you *never* get married. Believe me, that man isn't looking for you anymore: he's snookered someone else into marrying his daughter."

They all began to offer advice at once, until Hali excused himself to take a walk and ease his aching belly. He didn't mean to be rude, but he couldn't understand them when they all talked at once. As it was, they went right on talking over each other and didn't seem to notice he had gone.

He walked behind the barn to gaze at the hills and pastures, wondering at the wealth of a man who could own all this. He kept on walking through fields grown high with native grasses, climbing a small knoll until he topped a rocky outcropping that looked down upon Gertie's ramshackle house in the distance. It looked like a palace to him. He stood with his hands in his pockets, struck by the joyous singing of meadowlarks. In the distance, grazing cows lowed softly, adding to the splendor of the sun-warmed landscape. Never before had he seen such beauty as these sweeping golden hills, dotted with towering eucalyptus and majestic oaks. Never had he been serenaded so sweetly, and the familiar sound of cattle was a balm to his ears. He couldn't remember ever having eaten so well. He knew this was it: the American Dream.

He hurried back to the picnic area to find the women cleaning up and gathering their things to go home. Hap had been looking for him, for he had promised to teach him to play checkers and the harmonica. But it would have to wait for another day. Hali's passengers were ready to leave.

The mid-afternoon sun was still warm and bright, glaring off the windshield as Hali made his way back down the gravel lane. He had to coax his cab to start, but it finally roared to life in a gritty cloud of exhaust, and, with everyone waving, they clattered out of the driveway and down the bumpy dirt road. Tired from a full day outdoors, they rode quietly until they reached Gertie's. Hali helped Gertie up the stairs and into the house, but stayed clear of Waldo, who hung on to Gertie and glowered back at Hali.

Mabel and Josie nodded off in the cab as it sat idling. But it was impossible for them to sleep when the car resumed bounding and lurching over the potholed lane that led back to the main road. It wasn't long before they began barraging him with questions.

Hali," said Mabel, "I know this is a very personal question, but are you close to having enough money to buy your little house yet?"

He looked at her in the rearview mirror and smiled, saying, "I dunno, I t'ink I got about ten, maybe fifteen t'ousan' dollars in my bag, if I don' be rob again." He laughed. "Dos guys, dey always fin'in' dat bag." Again he burst out with a laugh, as though he and "dos guys" played an elaborate game of hide-and-seek.

"Your bag?" asked a puzzled Josie. "Don't you have your money in the bank?"

"Oh, no, ma'am," he replied solemnly. "If de law still lookin' for me, dey may fin' me dere. So I jis' keep my money in a bag in de trunk of my car. An' when she git too heavy, I trade in for bigger money. Works pretty good, except when dos guys fin'in' it and takin' some out." He shook his head, again unaccountably laughing at what sounded to the women like a ridiculous situation.

They looked at each other, not sure what to make of it.

"Well, Hali," offered Josie, "I don't know about 'those guys,' but you simply *must* put that money in the bank. The law *isn't* looking for you *anywhere* and never was. Your money will be safe in the bank, and it will grow to where you can have a house someday. Certainly it's a better investment than those lottery tickets you buy every week."

Both Josie and Mabel began to talk at once, going on to stress the power of compounded savings in the bank. Hali was amazed to find that the bank would actually pay him to leave his money there and was forbidden by law to cheat him.

They were so involved in conversation that they overshot Chapman Avenue and ended up in Villa Park. Hali found his way back to Mabel's with both women chattering about how easy it was going to be for him once his money was safely in the bank.

"Maybe by the time you get enough money together, Gertie and Waldo will want to sell their house and move into town," offered Mabel. "I think they have about twenty acres there. It hasn't been farmed for some time, but I bet you could bring it to life."

Hali had no idea how one bought a house or how much a house cost, but his head spun with the possibility of owning his own farm.

He dropped off first Mabel and then Josie, who reached into her purse and produced the one-hundred-dollar bill she had taken from their war fund. "We owe you more, I'm sure," she said, "and I'll take care of it later. But whatever it costs, it was worth every penny of it."

"Oh, boy," he said. "Dis feelin' like my lucky day. I buyin' dem lottery tickets fer sure."

Even his cab seemed to feel the magic of the moment. As soon as he drove out of her gate, it took off in a burst of power.

By five o'clock the yard sale had thinned out and Bliss took down the flag and sale signs. They couldn't remember having had more fun in ages. The men lugged the few things that hadn't sold back into the barn while Betty Jean and Mil counted the money. They were amazed to find that their till, an old tackle box donated by Betty Jean, now held well over $3,500 including a few IOUs to be paid when some purchases were picked up later. Bliss had again offered to split whatever they made with Mabel, but, as before, she wouldn't hear of it. So instead he offered half of it to Betty Jean, figuring she could use it. On that promise, she worked hard all day.

On Monday, Bliss let some sale stragglers pick through the things in the barn but called it quits when they had to take Keith to the airport. They'd had a good visit, working together as they had when their sons were boys.

Mil and Bliss had been home from the airport about an hour, watching the news with their dinner on TV trays, when there was a knock at the door. Bliss got up to answer it. There stood two men, a blond, curly-haired one in tattered overalls and another, taller and bearded, in faded jeans and a worn Raiders' sweatshirt. They reeked of body odor and stale alcohol. Bliss's heart jumped when he thought he recognized the truck in the driveway behind them as the one he'd shot at a week ago.

"Are we too late for your yard sale?" the tall, bearded one asked, standing first on one foot and then the other.

It seemed to Bliss the man was attempting to see past him into the house. Unnerved, he abruptly told them they were too late. It had been held yesterday. He wanted only to close the door and call the police.

"Well, how about them piles of pipe and lumber over there?" the shorter one in the overalls asked, pointing to the neat stacks beside the driveway.

"The fella's coming for it in the morning," Bliss replied. He had a powerful premonition that these men were trouble. "You're wastin' your time," he said and started to close the door.

"Well, uh, is it paid for?" asked the bearded man, wedging himself in the doorway.

"Cash on the barrelhead," Bliss answered curtly, and was about to ask them to leave when they sprang into action.

"Well, how about that, ol' man. It looks like you done our work for us!" He elbowed his pal with an I-told-you-so look while pulling a revolver from his belt.

They burst in past Bliss, knocking him down, and then kicked him out of the way to close the door behind them. The bearded gunman jammed his boot on Bliss's neck, holding him down, while keeping the gun aimed at his head.

Mil was so startled she choked on her food, nearly strangling. Making no attempt to help her, the bearded man demanded that she produce the cash from the sale or he would blow Bliss's head off. "You couldn'a got to the bank with it yet 'cause it's a holiday," he said, "so don't play innocent with me. You have two minutes, or we'll blow your fuckin' brains out, too, and burn the whole goddamn place down."

Still gasping for air, she stumbled to the kitchen, coughing and wheezing and steadying herself on whatever she could grab along the way. The shorter man followed closely. Opening the cupboard, she struggled to pull down the heavy tackle box. He grabbed it from her hands, smiling when he opened it and saw the stacks of bills and piles of neatly rolled coins.

"You wouldn' be holdin' out any on me, would you?" he asked slyly.

All Mil could do was shake her head as she attempted to draw a glass of water at the sink. Choking and clammy with sweat, she was shaking so hard she could barely hold the glass.

He left her in the kitchen and returned to the living room, jerking the phone cord out of the wall as he passed the little table beside Bliss's chair. He gave the tackle box and phone to his companion and then made a quick search for another phone. Finding none, and satisfied that they had what they'd come for, they abruptly left, with Mil choking in the kitchen and Bliss in full cardiac arrest on the living room floor.

FIFTEEN

MAYORS DEMAND ACTION WITH 18TH BAG MAN screamed the headline for tomorrow's *Orange County Register*, followed by SOUTHLAND FORCES UNITE IN SEARCH OF GROCERY BAG KILLER.

Andy Krach hunched over his newsroom desk, elaborating on the eighteen bodies found with paper grocery bags thrown over them. All were men with police records of one kind or another. A pin map, with the date and location of each body, would appear with his article.

California and its serial killers, he mused. The Night Stalker, who seemed to have a pathological hatred for women, and the meek engineer awaiting trial, who dumped his male victims along freeways after hacking off their private parts—to *eat*. Sautéed in butter, with button mushrooms, for God's sake! Now *there* was a pervert. He shook his head as he pondered such wackos as these. He knew that between the Methodists and the Baptists, freaks like that never would have made it where he came from in Ohio.

And now they had this Bagman thing. Well, he thought, the Night Stalker's safely in prison and the engineer's cooling his heels in jail. But the Bagman thing is out of control. And whoever the killer is, he's still on the loose.

He studiously ignored the commotion of other frenzied journalists that spilled over the banks of slate-gray work cubicles. So much for acoustical engineering, he thought, and the advice about doing your best work in a quiet place. But the urgency of it all made him feel incredibly alive.

He had been with the *Orange County Register* for a little over a year now. It had been his dream to move up to the big-time in California from his little hometown paper in Ohio. He'd felt hopelessly stifled there: everything exciting seemed to be happening in California. He looked forward to the hectic pace and tricky brushes with the law, as he'd seen in movies, in his search for the big scoop. It had taken a lot to convince his wife, Beverly, to leave their families in Ohio. But considering how much he loved his profession, and how much she loved him, she'd made the sacrifice.

Krach hadn't been with the *Register* long before he made a name for himself. The first time he attempted to use his bank's ATM he instead found himself in the cross fire of a police shoot-out with a pair of fleeing bank robbers. Peering from between the parked car and the mailbox that shielded him, he was able to give excellent witness. He then followed it up with well-written accounts of the checkered pasts of the perpetrators and their ensuing trials. This launched his reputation as an on-the-spot reporter, and Beverly couldn't have been prouder.

However, he hadn't reckoned on being betrayed by a spastic colon. The drastic change of pace, complicated by his discovery of California's highly seasoned ethnic foods, often left him painfully bloated and embarrassingly flatulent. And this was one of those times. Even though he had a deadline to beat, he'd defied his better judgment and had eaten onion and sausage pizza with jalapeño peppers for lunch. He popped another antacid, hoping to forestall the inevitable aftermath of diarrhea. He'd become well acquainted with the old saying that while the spirit may be willing, the flesh could be maddeningly weak.

He began writing, then had a better idea and picked up the phone. Wisneski should be home from Hawaii by now and have an up-to-date, inside track on this Bagman guy. He congratulated himself that his new friend, met while enjoying a few beers at the Wild Goose Bar in Anaheim, just happened to be an investigator for the Santa Ana police.

SIXTEEN

A tanned and relaxed Mark Wisneski strolled into the station, handing out macadamia nuts and alohas all around. Paige was so glad to see him that she had to restrain herself from jumping up to hug him. She could see it was going to take some doing to get him fired up again: after two weeks in Hawaii, he was definitely on island time. They made a date for lunch and went their separate ways.

At noon they met at Denny's on Seventeenth Street, and spent the first few minutes extolling the wonders of Hawaii, agreeing it was a bummer that vacations were so short and far between. Paige assured him that much as she needed a vacation, it would have to wait until she could resolve this Bagman thing. It was consuming her.

She didn't tell him she'd even tried meditation, candles and all, attempting to grasp the thoughts that eluded her. He'd laugh her out of town. By now she was convinced it was something he left with her; an idea, a vision, something they'd talked about before he'd left for Hawaii.

They had lunch at Denny's often and were favorites with the waitresses, who all came to their table to exclaim over his tan. To the delighted protests of the waitresses, he made a big display of unbuckling his belt as though to pull down his pants and show them his tan line.

Paige sat quietly, watching him have his fun. How lucky Alison was to have him, she thought. Crazy as he might act, she was certain he was a wonderful husband, unlike some of the men in their department. Enough of the married men had put moves on her that it made a working relationship with them difficult. But not Mark. Dear Mark. She didn't know what she'd do without him.

They ordered their usual turkey sandwiches, he with fries and a bottle of catsup, and she with salad and no dressing. While they ate, she brought him up to date on things that had transpired in his absence, and told him how fortunate they were to work the Bagman case together. She'd had to fight to get him on her team, speaking loudly for him in his absence.

He'd seen the memos. There were eighteen Bagmen now.

"What have you been *doing* while I was gone?" he teased. "Nobody sitting next to you to bother you and you still can't figure this one out?"

She gave him a withering look and then, with a little shrug of her shoulder, said, "That's what I'm counting on you for, Wisneski. Your newly refreshed mind. This Bagman thing has been driving me nuts. They're popping up like toadstools after a rain, but we're no closer to knowing what the hell is going on than we were in the beginning. Santa Ana to L.A. and all points in between. We think they're using the bus a lot, but our stakeouts at the stations haven't produced a damn thing."

Mark sat watching her anew. He'd almost forgotten how good-looking she was. He bet she'd be a knockout in a pair of spike-heeled shoes and a low-cut, see-through blouse. The comfortable shoes and easygoing outfits she wore to work did nothing for her figure. And she should take time to get a tan. She looked so pale compared to all the tanned bodies he'd become accustomed to in the islands. Maybe a little more makeup would do it. Her skin was so soft and unblemished that it wouldn't take much. But he couldn't say this to her. The last thing he wanted was for her to think he might be making a move on her. And ruin their relationship.

"The MO never changes," she was saying between bites of her sandwich, oblivious to his gaze. "Thirty-eight caliber, close range, no signs of a struggle. Money and jewelry intact, bag over the bullet wound. All races, all ages, all men—and all losers. Which must be why the DA hasn't leaned on us any harder than he has. But now that the media is blowing it up to be the mystery of the century, that's going to change. Did you see the morning paper? MAYORS DEMAND ACTION. Weird, isn't it, that anyone should want us to catch 'em? You'd think they'd cheer 'em on till they cleaned up the whole country."

"Yeah, my friend at the newspaper, Krach, left a message. Wanted some information for that story," said Wisneski, dragging the last of his french fries through a pool of catsup and then licking his fingers before using his napkin. "My guess is it's 'cause they think it's *foreign* drug connections horning in. You know the American mind-set. They're certain foreigners, commies and gays are out to destroy the country, but they're comfortable with our own, regular brand of murder and mayhem."

They sipped their coffee in silence.

"It's the damn *mystery* of it all," she began again. "It's inconceivable that anyone could commit all those murders, right out in the open, and not be seen by *someone*."

"You mean there is actually nothing, the tiniest thing?" asked Wisneski, busily folding his rumpled napkin into a bird of paradise, a popular style in Hawaiian restaurants. "A footprint, a discarded tissue one of 'em might have dropped? There's a lot of good DNA in snot, you know."

"Yeah, there is one thing," said Paige, ignoring his attempt to repulse her before he became even more graphic. He loved trying to make her squirm. "The original two sets of fingerprints have been joined by a third. Also not on file."

Wisneski looked up from his artwork. "Ho! Called in the reinforcements, have they?" he cried. "Well, honey, don't let it get you down. You know these men and their testosterone surges." He returned to his napkin folding. "Remember, they don't have PMS releases like you women do, and every now and then another one of 'em has to go on a spree to work it out."

He expected her to remember the conversation they'd had before his vacation about serial killers, testosterone, and PMS but wasn't prepared for the look that came over her face. She looked as though he'd slapped her.

"Hey, Turner, you aren't mad, are you?" he said. "Come on, Turner, hang loose. I wasn't making fun of you. I was only kidding!"

"Wisneski," she breathed. "That's it. The thing I couldn't put my finger on. PMS … and postmenopausal women. Old women who save grocery bags … and ride buses. Old women who go unnoticed and are mad as hell about something!"

She held up her hands as though framing a newspaper headline. "You said it, yourself, Mark: KILLER GRANNIES STALK CITY!" She stared at him, in awe of her revelation. "Wisneski, I think you just found the missing piece of the puzzle. *Old women*"

She scrambled to scoop up her purse and jacket, threw some money down on the table, and jumped up, saying, "Hurry back, Wisneski. We have a lot to talk about."

She left him staring after her, holding his fancy napkin.

Shit, he said to himself. I hope she doesn't blame that "old woman" idea on me. She needs a vacation, all right.

Flushed with enthusiasm, Paige waited for Wisneski in an interrogation room she'd commandeered. The contents of her Bagman file were spread on a long table in the center of the room. The chart from the morning paper hung on the wall, bristling with pins to show the location of each body.

Mark dejectedly joined her. He didn't want to hear her "old women" idea and didn't want to be the one to tell her she was crazy. He'd never challenged her before; they'd always seemed to think as one. He had barely entered the room when she launched into her theory.

"Look at this, Mark," she began. "They never stray far from the bus route. They seem to pick on known predators, so their hits probably approach them first, which accounts for no struggle, close range. You know, no one's afraid to approach an old lady. Actually, people hardly notice them. Picture a mugger approaching an armed—"

"Whoa, Nellie," he broke in, bracing himself in an exaggerated karate stance against her onslaught. "Slow down, Turner. Even you have to admit it's a pretty big jump from drug dealers to old women. Give me a break, here. Now, I might consider hookers taking revenge on customers who stiffed 'em, or some Bible-thumping cold-ass who wants to punish Johns, or something like that. Yeah, I could buy into that, maybe. But *old women.*" He looked at her in dismay. "Why in hell would an old woman give up the comfort of her rocking chair to do a dumb thing like this? Chasing around the worst parts of town, sometimes at night?"

"Who else saves grocery bags and rides buses, Wisneski?"

"Christ, everyone has access to grocery bags, Turner, especially anyone who works at the market they come from." He anticipated her objection and again shielded himself behind upheld hands, adding, "I know, I know. They've checked every hair on the ass of every employee who works at that market and come up with nothing. But that's only *nothing so far*. They're all still under the microscope."

He wanted to let her down easy, but she seemed totally wrapped up in her theory. He pushed her display aside, barely glancing at it. "Think drugs, Turner, and you'll be closer to solving this. Remember all the figuring and numbers we found on the bag of our first hit, in Santa Ana? Big numbers, Turner. Not the amounts old women deal with."

"Yes, the grocery bags, Mark. The one link to all the hits. Why the grocery bags? Kindhearted old ladies. Think about it, Wisneski. Angry but caring old women who are horrified at the grisly remains. Old women who can do almost anything right in plain sight and not be noticed. Old women who might live near, and shop at, that market."

Wisneski searched her eyes. She was deadly serious, convinced she was on the right track. She'd been working too damn hard, and it had taken its toll. The pain of what he had to say was etched in his face, and he chose his words carefully.

"Turner, I hate to disagree with you. We've followed each other's hunches and been right-on too many times. But you'll never get anyone to back you up on this crazy idea. In fact, maybe you should take that vacation. I think it would do you good."

She knew what he was implying and that he was trying to be kind. Work had been her life since her divorce, and he was afraid the long hours and stress had sent her around the bend.

"But Mark, if our stakeouts in the bus stations would just check out old ladies while they're at it …"

This last suggestion was too much for Wisneski.

"Good God, Turner," he exploded. "Do you know how many old ladies ride buses? We don't have enough men to check 'em all out! Besides, it's such a far-fetched idea that I wouldn't be crazy enough to suggest it to anyone." He'd been standing across the table from her, ignoring her charts and diagrams. Now he stepped around to take her elbow in a firm grip. "Come on, Turner. I hate to bust your bubble, but this 'old woman' thing is just going too far."

She gave him a cold, hard stare, and then turned to gather up her papers. He had barely looked at the presentation she'd set out and the pin chart she'd hung. Her head reeled from the sting of his unaccustomed dismissal.

"Okay, Mark," she said, trying to hide her bitter disappointment. "Forget it. Your Hawaiian vacation has dulled your instinct. I'll stake out the bus stations on my own time. Forget about old women and chase your phantom drug runners. I won't bring it up again."

"Are we still friends?" he asked, taking one of her hands in both of his.

"We're still friends," she said quietly.

SEVENTEEN

June came and went, and with it the rain. It is said that, no matter what, in Southern California the sun can be counted on to burst out of its infamous "June gloom" by the Fourth of July. May and June may be unpredictable, but no one remembers bad weather on the Fourth of July.

And with the rain went Mabel's squatter, just as Officer McClung had predicted. No longer able to justify a surveillance of her home, McClung assured her she needed only to call, at any hour of the day or night, and someone would be there in a flash.

McClung and Mabel had grown fond of each other. Her name made him think of a plump, rosy-cheeked grandmother from a Norman Rockwell painting, and he could always count on a refreshing glass of lemonade when he stopped by. Her thrill at having her own "trusty Irish cop" was so complete that he didn't have the heart to tell her the name McClung was Scottish, not Irish.

She hated to have the surveillance team go. She felt lost without their reassuring phone calls when returning from a mission after dark. It was a great comfort when Mil came to live in the guest room.

With the tender ministering of Josie and Mabel, Mil survived the trauma of Bliss's terrible death. His killers had not yet been found.

Her sons, Keith and Jimmy, intended to see that she was well cared for, but with one living in Phoenix and the other near San Francisco, it wouldn't be easy. They were immensely relieved when she left her home in the canyon and moved in with Mabel.

But they didn't understand why she abruptly deeded her property and possessions to them. How was she going to live? Of course, she couldn't tell them she planned to join Mabel and Josie in their war on crime, with the goal of living safely in prison. She knew they'd surely have had her committed. Until then, she would live on her Caltrans widow's benefits. Her needs were few, and Mabel charged no rent. With her affairs in order, she jumped wholeheartedly into her friends' campaign.

Within a few weeks, the outraged women, now three strong, had added a string of new purse-snatchers to their list of Bagmen. They had also inadvertently blown up a crack house in Los Angeles, killing an unknown number of gang members in the process. But that was purely by accident. They had intended only to shoot some drug dealers pointed out by Mrs. Ophelia Jackson, the woman they'd met earlier on one of their bus rides.

Mabel remembered Mrs. Jackson's complaint that her neighborhood was virtually held hostage by a gang of thugs and drug dealers calling themselves Simbas. So Mabel called Mrs. Jackson one day, confessing to being very curious about what a crack house looked like. Mrs. Jackson graciously invited her and her lady friends to come for a visit and see for themselves. However, she warned, they were taking a risk. Her neighborhood wasn't safe.

They knew what she had meant when they arrived after half a day's journey on the Greyhound bus from Santa Ana to Los Angeles and then on a city bus that dropped them off within a block of her house. Her neighborhood of small, single-family homes teemed with people of color and suffocated under an air of hopelessness. Those who could afford bars on the windows had them; the others simply nailed shut everything but the fortified front door. Stunted trees and shrubs drooped from neglect. Only a few hardy weeds showed green here and there through a palette of dusty browns. Trails of litter replaced what once might have been flower beds, tended by the original occupants when the area was new and full of promise. Children roamed freely, idle men stood gossiping, and the sound of too many people living in close proximity dulled the senses.

Mrs. Jackson, a plump, bighearted woman, greeted them warmly, seated them on mismatched lawn furniture on her front porch, and treated them to iced tea and cookies. She told them she spent most of her time there on hot summer days, because the interior of her cramped little house was too dark and stuffy. Every opening was nailed shut against intruders, and plywood was secured in the front windows that had twice been shattered by flying rocks and bullets. The fact that all three of her guests had been widowed by hoodlums had her clucking and shaking her head.

"We can jus' call this the Ol' Widow's Tea," she lamented. She told them that her husband had been run over by a car and killed three years ago while running from the vicious pit bull that guarded her neighbor's home. She was sure one of the local kids had let the dog out of the yard as a prank. She wasn't mad at the neighbor. People had to do whatever it took to protect themselves in this neighborhood.

"He was such a good man," she said of her husband, "'specially when he got too old for all that womanizin'. Went to church reg'lar wit' me, made the coffee ever' mornin', an' always bringin' me little presents. Not a day goes by I don' miss 'im."

Her eyes briefly scanned the neighborhood as she leaned closer to the women. She seemed to think they would be shocked by what she was about to say.

"It's hard livin' alone aroun' here. Bad stuff happenin' all the time. If I could jus' figure a way outta here, I'd be *gone*," she said, with an emphatic jerk of her head. But she held the hope of the Almighty in her heart.

"I've tried to work with those men over there," she said ruefully, rolling her eyes in the direction of what she said was the crack house across the street. "I invited 'em to come to church wit' me, an' tol' 'em

I'm prayin' for 'em, an' they jus' laugh at me an' say, 'Oh, now, Mama, you spendin' you money on the sweet spell a'the church ain't no diff'rent from folks spendin' they money on the sweet spell a'crack. It ain't no different, Mama,' they say. 'Whatever way folks wanna feel good, why, it's a free country, an' they free to use they money for whatever makes 'em feel good.'

She shook her graying head, big brown eyes full of sorrow.

"That Sunshine. No use talkin' wit him. He can charm the socks off a snake. It's the li'l chil'ren I worry about. Can't do nothin' wit' those big dummies, but they get the li'l chil'ren into buying that nasty stuff, an' before long all the little ones be jus' as dumb an' mean as the big ones."

They sat on her porch until late afternoon, watching the parade of strutting young men who openly engaged in the sale of drugs and bullied those who didn't want to buy. When a vanful of Simba members pulled up and began carrying large boxes into the house across the street, Mrs. Jackson pointed out the ringleaders.

"That'd be ol' Sunshine hisself," she said accusingly, "an' Pretty Boy an' Sam an' Gooseneck. You don' want 'em to see you. They nothin' but trouble."

She grabbed the pitcher of iced tea and struggled to her feet, urging the women back into the house, hoping to stay out of sight and out of harm's way. The three women arose from their chairs but lingered just long enough for Mrs. Jackson to disappear ahead of them into the darkness of the house. It was now or never.

They could see that the afternoon sun shone directly into the men's eyes, blinding them to the women's presence. Giving each other the nod, they quickly pulled stocking-encased guns from their purses and braced themselves against the porch railing. On the count of three, they opened fire, rapidly emptying their guns at the unsuspecting men from the shadow of the porch overhang.

Whatever was in the boxes blew sky-high, taking the men, the van, and the house with it, as well as the power transformer attached to the utility pole out front. The explosions slammed all three of the women backward against the wall of the porch, leaving them piled in disarray with their ears ringing, choking on the acrid smoke that hung heavy in the air.

The blast, they found out later, had left the area without power for almost three days. This discovery made them feel even worse, for they were already wracked with guilt about perhaps killing innocent people, as well as having so abruptly left Mrs. Jackson's generous hospitality.

Mrs. Jackson had no idea they were involved and didn't blame them a bit when they struggled to their feet, thanked her profusely, and left for the bus stop. The explosion and raging fire, compounded by the flurry of police, firemen, and rubberneckers were the last straw for Mrs. Jackson. She would have left, too, if she'd had somewhere to go.

The "crack house campaign" and its resulting chaos were far more than the women had bargained for. But that was before their most impressive, and last, mission: the virtual eradication of the First Street Gang in the park near Josie's on the Fourth of July. The only gang members who survived unscathed were the ten or so who happened to be in jail at the time.

The First Street Gang seemed an odd name for a gang that didn't operate anywhere near First Street. But they had a long history in Santa Ana and, thinking themselves to be the first street gang organized in the area, had simply called themselves the First Street Gang. They liked the sound of it, like First National Bank or First Presbyterian Church. They had only recently expanded their turf to take over the park by Josie's house.

The Fourth of July had burst forth a beautiful, summery day. Mabel and Mil were to pick up Josie for an old-fashioned celebration at Mabel's house, which they had decorated with little American flags and red, white, and blue streamers. Josie proclaimed they must have watermelon, which she offered to bring, and Mil tried her hand at making homemade strawberry ice cream in Mabel's old Kelvinator. The aged freezer couldn't get the ice cream much beyond the soupy stage, but Mil thought it would be good scooped up on sugar wafers.

Mabel, of course, would provide lemonade to complete the traditional Fourth of July menu of hot dogs and corn on the cob. She also had a supply of sparklers they'd discovered in the basement, which they planned to light and wave around after dark.

They picked up Josie at two, excited about the party they had planned. However, as they drove past the park on their way back to Mabel's they met a roadblock of two souped-up vans in the middle of the street. The occupants were idly sharing joints and shooting the breeze, oblivious to the fact they made the street impassable. Others of them milled around, drinking beer from cans camouflaged with removable soft drink labels and challenging each other to spitting and knife-throwing contests.

When Mabel slowly approached and made an attempt to squeeze by, several of them began pounding her car with their fists, yelling that this was a private party and for her to get the hell out of there. Wincing in fear, she paused to assess the best plan of retreat when bottles and cans began bouncing off her car. Then one of the men leaped up on the hood and began jumping up and down, rocking her old Buick like a bucking bronco.

She struggled to put the car into reverse, with Josie scrunched down beside her, hanging on to the dashboard and door handle for dear life. In the backseat, Mil managed to open her purse and remove the gun she always carried now, in one of Bliss's socks. In spite of the fists, cans, and bottles pelting the car and its disorienting lurching, she was able to roll down her window and take a sideways aim at the nearest van, which had a rag stuffed in the gas tank.

Just as Mabel's car shot wildly backward, Mil began firing in the direction of their tormentors. Of the five rounds fired at least one found its way to the rag-stuffed gas tank. The enormity of the hellish blast that followed flattened them against their seats and shattered Mabel's windshield into a kaleidoscope of jagged splinters. Stunned by the repercussion and the searing heat, they could only stare, wide-eyed, as the vans become engulfed in immense balls of orange flame. Billows of black smoke obscured the blazing inferno as bloody, screaming men ran every which way.

It took a moment for Mabel to regain her wits, but then she again jammed her foot on the gas pedal. They careened backward, out of control, until the car ran up over the curb and slammed into a tree. By this time they were far enough away for her to risk the time it took to shift into a forward gear and turn around. With a crushed rear end and trailing pieces of metal and a broken tailpipe, they beat a hasty retreat back to Josie's.

There they huddled in the living room, assaulted by the screaming of sirens that rent the air without letup. They expected the police to come banging on the door at any moment. Fire trucks, ambulances, police cars—they were certain every disaster vehicle in town had been called out, and shouting voices seem to come from everywhere.

Mil, however, could never sit still under any circumstance. While the other two sat motionless, afraid to breathe, she pacified herself with a cigarette, nervously tapping the ashes off between each puff. "Talk about fireworks on the Fourth of July," she muttered.

Her remark broke the strained hush and angered Josie, who was still struggling with the enormity of what they had done. "This isn't funny," she cried shrilly, her face flushed with intensity. "Didn't you learn *anything* when we blew up that crack house? We're supposed to be engaged in a war on crime, not just blowing things up, willy-nilly! What if there were innocent people in those vans? That would make it *murder* instead of war. Mil, whatever possessed you?"

Mabel jumped in to defend Mil, straining to speak over the screech of a newly arriving siren. "You can't be serious, Josie," she cried. "No innocent person would get mixed up with *that* bunch. And if he did, he wouldn't be innocent for long. They *needed* to be stopped. Who knows what else they might have done to us."

Shouting voices and pounding feet near Josie's door silenced them again, for right outside sat Mabel's wrecked car, clear evidence of their involvement. Mute with fear, they reached for each other's hands, prepared to meet their fate. To their relief, whoever they were raced off to join the crowd in the street.

After they dared breathe again, Mil continued, whispering for fear of discovery, explaining that she had no idea her shots would cause an explosion. "All I wanted was to scare them off before they dumped your car over," she said, reaching for the solace of another cigarette. "I must've hit a gas tank or something."

"The important thing, ladies," declared Mabel, "is that they were the enemy and this is *war*. Don't forget that. Terrible things happen during a war. Things get broken, and people get killed. We could have been killed, too, you know."

"You're right," Mil replied, puffing furiously on her cigarette. "I could've got all three of us blown up right along with those guys. I'm really sorry ... but ... it's not something I'm going to dwell on. I'd rather think about how lucky we were to get a whole *platoon* of the enemy, instead of just picking them off one or two at a time."

Josie wrestled with her conscience, the sight of the injured men and awesome conflagration indelible in her mind. At last, sighing deeply, she said, "Well, we can't undo it, so I guess we'll have to assume there were some really bad guys in those vans and that we've done a public service by getting rid of them."

She fell silent, morally compromised and badly shaken.

All three of them jumped when the phone rang, adding to the clamor of the sirens. It went on ringing, with all three women staring at it as though they'd never seen a phone before, until finally the ringing stopped.

"It was either the police or Mrs. Flannery," said Josie flatly. "One or the other of them must have seen the damage to Mabel's car and put two and two together, and it added up to the three of us. Well, even if we *are* ready to give ourselves up, we're certainly not ready to talk to either of them. How can we ever justify what we just did?"

"Josie," cried Mabel. "*This is war. And they were the enemy.* They didn't have to attack us like that!"

Mil began to pace, wishing there were a window that looked out over the street. From the sounds of the running feet and loud voices, she knew there must be a crowd out there. "I hope we haven't set the whole town on fire," she said.

Josie threw up her hands, saying she was through with their war. "I just know we went too far this time. If we burn the whole town down and innocent people die, we won't be taken seriously anymore. We will *deserve* to rot in prison."

Mabel again became the voice of reason.

"Ladies," she said, struggling up from the daybed, "you know we haven't set the town on fire. This is no worse than blowing up that crack house by mistake. That was an awful explosion, too. But it didn't burn the town down, now, did it? I agree this thing today was ... well, it was terrible. But just think of the irony of *this*." All eyes on her, she enjoyed the momentary suspense. "We were *meant* to end our war today, on the Fourth of July. The day for celebrating freedom from oppression. Think of the significance of *that*. Between those two vans, there should have been enough men to put us way over the top of our goal. We can turn ourselves in ... and be taken care of for the rest of our lives. And of course this thing today was scary—it was the decisive battle of a real war."

Josie pondered that thought for a moment and then groused, "Any way you put it, it's still terrible. There must be some way to make people behave without killing them and blowing things up. I agree we did what we set out to do, but I'm still upset about it. They were all mothers' sons, you know, and those mothers must be devastated."

"Well, those mothers should have thought about that when they were raising those boys," cried Mabel. "They should have made sure they wouldn't grow up like this."

Mil ended the argument by yelling, "Wait a minute. We stopped those guys from doing worse stuff, and that's the important thing. Now get over it. It's done."

Chastened, no one spoke again until they couldn't ignore their hunger. When they hadn't heard sirens for a while, they risked sneaking out to Mabel's car. Leaving the smell of burned wreckage that hung in the air near Josie's, they took a different route to avoid the park and were relieved to see the town still intact.

By the time they reached Mabel's, even Josie was reveling in the fact that their war was actually over. They enjoyed their little party, which now had a whole new meaning, in spite of their fear of capture. But they decided they'd seen quite enough fireworks and didn't use the sparklers. At nine thirty they dropped Josie off at her apartment. All seemed quiet near the park.

Because the explosion was thought to have been an attack by a rival gang, turf wars erupted in the city. Reinforcements arrived from everywhere. Gunfights raged and the city howled with sirens. The women stayed home, glued to their radios and TVs, shocked to find that their latest victims had been the infamous First Street Gang.

But three days of separation was all they could endure. They gathered for the luxury of air-conditioning and lunch at Josie's apartment, where they hung on every word of the TV news. Newscasters warned of the danger of being caught in the cross fire while gang wars continued, and cautioned listeners to avoid certain parts of town. The death toll from the exploding vans had now reached nineteen, and from related gang warfare, eleven.

Josie gasped in disbelief. Among the pictures flashed upon the screen of those who perished in the Fourth of July explosion appeared the slack-jawed Gordo and the bandanna-clad leader of the group that had attacked her—all of them pronounced to have been members of the First Street Gang.

"Gordo and that one with the thing on his head," cried Josie, pantomiming the tying of a bandanna. "But they couldn't have been more than thirteen or fourteen. *Gang members*. No wonder they were so mean. Their poor mothers. I wonder if they knew. Well, I guess no one taught them any better." She shook her head sadly.

"I wish I could say I feel bad about it," Josie continued. "I used to dream of revenge, you know. Now all I can say is they won't be causing any more trouble. We've saved a lot of good citizens from any more of their dirty tricks. It's a sad victory, but this thing puts us well over our goal. Thanks to Mil, our war is really over."

Mil scooped up Josie in a grateful hug. "We're just lucky *we* weren't blown up, too. Apparently, anyone who could have identified us was killed in the blast, or we'd have had a visit from the police by now. And no one seems to notice that Mabel's car is wrecked. We're *so* lucky they think another gang started this ruckus"

Relieved, Mabel said, "I can't wait for the security of prison. I'm tired of all the bad people and scary places. This town has just become too dangerous to live in."

The others agreed with her, not giving a thought to their being at the root of the current mayhem.

They spent the afternoon playing cards, which just wasn't the same without Bliss. At one point they had to stop the game and have a good cry. They had taken up his victorious shout of "R-r-r-r-*ipp* went my new dress!" in honor of him but changed "D-ow-w-wn-n with hot pants!" to "D-ow-w-wn-n with scumbags," a word Mil had learned from her grandchildren. They were sure he would have been proud of them.

They hadn't finished the tuna casserole at lunch, so they shared an early dinner of leftovers before Mabel and Mil decided it was cool enough to go home. Earl had never installed a cooling system in their home because they spent most of their time at the air-conditioned bakery.

Awaiting them, plastered on Mabel's battered windshield, was a large note. Terrified, Mil snatched it and jumped into the car while Mabel got the old Buick revved up. They slunk out of the apartment complex with Mabel straining to see through cracks in the windshield. Mil gingerly opened the note to read it aloud.

"Get this piece of junk out of here *now*. If we see it again, we'll call the police. The Management." Relief that it wasn't a summons of some sort left them weak with gratitude.

Josie was ready for bed and had settled in to watch TV when Mabel called to say that the cat had climbed into her car through one of the open windows and stowed away for the ride home.

"I'll bring him back in the morning," she said, knowing Josie might need him to talk to Theodore. She told her about the note on her car, saying, "I guess we'll have to use Hali from now on." They chuckled over the curiosity of cats and how lucky they were to have nine lives. "We're melting over here in this stuffy house," Mabel added, "and so is the peanut butter. I'll bring it along tomorrow for sandwiches. We may as well use the time to plan Pearl's farewell party."

Josie looked forward to another lunch with her friends. No one was prepared for what the morning would bring.

Mabel struggled to consciousness. It was still dark out, and the house was deathly quiet. Hadn't she just heard a horrendous noise? It couldn't be the clocks; she hadn't wound them since Mil moved in. So what had awakened her and caused her heart to pound in her throat? Her mind flew to her worst fear: the backyard.

"Mil, was that you?" she called in a hushed voice, afraid to move.

A little voice came from the other bedroom, "No … I thought it was you …"

It seemed an eternity before Mabel could will her frozen limbs to move. She groped in the darkness to find the bathrobe and slippers that lay at the end of her bed, and then opened the drawer of the nightstand for the gun she kept there. She stealthily made her way to the door, quaking with fear at what she might see. She was sure the pounding of her heart could be heard a block away.

She paused at the doorway and took a deep breath, and then carefully poked her head out. Her screams mingled with those of Mil's as they met head-on, arms thrashing, in the hallway. Shaking and shushing each other, they clung together like drowning swimmers. It took a moment for them to regain their equilibrium. Moving to the doorway of the dining room, they strained their ears and eyes for an intruder. They saw him at the same time.

In the living room. In front of the window. They stood rooted to the floor, staring at the shadowy outline of a man.

Mabel hardly trusted her shaking hands to take aim. Knowing she had only five rounds, each one had to count. Remembering Bliss's words, she had to take the intruder down before he lunged at them. Arms out in front of her, she wildly opened fire in his general direction, desperately hoping for the best.

Mil cringed as shots shattered the stillness of the night. Flattened against the wall, she couldn't decide whether to run and get her gun, too, or trust that Mabel could do the job. In seconds, it was over. Neither of them knew what to do next, so they just stood clinging to each other, half-deaf from gunfire.

Nothing moved. They heard no sound whatever. And the man still stood, right where he had been, in the living room. The pitiful mewling of the cat brought them back to their senses.

Mabel slid her hand along the dining room wall for the light switch. Squinting against the burst of light and still holding tightly to each other, they saw what it was that had awakened them. Broken glass and figurines littered the living room. The lamp had been tipped over by the falling whatnot stand, which had dumped its trinket-laden shelves onto the glass and porcelain figurines on the coffee table. Mouths agape, they looked to where the terrified cat sat staring back at them from atop the curio cabinet.

The breath went out of them. They sagged to their knees, weak with relief, and let themselves collapse to the floor. "It was just the cat," Mil cried, "jumping up on the cabinet … knocking over the whatnot stand! Oh my God!"

Mabel could only repeat, "The cat. Oh, Mil, and I shot poor Mr. Moonbeam!"

They sat on the floor, laughing helplessly. It was useless to go back to bed. They were thoroughly awake now, and there was this awful mess to clean up.

"I should have listened to Josie and got rid of all those trinkets in the first place," said Mabel, returning from the kitchen with a broom and a dustpan. She offered the broom to Mil. "I was saving them for you, Mil. I thought you might want them when Josie and I went off to jail. Well," she teased, "they're all yours now. But I'll help you clean them up."

"You know, it's no wonder so many people shoot each other," Mil added over the clatter of shards being swept into the dustpan. "You're just not thinking right when you're awakened from a sound sleep."

"It's a good thing you didn't go for your gun, too," answered Mabel. "We could have shot each other, right there in the hall."

It was a very sobering thought.

The inky blackness of night was just giving way to the faint grayness of dawn when silence again descended upon the house, except for the chorus of snoring that echoed between the two bedrooms.

The cat awakened them just before seven with his yowling. He needed to get out to "do his thing," as Mabel called it. The day was already warm and promising to be another hot one. Mabel groggily put on her slippers and robe and picked up the cat to carry him through the weeds to the backyard. Mad as she was at Buzzy for scaring them half to death last night, she couldn't risk losing him by letting him out alone.

The knee-high weeds scratched at Mabel's legs and crackled against the sun baked earth beneath her feet. She hoped he could find a soft enough place to dig. Earl always complained about the difficulty of getting anything but that stubborn old lemon tree to grow in the adobe soil that dried up like brick in the summer. She picked her way, with Buzzy in her arms, looking for a little clearing. The sun worked with the dew on the dry weeds to produce the sour, nose-tingling aroma of moldy hay, and grasshoppers flew up at every step.

Nostalgia flooded over her at the familiar sight and scent. She was again a child, playing in the weeds on the dusty wheat farm in Kansas. She could see herself catching grasshoppers and holding them until they spat brown bubbles of what her ornery cousin, Chuck, told her was tobacco. She wondered if children still did that. Chuck pulled their legs off, too, which was one of the reasons she never liked him. She remembered the time he tried to get her to put her finger in an empty light socket in the barn. He was always experimenting on his younger cousins. Fortunately, no one got hurt.

Chuck. She hadn't thought of him in years. She guessed he'd grown up all right, becoming a science teacher and all. Maybe she'd like him now. But she certainly hadn't then.

Her search ended behind the shed. She stopped short at a patch of clumsily turned earth, where once again she had the ominous sensation of hair rising on the back of her neck. The cat struggled to get down and flew from her arms.

"Now what," she cried, her hand grabbing for her heart. She knew that plot of freshly turned soil shouldn't be there. She fidgeted while the cat squatted in relief, and waited, heart pounding, while Buzzy began to dig around. She wanted only to flee with him back to the safety of the house.

The wind went out of her in a rush when the cat growled, ceased his digging, and sniffed at something he'd unearthed. He slowly backed off, ears flattened and fur bristling. Mabel looked in horror at what were clearly human fingers.

Mil came running at Mabel's screams and found her lying in the weeds behind the shed. The cat sat at a safe distance from his discovery, tail twitching, keeping an eye on something in the patch of disturbed earth.

"Mabel," she called, shaking her. "Mabel!"

Mabel stirred and moaned, "Get the cat. Call 911."

Mil followed the cat's gaze and bent to inspect what looked like upturned roots. The blood drained from her head. It wasn't roots. It was a human hand.

She stood momentarily glued to the spot. Then she grabbed the cat and ran as fast as she could through the weeds and back to the house. She had barely sagged onto a kitchen chair and dialed 911 before the dark spots gathering before her eyes joined the ringing in her ears to encompass her in a whirling, velvety cloud. In a faint, Mil gently slid to the floor.

EIGHTEEN

Just as Officer McClung had promised, help was only a phone call away. Mabel's number had been flagged with "premise history" as a result of her suspected squatter, so when the dispatcher found no one on the line at Mil's call, what law enforcement called a "welfare check" was mobilized immediately. Two officers responded within minutes of Mil's collapse onto the worn linoleum floor of Mabel's kitchen.

They found the two women huddled on the concrete stoop outside Mabel's kitchen. Clinging together in their robes and nighties, faces ashen and hair a mess, they must have looked to the arriving officers almost as scary as whatever had frightened them in the first place. Eyes locked on the backyard, they were poised to flee whatever awful thing lurked there. Inside the house a cat yowled to get out. Dazed, both women began a jumbled tale of fingers in the backyard.

"You can find them," quavered Mabel. "Just look where the cat dug ..." She waved her arm in the general direction of the backyard, overjoyed to turn the whole thing over to someone else.

"Behind the shed," added Mil, holding out an upturned hand with fingers projecting stiffly. "They look like roots."

One of the officers stayed with the rattled women, trying to calm them down. The second officer cautiously headed down the driveway toward the garage, looking for a shed. He disappeared from view and returned a few moments later, grim-faced, heading for the radio in the squad car.

It wasn't long before wailing sirens led a parade of paramedics, police, and homicide detectives, followed by a fire truck and two photographers. The cars converged around Mabel's car in the grassy driveway, spilling out onto the street and clogging morning traffic before officers could seal off the area with bright yellow crime scene tape. A crowd of curious office workers soon gathered and had to be restrained from crossing the tape barrier.

Part of the assemblage disappeared with the photographers behind the shed. The rest milled around, taking peeks at the body and comparing notes. Last to arrive, muscling its way through the police cars and crime scene tape, was a TV camera crew.

Two young paramedics helped the women off the stoop and into the house. Feeling safe now, the women thanked them profusely and told them they were free to leave: the women didn't want to cause any more bother. Still woozy from shock, they unconvincingly declared themselves to be just fine. The cat had stopped his yowling and contented himself by weaving between their bare legs, purring like the buzz saw for which he was named.

In the short time they had waited for the police to arrive, their thoughts kept returning to Pearl's party. Nothing must get in the way of Pearl's farewell celebration. If it weren't for the promise of that party, they would have been eager to tell everything right on the spot and trade the murder and mayhem around them for the peace and quiet of prison.

They hadn't imagined such a flurry of response: police, paramedics, detectives, cameramen, a fire truck. Why a fire truck? they wondered. Mil didn't remember that much hubbub when Bliss died. But, she had fled to Betty Jean's and really didn't know what had gone on back at her house. The problem now was to avoid getting dragged into this mess any more than they had to. Mabel felt faint every time she wondered how long she'd been living with a body in her backyard.

Reluctant to leave while the women still seemed in distress, the paramedics propped them up among the pillows on the sofa and brought glasses of cool water. Once their heads cleared, Mabel and Mil began talking circles around each other, pouring out garbled accounts of how they had come to find the fingers, about the murders of their husbands, and about the strange goings-on in Mabel's backyard.

Midway through a sentence Mabel nudged Mil and gave her a follow-me look. Professing to help each other to the bathroom, they left the paramedics in the living room and shuffled their way down the hall.

Once the bathroom door was shut, Mabel leaned against it to support her sagging body and frantically whispered, "Mil! What if they think we did it? What if they think we killed and buried that person? We might be put in jail before Pearl's party." Her panic at the idea had drained the last remaining starch out of her.

Mil went blank. She hadn't thought of that. The ghastly sight in the backyard had completely filled her mind with the still raw and painful memory of Bliss's tortured death. As for the poor soul in the shallow grave, she hadn't allowed herself to think beyond the horror of anyone disposing of a human being in such a callous way.

Mil whispered, "Oh my gosh, Mabel, you might be right. If we keep trying to avoid their help, they might think we're trying to hide something." Her eyes clouded with the attempt to think through this latest complication. What a bitter pill it would be to have it all go wrong now and leave Pearl in the lurch. Finally she said, "I don't know how we're going to do it, Mabel, but somehow we have to convince them to leave us out of this."

At the same moment they caught sight of themselves in the mirror: pale arms and legs protruding from rumpled cotton robes, hair frazzled from sleep, and pasty faces slathered from the night before in the greasy cream Earl used to call "Oil of Old Lay."

"Good grief," croaked Mabel. "We look awful. No wonder the paramedics are reluctant to leave. Quick, the hairbrush ... and a washcloth ... and some rouge."

Mil kept flushing the toilet for background noise while they made a slapdash attempt to groom themselves. "Why are we so scared, anyway?" she asked, her spunk returning. "We had nothing to do with this business in your yard. Let's go back out there and let them see we have nothing to hide. I'm sure the police will want to talk to us some more. So, let's get it over with. As Theodore used to say, the sooner the quicker!"

Mabel reminded her they must also return the cat to Josie. "We have nothing to feed the poor thing, and Josie's expecting us for lunch, you know. We'd better call. Oh, dear," Mabel moaned. "How are we going to break this to her?" Dejected, she led the way back to the living room.

"Ladies, this is Inspector Turner, Santa Ana Police. If you feel up to it, she'd like to talk to you."

The one who appeared to be the head paramedic hovered protectively while making the introductions. He thought the women looked much better than they had a little earlier, but, at their ages, he knew things could fall apart pretty fast. The women had the right to refuse further treatment, of course, but he decided to hang around for a few minutes, just in case. They still seemed pretty frail to him. His partner waited in the ambulance.

Paige would never forget this meeting. Before her, in their simple cotton print robes, sat two old women, hair silvered with white, one short and plump, the other tall and slender. The short, darker one wore her hair in a knot at the nape of her neck and looked back at Paige with questioning brown eyes. The tall one puffed nervously on a cigarette. Her graying auburn hair was stylishly cut, and her impish green eyes couldn't resist a tentative smile.

Paige's heart went out to them. It was a shame they had to endure this nasty business. Sweet, sheltered gentlewomen, she thought. No wonder they'd passed out at the sight of a human hand sticking up out of the ground.

"Good morning, ladies," she said, consulting her watch. "You've had quite a time of it this morning. It's not even eight thirty, and you must feel you've already put in a full day."

She settled into Mabel's saggy goose-down chair, plumping the pillows a bit for support. The women only nodded sweetly at each other and then at her.

"Is there anything we can do for you? Contact someone? Bring in breakfast? If you'd like to get dressed first, I'll wait for you."

"Oh, could you?" It was Mil, thrilled to be talking to another woman instead of a policeman. "It's okay if we stay in our robes, but we do need to get hold of Josie, who's counting on us for lunch with her cat and the peanut butter. Well, it's not really her cat, but she has air-conditioning, you see, and since we're taking the cat, we thought we might as well take the peanut butter."

She put out her cigarette and nervously resisted the urge to reach for another.

"I hope you don't mind if I smoke," she said. "When I get nervous, I can't seem to help myself. My husband died trying to get me to quit. Well, actually, he died of a heart attack when he was killed, but ..."

Mabel saw the puzzled look on Inspector Turner's face. She leaned closer in an effort to help explain.

"You see, Inspector Turner," Mabel began, hoping to make clear with the waving of her hands what Mil hadn't been able to with words, "Josie needs the cat to talk to Theodore. She's a widow, too ... we're all three widows, but Mil's the newest one. Such a shame. Bliss was the finest man." She turned sorrowful eyes to Mil, reaching for her hand.

"Well, anyway, that burglar came right through Josie's bedroom window during the night. But she doesn't live there anymore. Now she has guards and everything. But she still needs Theodore's advice now and then. You see, he was her husband before the burglar shot him, right there beside her, in their own bed. Well, when the cat's in the room, people don't think she's crazy, so we're taking the cat back to her, and because it's melting, we're taking the peanut butter, too."

Mabel could see she hadn't made things any clearer. Inspector Turner looked more bewildered than ever. She tried again, hands now working in earnest, with Mil nodding in agreement at everything she said.

"Actually, the peanut butter doesn't have anything to do with it," she said, smiling sweetly, as though removing that one factor from the equation would make the rest of it add up. "Forget the peanut butter. But, you see, Buzzy … he's her cat … well, he's kind of the neighborhood cat, but he purrs so loudly, and Josie didn't want to say Beefheart … Uh, well, anyway, he stowed away in our car last night and gave us a terrible fright when he sent things crashing all over the room in the middle of the night. What a mess! But it was poor old Mr. Moonbeam who got the worst of it."

Mabel grimaced, reliving their midnight adventure.

"Anyway, Buzzy wanted out early this morning, so I took him to find a soft place to dig—and he dug up that person right where I put him down. And you know all the rest. So we're taking him and the peanut butter to Josie's for lunch—that's the only reason we brought up the peanut butter in the first place."

She suddenly remembered the offer of food.

"Did you say you can bring in breakfast? We haven't eaten yet, now that you mention it."

She turned to Mil, as though that explained everything.

"No wonder we fainted, dear," Mabel said. "We haven't had anything to eat since Josie's tuna casserole. Was that only yesterday? Wait a minute … is this today?"

Turning back to Paige, she added, "I'm sorry if we seem a bit confused, honey. You see, we thought we had an intruder last night, but it was just my figurines smashing together all over the living room. Poor old Mr. Moonbeam over there," she said, pointing to where a bullet-riddled Mr. Moonbeam kept vigil at the window. "He was doing his best to protect us, and he got the brunt of it. You can see, with all that going on, we didn't sleep much last night. And now we wake up to *this*.

She drifted off, trying to reconstruct the order of events.

"I was carrying the cat through the weeds, thinking about how grasshoppers spit tobacco juice and remembering how my cousin, Chuck, used to experiment on them. He experimented on little kids, too. But I didn't like it when he pulled their legs off. Anyway, the cat found fingers when he dug around out there …"

Mabel looked at the concerned faces staring back at her as if seeing them for the first time and attempted to rise up off the sofa.

"Oh, I've forgotten my manners. I can get some lemonade …"

"No, no! Stay there," stammered Paige, reaching out to restrain her. "We can get it for you." Her mind raced. Low blood sugar, she said to herself. And shock. The poor things are clearly weak and disoriented. Doughnuts and orange juice should help. "In fact," she added hastily, "I'll send my partner, Wisneski, down the street for doughnuts and orange juice. He loves doughnuts, so he won't mind going."

She made a mental note to ask about the significance of this oddly dressed dummy called Mr. Moonbeam. He looked as though he might have been used for target practice. As difficult as it was for them to explain anything, however, she didn't want to get caught up in something obviously extraneous just yet.

The paramedic made himself useful and produced glasses of cold lemonade from Mabel's kitchen. Then he hunted up Wisneski and told him he was wanted inside. Not finding anything else to do, he and his unit headed back to the fire station.

Wisneski quickly agreed to go for doughnuts and orange juice. Otherwise, he would have to stand around waiting for the lab techs before they could exhume the body, and it was getting hotter by the minute in the searing July sun. He returned with enough bakery goods for an army and almost as much juice, to share with those who were working outside.

Andy Krach arrived while Wisneski was gone, and busied himself taking notes. When Wisneski drove up, Krach thanked him for the call tipping him to a scoop and helped distribute the treats among the crew in the yard. Then they both went into the house to confer with Paige.

Mabel and Mil delicately partook of the unexpected feast while the others talked. Wisneski enjoyed watching the women nibble at the doughnuts in the most ladylike manner, dabbing at their mouths with embroidered napkins. Rotten luck, he thought. Well-bred old ladies with no one to care for them, living in a neighborhood like this. Too old to change their ways and move. Probably too poor, as well, with no one to provide the muscle a move would take.

His mind flashed ahead in time. He wondered what the future held for him and Alison. He couldn't imagine them old and frail—and alone. Maybe it was just as well. It was too damn depressing to think about.

Andy felt right at home in Mabel's old house. For the first time since leaving Ohio, he felt a twinge of loss. The house was like many of the homes on his boyhood street in Ohio and had the same warm, musty odor he'd loved at his grandmother's house. He listened and took notes, finding himself utterly charmed by the two old ladies.

With patience, Andy and the inspectors were able to piece together Mabel's and Mil's disjointed stories, although the story of their also-widowed friend, Josie, was confusingly intertwined. They found the women utterly endearing, even if their thoughts were hopelessly scattered. They were a refreshing change from the unsavory sorts the cops usually dealt with. The inspectors remembered Bliss's recent and still unsolved death, as well as Earl's death in the bakery four years ago.

"But where is Officer McClung?" asked Mabel, eyeing the last of the doughnuts, a gooey thing oozing with chocolate. "He was keeping watch over me, but I guess not long enough."

She was assured he'd be there as soon as he could. The inspectors were waiting for him to arrive before inspecting the shed, because as far as they knew, he had been the last to see inside it.

Satisfied, Mabel wiped the last of the chocolate doughnut off her mouth and waited to see what would happen next.

Andy thanked them for the interview and left, hoping to beat the deadline for the afternoon paper. With him went the staff photographer, who had taken pictures of the women to add to his shots of the body in the yard. No sooner had they gone than the TV crew prevailed upon them to be videotaped. The women agreed, even though they were still in their robes. They found it quite exciting to be at the center of so much commotion.

Now the question for Turner and Wisneski was what to do with the women while further investigation and exhumation took place.

"We could go to Josie's," offered Mabel. "It's not very far, and it's air-conditioned. She's expecting us, anyway. But we can't stay there overnight, because she has only a little daybed." She looked out the window at the array of vehicles parked around and behind her car in the driveway. "I don't think I can get my car out, though. And I'm not sure I'm fit to drive."

Wisneski had been momentarily distracted, interested in her collection of clocks and antiques, but when she mentioned her car he spoke up.

"I did notice your windshield is badly shattered," he said, "and there's some pretty heavy damage to the rear of your car. You aren't still driving it, are you? How'd it happen?"

The two women looked at each other nervously.

"Well," Mabel began, "that's a long story. I haven't had it fixed because I won't be driving much longer. You see …"

Wisneski didn't want to get into another of her confusing and often pointless stories, so he interrupted her to say that he and Inspector Turner would personally drive the women to their friend's house and be back for them sometime after dinner. "We should have the premises restored by then and won't need to bother you anymore."

"Good idea," Paige said. "Go ahead and dress, get what you might need for the afternoon, and we'll take you. There's no sense in your having to witness all this ugly business around here."

Actually, she hated to abandon them. They seemed so helpless. An anachronism in today's world, she thought. Violence should have no place in their old-fashioned lives of quiet civility.

"Shouldn't we call Josie first?" asked Mil, reaching for the phone. "She's going to be awfully shocked to see us drive up with two policemen." She smiled at Paige and corrected herself. "I mean, two police persons."

After a short discussion it was decided that Josie would have less time to stew if they just drove up without calling first. Because the detectives weren't wearing uniforms, Josie might not be so shocked.

"She's become such a worrywart lately," explained Mabel. "No sense upsetting her till we have to."

They dressed while Turner and Wisneski took care of other matters. Then, clutching their gate pass to Josie's, the women enjoyed the ride to the Glendon Arms Apartments in the backseat of a squad car. They felt deliciously wicked, sitting where many a felon had sat. Mabel carried the still-purring cat, and Mil, the jar of peanut butter.

Josie happily prepared lunch for her friends, decorating the table with a bouquet of fading stock and snapdragons cut from the apartment grounds. She would never cut the fresh, fully bloomed ones, for that would be rude to the other tenants. But she didn't think they'd miss the dying ones. She was setting out lunch, with many little saucers of tidbits, when a police car pulled up to the curb.

Josie was astounded to see Mabel and Mil helped from the car and escorted to her door. Who were those other people? The sight of a police car took her breath away.

Mabel dropped the cat and rushed in ahead of the others, knowing Josie would immediately assume the worst. "Now, Josie, dear, don't worry. Everything's okay," she said, enveloping a white-faced Josie in her arms.

Mil followed closely, mindlessly adding, "Well, everything isn't *really* okay, but *we're* okay."

Behind them stood Turner and Wisneski, waiting to be introduced. Upon hearing they were police inspectors, Josie seemed to shrink before their very eyes.

"Are ... are we going to jail?" she asked, tiny hand to her brow. "Before Pearl's party? Oh, dear! How did it happen?"

Turner and Wisneski looked at each other in wonder. This old lady seemed as addled as the other two, and she hadn't even been near the body. She really was a worrywart.

"Come sit down, Josie," urged Mabel, leading her to her little chair. "We have quite a story to tell you. And, no, we aren't going to jail. These nice people gave us a ride because my car is buried in the driveway, and we had to be gone while they dig up the body."

Hand groping for her heart, Josie burst out, "Body? What body? Mabel, what are you talking about? And why—how in the world did your car get buried in the driveway?"

As usual, Mabel and Mil both began to talk at once, telling her the events of the morning, correcting each other and leaving Turner and Wisneski to wonder how Josie would ever make sense of their convoluted tale.

"In your backyard!" Josie was wide-eyed. "Oh, you poor things." She reached out for her friends' hands. "I wish you could stay here ... you aren't going *back* there, are you? Oh, dear! Who is it, the body? And how did it get there?"

Paige replied that they didn't have the answer to either question yet and assured her that her friends would be taken care of. "But you ladies might start thinking about a change of address," she said to Mabel and Mil. "It's a crazy world out there. Your friend here has the right idea." She nodded to indicate Josie. "Have you thought of moving into a high-security place like this?"

At this, the irrepressible Mil blurted, "Have we ever!" and began to laugh.

Upon hearing her, Mabel also had to laugh. Josie, who was still giddy with shock, met their eyes, and she, too, burst into laughter. Every time they caught sight of each other, they erupted again.

Turner and Wisneski watched in awe. What was so damned funny? Either the shock had made them hysterical or these women were crazy as loons.

The women tried to apologize to their guests between outbursts. Finally, they refused to look at each other while wiping their eyes and sputtering more apologies.

Turner and Wisneski knew it was time to leave. Sweet as these old ladies were, they'd had just about enough of their eccentric behavior. "We'll be back after dinner," Paige promised, edging for the door. "And we'll have set up a surveillance of your house. Or, if you'd rather go to a hotel ..."

Wiping tears of laughter from her eyes, Mabel quickly assured them, "Oh, no, thank you. We'll be all right. As long as that body is gone and someone is keeping watch over us, we'll be okay. Till we move to a safer place."

At this, she again fought back laughter, which got Mil going once more.

"Oh, dear," Mil wheezed, hiding her face behind her hands. "I'm sorry. This really isn't funny." She turned away from them, still laughing and thoroughly embarrassed by her lack of control.

Josie managed to contain herself till she saw the inspectors to the door, and then the three of them, lost in the irony of Inspector Turner's suggestion, laughed until Josie was in danger of wetting her pants.

On the way back to Mabel's, Wisneski couldn't resist teasing Paige about her "old women" theory. They hadn't talked about it since that first day in the interrogation room, but he knew she'd been spending a lot of free time haunting the Santa Ana bus station looking for suspicious old women.

"Well, Turner," he drawled, "maybe you've just found your old women murderers. Those three old ladies seem pretty dangerous to me. It'd be easy for them to confuse their prey with all that nonsense then jump 'em when they least expect it."

Paige laughed. She knew she had it coming. He'd restrained himself so far, but she knew his sense of humor could be bottled up only so long. Shaking her head in dismay at the mental image he painted, she guessed those three were barely capable of maneuvering through a day, let alone stalking the city with loaded thirty-eights.

"Well, I didn't mean *old* old women. But," she added slyly, "you never know."

Subdued from the events of the morning, the women set about their lunch of peanut butter sandwiches, grapes, and little bits of things from Josie's refrigerator. All they could talk about was the body in Mabel's yard. However, the conversation became so distressing to Mabel that they had to change the subject. It was bad enough when Josie suggested this could have been the work of the Mafia; the tortured body of someone who wouldn't cooperate. But Mil's suggestion that it might be hacked-up pieces of several bodies sent Mabel over the edge.

They tried to think about Pearl's party. But their minds kept returning to the body and the exhilarating fact that they had somehow survived their war on crime all in one piece. They were about to begin a whole new chapter in their lives.

The women saw themselves on the news twice that afternoon. Mil was shocked to see how old and frail they looked.

"How can that old woman be *me*," she exclaimed, "when *I'm* still me, and I'm not that old!"

"It's either trick photography or we *do* look that old," said Mabel. "We know we're not young anymore, so that must be how the world sees us: frail, useless old women. What an awful thought."

Turner and Wisneski arrived at dusk, assuring Mabel and Mil there would be around-the-clock surveillance of their home and reminding them they still had the option of going to a hotel. But the two women couldn't wait set off for home, leaving Josie behind with orders not to worry.

Not to worry, indeed, Josie thought, knowing she would worry the night away. She didn't know how they could go back to Mabel's defiled house even in broad daylight. As for her, a team of wild horses couldn't drag her over there after dark.

NINETEEN

Going over the events of the past weeks, the women realized how much they missed the quiet days of playing cards, watching soaps, and planning get-togethers. They needed one last fling before being imprisoned forever: a potluck visit to the canyon with Betty Jean, Hap, Gertie, and Waldo.

They hadn't been back to the canyon since Bliss's death and missed their old friends. But Pearl's farewell party was only three days away, and they had already invited Inspector Turner for tea the day after that. Once they confessed to her over finger sandwiches and tea cakes, they would never visit anyone again.

Luckily, they were able to squeeze in a date with their friends the day before Pearl's party. But Josie's faithful cab driver, Hali, couldn't help them. His dilapidated cab was undergoing repairs and wouldn't be ready until late afternoon.

"Heck, *I'll* drive us out there in Bliss's old truck," volunteered Mil. It was one of the few things her son had been unable to sell for her. It now sat parked in Mabel's garage, waiting for him to decide what to do with it. Mil hadn't driven it in years, but they knew they couldn't count on Mabel's car.

With the other two sputtering their protests, Mil managed to back the truck out of the garage without hitting anything and drove it around the block a few times to bone up on the art of gear shifting. Before long, she roared up into the driveway and announced she was ready whenever they were.

Josie and Mabel had to use a stool to climb up into the cab. They laughed at the spectacle they must have made, pushing and tugging at each other to find a perch on the hard leather seat while juggling containers of food. Then, with a grinding of gears, they were on their way.

The truck alternately bucked and died and lurched back to life again on the way to Chapman Avenue. At the turnoff to Modjeska Canyon, the highway became narrower as it began winding through the golden, tree-studded countryside. Mil struggled to keep the truck in her lane. When she came close to sideswiping a car or running off the road, Mabel and Josie shrieked and hid their eyes. Josie finally threw her skirt over her head to avoid having to see, and stayed that way for the rest of the trip.

Mil basked in the familiar sights. She looked forward to driving by her old home for one last look at the end of the day.

Soon they came to the gravel lane leading to the Scheidler's. Mil braked and did her best to gear down. The truck leaped and screamed with the stripping of gears. Miraculously, she made the abrupt maneuver without overturning or falling into the drainage ditch below. Mabel was too shocked to speak. Even Mil was white-faced. This was too close for comfort.

"We should have asked Hali to drive your truck!" came Josie's voice from beneath her skirt. "We shouldn't have let you do this, Mil."

They continued slowly along the rutted gravel road until Mil recovered her spirit of adventure. She ground to a higher gear, saying, "hang on, ladies! This is fun!"

Josie and Mabel held tightly to their covered dishes and each other as they bounced through the old berry field. Tangled branches again reached out to greet them with a screeching of thorns along the sides of the truck. After pitching down through the hollow with its stand of old trees, the road turned and they were in the clear again. Mabel alerted Josie that they were nearing Gertie's, and Josie came out warily from beneath her skirt.

Hap saw their cloud of dust and went to help them down from the truck. Gertie stood in the doorway, with Waldo hovering over her shoulder. Their loud chatter as they made their way up the stairs and into the house brought Betty Jean running from the kitchen. Everyone hugged everyone else, all talking at once. Their friends immediately wanted to know about the body in Mabel's yard. Mabel told them Officer McClung had called this very morning to hint a solution was imminent. But that was all she knew, and she didn't want to think about it.

The women had offered to bring all the food: Gertie had her hands full now that Waldo was home again. Josie brought Parker House rolls and a fruit salad, Mil had baked two meat loaves, and Mabel, of course, brought her famous lemon meringue pies. Betty Jean whipped up a casserole of scalloped potatoes, promising it contained no marijuana, and Hap made a salad from the vegetables in the garden. He'd also decorated the table with an enormous bouquet of flowers that burst from the milk carton in which he'd brought them.

Waldo was as excited at the prospect of all that food as he was at seeing his friends. Gertie had laid out a fresh pair of overalls for him, hollering that she expected him to behave himself—no making a mess at the table or wandering off and scaring her. He had gruffly agreed. He didn't want to go back to that care facility. He also paid a visit to the spice cabinet, fumbling around until he found the vanilla for his hair. It wasn't every day he got to entertain ladies.

Gertie had set the dining room table with her best dishes. Few of them matched, and any chipped parts were turned to the back. She'd also made a pot of her delicious baked beans, which had baked all morning in the oven of her old woodstove and scented the house with the irresistible aroma of bacon and bell peppers steeped in molasses and onions. Figuring not to waste the heat of the hot oven, she'd also baked a berry cobbler from the first wild fruit of the season. Waldo seemed more interested in the food than anything else, so they placed everything on the table and bustled around taking their seats.

Waldo stuck to his eating, smacking his lips and grunting his satisfied "yup … yup" while the others talked and laughed. The moment he was through he pulled himself up, letting the food from his lap fall where it may, and went out to the porch to have a smoke. They hadn't let him smoke in the care facility, so in order for Gertie to bring him home again he'd had to promise to be more careful with his cigarettes, and to stay put and be quiet when she told him to. After a few shouting matches and threats of packing him back off to the facility, he'd grudgingly given in to her rules.

Hap picked up his checkers set and dutifully went to join him. His mother had given him the job of keeping track of Waldo today so Gertie could visit. Maybe old Waldo would still enjoy a game of checkers if he could keep his mind on it. Hap knew not to lock horns with him. They'd play by whatever rules Waldo made up as they went along.

With Hap and Waldo safely out of earshot, Mil turned to Gertie and asked, "How did it happen that you brought Waldo back home, anyway? It has to be awfully hard for you."

Gertie woefully shook her head. "I tell ya, Mil, it like to broke my heart when I seen that fine man, all sedated and droolin' like a baby in that damn place. No fire in 'im, nothin'. Jist a broke down ol' man. Had to be sedated or tied to his chair, one, an' I jist couldn' take it no more. So, I tol' 'im the rules an' brung him home. An' my son, Orvul, sends me money for a lady to hep me." She began fussing with her dentures, obviously unaccustomed to wearing them for any length of time.

"Where is she?" asked Josie. "Does she stay with you? Certainly you have enough room."

"Well, I tried t'git her to, but she said she wasn't stayin' here with no crazy man. She met him, you know, when I in'erviewed her. Trouble is, she don't come ever' time she's s'posed to." By now she'd had enough of the trapped berry seeds in her dentures. She pried them out of her mouth and slapped them down on the table, covering them with her napkin.

Waldo began yelling out on the porch. Hap had to agree that Waldo could move his pieces any way he wanted before they settled in again to play.

"Jish lishen to that damned ol' ffhart," crowed Gertie, tossing a gargoylian grin of toothless gums in the direction of the porch. "He got the ffhire back in 'im, all right!"

The women zeroed in on Gertie's dilemma with all kinds of advice. Among other things, she must try to get the lady to live with them, or at least be more forceful with her so she would come when she was supposed to. And how about moving to town? Living way out here had to be a real inconvenience. Gertie listened politely for a short time, and realized they didn't understand the scope of the problem.

"Hold yer horshesh," she began, her lips flapping in and out of a cavern of gnashing gums. "You don' know how hard it ish t'git shomeone to hep ya way out here! She'sh the only damn fool anshered the ad. Showsh ya jish how bright she ish."

She stopped to laugh at herself, saying, "Ain't that shomethin'? *Me* shaying *she* ain't bright!" She held her head between work-roughened hands, laughing in her despair. True to form, this woman could find humor in anything.

"An' we cain't move out of a housh that'sh paid fer," she said flatly, with her Midwestern reasoning. "They'll have to take ush outta here in pine boxshes. Don't know where we'd go, anyway, that'd be any better for Waldo, an' me able ta shtay with 'im."

"There *has* to be a place where you could both stay, Gertie," said Mabel. "You know, where he could get the care he needs and you could get some rest."

"Never heard a'one," Gertie responded, leaning over to sniff the flowers in Hap's milk carton. "Beshidesh, them playshes wouldn't git rich off a people like me. They'd fill 'em up with folksh who kin pay for lotsha care. And that'sh the problem. When we git old, one of ush ish bound to need more care than the other, and when it gitsh to where one of ush cain't take care of the other, why, there's nothin' to do but sheparate ush. I tell ya, I don't know which is worsh: worryin' about 'im where I know he ain't happy, or tryin' t'do it all myshelf."

Betty Jean had little to say about Gertie's problem. She was content to live one day at a time, letting the future take care of itself.

They heard more yelling from Waldo out on the porch. He didn't want Hap's checker piece on the same square he was aiming for. Hap got him settled back down by letting him have his captured pieces back. In all their arguing, neither of them heard the brilliant singing of the meadowlark in the pasture or the lowing of cattle. But the sounds were the music of the earth to Mil's ears, the indescribably sweet songs she had missed since moving into town with Mabel. She willed herself not to cry. What was done was done.

The next outburst from Waldo was his disgust with the whole game. He threw his checkers across the porch, yelling that he was tired of being cheated by that damn fool, Hap. He wanted to hear Mil play the piano. Hap stood up and got out of the way. He didn't know what Waldo might do next.

Waldo stomped back into the house followed by Hap, who was glad the impossible checkers game was over. "C'm'in here, you ol' biddies," Waldo yelled. "Fire up that ol' pianer an' let's have a little music!"

He led the way into the living room and set himself down heavily in the frayed armchair that sat beside the ancient upright piano, causing billows of dust to fly up. The equally dusty top of the piano held rows of framed family photos from long ago, but they, too, were so dusty it was hard to tell who was in the pictures. The piano probably hadn't been tuned since their daughter, Velma, left home many years ago, but Mil always managed to pound out some pretty respectable tunes on its yellowed keys.

Everyone followed Waldo into the living room, which for years had been used only when Mil played the piano. Tattered sofas and chairs lined the walls. Rugs worn thin by the feet of stampeding children had long ago been taken up to let the sound of clattering shoes echo from the bare walls and ceiling.

Mil blew off the keyboard and took her seat at the piano. Hap produced his harmonica, and they soon had the room reverberating with music. Those who knew the words to songs joined in, and before long Waldo was enchanted out of his chair, dancing stiffly around the room. When they began to play the "Missouri Waltz," he gathered up Josie and gallantly circled the room with her, just as he had done years ago. It gladdened everyone's hearts to see a glimmer of the old Waldo. Betty Jean joined them, dancing around the room in an arm-flapping style all her own, her long skirt whirling around her sandaled feet. Eventually Hap decided he'd rather dance than play. He left the music making to Mil and followed his mother's lead, lumbering around the room like a big dancing bear.

After a time, they all sat down to talk and listen. Mil played on and on: fox-trots, polkas, and ragtime, anything anyone requested. She was at her best, knowing this was her final performance. She continued to play until her hands ached from the effort. Her friends applauded wildly. They had always been her best audience. How she would miss them and that funny old piano.

The women brewed more coffee and tea and arranged the leftovers from their feast invitingly around the flowers on the dining table. Waldo had worn himself out dancing and wandered off down the hall, saying he was going to bed. The rest of them visited for a time while helping themselves to leftovers. When Hap had licked the last crumbs from the pie pans and no one could hold another bite, it seemed time to go home.

Saying good-bye was hard for the three women. They knew they'd never be back to this rollicking old house, where in days gone by they'd danced and sung and played cards until the wee hours of the morning. Betty Jean and Hap might come visit them in prison, but they were afraid they'd never see Gertie and Waldo again. They stood in a clump in the doorway, hugging their friends and exchanging thanks for a most wonderful afternoon.

Hap boosted them up into the truck. With the late-afternoon sun glancing off the windshield and a lot of waving and hollering, they turned down the gravel lane and headed for home. Mil was having better luck handling the truck. Except for the ruts in the road, the ride was much smoother. However, Josie clutched the hem of her dress in her hand, ready to throw it over her head at any moment.

"That was the most perfect send-off," said Mabel, dreamily.

"Wasn't it, though." agreed Mil. "Good thing, too, 'cause this and Pearl's party are going to have to hold us for the rest of our lives."

"But isn't it sad to see how worn-out Gertie is from caring for Waldo," commented Josie. "What's going to happen to them? I wish there were something we could do ..."

They had cleared the berry field and were approaching the narrow passage over the drainage ditch when they saw the overturned pickup truck. It had smashed through the rotting post that Mil almost hit, and nose-dived to land on its side in the ditch. The truck's wheels were still spinning slowly, and its cargo was tossed all over the road. Two men, obviously not hurt badly, had crawled out and stood looking to the women for help as they drew near.

Mil slowed and stopped beside them. Through her open window, she caught the familiar odor of stale alcohol and tobacco wafting from the taller, bearded in as he leaned in to speak to her. The shorter one hung back, cradling his injured arm close to his body. She knew when her heart jumped into her mouth that these were the two who had killed Bliss and robbed them. She stared, mouth agape, into the cold eyes of the man who'd held Bliss down with his boot and threatened to shoot both of them. She didn't hear a word he said.

"... misjudged that driveway, I guess," he was saying. "Me and my friend here sure would appreciate your help. I think my friend's arm's broke. Maybe you can see about him while I wait here for a tow truck?"

He pointed to the contents of his truck, spilled out over the road and into the ditch: several TVs, a lot of machinery, and, entangled in snarls of black wire, what looked like a collection of electronic equipment. "I'd sure appreciate it if I could clean that stuff up outta the road and put it in your truck for the time bein'," he went on, still speaking to Mil's blank face.

When Mil didn't respond, Josie leaned across and said, "Why, of course. We'd help you, but I don't think we'd be any good at picking up that stuff. Do you suppose you could do that?"

"Yeah, okay," he said. "Just pull the truck up a little. It won't take me long."

He turned to his work. Mil remained frozen, unable to move. Josie had to prod her to pull forward, as the man had requested. The injured man still hung back, leaning against a tree and saying nothing while the taller man began the job of loading things into the back of Mil's truck.

Mil rolled her window shut and gasped, "They're the ones who killed Bliss. I bet that stuff in their truck is stolen!"

Josie and Mabel were dumbstruck. No one spoke while they struggled to overcome their panic.

"Are you sure? What are we going to do?" wailed Josie, followed by "Oh, dear—oh dear!" from Mabel.

The expression on Mil's face told that she knew exactly what she was going to do. "I still have a gun in my purse," she said. "I never took it out. Wait till he gets all that stuff in my truck. You'll see."

What might have been ten or fifteen agonizing minutes seemed like an hour as they waited for the man to finish. By the time he headed their way again, wiping his hands on his pants, Mil had her stocking-encased gun ready. She rolled her window down as he approached, but the man never had a chance to speak before the roar of the gun exploded from the cab of the truck. Without making a sound, he slumped out of sight. Twenty feet away, still under the tree, stood his horrified friend—the one who had followed her into the kitchen and taken their box of money. One more blast from Mil's gun and he, too, slumped to the ground.

Mil calmly returned the gun to her purse. Mabel and Josie sat speechless beside her. When she felt ready, Mil put the truck in gear and pulled slowly out of the driveway, edging by the dangling wheels of the overturned truck.

"What do we do now?" quavered Mabel. "Oh, dear." Trying to be brave, Josie put her arm around Mabel's shoulder and held her close. "It's all right, honey," she answered. "Those were Bliss's killers."

They drove, their minds a scramble, until Mabel asked Mil what she intended to do with the equipment in her truck.

"Just leave it there," she said, "and turn it in with the guns we're going to give Officer Turner at the tea party. If it was stolen, she can see that it's returned."

"I guess it's a good thing Hali couldn't take us," reflected Josie. "We wouldn't want to involve him in this. It turned out just right this way."

Mabel began worrying about the two men. "We didn't cover them up or anything. It doesn't seem very nice to just leave them there like that until someone finds them. Why did they want to put their stuff in our truck, anyway?"

Mil had been thinking about that, too, and felt certain she knew the answer. "Probably because they wanted to trade their smashed-up truck for ours. I bet they were just nice to us so they could load all that stuff in our truck. You know they were going to dump us out and take the equipment *and* the truck. But we didn't give them a chance, did we? Anyway, I'll call the sheriff's station on the way home and tell them where to find the bodies. They'll get the details later."

Being in the presence of Bliss's killers again had put a pall over seeing her old home. Mil decided she'd seen quite enough of the canyon and drove Josie straight home. At peace from settling the score, she was ready to move on. When they dropped Josie off at her apartment, they reminded each other that they couldn't talk about the two men or the truck at Pearl's party tomorrow. How could they explain everything? Josie promised to add two new marks on the wall for Mil.

TWENTY

Mil remembered from her previous experience with calling 911 that the system allowed the answering dispatcher to trace the call. The women couldn't risk giving themselves away on the eve of Pearl's party, so on the way home she stopped at a pay phone to call. She gave only enough details to make it possible to find the two men and hung up, leaving the startled dispatcher to take it from there. Much as they had enjoyed their visit to the canyon, they were grateful to be through with that traumatic day.

In the morning they called Hali and arranged to be picked up for Pearl's party at noon. Driving there in Mil's truck was out of the question. It was full of stolen equipment. The truck, minus the driver's-side mirror Mil had clipped off the night before, would have to remain just the way it was in Mabel's garage.

It was an oppressively warm day. When Hali arrived he found the two women waiting under the shade of the fruit-laden lemon tree with their bags of supplies for the party. He helped them into the cab after crossing himself and mumbling something about the body that had been found there, identified on the morning news as an old Mexican woman.

"Dos Cat'olics t'ink dis takes de spell away," he explained, continuing to cross himself. "I don' know if it works if you not Cat'olic, but you better be doin' it, too. How you brave enough to stay dere, where dat poor lady be foun'?"

Mabel assured him that the police had everything under control, and Mil eased his mind by telling him the woman's spirit had been consoled when her body was returned to her loved ones in Mexico. He promised to wait for their call at the end of the day.

Between the heat generated by the plastic seat covers of the cab and the walk from the cab to Pearl's door, the women thought they would melt. The blazing sun radiated off the concrete walks and walls of the apartment complex. Patches of brown had crept into the grass, and the shrubbery drooped. Nothing seemed to move or breathe.

Josie had walked the short distance to Pearl's earlier that morning and now answered their knock with a welcoming rush of cool air from the open door. Pearl's sister, Peggy, had returned from Chicago for the party, and came running to give them big hugs. Arriving at the appointed hour of two o'clock would be two more of Pearl's closest friends.

Mabel busied herself laying out her best linen and silver service, which she had brought, carefully wrapped, while Josie arranged flowers rescued from the merciless heat of the apartment grounds. She had already helped Peggy string swaths of brightly colored crepe paper throughout Pearl's apartment. Mil lost a few balloons while mastering the helium tank Peggy provided, but brought her usual enthusiasm to the task. They thought it looked gloriously festive, the farewell celebration of the year.

At two o'clock the other guests arrived, bringing their desserts and special messages of good-bye. Josie felt bad about not inviting Molly Flannery. She had been a champ in organizing the sign-up sheets for food and services. But they couldn't risk her need to tell everything she knew to anyone who would listen. Besides, she might insist on staying to help clean up and get in the way of the *real* party that followed.

Peggy had helped Pearl shower, shampoo her hair, and manicure her nails the day before. She had also helped her wrap a memento for each of her friends. The effort had left them exhausted. The plaster cast on Pearl's arm had been replaced by a softer, more supple one, but her arm was still of little use. Pearl's weakness and muscle spasms made things so difficult that Peggy had nearly given up, but Pearl fought her way through the pain to be ready for this big occasion. Now heavily medicated, she was the happiest she had been in weeks. It was a balm to her soul to find that dying could be beautiful, dignified, and celebrated.

Pearl gazed around her apartment, which was alive with color and chatter. She treasured these women friends, especially the dear ones who were putting themselves on the line for her. She basked in their love and the beauty of the day. Again she whispered to herself the powerful mantra of the Plains Indians: *This is a good day on which to die.*

The main topic of conversation was, of course, the identity of the body in Mabel's yard. It had been found to be that of one Maria Elena Rodriguez Salizar, a very old, very desperate woman from Mexico. This discovery was the crucial piece of a puzzle that had hounded police for over a year. Mil told how Officer McClung had led the search of Mabel's shed, where powdery traces of cocaine had been found up on the rafters, out of casual view. The bloodstains on one of the crusty blankets in the shed matched the blood of another old Mexican woman, found only months ago, buried in a shallow grave in the foothills near Riverside.

Maria Elena Rodriguez Salizar, bludgeoned to death and buried in Mabel's yard, turned out to be the eighth and last known victim of a very profitable drug ring operating out of a public storage space in Santa Ana. She was just one of a series of old Mexican women who had been living, briefly, in Mabel's shed. Undoubtedly there had been more, whose bodies hadn't yet been found.

"Those pitiful old women were just being used," declared Mabel, "and the drug runners were getting more brazen. Imagine! Burying the last one in my backyard, thinking I wouldn't notice." She rolled her eyes at the outrage of it all. "The poor souls were offered a place to live in the States, given fake green cards and Social Security numbers, and promised money in exchange for smuggling drugs into California. All they had to do was wear a nun's outfit, strap bags of cocaine to their bodies, and walk across the border in San Ysidro. No one messes with a nun, you know, especially an *old* nun. I'm sure those women thought it was too good to be true."

Everyone railed against the injustice, agreeing that in a country where there is little or no help for them, desperate old women would jump at the chance to ease their harsh struggle for survival. It was such a simple thing they had to do, with the reward of living forever in the land of milk and honey. Undoubtedly, there were more applicants for the job than there were drugs to run.

"But it was this last one, in Mabel's yard, that did in that nasty bunch," piped up Josie. "When the police found that bedraggled nun's habit in Mabel's shed, with traces of cocaine on it, they put two and two together and posted another drug-sniffing dog at the customs building at the border. The very next day, when both dogs seemed to bound out of nowhere, they nearly scared two pretend-nuns to death, growling and sniffing up their skirts. I guess the old women were glad to be rescued by Border Patrol agents."

Mary Lou, one of Pearl's friends from her teaching days, wrinkled her nose, adjusted her glasses, and asked, "But how did the police know who put them up to it?" She waited for the answer, front teeth protruding slightly as she peered quizzically down her wrinkled-up nose. She was unaware that this expression had prompted years of her fourth-grade students to secretly call her "Thumper."

"Well," said Mabel, "when their plan went haywire, those nuns led the police right to their would-be benefactors, who were waiting in a car on the American side of the border. I guess the women were supposed to play dumb, but they were too upset to carry it off. "Now, the law didn't really want to mess with those pathetic old women, so they were just defrocked, given a scolding and a Big Mac, and sent back to Mexico. It was their contacts the police were after. The trail led to that storage unit over on McFadden. But some of the women had to stay in my shed until their contacts could get the drugs to the storage unit. Then, I guess, the women were simply disposed of. Honestly, when I think of all that going on in my backyard, I just … well, it nearly makes me crazy!"

Pearl's other friend, Virginia, a plump, motherly-looking woman, listened in awe. Even though she'd seen it on TV and read about it in the morning paper, it was still a shocking story. Being in the presence of those involved made her feel further violated, allowing her to vent even more outrage.

She and Mary Lou would have been dumbstruck to learn that today's farewell party was not what they had been led to believe. They thought Pearl was leaving for Chicago to be taken care of by her sister, Peggy. They also thought the party would be over at four thirty. They didn't know that was when the main event would begin.

Mabel and Mil had organized a game of "This Is Your Life," with everyone bringing pictures and mementos of their shared past with Pearl. Josie and Peggy took care of the refreshments. Pearl was very weak, and for fear of overburdening her fragile condition, they kept interaction with her to a minimum. She was content to just watch and listen, enjoying all their prattle and laughter.

But she had her own thoughts. She wished Herb could have been here to appreciate this special day. They had vowed to help ease each other out of this world if it ever became necessary. They knew that other, more earthbound cultures didn't look at taking one's own life as a moral issue but rather as a matter of good sense when there was no more living to be done. They knew when it was time to let go, and celebrated their loved ones' crossing over into the next world.

Why is our culture so afraid of death, she wondered, if the afterlife were as wonderful as it was proclaimed to be? Why does the church skirt the issue of death with platitudes, while the medical world forces life upon people who would rather slip peacefully away? Where is the compassion when people preach that I should enjoy life in this broken body, when they can self-righteously walk away and enjoy life in their healthy ones? What do they know of the pain and the continuous onslaught of my affliction? Her visual and muscular impairment were becoming worse. She'd already lost the battle to a urinary catheter; loss of bowel control wouldn't be far behind.

Society's contradiction was beyond her understanding. Why should she be encouraged to become a burden to herself and society rather than be allowed to end a meaningless, difficult life? How could people be so certain that God, who honors the *giving* of one's life for another, doesn't also value the equally heroic act of *taking* one's life for another?

She had worked it out in her mind; she would die with God's blessing. She had assured Him it wasn't that she really wanted to *die;* it was just that she didn't want to *live* to become a burden to Herb's sons. They could have what was left of his estate and peace of mind, as well. The letters she had waiting for them, assuring them of her love, should put their hearts at rest.

Herb my dearest, because of my sister and these incredible friends, both my life and my death are being celebrated here today. This is a good day on which to die! She felt as though her heart would burst with the promise of release.

It was almost four thirty when the games were over and the desserts had been enjoyed. Everyone thought it had been a splendid day. Mary Lou and Virginia hugged and kissed Pearl good-bye, afraid they'd never see her again. They made promises to write and call, and begged her to cheer up. Things would surely be better at Peggy's.

As soon as they were safely gone, Pearl retreated to her bed, limp with fatigue. She didn't want to lose momentum. She was sure she could feel Herb hovering nearby, encouraging her to join him, and she was more than ready.

It was a sobering moment for her three friends and sister. But they had gone over it and over it, and were in accord as to how to proceed. Their only fear was of botching it and leaving Pearl even more disabled than she already was: a complete vegetable, kept alive by a respirator. That thought was too horrible to consider. They had to do it right.

Josie had earlier suggested singing "Nearer My God to Thee" and having a little prayer session, but the others voted it down as maudlin. They felt that if God were really as unreasonable as some said, no amount of singing or praying was going to make any difference. However, if He really knew their every thought and deed, and were the loving and forgiving God they hoped He was, He already knew this was an act of the utmost compassion and would be agreeable to receive Pearl on her own terms. This is what they had to pray for; that and the ability to tell the little white lie: that Peggy was totally innocent of any complicity. For Peggy's safety, they had also agreed they could never write, call, or see her again.

Pearl had requested that the stage be set by the playing of an audiotape she and Herb had brought home from Peru. It was hauntingly primitive music, a blend of guitars, wooden flutes of varying lengths, and simple percussion instruments. When she and Herb had first heard it on a street corner in Lima they had stood transfixed, prickled with goose bumps by the exquisite harmonics. It was as though they had transcended to another level. The searing memory of it stayed with them forever: Peruvian men in white cotton shirts and pants, their shimmering black hair in long, single braids down their backs; knowing black eyes shielded from the sun by equally black fedoras; bodies swaying sensuously with the music, weaving a spell upon Pearl and Herb as they stood glued to that enchanted spot. They never failed to thrill every time the tape was played, especially at the hypnotic rendition of Rodrigo's "Concierto de Aranjeuz."

This otherworldly music now permeated the room as the women gathered around Pearl's bed, where she lay waiting. Her eyes shone with love and trust as she gazed from one to the other. The rest of her wasted body simply lay there, as though knowing its work was done. They had brought all the balloons into her room and tied them to the bedposts and lamps. The floating splashes of color lent a false air of cheer to a room filled with apprehension.

Peggy and Mil propped Pearl up to enable her to swallow the sleeping pills that Josie and Mabel had poured into a waiting crystal bowl. Peggy had also placed a small drinking glass and a pitcher of water on the nightstand. As agreed, the empty pill bottles, with Josie's and Mabel's names on them, were to be left in plain view for the benefit of the police.

The women nervously joined hands with her, forming a tight circle at the side of her bed. They had already said most of what they had to say while playing "This Is Your Life," so their good-byes were simple and heartfelt. They spoke soothingly to her as they took turns reaching into the bowl, giving her a pill and a sip of water with which to swallow it.

"Nice and steady, dear," said Josie, who had drawn the long toothpick that let her go first. "Don't hurry. Just pop it in, drink it down, and let it sit a minute. There you go."

Mabel took her turn. "You're doing great, Pearl. I knew you would."

She passed the glass of water to Mil, who stood ready, pill in hand.

"Down the hatch. Here, just a minute, let's make it a double," she said, reaching into the bowl for another pill. "This one's on me!"

Pearl smiled as Mil placed the pills on her tongue. Dear, lighthearted Mil, she thought. She made both living and dying seem so natural, so easy. Herb always said she had a way about her, a kind of harmony with the universe.

"I love you, Mil," she said. "And you, Mabel, and Josie, and dear Peggy."

One after another they took turns until they could no longer rouse her. The music played on as the late-afternoon sun cast brilliant shadows through the tree ferns that screened the window, reflecting off the balloons to fill the room with color. Silently, the women stood over Pearl, holding her hands, feeling her life slip gently away. She seemed to glow, freed at last from the disfiguring spasms of her disease.

It had been difficult for her to swallow the last few pills as the lethal medication began to dull her senses. But they had planned it well, first making sure she had enough food in her stomach to avoid throwing them up, and timing it carefully so she was sure to take enough. The bowl of pills was nearly empty, and Pearl looked more at peace than they had ever seen her.

In a rush, the women gave in to their churning emotions, sobbing softly, caught between their relief for Pearl and the sorrow of losing their dear friend. They remained sitting on her bed, silently keeping vigil as the afternoon sun, too, slipped slowly away. The once-brilliant shadows grew deeper, finally leaving the room swathed in the lavender glow of evening.

And still the music played on. After it had swelled to the grandeur of "Concierto de Aranjeuz" one last time, Peggy quietly arose and signaled the others to follow. There was nothing more they could do.

No one wanted to turn off the stereo. They thought Pearl might still be able to hear it. Moving like sleepwalkers, they took down the festive streamers and balloons, picked up all the dishes, and cleared away any evidence of a party. Every now and then they checked on Pearl to make sure she was still comfortable. Only when her forehead began to feel cool to the touch were they sure it was truly over. Peggy turned off the stereo, retrieving the cassette and yanking every inch of tape out of it. That music, Pearl's music, would haunt her forever. She never wanted to hear it again.

They knew they should be horrified at what they had done, but strangely they were not. They had rehearsed it for weeks and were reconciled to the moral and ethical validity of their deed. It had been a perfect way, on a beautiful day, in which to die.

Subdued and emotionally spent, they sat talking quietly in the living room. At Pearl's request they had waited until now to open their gaily wrapped mementos. Mary Lou and Virginia had also promised not to open theirs until they were home. And when they opened them, they would understand why: Pearl's gifts would seem too generous to accept.

"Oh my goodness," exclaimed Josie, opening a little velvet jeweler's box. "Her gorgeous blue sapphire and diamond ring!" Touched beyond words by what it had meant to Pearl to give her such a gift, she clutched it to her heart and began to cry. "Oh, Pearl, you sweet thing. You knew how I love blue. Peggy, are you sure I should have it?"

Mabel had just opened her box. She gasped, breaking into tears. "Oh, Pearl—your beautiful ruby ring! With the moonstones! I don't know what to say. You kept hinting my gift had something to do with Mr. Moonbeam. But how can I possibly keep it?"

A shriek went up from Mil. "Her opal and diamond ring!" She just sat staring at it. "Her incredible opal and diamond ring," she repeated, her eyes welling with tears. "That's what she always said, that I had the flash of a fire opal. But, but ... oh, Peggy, I don't know if I should keep it."

Peggy had known what was in the little boxes. Pearl had selected and laboriously wrapped each one, finding joy in equating her cherished friends with her jewels. She knew they would treasure the significance. Of course they should keep them.

"And look what she gave me this morning, before the party started," Peggy said, rising to head for the adjoining dining room. She took two small boxes from the buffet, snapped them open, and gazed at their contents for a moment before returning to where the others sat in a hush of expectation.

The first box, which caused a chorus of gasps, contained her dazzling, diamond-encrusted gold wedding rings. The second box held the massive pearl and diamond ring that Herb had ordered crafted to Pearl's specification.

"She said she didn't want me to forget her, as if I could," Peggy murmured tearfully. "She insisted *I* was the *real* pearl, and she was just the one with the name. She didn't think the rings would have as much meaning to Herb's sons as they did to me, and she insisted I take them."

They sat there, each with her gift, until Mabel and Mil knew it was time to call Hali. Pearl lay peacefully, her dark hair just a lustrous shadow upon the pillow in the cool moonglow that flooded her bed. It was done. All that remained was for Peggy to call 911 after they had gone.

TWENTY-ONE

Elbows on her desk, Paige sorted through an ever-mounting pile of papers in an attempt to clear her mind as well as her work space. Her office, which normally hummed with activity, was blissfully quiet. She could actually hear herself think. The inspectors who shared her office, including Wisneski, claimed to be away on their own cases, but she knew they had probably just met for doughnuts at The Coffee Cup. None of them worked less than fifty or sixty hours a week. God knows you need a break now and then in this line of work, she thought, before you begin screaming at the walls in disgust at the human race.

The case of the Newport Beach bimbo had gone to the jury yesterday. Paige was glad to be through with that three-ring circus and the insults of the defense attorney, Lebanoff. She hoped the jury would see through his histrionics and bring in a conviction.

The next case to be tried, the homosexual serial killer, was going to be ugly. Psycho cases like this titillated the public to a lather. They hung on every word written about the testicle-eating murderer. The unsolved Bagmen murders had taken a backseat to coverage of the suspect, a brooding computer engineer who lived in a world of bits and bytes with his grisly inclinations.

She skimmed the pages of the file, shaking her head at the murky depths to which a human could go. The victims all seemed to be male prostitutes, unaware that this innocent-looking engineer's depravity was infinitely worse than their own. And, she thought, like so much of the pitiful humanity that coursed through her department, they found their addictions to be a one-way road to hell.

She read the latest lab report and gave a sigh of relief. The last victim, a young man who had been sodomized and murdered under a bridge in a nearby park—in broad daylight—held two different semen specimens. The killer had been spotted by a butterfly enthusiast, chasing what he thought was a Painted Lady. The butterfly enthusiast remembered the fleeing man's license number and was able to identify him in a police lineup.

This victim was her only link to the case. The prosecution wouldn't include him with all the others because the defense would, of course, challenge them to prove who had been with him last. She wouldn't have to testify.

Tucking the lab report back into the file, Paige glanced again at the thumb-worn Bagmen file on her desk. She had virtually memorized it and could almost recite it, page for page. It had been strangely quiet on that front. There hadn't been a Bagman found since early July, leaving them to wonder if the perps themselves had been killed, or, if it really were drug related, they had gone back to Colombia or wherever they had come from.

Damn the mystery of it all. Murders so clearly identified with their damn paper bags, right out in the open, and still no clues. It galled her to think this Bagman thing might never be solved.

She looked at her watch, regretting having promised to join those three old ladies for tea this afternoon. But they had asked so sweetly, and she hated to disappoint them. Maybe it could be postponed. She reached for the phone, and then changed her mind.

What the heck. They've probably gone to a lot of trouble, and I need a break. Those old ladies will be refreshing after all the sordid goings-on around here. Remembering the day the body had been found in their backyard, Paige smiled, recalling their scattered babble, their childlike innocence and giddy laughter. *This promises to be some tea party!*

When she had told Wisneski of the upcoming event, he grinned and assured her that the Mad Hatter's tea party wouldn't hold a candle to this one: riddles with no answers; conversations with no point; laughter at nothing funny.

"Call me if you need help climbing back up out of the rabbit hole," he'd said.

The heat had temporarily lost its grip under an overcast sky. It was a welcome break from the insufferable scorchers they'd had for the past month. Paige didn't know how people lived in the Southland without air-conditioning, but many of them did, including the hostesses of today's party. From her previous visit, she remembered the whirring fans aimed in all directions. Thank goodness for today's reprieve from the heat, she thought. It will make it easier for all of us.

She had barely knocked at the door when it was thrown open by her three enthusiastic hostesses. No doubt they had been watching for her from the window.

"Oh, Inspector Turner! Do come in," cried Mabel over the voices of the other two, who also warmly welcomed her. "Aren't we lucky the weather cooled down a bit," she exclaimed, "'cause I don't have air-conditioning like Josie has. Come in, come in! We've been waiting for you."

Paige felt swallowed up by their eagerness. *This must be what it's like to be old and out of touch. Just a little tea party has them all fired up.* They virtually towed her into the living room and urged her to sit in the same saggy goose-down chair in which she had sat before.

They couldn't do enough for her. Mabel brought a glass of cold lemonade, Josie made sure at least one of the fans was circulating the air in her direction, and Mil offered to hang her jacket in the closet. Then they all abruptly sat down on the sofa facing her, just looking at her and each other, not seeming to know what to do next.

Awkward. Really awkward. I wonder why I thought this would be easy. "Well, how is everyone?" she asked, hoping to get some conversation out of them. "You look lovely, all of you."

They were dressed in what was obviously their Sunday best, with their hair neatly groomed, noses powdered, and color on their cheeks and lips. They all spoke at once, varying themes of "Just fine, thank you. And you?"

The conversational ball was immediately back in Paige's court. *This is going to be painful. Could these be the same women who talked my ear off last time?*

They had begun a terse conversation about the weather when a police car went shrieking by. It gave Paige an opportunity to say that it was still business as usual in the crime world, although the gang wars seemed to be easing up. They listened attentively, nodding in agreement now and then.

Josie began to fidget and stood up, saying, "Tea is ready. Let's all go into the dining room."

Paige struggled out of the deep, almost formless chair and dutifully followed them. They seemed hell-bent on getting to the table, she thought. The tension in the air literally crackled among them, making her think of the dramatic bursts of electricity leaping between separated conductors at the Griffith Park planetarium.

The table was elegantly set with china, silver, and crystal on Mabel's best linen tablecloth. Fancy plates of finger sandwiches and pastries were artfully placed, decorated with the sweet faces of fresh pansies. Mabel hurried to light the four candles in the candelabra while Mil brought in silver pots of tea and coffee from the kitchen. Josie helped seat Paige at the head of the table. The whole event seemed rehearsed, with very little conversation, until everyone was seated and began passing around the plates of food.

Paige commented on the beautiful table setting, the delicious-looking food, and the colorful pansies. "I feel honored to be here," she said. "You've gone to so much trouble."

At this, Josie spoke up. "You don't know how important it is for us to have you here, Inspector Turner."

Mabel and Mil nodded their agreement enthusiastically.

"You see, when you were so dear to us, we knew we had a friend in the police department. And it's even better that you're a police*woman*."

"Believe me, you'll find we're going to need a friend," interrupted Mil, picking a cucumber and sour cream sandwich from the plate and passing it on. "Well, it's really nice to see you again, but beside that, we wanted you to know we've taken your advice about preparing to live in a safer place."

"There won't be any more tea parties there, you know, so we'd better enjoy this one," exclaimed Mabel, her brown eyes dancing.

"We'd like you to see that all our clothing and furnishings go to a women's shelter," said Josie. "We've discussed it thoroughly and decided they have the greatest need. I don't know if they want all this silver and crystal," she said, glancing around the table, "but maybe they can sell it and buy something more useful."

Oh no, here we go again! Where in the world could they be going where they wouldn't need their clothing and some of their furnishings? Wisneski was right. We're going down the rabbit hole again! Paige held a tea cake halfway to her mouth, staring around the table at them. She couldn't think of what to say.

"We have three beds among us," Josie was saying. "Well, mine is only a single, but anyway, I know that's one of the greatest needs in a shelter. Plus all the bedding and dishes and things. We didn't think the government would want them."

"And Mabel's house should bring a pretty good price," added Mil. "It's not in a very good area for a *home*, but the lot should be valuable to a commercial builder. That's Mabel's bonus to the government, you see, because we want to be sure we're not costing the government any extra."

If I can just be patient, they'll get to the point. Where in hell are they going? And why are they involving me? They can't seem to make anything

217

simple! She dabbed at her mouth with an embroidered napkin, careful not to stain it with her lipstick, and arranged it neatly back in her lap.

"I'm afraid you'll have to start at the beginning, ladies," she said. "You have me confused. Where could you be going that you won't need any of your things, all three of you, together? And what does the government have to do with it?"

"The beginning?" Josie asked vacantly, fidgeting again. "Well, I guess that was the day that bunch of juvenile delinquents attacked me in the park."

She went on to recap the story for Paige, with Mil filling in around the edges. "That was when we decided it just wasn't safe, living the way we were."

Mabel interrupted, "But Josie, don't you remember we saw Senator Farley on TV, making his pitch *against* Social Security and *for* prisons. And we'd already seen a special on TV about how comfortable prisons are ..."

Now it was Josie who interrupted. "And Mabel said we might as well be in prison if we had to stay locked up in our homes to be safe ..."

Then Mil got into it. "They told Bliss and me about their plan, but we didn't think they'd really do it, and I certainly never thought I'd join them ..."

Back and forth they went, becoming more animated, each taking a thread of the story and weaving it obliquely into a disjointed tapestry of events, correcting each other and leaving Paige holding her head. She felt as though she were watching a three-way tennis match, her eyes bouncing back and forth from one to the other. Her simple request to start at the beginning had resulted in a tidal wave of incoherent information.

"Wait a minute," she cried. "Now I'm *really* confused. Am I hearing about guns and bodies? And patriotism and prison? Ladies, give me a break here. Just speak one at a time. And may I have the sandwiches, please?" She knew the moment she spoke that tacking on a request for the sandwiches, in her urgency to get a word in edgewise, had made her sound as scatterbrained as they did.

"Relax, everyone," she said, helping herself to the tray Mil held for her. "Before our tea and coffee get cold, let's speak one at a time and don't anyone interrupt. I'd really like to hear what you have to say, but I'm afraid you're giving me a headache. Okay, now," she said, encouraged by their nods of agreement. "I got the part about the thugs in the park, and I'm really sorry that happened to you, Josie. But I think that bunch was virtually wiped out in an explosion on the Fourth of July. It should be safe to walk there now."

She turned to the others and continued. "And I understand your fear of living alone in this city and your concern over cuts in your Social Security. But you lost me in talk about prisons and things. Let's warm up our tea and start from there."

Everyone dutifully refilled her cup. No one said a word. They waited for Paige to say, "Okay, now, who wants to go first?"

Mabel volunteered and began to denounce the laws that made it easier for criminals than for law-abiding citizens. When she paused for a few seconds, Mil took over with the need, at their ages, to protect themselves by learning to use a gun. It was hard for the other two not to join in her comical description of their gun practice in Mabel's basement. Soon all three of them were laughing and embellishing the story.

They composed themselves under Paige's stern stare, and Josie went on to speak of their dwindling resources and their need for the vital services supplied freely in prison. "But we don't want to be a burden to the government," she hastily added. "We reasoned that for what it costs the government to imprison twenty or so criminals, it could be taking care of *us*, instead. So all we had to do was clear the streets of the appropriate number of criminals, and we'd not only be performing a public service but also earning our keep."

Paige felt a chill start at her shoulders and work its way down her back. Something was coming together in her head despite her reluctance to confront it—something she didn't want to hear.

Mabel picked up the story and told of their arbitrarily assigning each criminal a value of $100,000. "Of course, when it was all over, we had greatly exceeded our target. Now, with my house thrown in as a bonus, we don't have to feel bad about asking the government to take care of us."

Josie resumed in earnest. "And we never shot anybody unless he attacked us first, Inspector Turner. You can be sure of that. Well, except for those drug dealers at the crack house. But that was really a mistake. Anyway, we were as humane as we could be. We mostly fired at close range, so one shot would do it, and we covered them up with grocery bags. It made such a horrid mess …" Overcome with the ghastly images, her voice trailed off, and then she began again.

"Shooting those unsuspecting men at that crack house still bothers me, though. I don't know what we were thinking. They didn't threaten us or even see us. That wasn't very nice of us. We can only hope Mrs. Jackson was right, that all the people in that house were bad. Goodness, we didn't expect such a terrible explosion and fire! It would have blown the glass right out of Mrs. Jackson's windows again, but luckily, she still had plywood!

"We were sitting on her front porch, just visiting, you see, and we shot at the ones who she said were drug dealers. But she took the lemonade in the house and didn't know we did it. They were carrying big boxes into the house, those Simbas, you know? But it was the first time we tried to shoot anybody from a distance, and I guess our aim wasn't very good. We felt really bad about causing a power failure … I guess a transformer got in the way."

Mil couldn't wait to speak. "And when we blew up that gang in the park we didn't use paper bags, either, because the people were, well, sort of all in pieces. And we had to get out of there fast, before *we* were blown up, too. We didn't plan to do that, either."

Paige's chill had given way to a hot rush of blood to her head, which now just as rapidly drained away, leaving her clammy and light-headed. The Bagmen. These women were talking about having killed the Bagmen. And the First Street Gang. And blowing up the Simbas's crack house. They knew too many details to be making it up. Not only were these old ladies the Bagmen killers, but they were confessing to other, unrelated havoc.

Seeing Paige slump in her chair, the other three jumped up from the table and hovered over her in confusion. Mabel ran to the kitchen to get a cold cloth for her forehead, Josie readjusted one of the fans, and Mil helped Paige pull her chair out from the table and lower her head to her lap.

"I'm okay, I'm okay," Paige said feebly. "I ... I wasn't prepared for this. Just give me a minute ..." She lifted her head a few inches and tried to focus on them from that odd angle. "Are you ... turning yourselves in to me?" she asked, still woozy.

They nodded silently, their eyes riveted on her helpless figure.

"In that case," Paige said, "I'm going to need to make a phone call. Wisneski should be here."

"Oh, honey, let me call him for you," offered Mabel. "You just sit there and put yourself back together. What shall I tell him?"

She started for the kitchen, where the phone hung on the wall.

"Call this number," Paige said in a thin voice, reeling off a string of numbers. "Tell him who you are and that I'm with you ... and that I need him to pull me out of a rabbit hole. A *big* rabbit hole. He'll know what you mean."

The other two stayed with Paige, fanning and patting her with the wet cloth, while Mabel made the call.

Wisneski wasn't at the station, so Paige gave Mabel instructions for calling his pager and leaving her number. He returned the call within a few minutes. By this time, Paige had recovered enough to answer the phone herself.

"Wisneski," she said, "remember your offer to pull me out of the rabbit hole? Well, I'm in a big one. A really big one. Get your butt over here, and bring a recorder. You know where I am."

She hung up, and the three women joined her at the table, uncertain what to do next.

"Don't tell me anything more, ladies. Wait till Wisneski gets here. He's got to be in on this. I'll let him read your rights. In the meantime, let's not waste all this good food. You're right, ladies. This could very well be your last tea party." Her eyes gleamed with vindication.

By the time Wisneski arrived the three women were talking recipes and how differently they had cooked as young brides. Very few things came prepared in those days, and almost everything was made from scratch. Paige sat quietly, mostly just listening.

They had set aside a plate of goodies for him, and cleared the table to make it look lovely again. All four of them greeted him at the door and led him directly to the dining room. He kept looking at Paige with questioning eyes, but she avoided his gaze while helping the women seat and serve him.

He virtually inhaled the finger sandwiches and tea cakes while they continued to chatter of things that didn't interest him. Finished, he looked around the table, wondering what was coming next, intrigued by the expression on Paige's face. After all these years, he knew that smug look well.

"Okay, Wisneski," she began. "Please read these ladies their Miranda rights. They'd like to confess to the Bagmen murders."

She'd never seen him at a loss for words. But now his eyes blinked in disbelief as he strained to process what she'd just said.

"Bagmen?" he repeated. "They killed the Bagmen?" He stared at Paige and then softened, saying, "Turner, you're too much. I bet they blew up the park on the Fourth of July, too. Why didn't you just *say* you wanted me to join your tea party? You didn't have to play 'gotcha.' But I have to say, that's a good one, Turner."

No one spoke. They just stared at him. He pushed back his chair and stood looking down at them with an expression that would have had them laughing if it had been a trick. Four pairs of eyes stared back.

Finally Josie said, "Paige has instructed us not to say anything more about it until you've read us our rights. And we'd really like to talk about why we brought you here, so please get on with it."

He looked as though he'd suffered a blow to the stomach, slumping perceptibly and unable to speak. Paige turned on the recorder and smiled sweetly as he stammered for a moment before beginning to recite from memory the Miranda law.

When the women were sure he was through they all began to talk at once. Paige raised her arms over her head to get their attention and reminded them they were being taped, so they couldn't talk over each other. They would have to speak only when responding to a direct question.

The room grew quiet as Paige led the interview, documenting their names and the date. Each one solemnly stated that she didn't want an attorney and that she was giving this information freely and willingly. They also declared their intentions to decline a trial, and hoped their complete cooperation would grant them the right to stay together, wherever they were sent.

Wisneski hardly knew what to do with himself. He couldn't sit still, so he started pacing, flabbergasted by the statements the women were making. Paige finally asked him to sit down: he was making her nervous.

When he did, he couldn't contain his questions. "What in the name of sweet Jesus gave you the idea you were responsible for the Bagmen murders?" he shouted at them. "And if you are the Bagmen killers, why the hell didn't you tell us that when we were here at your house last time? Why now, for God's sake, with the pretense of this ... this tea party? I bet you don't know anything about the Bagmen!"

He'd wanted to say "silly tea party," but the shock on their faces made him hold his tongue. It was easy, scaring the three women with his yelling. And that was the idea. Maybe they'd admit it was a joke.

"And where are your weapons?" he continued, impaling them like squabs on a spit in his fierce glare. "If you really are the Bagmen murderers you must have a gun or two. And fingerprints. You should be on file with the Department of Motor Vehicles, and the fingerprints on those bags were not on record. And the numbers written on that first grocery bag? How about that? *Big* numbers. Who wants to try to explain these things?"

Paige had to stop them from all talking at once when they got over the shock of Wisneski's assault. She allowed a wrought-up Josie to answer first.

"To start with, you don't have to be so mean," she cried. "We didn't confess last time because we hadn't helped Pearl die yet. If it hadn't been for her counting on us so much, we'd have been glad to, believe me. We were tired of the whole thing." Mad as the proverbial wet hen, she sat in a huff in her chair, glaring at this man who might not be their friend after all.

"But poor Pearl trusted us to help end her life," she continued, "and we were committed to seeing the job through. We made it as nice as we could for her, but we're still upset over it. And you're making it worse by yelling at us. As for our guns, we've gathered up a whole suitcase-full for you."

Paige and Wisneski stared at each other. Helping someone end her life? They euthanized someone? They hadn't mentioned that before. And a suitcase full of guns? God only knew what else they would confess to.

Mil went on to tell them of the guns they had collected from their victims along the way. "We certainly couldn't use all of them, so we saved a whole bunch for you. It's just that many more guns off the street," she said proudly.

Mabel asked what fingerprints had to do with the Bagmen. She didn't recall touching any of their victims.

Wisneski reminded her that unidentified fingerprints had been found on the grocery bags covering the Bagmen. If they had belonged to any of the three women, they would have been traced through the Department of Motor Vehicles. He knew that at least she and Mil were still driving.

"Oh, *that*," said Mabel. "I haven't renewed my license in over twenty years. And I don't think Mil or Josie has, either." She seemed elated to find it was no larger a mystery than that. "No one ever took my fingerprints. But it hasn't seemed to make any difference. The DMV sends me registration papers for the car every year, so I just fill them out and send them back with a check and nobody ever says anything about a license to drive. Goodness, I'm sure I couldn't have passed the test, anyway, so what was the point of taking it?"

The three women beamed at him, nodding their heads in agreement. Wisneski knew he should have expected just such answers to his questions.

Josie suddenly remembered the first grocery bag, the one she'd used to cover the young man in Santa Ana. "The numbers scribbled on that first grocery bag? We were just trying to figure out how much it would cost the government to keep us in prison, and how many criminals we'd have to get rid of to pay for it. Remember, Mabel, we did that in the car?"

She had begun to simmer down from her huff, and hurried to offer further proof of their guilt. She also volunteered to show them the marks on her wall, where they had tallied up their hits as they got them.

"We started out with just an *M* for Mabel and a *J* for me," she explained, "but when Mil joined us, we added *MS* for Mildred Steinberger. And Mil got the most, from blowing up that whole gang in the park."

Her face lit up with another recollection. "Mil got two more a couple of days ago, out in the canyon. We have their stolen stuff for you. But I'll let her tell you about it. I can give you the money I took from that man in the alley in Los Angeles. It's in my dresser drawer."

"What!" shouted Wisneski, turning to Mil. "Wait a minute. I want to hear about the two men in the canyon. The ones we found night before last? And what stolen stuff?"

Mil told about meeting the two men who had killed Bliss on their way home from visiting the Scheidlers, but with Josie and Mabel trying to help with the details, he soon became confused. He held up his hand to shush them. He'd heard enough. He couldn't deny they knew what they were talking about.

The interview went on for another hour, the women helping each other with dates, places, and circumstances. They called it quits around seven, when Paige ran out of tape for the recorder. But they had already said everything there was to say.

Paige looked at Wisneski. "Well, what do you want to do with them?" she asked. "We can't just leave them here, can we?"

"Not if we don't want our butts kicked all over city hall," he replied. "For my money, I'd leave 'em alone and let 'em finish the job on this town, but I don't think that would sit too well with the DA."

Mabel looked as though she might cry. "But we *want* to go with you," she cried. "I've had enough of people in my shed and hoodlums on every corner."

Mil rose from the table and headed for the living room. "We've already packed our overnight bags," she called over her shoulder. "We really expected to go with you to jail. After telling you all the things we've done and the people we've killed, you can't just leave us here."

She returned with the three tidy bags Paige had noticed earlier, sitting in a row beside the sofa under Mr. Moonbeam's watchful eye. "We didn't know what to bring," she said, "'cause we think you'll be supplying most everything. But we have our cosmetics and toothbrushes and a fresh change of undies. Shall we get our nighties and a change of clothing, too, or will we need them?" She plunked the bags on the table and stood, awaiting a reply.

"The big suitcase in the living room is the one with all the guns," she continued. "It's too heavy for me to lift, so Inspector Wisneski, you can take it to your car when we go."

Wisneski almost choked. They were packed and ready, guns and all. They were so damned logical about this and so scatterbrained about everything else. He had finally accepted their guilt, but how could they be so damn matter-of-fact about it? They really must be crazy if they looked forward to going to prison.

"You won't need your overnight bags, ladies," he said wearily. "We'll be providing everything."

They exchanged smiling I-told-you-so looks and waited for him to tell them what to do next.

He frowned, thoroughly perplexed. Under his breath, he asked Paige, "Do we need cuffs? It doesn't seem decent to put old ladies in handcuffs." But he worried about explaining the lack of them to the booking officer. It was going to be hard enough to explain bringing these sweet old ladies in and announcing they were the Bagmen killers, as well as the perpetrators of other major mayhem.

Paige shook her head. The women would be no trouble.

"We don't need handcuffs," said Mabel. "We just need a ride to the police station. We were going to turn ourselves in there but decided instead to treat you to a little party, to show you how much we appreciate your kindness, and tell you about it right here."

"We knew you'd treat us fairly," said Josie, "and we wanted to be sure you got credit for solving the case. Just imagine," she added, smiling impishly at Mabel and Mil, "from now on we'll have three square meals a day and somebody else will do the cooking … and the cleanup! And we won't ever have to go out where it's unsafe again, or worry about making ends meet."

"I imagine we've missed dinner at the jail," said Mabel. "Let's finish up all the sandwiches and things. I'll see what else I have that would just spoil after we leave. It's a long time till breakfast."

With Josie's and Mil's help, the table was reset with the remains of their tea party, as well as little bowls of leftover spaghetti, applesauce, green beans, bread and butter, and the sizable remains of a crunchy Jell-O salad. Wisneski couldn't believe he was going along with this, but Paige seemed to be getting a kick out of it.

The five of them sat around the dining table, recapping the women's exploits, and making short work of their dinner. Wisneski wanted to hear more anecdotes of their missions, such as their sneaking away from under McClung's nose to do in a few of the Bagmen, and the times when passersby had come upon them before they'd made their escape and tried to protect the women from the gory scene. Even he had to laugh. But he felt as though he, too, must have plunged down the rabbit hole. Sitting here chatting and dining with these women, the admitted Bagmen killers—he must be as crazy as they were. All he could think about was what they were going to say back at the station.

It was almost ten by the time the women had fussed around cleaning up the kitchen to their satisfaction. "Can't have the government thinking I'm a bad housekeeper when they come to take over," Mabel said. As they worked, they showed Paige around the house, offering information about the dishes and furniture and things she was to dispose of for them.

"Oh, we almost forgot," said Mil, going to the coffee table in the living room to get a small package wrapped for mailing. "Would you please take this to the post office for us? It's the three beautiful rings Pearl gave us at her going-away party. We want her sister, Peggy, to have them." She paused, gently kissing the package and whispering, "Goodbye, Pearl. We miss you," before passing it to Mabel and Josie for their tributes. Then she handed it to Paige.

Paige drove the three women across town to the Santa Ana police station with Wisneski following them, a suitcase full of guns in his trunk. In the backseat, the women carried on more like vacationers headed for a weekend at Disneyland than felons about to embark on a life in prison.

Paige smiled to herself, imagining the disbelief and commotion awaiting them at the station. If she lived to be a hundred, she would never have another case to top this. It was just as she had said: You never know.

TWENTY-TWO

Andy and Beverly Krach were rehashing the same old argument. She wanted to quit her job as a systems analyst for Loral in Newport Beach and move back to Ohio. She wanted to start a family *now*. He wanted her to keep bringing home those big paychecks until he could figure out what he wanted to do, professionally.

He loved to write. He knew he was good. Unfortunately, the stress of this new job in California kept his insides in an almost constant uproar. Beverly thought the answer was to move back to Ohio. Besides, she was tired of being called Mrs. Crotch, or Mrs. Crack, or Mrs. Cratch. Everyone in their hometown in Ohio knew their name was pronounced "crock," as in "rock." She hoped her work associates wouldn't discover her maiden name had been Black, because here in California, women often seemed strangely compelled to hyphenate their maiden and married names. She cringed at the fun they would have calling her Beverly Black-Crotch or Beverly Black-Crack.

But for Andy, Southern California was everything he had hoped for. He couldn't imagine returning to small-town life and not having access to the spicy foods for which he'd developed a profound love-hate relationship. He didn't think a spastic colon could kill him, although it had certainly put him in some desperate, to say nothing of humiliating, situations. It was during those spells he began to dream about freelancing. He thought being on his own should relieve the stress while he wrote feature articles, travelogues, or, God help him, every writer's dream: the Great American Novel.

As usual, their discussion hadn't resolved anything. They were just getting ready for bed when the call came from Wisneski. Andy was always glad to hear from him. They had forged a tenuous friendship, based on their willingness to share confidential information, and Andy hoped to get a great story out of it one day.

He picked up the portable phone in the bathroom, dressed only in his socks and shorts, and strolled into the bedroom. Beverly sat propped up in bed, reading "Your Baby's First Year," in the *Reader's Digest*. She ignored the call; at this hour, calls were always for him.

"Krach here," he said, glancing at his watch. "Hey, Wisneski. What're you doin' up at this hour?"

He pushed copies of *Ladies' Home Journal* and *Parenting* to the floor and settled on the end of the bed, avoiding the tangle of Beverly's legs. As he listened, his eyes grew wider until they were bulging in disbelief.

"Wisneski, are you bullshittin' me?" he yelled. "What're you on, anyway?"

Beverly lowered her magazine and watched with curiosity as he got up, wild-eyed, to pace the floor. After a few moments, he said, "I'll be there as quick as I can. If you're pullin' my leg, Wisneski ... ," and he threw the phone on the bed.

"Don't ask me to explain now," he called from the closet as he hopped around pulling on his pants. Hastily throwing a T-shirt over his head, he croaked, "Either I've got the scoop of the century or Wisneski's gone nuts."

He brushed at his hair with his hands, grabbed his billfold and keys, and was gone.

Beverly dropped her magazine.

"Andy," she called after his disappearing figure. "Your Imodium!"

Paige wished she'd had a video camera to record the shock and disbelief at the booking desk. At first the booking officer thought it was just another one of Wisneski's pranks, like the time he'd cozied up to a flashily dressed transvestite and introduced him, to the transvestite's delight, as his cousin Sally, visiting from Cleveland. Or the pair of hookers he had claimed with a straight face were the captain's sisters.

Paige had to convince the booking officer that this was no joke. These women were indeed the Bagmen killers, among other things, in spite of the fact they were not in handcuffs.

The three old women looked woefully out of place, befuddled and blinking into the harsh lights of the police station. Officers began arriving from all over the building to have a look at them. Other bookings had to wait in the confusion. Everyone wanted a peek at the notorious Bagmen killers. No one could believe it.

"Man, you guys are really hurtin' to hafta start settin' up ol' women," said a sour-faced, stringy-haired young man brought in for an attempted home burglary. "Stupid pigs," he muttered.

"Bagman killers, my ashh," shouted a disheveled old drunk, eyeing the well-groomed, grandmotherly women huddled between Turner and Wisneski. He shot bleary, disbelieving glances from one officer to the other. "Sheesh, even I c'n see you're barkin' up the wrong tree, an' ya can't get much drunker'n me."

Attempting to focus his alcohol-fogged eyes, he peered at the women, first with one eye and then the other. "Humph," he snorted. "I'm s'prised you didn' try layin' that bag thing on me, too. Always draggin' me in here for somethin' er other. Well, I hope ya fired that last cook. An' I'd like a private room ... with a view a' them ol' women."

He cackled at his own joke and trailed off with a string of his usual halfhearted protests at being locked up again. Craning his neck to get a better look, he burped and nearly toppled over. His arresting officer leaned him up against the wall, telling him to cut the comedy and wait his turn. They all knew his routine of staging a little "drunk and disorderly" when he needed a safe bed and a hot breakfast. He was one of their more harmless habituals, and they didn't mind his company when space allowed.

Everyone seemed to have something to say. The hallway had become a traffic jam of rubberneckers. Turner and Wisneski completed the booking process as quickly as they could, before it could get any crazier. The sooner they could get the women safely into their cells, the better.

The women's first night in jail was short and full of surprises. They were photographed, fingerprinted, questioned, strip-searched, and finally issued ID bracelets, bedding, and jailhouse garb.

Paige pulled every string to make their strip searches as dignified as possible. It seemed the least she could do for them. She'd never faced such a perplexing situation as this: she genuinely cared about her suspects. Then she appropriated an overflow cot to make it possible for all three of them to be in the same two-woman cell. Helping them make up their beds, she explained the system.

"Your other door opens up into the dayroom. It's for your use from seven in the morning until eleven at night. You can play cards and watch TV and visit with the other inmates in there. Your meals will be brought in there, too. It's locked now, so I can't show it to you, but you'll learn all about it in the morning."

Like the first day they met, she hated to leave them. They seemed so in need of assistance and so appreciative of her help.

"Look at this—it's air-conditioned! With sliding glass doors instead of bars," said Mabel, touching the glass in amazement. "And it's so clean!"

"I don't know about these shoes," said Mil, frowning at the rubber shower-type footwear. "I can't imagine not wearing nylons, but if nobody else can wear them either, I guess we'll be right in style."

"I know I promised I wouldn't complain," said Josie, looking dejected in her baggy two-piece, short-sleeved uniform, "but what on earth do you call this color? Pea green? Olive drab? Well, Theodore would have had a good name for it, like his sky-blue-pinks and you-know-what brindles." Naughty words such as "shit-brindle" were impossible for her to utter, although it had secretly tickled her when Theodore used them.

The other two could only laugh at her dismay. They frequently wore slacks, and the sight of them in their uniforms wasn't as strange as the sight of little Josie, swallowed up in the pajama-like garb, wearing pants for the first time in her life.

"If only they could have been blue," she lamented. "But," she was quick to add, "we'll just have to get used to it. At least we don't have to wash and iron them."

The women's module of the Santa Ana jail was built to house ninety-six inmates. It held sixty-three sleeping women tonight. The disrupted occupants of the cells near theirs had begun loudly protesting, yelling for them to be quiet.

"Turn off the damn lights," came one voice, and "Have your meeting in the morning," came another. Even through the glass doors, cries of "Maybe you don't need your sleep, but we do" and "Shut up over there" began to resound through the corridor.

Paige put her finger to her lips and softly said, "Try to get some sleep. I'll be back in the morning. I don't think you'll need anything till then. You should be warm enough, and you'll have a good breakfast."

She found herself wanting to hug them good-bye, but instead just gave their hands a warm squeeze and hurriedly left. This had been quite a day for all of them.

KILLER GRANNIES STALK CITY blared the morning headline in banner letters. Subheadings read ADMIT TO BAGMEN IN LA AND ORANGE COUNTIES, OTHER ATROCITIES and WOMEN CONFESS FREELY, DECLINE JURY TRIAL.

The article was short, but it was all Andy had time for: they had held the press for him, at that. His information came straight from Wisneski, because by the time Andy arrived at the station, the women were already locked up. Their mug shots and more information were promised later.

By the time the afternoon edition of the *Orange County Register* hit the streets, news of the Bag Ladies, as Andy chose to call them, had aired on every radio and TV station in the nation. The concept of old women clearing the streets of criminals was utterly bizarre, as was their desire to live forever in the safety of prison. The euthanasia part and the disposition of their possessions were of small interest in the first rush of information.

Mug shots and news clips of Mabel and Mil from the day the body had been found in their yard, along with allusions to the information on Paige's tape, were all the media had to work with. Interviews with friends, neighbors, and one of Mil's sons followed. In the dayroom, the women watched Molly Flannery on TV, where she wiped tears from her eyes and appeared baffled for the first time in her life.

"Such a sweet lady," she said, referring to Josie. "I don't know what to tell you. It simply isn't in her to go around killing people. Especially Pearl—she helped that woman every way she could. Now, if you want my opinion ..."

The film editors cut short her opinion to move on to an interview with Betty Jean, who was convinced it was the usual police bungling, nothing new. "Those women are the dearest people you'd ever meet," she said. "This is a lot of phony baloney. The cops have *really* screwed up this time."

The manager at Mabel's bank looked as bewildered as the others. "She's banked here for years, and, why, she's simply not capable of ... of such a thing. This is all so confusing ... "

It was harder for Mil's son, Keith. He had talked on the phone at some length with his mother and still couldn't make sense of it. He cut the interview short. "This is so out of character for her. For all of them. I won't have anything to say until I see them, and I'm on my way now."

His brother, Jimmy, declined to be interviewed at all.

"Such a handsome man," said Mil, smiling proudly at Keith's image on the TV. "He and his brother just have to understand that I can't complicate their lives by expecting their wives to take care of me one day. They're all so busy, everybody working, running in all directions. They'll soon realize I'm better off right where I am, with my very best friends, and they can visit me whenever they want."

The women enjoyed their stay in the pre-arraignment facility, playing cards and watching TV, but keeping mostly to themselves. The other inmates seemed too busy complaining to take any interest in them. Although Josie, Mabel, and Mil thought the setup was wonderful, the other women proclaimed the place to be a hellhole. It made the old women rethink their notion that the company of younger women in this setting would be an advantage. Nevertheless, they basked in the easy pace and complete care given them, cheered by Paige's visits.

"You're going to be tried by Judge S. Carter Thompson," Paige told them. "He's assigned an attorney to each of you. They'll be in to talk to you this afternoon, so they can represent you properly."

"Attorneys?" they all said at once. "We told them we don't want a trial!"

"That's just an unnecessary expense," cried Josie. "We *chose* to be here. We don't want anyone trying to get us out."

"I don't know what we could tell an attorney that we haven't already told you," said Mabel. "Tell them for us that they really don't need to bother."

Mil was about to add her protest when Paige assured them it was a formality over which they had no control.

"Save your protests for your attorneys," she said. "They'll tell the judge you're not cooperating and ask to be excused. It will be up to you and the judge from there on out. You'll be taken to the county jail after arraignment, awaiting bench trial. It's much the same over there, only much larger and not quite as nice as it is here. You'll stay there until the judge decides what to do with you."

Turning to Josie, she added, "I think you'll like the uniforms much better, though. They're bright orange."

The day of their arraignment produced pandemonium. Andy had agreed to represent the ladies for an exclusive with the TV tabloid, *Current Edition*, with payment to benefit women's shelters in Orange County. But those journalists and photographers were not alone. The hallways of the courthouse bustled with cameras and reporters from all over.

In the updated courthouse a suspect was usually given a video arraignment, with the inmate in one room and the judge in another, able to see and hear each other clearly. But Judge Thompson wanted a good look at these women who freely proclaimed their guilt, refused a trial, and demanded to be kept in prison. Intrigued with the thought his name could become a household word, he quickly bowed to media pressure to let a TV camera into the courtroom, for people clamored to hear every word of the proceedings.

Wisneski had persuaded the judge not to insist on having the women brought before him in chains. "Cross my heart and hope to die, Your Honor," he had said, crossing himself as he spoke, "you'll have no trouble with them. They're dying to get into jail, and they'll comply with your every wish. Trust me, Your Honor, I know these women."

Judge Thompson had finally agreed, but only after telling Wisneski, "I'll have the bailiff instructed to shoot *you* before restraining *them* if any one of them even *looks* like she's going to be a problem."

Paige and Wisneski sat in the front row at the hearing, right behind the three women. Paige hoped her presence would be a comfort to them. Behind them sat McClung and Davini, the officers who had aided Mabel and Mil after reports of prowlers on their property. Andy Krach, with notebook at the ready, sat nearby.

When the room was filled to capacity, a scowling Judge Thompson called the court to order, admonishing everyone that he didn't intend for this to be a three-ring circus and that he would eject anyone who even made a peep. It was well known he would do just that. What he lacked in size, he made up for in show. From his elevated position at the bench, his rather large head and shock of prematurely graying hair made him look much taller and more dignified than his actual, scrappy five feet seven inches.

The routine preliminaries took a little time, then each woman replied, "Guilty, Your Honor," when asked how she wanted to plea to each of the many counts lodged against her. Each one also reaffirmed her choice to decline the right to a jury, throwing herself upon the mercy of the court. The courtroom quivered with a strained hush. It stretched the mind of every person present to see these three frightened, grandmotherly ladies, dressed in their bright orange uniforms, bravely confessing to a stunning string of murders and felonies.

The attorneys assigned to the women gathered their papers and reported that their clients had no intention of cooperating, entitling Judge Thompson to dismiss them. With cameras rolling, the judge puffed himself up to look even more menacing than before and scalded the three frightened women who stood before him with his piercing glare. He hoped the camera had him at his best angle while he scored a few tough-on-crime points with his conservative constituents.

"So you think you can represent yourselves," he boomed, mocking their naiveté. All three women jumped and seemed to shrivel in the wake of his explosive voice. He obviously enjoyed having startled them.

"Well, that's your choice. Since we've saved the time it would take to select a jury, we're going to hear this case two weeks from today." Glaring down at them over the top of his glasses, he added, "And it had better be good. Murder, mayhem, so-called mercy killing … It had better be *better* than good." He sealed his words with the resounding slam of his gavel.

The day of their trial produced even more commotion than the day of their arraignment. Many people were turned away and had to console themselves with seeing the trial on TV. Journalists vied for seats and jockeyed for wall space at the back of the room.

Judge Thompson started the trial right on time, a habit for which he was famous. He made short work of the preliminaries, reminding everyone in the courtroom that he expected total silence from them or they would be summarily ejected—no cameras, cell phones, or tape recorders. The look on his face showed that he meant it. Leering down at the three cowering defendants, he began.

"So, can you tell me, one at a time, what was on your mind when you decided to be a three-woman vigilante movement? Are you that dissatisfied with the way we run things? And do you really think life in prison is better than in your own homes? You three have some explaining to do, and, as I told you before, it had better be good."

He continued to glower at them while his fingers searched for the paper listing their names. Once he found it, he adjusted his glasses and boomed out the first name.

"Mabel Esther Rockwell? What have you to say for yourself?"

Mabel stood up and looked around nervously. Being called on first had been her worst fear since grade school. She felt too rattled to speak.

"Well, Your Honor," she started in a thin voice, "I'm sure you've listened to our taped confession, and I don't know what else to add to that. Except that I'd like to give my house ..."

"Speak up," roared the judge. "How can you defend yourself if we can't hear you?"

Mabel gulped and cleared her throat, faint with fear and wishing she were anywhere but here. "I'm sorry, Your Honor. I'll try to do better." But her mouth seemed full of quicksand. With a great effort, she continued.

"I was saying I'd like to give my house to the government, to help defray whatever it costs to keep us in prison. And I'd like to ask you to please keep us together, wherever we go, so we can take care of each other."

She stopped, completely unnerved by the judge's glare and the stressful setting.

"You can keep our Social Security money to help pay for our room and board," she stammered. "Uh, and I want to thank you, Your Honor, for a nice stay in your jail." Her legs were about to buckle from fright. She unceremoniously sat down for fear she would collapse.

"Thank you for a nice stay in my jail?" the judge thundered back at her. "Thank you for a nice stay in my jail!" He rolled his eyes, slapping his forehead in disbelief. "And you think if you give us your house it will make it all better?" He shook his head, staring at her in outrage.

Looking fiercely again at his notes, he called out, "Mildred Edith Steinberger, what have you to say for yourself?"

Mil desperately wished for a cigarette. She stood up, smoothed out her uniform, and timidly echoed what Mabel had said. She did her best to speak up. She didn't want the judge yelling at her, too. "But I want to add that I couldn't wait for our war on crime to be over. It took a lot out of us, you know. We took courage from the words of John F. Kennedy, sir, to ask not what our country can do for us, but instead, what we can do for our country. And we think we've made the streets a little safer for other people now."

Light-headed in her fear, she stopped, not sure how much the judge wanted her to say. The judge seemed to wait for her to continue, so she went on.

"All three of our husbands were killed by burglars, you see. We've lived in fear ever since. It's pretty scary out there, you know, for older folks who live alone. I mean, to be safe, we have to live behind locked doors with bars on the windows. So we decided, since we have to live behind locks and bars anyway, we may as well do it where there's food and laundry service, too. It's been such a relief to feel safe in your jail!" Quivering in terror, she managed to say, "We sincerely thank you, Your Honor," before abruptly sitting down.

The judge could not hide his bafflement, even though the look on his face could have pierced steel. He loudly cleared his throat as he readjusted his glasses and scanned his notes.

"Josephine Ellen Winkworth!" he barked. "I hope you have a better story than these other two!"

Josie stood up, meek before him. *He wants a better story? The whole story, maybe, right from the beginning?*

"Thank you, Your Honor," she said, speaking in her best teacher voice. "It's kind of a long story, but I'll try to make it as short as I can. You see, on the same day those young men attacked me in the park, Mabel and I heard Senator Barley ... er, I mean Farley ... talking about doing away with or cutting our Social Security. He said he needs that money to build more prisons." She took a deep breath, uncomfortable with all those eyes on her in the crowded courtroom. After a moment she resumed.

"We'd also seen a special on TV about prisons, telling how the ACLU makes sure everything is first-class there. It's safe and better monitored than nursing homes, too. And you get your meals and medical care and everything you need."

She waited for him to agree with her. He only continued to glower. Disappointed, her arms held out in supplication, she went on. "Can't you see the irony of this, Your Honor? Here we were, being good citizens and doing our best to hang on with just our Social Security— which we'd paid for, mind you, for over forty years—while criminals like the ones who killed our husbands were getting a free ride, almost a reward, for making trouble for everyone else. And Senator Farley wants to take money away from us to build even more housing for them instead of stopping them. Well, inflation has reduced to pocket change the savings we thought would carry us through our later years. We simply can't do without our Social Security. And whoever thought we'd have to deal with drugs and gangs and crazy people in our old age.

Some way, we must make our streets safe again without having to lock up half the country."

She paused, waiting for his response.

"So?" challenged the judge. The room remained eerily quiet: no coughing, no shuffling of feet, nothing.

"Well," she continued, "in spite of what Senator Farley says, we reasoned that it was criminals, not Social Security recipients, who were bankrupting the country, with all the money spent on them for courts and jails and prisons. It finally dawned on us that it didn't make sense for all the safe, free accommodations to be reserved for bad people. We good citizens need those same services. But if Senator Farley has his way, many of us will end up out on the street or wards of the state in those depressing state-run old folks' homes, where everyone is old and ill and just 'waiting for the last bell to ring.'" She punctuated the thought with a grimace.

"When Mabel and I found we'd receive better care in federal custody than in those bottom-of-the-line old folks' homes, we decided to earn our way into prison by becoming one of President George H. Bush's 'thousand points of light.' We could make a difference!"

She turned to point out Mil with a gentle sweep of her arm.

"Mil joined us later, when her husband was killed by robbers, too. Our mission was to make a dent in the number of outlaws who never learn, people who think democracy means the freedom to behave as badly as they want. And you have to admit our laws protect their right to do so. It's like they count on the rest of us to be civilized so they don't have to be.

"Anyway, at our ages, and in our financial fix, we certainly had nothing to lose. Our lives weren't worth much. But, don't you see, we could give our lives *value* by making the streets a little safer for others. And by reducing the number of troublemakers the government has to keep locked up, it offsets the cost to the government of taking care of *us* in prison."

If anyone had dropped a pin, it would have sounded like a bomb exploding. All eyes were locked on the tiny body in the oversized orange uniform standing stoically before the judge. She looked so fragile, so incapable of the deeds ascribed to her. After a slight pause, she continued.

"The only thing we ask of you is to keep us together, as Mabel said, so we can look after each other. If you turn us loose, I'm afraid we'll just have to continue our war on crime—or go on a hunger strike or something—until you agree to keep us safely in prison. We don't want to prolong this trial or do anything that would cost extra, and we promise we won't run away or get into any trouble."

Judge Thompson looked stunned.

"*You're* threatening *me?*" he cried. "Telling *me* what you will and won't do? Giving *me* the terms of your judgment? On the promise you'll be good? I can't believe I'm hearing this. Why should I believe a promise from *you*, when you've clearly demonstrated you're not to be trusted? Ha!" His scowl almost, but not quite, gave way to a laugh.

Josie absorbed his humiliation.

"I know what you're thinking," she said quietly, "but I want you to know my word is, and has always been, my honor. And that goes for Mabel and Mil, too. We don't lie or cheat or steal. We only want to be together in one of those prisons we saw on TV."

The judge's glower had given way to a look of disbelief.

"And what makes you think I'm not going to sentence you to death instead of life in prison? Do you realize I could make an example of you, have all three of you executed for taking the law into your own hands? Killing people, blowing things up, possession of questionable stolen property... And don't think so-called mercy killing isn't murder, too!"

Josie hung her head. *Execution!* They'd never thought of that.

She looked thoroughly defeated and tinier than ever. Raising her head, she met the judge's eyes. Her voice was soft but firm when she said, "In that case, I would like to call upon the words of Nathan Hale, Your Honor, and I know I speak for all three of us. If you choose to have us executed for trying to make a difference, then I would regret that I have but one life to lose for my country." She hesitated, as though she might have something more to say, and then sat down.

The courtroom erupted as reporters headed for the door. This was sensational stuff. It was all Paige could do to keep from throwing her arms around this splendid little woman who sat beside Mabel and Mil, unaware of the stir she had caused,

This ought to set the constipated system back on its ass, Paige thought. Just like the classic fairy tale, the least of us had pointed out that the emperor has no clothes—the Emperor of Justice, anyway, whose shortcomings were left stripped for all to see.

Judge Thompson loudly restored order to the courtroom, banging his gavel and instructing the bailiff that if anyone else even moved a hair he was to be thrown out. "We're going to take a continuation on this," he shouted. "I want to see anyone who had anything to do with this case in my chambers." Turning to the bailiff again, he said, "I am remanding these women back to your custody. I'll call for them when I've determined their sentences."

Josie, Mabel, and Mil stared at each other, pale with fear. *Execution!* Their planned retirement in prison may have just taken a sharp turn. For the worse.

TWENTY-THREE

Officers Davini and McClung hurried to join Paige and Wisneski in the judge's chambers. Nothing could describe their shock at finding these respectable old ladies responsible for the Bagmen murders, as well as blowing up both a crack house and the First Street Gang—and euthanizing their dear friend.

The four of them stood in front of the magnificent mahogany desk that once belonged to the judge's grandfather, the Honorable S. Carter Reed. Now deceased, he had presided over superior court in Chicago during the time of "Scarface" Al Capone and George "Bugs" Moran. A large portrait of Judge Reed, solemnly draped in black judicial robes and returning the same unrelenting stare for which Judge Thompson was famous, occupied most of the wall space across from the desk.

"Absolutely harmless without their weapons," Wisneski assured the judge, who half-reclined in the leather chair behind the desk. Arms folded across his chest, Judge Thompson's severe look had been replaced with one of complete frustration.

"Perfect ladies under any other circumstance," added McClung.

"And I thought I'd seen everything." the judge replied, as stunned as though it had just been confirmed that the earth was flat. "What in the hell do you make of this. Those old ladies really want to go to prison! They have it all figured out. *Now* what do we do? A life sentence at their ages doesn't mean anything. No sense giving them death, though. It would upset too many voters."

He turned pleading eyes to the portrait of his illustrious grandfather.

"What do I do now, Grandpa?" he asked, in a meltdown of his tough-guy demeanor. "They've stacked the deck on me. *Three old ladies, yet.*" He looked from one of the officers to the other, hoping they had the answer.

The first to speak was Officer Davini.

"You can't say they didn't hit the nail on the head, Your Honor. From what I hear, they've been through hell at the hands of the crap whose rights we're supposed to protect. Let's get real. We've all dreamed of doing the same thing. The only difference is they thought it was a *helpful* thing to do—and had the guts to do it."

"But remember, they've given no one any trouble and turned themselves in voluntarily," Paige hastily added. "Quite clearly, they had the good of their fellow man in mind, however odd it may seem to a man of the law. I can absolutely guarantee their good behavior. I'm not asking you to pardon them, but I *am* asking you to just put them together somewhere, for the rest of their lives. I mean, what other punishment can you give to women that old, for heaven's sake? And they're not going to try to run away or be any trouble. Can you imagine the national furor if you sentence these sweet old ladies to death?"

As it turned out, Judge Thompson had wanted only to give the women, and the press, something to think about when he threatened them with the death penalty. His reputation as a hard-nosed adjudicator had served him well with the voters during three elections. Clearly, he couldn't turn them loose, and bail was out of the question. They'd promised to keep on killing if not incarcerated or, maybe worse, stir up the public with a hunger strike. A life sentence without possibility of parole was all he could come up with, and that was just what they wanted. Thoroughly embarrassed at being outsmarted by three

246

old women, he snapped forward in his chair, ready to dismiss the assemblage.

"But no matter how we feel, we can't let the public think we're soft on crime," he reminded them. "Can't risk some other old people getting the same idea, for a free ride as guests of the state." He'd never felt so compromised.

"You know," he mused, "I have to admit, it's not so crazy. I guess it was just a matter of time until some of our desperate old folks figured things out and turned the system around on us. You know, like our repeat offenders do, when life on the outside gets too tough. When the safe routine of prison seems easier."

He nodded his head thoughtfully. "Old women, willing to ignore the shame of prison for free room and board. What in hell have we come to. But I guess it's not much different from the boom we've seen in illegitimate children. Wasn't too long ago it was a disgrace to have a baby out of wedlock. The mothers were shunned and lived in poverty. Now it's done all the time because it pays, and nobody thinks too much about it."

He strained to think of any legal precedent he could use against them. But they had him off balance. With the wild card of their twisted logic, they had just breached, and even embraced, civilization's greatest restraint: the fear of death or imprisonment.

"Folks," he said, "those three old ladies have us in a no-win situation, and we can't do a damn thing about it. They're going to get just what they wanted. And we'd better pray it doesn't start a trend."

He snorted at the irony of it.

"Women and their logic. God help us all! Any of you remember *Arsenic and Old Lace*?" he asked, as they turned to go. "Some other kindly old women on a mission to kill misfits. They belonged in the loony bin, but these three know exactly what they're doing. And damned if that little bitty one doesn't remind me of my grandma. A perfect lady, but back her into a corner and look out! Oh, boy," he said wearily, "Grandma would've loved this."

Between their arraignment and bench trial, the three women spent only two weeks in the county jail. Other prisoners could spend months, depending on how long it took to prepare their cases. They thanked their lucky stars for their life-instead-of-death sentences, and were grateful to be through with all that terrifying court business. Now they looked forward to being taken to the California Institution for Women at Frontera, in San Bernardino County. They didn't know that Judge Thompson was equally grateful to have them removed from the public eye. He realized he never should have allowed a TV camera in the courtroom, and hoped the furor surrounding them would fade before other oldsters would follow their example.

Outfitted in their bright orange jail clothing and the obligatory waistband-to-wrist cuffs for the ride to the prison, they felt like criminals for the first time. Because of their ages they were not required to wear leg irons like the other women. However, they were excited about the trip. They had been indoors way too long.

The sheriff's bus made several stops, picking up the day's batch of women from jails along the way. Josie, Mabel, and Mil clung together, feeling completely out of place among the decades-younger women who filled the bus. Surprisingly, some of them seemed as cheerful as though this were the bus to YMCA camp. They watched the bustle of Orange County disappear behind them, and marveled at the part of Southern California they'd never seen. They remembered when Orange County enjoyed these kinds of open spaces, dotted with orchards and dairy farms, before its skyrocketing population had claimed most of it for homes, shopping centers, and freeways.

It was almost noon and over ninety degrees when they arrived in a wavery cloud of diesel exhaust at the Reception Center. They learned that the prison had no air-conditioning. The only relief for staff and inmates alike was huge fans that blew the hot air in all directions. Their last experience with air-conditioning would be here, on this bus, which had just rumbled into Receiving and Release. They gaped at the ominous, tall fences topped with double coils of razor wire, but were overjoyed at the sight of the well-tended green lawns and flowers within the enclosure.

"This doesn't look like a prison," said Josie breathlessly. "Take away the fences and it's beautiful. Look at the bougainvillea, and impatiens, and geraniums … "

They were herded along off the bus into the enclosed reception area and freed of their restraints. After checking ID bracelets and logging in, they were directed to another door at the opposite end of the receiving room, which opened into a fenced compound. As the other women began to file through it, Mabel stopped and motioned to Mil and Josie.

"Ladies, mark this moment," she said, her voice hushed as she pointed at the door through which they had just come. "Do you realize we'll never again walk back through that door? The minute we walk out into the compound, we're in here *forever*." The three of them stood staring behind them at the entrance to the prison until one of the guards, a no-nonsense-looking black woman, barked, "Step it up, ladies, and stay in line."

A sense of adventure overcame any trepidation they might have had. They stepped back in line and, without another moment's hesitation, walked with heads held high into the California Institution for Women at Frontera.

PART TWO

TWENTY-FOUR

In 1952, the opening of the California Institution for Women at Corona, on 120 acres near the city of that name, climaxed a century of efforts to build a facility for convicted female felons. For the previous one hundred years California's women convicts were housed first aboard a ship in San Francisco Bay, and later in overcrowded quarters above the captain's office at San Quentin, and finally at an isolated prison in Tehachapi, which was devastated by an earthquake in 1952. This new facility was designed to be reformative, not punitive. Rehabilitation was the key word.

But the citizens of Corona objected to the use of their city's name for a prison, so its name was changed to California Institution for Women at Frontera. Frontera was a feminine derivative of the word *frontier*, signifying a new beginning. It was clearly different from all the other prisons. There were no gun towers, and was so lovely that it became known as "the campus."

Originally able to house 300 women in individual rooms, the inmate population rapidly grew and women were soon forced to share rooms, even as the facility was expanded. In the early 1960s, the small hospital wing was enlarged and equipped to become a fully accredited teaching hospital, able to meet all medical and surgical needs. Babies were born here and allowed to stay with their mothers for up to ten days while their custody was being determined.

In 1962 the reception center was built, along with its associated Psychiatric Treatment Unit, where arriving inmates would be evaluated and processed for placement. It was a separate, fenced compound adjacent to the main campus. By the mid-1980s, AIDS and tuberculosis, both major public health concerns, had become important management issues, and areas were set aside to quarantine inmates testing positive for these diseases.

By the 1990s the exploding prison population had swelled Frontera to approximately two thousand inmates, with about 18 percent of that number processing through Reception at any given time. The median age was thirty-four; less than 1 percent of the population was over sixty. Eighty percent of the inmates were in for drug-related offenses, whereas the remaining 20 percent were there because of something to do with a man. However, it was often difficult to establish a clear line between the two categories. Men seemed to be involved one way or another in most cases, and it may be more accurate to say that only 20 percent of the inmates were not convicted of drug offenses.

The new arrivals, including Mabel, Mil, and Josie, were given this information at a short orientation for what appeared to be two busloads of women. They were also told that their stay here in Reception would be temporary while they were being evaluated, physically and mentally, for permanent placement. Their hearts nearly stopped when they were told that everyone would not necessarily stay at this facility; most would be sent to other prisons in northern or central California, depending on the results of their evaluations and available space.

Before they had a chance to dwell on the horrid thought of being separated, they were issued jeans, shirts resembling baseball jerseys, flowered muumuus, socks and rubber sandals, underwear, and toiletries and assigned to their rooms. In consideration of their ages, each was assigned to a lower bunk in a different room. They'd hoped to stay together, but things were happening so fast there was little time to stew over it.

To their surprise most of the guards and inmates were courteous and helpful. Some of the new inmates seemed to know the guards and each other, and carried on animated conversations. Others looked traumatized, standing forlornly by themselves. The women were to find that everything they did from that day forward was regimented by the clock, which kept the organization running like the well-oiled machine it was.

Finally, when everyone seemed sorted out to the director's satisfaction, they were escorted to the dining room for what was to them a sumptuous lunch of potato soup, turkey sandwiches, and chocolate pudding. It was a large, stuffy area, set up to serve all the inmates of the Reception Center at one time. They were given the same food as the general population of inmates, but separately, in their own facility.

The women found that although there was no assigned seating, they were to fill their trays in the food line and take their seats in a prescribed manner. Each table of four was to be filled before they could move on to the next, in rows ten tables long. It was obvious that some of the women knew the ropes already, but most of them stood waiting to be told what to do. When the three women caught on to the system, they hung back until they were sure of being seated together.

Their tablemate was a bewildered, sweet-faced Hispanic woman who spoke very little English. She ate quietly, making it clear that she preferred to be left alone.

"This place can't be too bad," Mabel whispered to the other two. "So far, everything's been great. Even the food. Too bad they don't have air-conditioning, though." Like everyone else who wasn't directly in front of a fan, she glistened with a fine sheen of perspiration.

"This is like no prison I've ever seen in movies," agreed Mil. "Everyone is so nice. They're even letting us sit together. And I don't see bars anywhere."

"Just look at all the flowers," exclaimed Josie. "Even in this heat. But there certainly are a lot of flies. From the dairy farms, I guess." She looked down at the baggy orange jumpsuit she'd finally become accustomed to. "I hope they don't expect me to wear those jeans—and that shirt. I'd prayed for blue uniforms but never thought about blue *jeans.* Guess I'll have to get used to myself in a muumuu."

The days in Reception flew by in a whirl of physical examinations, evaluations of one sort or another, personal analyses, and learning to live with the rules. The three women marveled at the respect shown them by the other inmates, many of whom had never known their own grandmothers. The main topics of conversation were assertions of innocence and wondering who got to stay at this prison, near boyfriends and family, and who was to be sent elsewhere.

They could watch the regular inmates going about their work and class-filled days through the razor wire–topped fences that separated them. They were told the rooms were much nicer over there, and that the larger dining hall on that side was called the Village Cafeteria. Amazing things for the first-timers were the total lack of bars and the amount of freedom they had. If it was even nicer on the other side, that's where they wanted to be. Some of the old-timers enjoyed terrifying the newer ones with horrific prison stories. But like most scary stories, these things always seemed to have happened somewhere else, and to someone somebody else knew.

Josie's roommate, Esperanza, was only twenty-one. She was here because of a string of burglaries she and her boyfriend had committed to support his drug habit. She missed him desperately, for he had ruled her life since she was fourteen. Her English was halting, but she told Josie she would do anything for that man. She had prostituted herself for him many times. She was a good roommate, painfully quiet, and followed Josie around like a little dark shadow.

A solidly built young woman named Connie was Mabel's roommate. She was boisterous when with her friends, and Mabel could see she had it in her to be a real troublemaker. She mostly ignored Mabel and often got in trouble for not following the rules. Mabel was glad their only real contact was during lockdown, between nine in the evening and six in the morning. She hoped Connie would be one of those sent elsewhere.

Connie had never clearly defined what had brought her to prison, saying only that "some shitty-assed cop had nothing better to do." Mabel found out later that she had been arrested for one barroom brawl too many, in which she had broken another woman's nose and slashed her face with a switchblade knife.

Mil's roommate, Tina, was a well-mannered young woman who could easily have been a model with her long blond hair and shapely body. She was proud to say she was from La Crescenta, a posh neighborhood in the foothills north of Glendale. Her crime had been cocaine trafficking at Glendale City College to support her BMW and love of designer clothing. She clung to Mil the way Esperanza clung to Josie, terrified by the catcalls and whistles from some of the other women. She'd heard of homosexuality in prison, and could hardly sleep for worrying about what might happen to her.

Tenuous relationships were formed, with everyone knowing it could all change at the end of their four to eight weeks in Reception. And change it did.

Josie, Mabel, and Mil were ecstatic to be scheduled for minimum security at this very prison. Esperanza, Connie, and Tina were slated for transfer to the much larger women's facility in Chowchilla. Josie and Mil worried about Esperanza and Tina, who had prayed constantly to be kept safely in the company of the three older women. Mabel worried about the inmates at Chowchilla: they'd have to deal with Connie.

No one was given time to mourn or celebrate her placement. When a decision was made, it was executed immediately, to make room for busloads of new inmates arriving regularly. No army operated with greater precision than the staff of Frontera.

Any ideas the women had about a life of leisure in prison were quickly dispelled. Their days among the general population in the minimum-security module were busy with classes, work details, volunteer programs and meal schedules, although they were thrilled to find they could have a TV in their rooms and decorate with things from home. Between Mil's sons and Paige, the women were brought whatever they asked for. When they weren't required to be somewhere else, the women could relax in the lounge of their "cottage" and watch TV, play cards, or work on projects of their own.

Each cottage housed up to 200 women, bunked two to a room. The rooms were just large enough to accommodate a set of bunk beds placed against the heavily screened window, two small wardrobes, two dressers, a toilet, and a sink. There were no bars in sight. Instead, a heavy wooden door with a small cutout window led into the common hallway. If they had an emergency or needed the guard during lockup hours, they were to signal by hanging a towel through the cutout in the door.

Although the three women were assigned to three different rooms, they at least were in the same cottage. They understood that their roommates would change as inmates came and went, but they expected to live and die there. They were delighted to find that all three of them were assigned to work in the kitchen, or "culinary," as it was called.

Josie shared a room with LaShondra, a slow-witted young black girl who was due to give birth in five months. She was in for drug trafficking.

"After what I learnt here," she told Josie, "I don' want this baby. Might have two heads or somethin' from all the crack. Don' know what I'd do with it, anyway, even if it has jis' one head. The gov'ment don' give ya enough t'live on for jis' one baby, but a bunch of 'em slows ya' down. Ya know, like that TV ad says, 'I gotta lotta livin' t'do!'"

Josie followed LaShondra's example and placed both her thirteen-inch TV and her compact radio on the small wooden projection at the end of her mattress. Wall space was limited, but she hung her wedding and anniversary pictures where she could see them from the end of her bunk. She felt almost at home with Jennie's and Bobby's pictures once again in place on her small dresser, flanking Theodore's army picture with its little American flag. LaShondra didn't seem to notice when Josie conversed softly with them on occasional mornings or evenings.

Josie loved how LaShondra sang and hummed to herself in a rich alto voice. She presented an immediate challenge to the teacher in Josie; she was sure she could help LaShondra master better skills for her return to life on the outside. She decided that would be her new mission.

Mabel's roommate was Elsie, a pudgy, pimply girl who had simply got in with the wrong people. She'd never had a boyfriend and had been thrilled when a fast-talking con man flattered her into running errands for him. These errands consisted of picking up and delivering what turned out to be drug money in the metal file box she was given to carry in the trunk of her car. Because she accepted small gifts from him, as well as money from time to time, she was considered to be his accomplice. When he went down, she went down with him.

"And he never even kissed me," she lamented. "All that time, telling me he loved me and needed me. He said he was divorcing his wife but going to stay true to her till then so I'd know he could be a faithful husband. Oh, God, I feel so stupid."

She cried every time she talked about her betrayal, but Mabel suspected she'd welcome him back in a minute. Such as their relationship was, he'd been the only one who'd ever paid attention to her. But he undoubtedly found the inflamed pustules on her face and her soft, bloated body repulsive. He needed her, all right, and led her on by appealing to her gullibility and lack of self-esteem.

Elsie was a quiet, considerate roommate—a big improvement over Connie. After lockdown in the evenings she would sprawl on her top bunk either watching TV or talking with Mabel, but always twisting a strand of oily hair around her finger, and sometimes chewing on the bushy ends of it. "At least I'm getting out of here in a year and he'll be in for four more," she kept saying. "Sure wish he could'a got the death penalty, though."

Mabel didn't know if she could stand a year of Elsie's bad grooming and hair-fiddling. It occurred to her that she might work on Elsie during their year together—sort of polish her up to be ready for a new life on the outside. Heaven knew the poor thing could use all the help she could get.

Mil immediately loved her roommate, Betsy, who had been convicted of trying to kill her abusive husband. She had a sense of humor to match Mil's.

"It feels so *good* to be away from that bastard," she would say. "He wouldn't let me leave him, beat me up every time I tried. So I didn't have nothin' to lose. It was either me killin' him or him killin' me. But I didn't plan on botchin' it."

She'd shot him twice one night when he was in a deep, drunken sleep, and run to hide at a girlfriend's house, prepared to say she'd been there all evening. When her husband awakened in the morning with a couple of still slightly oozing bullet wounds in his shoulder, it was all over for Betsy.

"The bad part is he's just waiting for me to get out," she said. "He's gonna beat the livin' shit out of me and kill me, for sure. And there's nothin' anybody can do to stop 'im. So, I'm gonna live it up in here. At least I'm safe from him." She was a model prisoner, good-natured and always helpful.

Paige came to visit them on weekends when she could, and they looked forward to seeing her. She brought them news from the outside, including letters to the editor regarding their escapades. Most of them applauded the women as heroes, but others branded them as despicable.

Mark Wisneski came by once and was so dispirited at seeing them locked up that he never came back. He had no trouble getting them to agree that Andy Krach was to have exclusive interviewing rights, and cleared it with the warden before he left. From then on, he sent his regards via Paige and Andy.

Surprisingly, one of their first visitors was Molly Flannery. Although Josie was touched that Molly would come all the way to see her, she surmised that the visit was more about making herself seem important than her desire to see Josie. Nevertheless, it was nice to see her and catch up on what was going on at home.

After settling into the stark, glass-walled visitation room and voicing her disapproval of Josie's actions, she gave a long-winded account of having been on TV and quoted in the newspapers. Then she launched into reporting the current gossip about her neighbors. Josie thought Molly would like to hear about life in prison, but, as usual, Molly had no interest in anything Josie might have to say. As gossipy as ever, she couldn't wait to tell the shocking story about Ms. Atkinson and Mr. Tweedy, the couple who had sparked up a romance in the laundry room.

Leaning close to Josie for emphasis, Molly vowed, "I knew there was something wrong with that woman the moment I laid eyes on her. And poor Mr. Tweedy just walked right into that mess. Josie, you should have seen it. That woman had twenty-two credit cards, most of them charged up to the limit. Her place was stuffed to the gills with the expensive dolls she'd never had as a child, junk jewelry, and pretty things from all those catalogs she gets. Plus, she ordered a lot of gadgets off the TV. Paid the minimum every month, and when one credit card company cut her off, she'd just use another one. New cards came in the mail all the time, so she was never without six or eight good ones."

"How in the world did she get twenty-two cards?" Josie asked, astounded. "It was all I could do to get one."

"Well, that's the part that tells you just how crazy she was. She said she was so flattered by all the different companies sending her cards out of the blue, and telling her what a valued customer she was, that she would have felt bad for not using them. Didn't want to play favorites among them when they all seemed to think so highly of her. And on top of that, a bunch of them included life insurance for a few dollars more each month. But between the fine print and the cards that were blocked for lack of payment, they all turned out to be worthless."

Josie was flabbergasted. "How do you know all this?"

"Well, as I said, that poor Mr. Tweedy just walked right in on it when she invited him in for coffee. He couldn't believe his eyes. Believe you me, it didn't take him long to figure out something was *wrong* with that woman."

"So what did he do?" urged Josie, unable to imagine what would happen next.

"He's such a timid man, you know, you'd think he'd just walk out, shut the door, and not get involved. But he went right over to the manager and explained why he needed the phone number of her next of kin. Then he called her son, John, who lives in Phoenix, and got him right over here. It must have been an awful shock for John when he walked in on it."

Josie labored over Ms. Atkinson's dreadful plight. "So what did John do? Poor Ms. Atkinson! Did she have to give it all back?"

Molly leaned in closer, gleeful to share her story. "That's another crazy thing. When she received notice that the cards would no longer be honored for lack of payment, she just stashed them away in the cupboard. She always had a few new ones to use. John totaled up all her bills and found she was over $100,000 in debt. And the credit card companies didn't want the merchandise back; they wanted *money*.

"Well, John could see that his mother had slipped a cog or two, and he was left in a terrible dilemma. His mother couldn't live alone anymore. Her place was a shambles, and she wasn't eating right or taking care of herself, either. But if he took her home to live with him, he was afraid he would be legally responsible for her debts. Turns out his ex-wife had wiped him out in a nasty divorce a few years ago, so he didn't have the money even if he'd wanted to pay those bills."

"So what did he do?" asked Josie, hanging on her every word.

Molly sat back with a satisfied look on her face. "I guess he did the only thing he could do. The woman was totally incompetent, so he put it in the hands of the fraud unit of the FBI, and now she's over in that Alzheimer's home in Garden Grove, paid for by the state. Seems her sister is somewhere in one of those homes, too. Poor thing. She doesn't know she did anything wrong. If you ask me, those credit card companies had it coming, sending out cards willy-nilly to people who don't understand the first thing about them."

Molly abruptly took off in another direction about the Tustin Marine Base closure, which meant her husband would lose his civil service job there. "He applied at the El Toro Marine Base, in Irvine, but now they're talking about closing that one, too. So that'll make two bases, small cities, you might say, being boarded up when it seems like they could be converted to provide low-cost housing, and even jobs, for people. Whoever lives there could help with the maintenance and maybe run a few services, you know, as part of the privilege of living there. If you ask me, the government doesn't think things through very well."

Josie was exhausted when Molly left. She'd heard enough gossip to hold her for awhile. She guessed this was the last she'd see of her, for Molly had what she'd come for. She could go on forever bragging about being such a dear friend of one of the notorious Bag Ladies that she'd even visited her in prison.

The three women were overjoyed, however, when Betty Jean brought Gertie in her old Volkswagen van to see them. Hap stayed home to look after Waldo, who couldn't come because he refused to wear anything but blue jean overalls. Gertie had given up trying to explain to him that visitors would not be admitted if wearing jeans, which had become a no-no in the early days of Frontera. Back then, guards, guests, and inmates alike were allowed to wear them. But when a hair-pulling fight broke out between two women in jeans, it took staff members awhile to realize an inmate had attacked a guard. Guards were now required to be in uniform, and for everyone's safety, only inmates could wear jeans.

They visited outdoors at a picnic table under the shade of a broad old sycamore tree. Munching on goodies from vending machines in the visitor's room, they caught up on everything that had transpired since their potluck party.

"The cops were all over the place," exclaimed Betty Jean, "asking questions about those dead men found in the road, but none of us knew anything about it. Then we find out *you* killed 'em, and the Bagmen, too. We watched it all on TV. We were so *proud* of you"

Gertie said she was trying to figure out a way to join them. "Wish you'd a'let me an' Waldo take credit for the ones out t'my house," she joked. "Then I'd be in here, too. An' since Waldo don't care much where he is as long as he's with me, maybe they'd a'let me bring 'im along."

Worried about leaving Hap alone with Waldo, they didn't stay long. But they promised to come back.

Sergeant Davini paid a brief visit to see how they were doing. He had smuggled in a few magazines with pictures of the women on the cover for them to autograph. It was highly irregular, of course, but they were pleased to oblige. He planned to store them in a safe place, considering they would eventually be collector's items. His twin sons were only five years old, but he knew they would appreciate the magazines one day, knowing their dad had actually been involved with these notorious women.

Andy Krach knew he owed Wisneski big-time for his exclusive permission to interview them, both for his newspaper and for the book he planned to write. He didn't know how lucky he was that the contract specified talking to them individually: with his spastic colon, no amount of Imodium could have helped him interview all three of them at once.

The women took an immediate liking to Andy. Wisneski had promised them the young reporter could be counted on to do justice to their story. They were delighted to tell him everything he wanted to know, and a whole lot more.

In turn, he kept them apprised of events in the DA's office concerning their case. They were thrilled to find that Peggy, who had returned to Chicago after arranging Pearl's small funeral, escaped prosecution in Pearl's death. Only Paige and Mark Wisneski suspected the truth of her involvement, and they wisely left well enough alone.

Andy kept their story very much alive in the newspaper, prompting ever more responses from the public. PATRIOTS OR CRACKPOTS? one headline asked, and THE NEXT DESPERADO: YOUR GRANDMOTHER? asked another. His articles made compelling reading for old folks and lawmakers alike, and sparked a firestorm of public reaction.

ON THE BRINK OF ORWELL'S *BRAVE NEW WORLD* was one of Andy's favorites. He also borrowed from Virgil's *Aeneid* to write BEWARE OF OLD LADIES BEARING GUNS and had fun writing A SHOT OF *ARSENIC AND OLD LACE*—WITH A TWIST. He did a lot of research for an article he entitled PRISON: THE ULTIMATE SOCIAL SECURITY. But when all was said and done, he didn't have the answer, either.

Talk shows rehashed what had led to the women's decision to live in prison. The ACLU was called upon to defend country club conditions in jail, and the NRA stoutly proclaimed that, no matter what, it was everyone's right to have all the guns he wanted. Most of the clergymen interviewed took a hard stand against euthanasia, as they did killing of any kind, and generally urged turning the other cheek to criminals, who would, of course, repent if people were nicer to them. Senator Farley got a lot of air time talking about Social Security but backpedaled furiously when the issues of government pensions and perks came up.

More and more, the plight of the elderly and the cost to the country of runaway crime, both financially and emotionally, were fodder for debate. Newspapers everywhere were flooded with letters to the editor. It seemed everyone had an opinion, but no one really knew what to do about the many conflicting and seemingly irresolvable issues the Bagmen case presented.

One thing was certain: nothing would be the same again. A Pandora's box of laws and morals at odds with each other had been opened. And the public was consumed with it.

TWENTY-FIVE

Elmer and Opal Hodgkins, both sixty-nine and struggling with emphysema after a half century of smoking, got up one morning, fed their cats, and left their run-down mobile home in rural Flint, Michigan. Carrying a handful of foreclosure notices, they drove straight to a local branch of the First National Bank and asked to see the manager. They were ushered into his office and sat waiting nervously until he appeared.

The manager, a Mr. Albert Grossman, professed to be deeply sorry about last year's tragic deaths of their daughter and granddaughter, who had lived with them in their tiny trailer. "Such a shame," he said. "Innocent victims, in the way of a gang shoot-out." His eyes flicked to his Rolex. "The wrong place at the wrong time sort of thing, you know."

He offered a terse apology that foreclosure on their property should be necessary, but he could no longer overlook the $947.84 in delinquent payments on their home loan. And there was also the matter of five years' unpaid property taxes, amounting to something over two thousand dollars. "Most unfortunate," he said, "but business is business, you know." He reminded them that the bank had repeatedly extended their grace period to where it was way beyond the limit: only a cash payment could spare them eviction.

They nodded and started to mumble something about all those funeral expenses when the phone on Mr. Grossman's desk rang. Ear to the phone, Mr. Grossman handed them back their sheaf of papers and gestured for them to leave, appearing only too glad to dismiss them and their troubles.

"Call us if we can be of further help," he called as they closed the door behind them.

Opal and Elmer gave him a Bronx cheer through the closed door, climbed into their beat-up old Ford Fairlane, and headed for town. They took their time, scanning the streets near the defiled spot where their loved ones had died, until they saw the men they were looking for. In a squeal of worn-out brakes, Elmer dived into a no-parking zone near the corner, and, each packing a twenty-gauge shotgun, they made their way through lolling groups of street people to where two men stood bantering with passersby, offering to sell drugs and hot merchandise. The very sight of them, their loved one's murderers, set the Hodgkinses' blood to boiling. A neophyte prosecutor had bungled their trial into a mistrial, and here they were, back on the streets, business as usual.

Opal and Elmer had already made up their minds. If they were going down for something as simple as running out of money, they weren't going alone. These miserable excuses for human beings were going down, too.

As bystanders backed away in horror, Elmer and Opal each took aim and calmly emptied their shotguns into their two astonished victims. Then they stood quietly, holding hands and praying in the midst of the resulting chaos, certain those old gals in the newspaper had the right idea; the streets could use a good cleaning of punks like these. And, in their circumstances, a guaranteed life sentence in the safety of prison sounded pretty good. It meant they would be separated from each other, but with all their health problems, they had known that day was coming, anyway. And those Bag Ladies made prison sound a whole lot better than a nursing home. At the very least, they couldn't be evicted.

In Salem, Oregon, at about the same time the Hodgkinses were forging their destinies in Michigan, seventy-four-year-old Sara Adler kissed her poor, demented husband for the last time and began cleaning up his room. The haunting voice of Marty Robbins singing "El Paso" filled the air. With the cassette tape set to continuous play, she chucked his array of sickroom supplies into large trash bags and tied them securely while Marty sang "Cool Water." She had already bathed and changed him to every other song on the tape, appropriately starting with "Devil Woman." His sheets and towels churned away in the washer and dryer.

Richard was crazy about Marty Robbins. When she had read that the Bag Ladies played their friend's favorite music while administering sleeping pills, Sara knew right away that the music for Richard to die to would be Marty Robbins. She stopped to check for a pulse, testing the temperature of his forehead with her wrist.

He had been such a good man before dementia took his mind away. She had cried and railed against the injustice of it all until there were no more tears, but only the resolve that he must not suffer. She would take care of him in her own way, rather than subject him to bedsores and rashes and indifferent care at the nursing home.

Finally, when everything met her satisfaction, she lay down beside him and took his limp hand in hers. Stroking his arm, she recounted the good times they'd had and the love they had shared, while the plaintive music played on and on.

There had been no struggle—nothing at all. He hadn't even opened his eyes when she propped him up in the feeding position and began poking applesauce, mixed with the contents of sleeping pills, into his mouth. As he did with whatever pureed food she placed in his mouth, he gummed the mixture around until she placed a drinking straw between his lips. This somehow triggered his primitive reflex to suck and swallow. Laboriously, he polished off an entire bottle of sleeping pills.

Accepting pureed food and doggedly swallowing it was the only skill left to him. He'd been a bedridden vegetable for months now, after a hellish year of not knowing who she was. That year had been the hardest, when he had been the most abusive. Now his diapering and feeding were the center of her life. The doctors assured her that his heart was strong, and with good care he could go on like this for a long time.

Sara had poured over every word written about the Bag Ladies and knew they were right. A loving God would know that Richard's living on and on in this way was inhumane to both of them. She couldn't do this to him—or herself—anymore. Even though Richard would never know the difference, *she* would. She was physically and spiritually drained from his constant care, and the expenses Medicare didn't pay for had her financially strapped. Their savings were almost gone, and by month's end she went without what she needed to care for herself. The thought of a sheltered life in prison, in the company of other women, was like the rainbow's promise at the end of a very long storm. The government was welcome to everything she had in return.

On that very same day, Lucinda Freeman and Murielle Joplin tidied their little walk-up flat in Harlem in preparation of leaving it forever. Over the past few days they had sorted out who of their family and friends was to have their few treasures, and attached notes to these select items. They wanted the government to have the rest in exchange for the safe life they envisioned in prison.

Widowed sisters in their eighties, Lucinda and Murielle were scared to death of the young people in their neighborhood. These kids would just as soon rob you as look at you; leaving their home to run simple errands had become a hazard. Although failing health made it more difficult every year to climb the flight of stairs to their apartment, for security reasons a ground-floor apartment was out of the question.

Neither wanted to be the one left behind to fend for herself when the other one died. They blessed the Bag Ladies for showing them the way.

They showered and put on fresh cotton dresses and clean underwear before stepping out the door. Each carrying a Saturday night special, they laboriously descended the stairs and settled their ample girths on the concrete stoop in front of the building. They knew just who they were looking for.

It wasn't long before a group of five insolent-looking youths strutted toward them, elbowing others off the sidewalk as though it belonged to them. One wore dreadlocks, two had shaven heads, and all glistened with gold jewelry. It was the same bunch who regularly terrorized the neighborhood and who had more than once wrested from the two women whatever money they carried.

When they were close enough for Lucinda and Murielle to see the looks of shock on their faces, the women raised stocking-encased guns from the folds of their dresses and mowed them down. Then, fumbling with arthritic hands, they reloaded and emptied their guns into them again, just in case they weren't quite dead. Numb to the ensuing pandemonium, they hoped it wouldn't take too long for the police to arrive. It was hot, sitting there in the sun.

"My worst nightmare," growled Judge S. Carter Thompson, scanning the morning paper over breakfast. Every morning it had been the same. Scattered across the country, desperate old folks were picking up guns and blowing away criminals or euthanizing ailing spouses and friends. All threw themselves upon the mercy of the court and hoped for a secure life in prison. He imagined it was going to get worse; the three women's story was due to air tomorrow night on *Current Edition*. He'd forbidden a live interview, but he couldn't stop the media from making a circus of it.

The three women continued to adjust to the routine in prison, finding life in the general population easier and more predictable than what they had experienced in Reception. They made a hit with the other women in culinary with little tricks they had learned through the years, such as the magic of storing a piece of bread with brown sugar to keep it from hardening. Their conversion rhymes were a help, too, for the women who had never before spent much time in the kitchen:

"A pint's a pound the world around" was the easiest to learn. A little more complicated was:

"Two cups make a pint, two pints a quart, and then we change to four.

Four cups make a quart, four quarts a gallon, of anything you can pour."

They had to remember things like their assigned laundry and phone times, which were displayed on large sign-up sheets in the laundry room and by the telephone. Each cottage had only one washing machine for personal items, and laundry was dried on the clothesline stretched across the grassy atrium within the four wings that made up each cottage. Prison-issue linens and clothing were, of course, sent to the prison laundry.

With only one phone booth and one washing machine, if they missed their turn they had to wait until the following week.

Once they had everything firmly in mind life became easy for them. They began to enjoy interacting with the other women. Because they were good-natured and respectful, they, in turn, were treated with respect. The food was good, they got plenty of sleep, and they had no complaints. In the beginning, when they had time to think about it, they missed keeping up with their soaps. But it wasn't long before they had forgotten all about them.

They were thrilled to be interviewed by the lovely TV anchor, Carrie Bryan, for *Current Edition,* and couldn't wait to see the interview when it aired on TV. State prison laws allowed interviewers no camera or recorder, so the young lady had to rely on her ability to take copious notes.

"The state doesn't want us making celebrities out of inmates," she explained to them. "Although I think it's too late for that. You *are* celebrities."

She and the film crew would later add shots of the various crime scenes as well as exterior shots of the prison, where Carrie would stand and broadcast. These shots, spliced with film clips from their trial and footage from the body's discovery at Mabel's, would yield a satisfactory format.

Carrie led them, one at a time, through the events that had brought them here, starting with a brief account of each husband's death. Few words were wasted on their war on crime. It was much too nasty a business, they declared, vowing the whole thing would have been unnecessary if the system had been running right in the first place. But they spoke glowingly of life in prison, from an old person's point of view. Josie was interviewed first.

"The younger women all treat us with respect, and even the guards are nice," she said. "The food is good, and the work isn't hard; they let us old folks sit down a lot. Once you get used to it, the routine is pretty comfortable. I'm looking forward to separating the bulbs in the garden this fall and doing some planting in the spring. I'm also helping some of the girls study for their GEDs. I hope it will give them the skill to make better choices when they get out of here."

Carrie noted that Josie had once been a teacher.

Mil was ecstatic about the keyboard she'd been allowed to play in the combination music and craft room.

"I've been in great demand, giving lessons to the other women," she said. "There's a lot of untapped talent here. I have to say, I miss cocktails at five, and I've quit smoking because the rules are too strict about when and where you can smoke. But I guess, in the long run, it's for my own good. I feel bad about embarrassing my children and grandchildren like this, but, if they look at the *good* side, they're spared the burden of caring for me when I get old."

Spliced-in film clips from their trial captured the twinkle in her eye. When the program later aired, it resulted in several letters proposing marriage if she should ever get out of prison.

Mabel reported that the medical care was wonderful.

"I have new glasses," she said proudly, "and they'll perform knee surgery if this darn knee keeps flaring up. I'm learning to paint, which I've always wanted to do, and I'm having fun teaching stitchery to some of the girls. Of course, it takes a while to get used to the regimentation, and I know I look funny in jeans. But, all in all, prison life can be kind of cozy. I was getting too old to live by myself, anyway. Just getting to the store had become a chore, and I could see it was only going to be downhill from there. Now I don't have to worry about a thing" She looked quite upbeat in her jeans and baseball jersey.

She concluded by telling Carrie, "My only regret is that living on the outside had to be so scary. Take my word for it, young lady: you'll find that security becomes one of your highest priorities when you reach our ages!"

Promptly at seven on the evening of the broadcast, scores of their cottage-mates gathered in the lounge to see their famous friends on TV. Some of the women, the hard cores who didn't see anything wrong with a life of crime, hung around just long enough to set up a loud chorus of boos and jeers. But the rest of them cheered loudly and were proud to know these famous ladies. They couldn't have imagined the stampede it would incite among old folks on the outside.

"Yes, sir," stammered Andy.

Phone in one hand and coffee cup in the other, he was being blistered by Orange County District Attorney Rupert T. Bennings III.

"Yes, sir," Andy repeated. "It's all over the wire service. I know. Just about every city in the nation is reporting. I know ... but I'm not sure what we can do about it, sir. Freedom of the press, you know."

He whirled around in his office chair to look out the window. Funny how sane it seems out there, he thought, even though the nation seems to have erupted. Old people on the warpath. Either killing their way into prison or amassing hunger strikes on the steps of city hall, demanding to be kept in the safety and comfort of prison. Absolutely bizarre.

The district attorney continued his diatribe, calling it an insurrection and declaring his certainty that the whole thing was the media's fault. Andy held the receiver out in front of him, not listening, until the word *insurrection* called up images of famous events in history. He wondered if the nation had also seemed to erupt after the insurrection later called the Boston Tea Party.

He laughed to himself. Instead of the cry, "The Red Coats are coming!" folks might call out, "The White Hairs are coming!" With a jolt, he realized that the Bagman saga had a tea party in it, too. The women had confessed at one.

That was it! *Tea Parties and Turning Points.* The title for his book! The concept of blending historic events into the women's story immediately began to germinate in his mind and flowered into the spine-tingling thought that history might be being made at this very moment, and he was right in the thick of it.

He let District Attorney Bennings vent for a few more moments and then simply said, "Gotta go, sir. Nice talkin' to you."

He wasn't going to let anyone harangue him into another intestinal upset. If he learned nothing more from this whole crazy thing, he was determined to capture the calm with which those little ladies had met their fate in the courtroom. He had great admiration for all three of them. He knew if he'd been the one facing Judge Thompson in that courtroom, his bowels would have emptied themselves all over the floor.

But no more. He was enjoying national acclaim for his newspaper articles and making great strides on his book. He was living and breathing Bag Ladies and loving every minute of it. And who knew:

this was the kind of story that, if he were lucky, just might earn him consideration for the coveted Sigma Delta Chi award in journalism. Well, he thought, I can dream, anyway.

He swiveled around and resumed pecking away at his keyboard. This is going to be a great article, he thought. The DA trying to stem the tide by censoring the newspaper Of course, he wouldn't say it quite that way.

TWENTY-SIX

Paige was the next to receive a call from District Attorney Bennings.

"They'll listen to you," he growled. "I want you to get out there and tell those women to shut up. They're making prison sound so good that we have an epidemic of old folks doing whatever they can to get in there. They'd like us to think they're patriotic, but those old folks are out patrolling the streets like a bunch of damn storm troopers—or draped all over city hall, refusing to eat. We have the ACLU goin' nuts, and jails are bustin' at the seams. All I need is the kiss-of-death call from the attorney general if I can't handle this."

Paige assured him she would enjoy seeing them on the DA's behalf, but felt sure those three old ladies weren't going to be told what to do. She took a chance and called Rex McClung and invited him to go with her.

He and she had hit it off during the women's trial. Once she discovered he was single, she'd found him haunting her thoughts. She sensed that he felt the same about her, because he rearranged his day to go with her. Andy would meet them there.

The rest of the week, she worried that it might have been a big mistake to invite Rex. It could become terribly awkward. *Damn. Why am I so nervous about spending a day with him?*

When she picked him up at the station Saturday afternoon, he smelled faintly of Old Spice—her favorite men's fragrance. Fighting the sense of giddiness that came over her, she forced herself to speak as casually as she could. Rex knew about her ex-husband and had heard of her many contributions to the department. At first he didn't want to talk about himself, but by the time they reached the prison he had shared a few personal things with her.

He had a daughter in her second year at UCLA and a son in high school who lived with him. His wife had left him some years ago, but he didn't want to elaborate on it. Fortunately, they arrived at the prison in time to change the conversation to mundane things like where to park and how much hotter it was out here and to curse the flies that attacked them the moment they stepped out of the car.

A guard showed them to the visitation suite, upstairs over the warden's office, where the three women and Andy awaited them. The women were all atwitter to see the two of them arriving together and greeted them with broad smiles and furtive little nods of approval among themselves.

The stark, two-bedroom family visitation suites were originally used as staff housing when Frontera was new. Now they were reserved for the two or three-day visits granted to inmates and their families. "Lifers" like the three women were not granted the privilege of their use. But the warden and the DA had considered this a special occasion.

Rex and Paige joined the others on the scattering of industrial-strength chairs and sofas. Soon Rex and Mabel were recounting their days together, when he had been her "trusty Irish cop." He had them all laughing at his description of the pungent odor that assaulted him on his first visit. "She made it even worse by throwing pickle-brine-soaked boxes in the blaze of her fireplace. And those women were sneaking off right under my nose to conduct their missions. Hell, they were more dangerous than the people we were trying to protect them from."

Paige watched and imagined herself alone with him. A warm rush she hadn't felt in what seemed like ages flooded over her. She knew she'd better get on with what she'd come for. Besides, the room had been closed up all morning and was terribly hot and stuffy. She wanted to have their meeting and get out of there. The afternoon visiting session was nearly over, and they had important things to talk about.

"I want to qualify the statement I'm about to make, ladies," she said, when she had everyone's attention. "I'm here representing the district attorney's office, and I've been asked to 'suggest' you tone down your glowing reports of prison life. I don't know if you're aware that a lot of people have been copying you, and it's putting a real strain on jails and services. Its also has the ACLU in a flap over who they are supposed to be protecting, the old folks or the criminals. The DA, I might add, has hinted he'll see that you're separated, or revoke your visitation privileges if you don't comply."

The three women were stunned. Paige didn't think she'd ever seen them when not one of them knew what to say. But, of course, their silence was only temporary.

Mil got her wits together first. "Don't talk about how nice it is here? I don't get it. These people are doing their best to take care of us, and we're supposed to say it's awful?" She appeared flabbergasted at such a notion.

"They want us to lie?" cried Mabel. "Why on earth would I speak badly about all the people who have been so good to us?" She looked around at the others in disbelief.

"Surely we're allowed to speak freely, even if we *are* in prison," said Josie. "You don't have to print what we say, you know, but we are the happiest we've been in a long time. We're safe and well fed, and I haven't had a nightmare since I've been here." No longer reliving Theodore's death was proof enough for her.

Mil lowered the folded paper towel she'd been using as a fan and asked, "What more can they do to us if we don't comply? Put us in solitary confinement? Torture us? You know, bamboo splinters under the nails and things like that? I still don't get it. They should put bamboo splinters under the nails of the lawmakers who've let the country come to this, where the only safe place for old folks is in prison."

Mabel had been thinking. "If we're looking for negatives, I admit I didn't like the strip search we had in Reception. But, you know, by the time a woman reaches *our* ages, private parts haven't been private for a long time."

"Speaking of private things, I'm sure we'd all rather have private bathrooms," added Josie. "But when I was young I got used to sharing a three-holer outhouse with my Aunt Beulah's family when we went to visit. And this isn't that much different. It's all in getting used to it. And, let's see, I guess I could say I'm getting tired of wearing a muumuu. But it sure makes dressing in the morning easy."

"Listen, from what my roommate tells me, this place beats *freedom* in Cincinnati," said Mil, laughing. "And people live *there* because they *want* to. Shoot, other than being a little hot at times—and those darn flies—we're glad to be all together and in good health. As Josie says, our needs are being met, so how could we complain?"

"I don't have the answer, ladies," said Paige, "but you and Andy can work out a deal with the DA. He might let Andy continue to interview you for his book, if Andy promises no more clever newspaper articles to incite the public."

Rex had been sitting quietly, just watching and listening.

"Maybe you can do more than that for the DA," he said. "If people are reading everything you say, they might appreciate some words of wisdom. Ideas that might turn this thing around. Along with an apology for taking matters into your own hands."

His intense blue eyes searched their faces for a response. "He'll need that apology," he said quietly. "Andy here could probably help you put together a statement."

"Sort of like a manifesto?" Andy asked, wide-eyed. "With 'whereases' and stuff?"

His eagerness had him on the edge of his chair. This was sounding more like the Boston Tea Party all the time. His insides began to churn as he assessed the increasing impact of these women's rebellion and his role in it. For a few agonizing moments he tried to fight the unmistakable urgency building in his bowels.

*Oh no! Pull yourself together, man. Meditate. Mind over matter …
Shit!*

He excused himself and hurried to the small bathroom that
separated the two rooms of the visitation unit. *Damn. Between the tacos
for lunch and letting myself get carried away with this thing, I've brought
it on myself.*

While he was gone, Paige and the three women arrived at an
agreement. They certainly didn't want to be separated. They would
work with Andy on a statement and stop talking to the media about
life in prison. And they must make their apology profound. For Andy's
sake, Paige reminded them to speak to him one at a time.

"The matron is waiting to see us," she said. "That's her proper title,
but people usually refer to her as the warden, her male counterpart.
She'll be interested to know we worked it out."

They wrapped up their visit when Andy returned, looking a little
peaked but no less eager. It was almost three o'clock, the end of the
Saturday visiting session, when they descended the stairs to find it was
not much cooler down there. Only slightly cooler air churned from
fans at both ends of the hall. The warden, Susan Metcalf Sigurdsson,
was waiting for them.

She was an imposing, Nordic-looking woman. Andy immediately
thought of the buxom Valkyries of opera. All she needed was a flowing
robe, a shield, and a horned helmet.

Warden Sigurdsson had been in charge of the prison for three
years, and it was she who was responsible for its congenial atmosphere.
She brought an element of respect with her and saw that it worked its
way down through the staff and on to the inmates. Staff who couldn't
comply didn't last long. And inmates who behaved respectfully were
rewarded with extra privileges. There had been fewer "inmate incidents"
during her tenure than ever before.

She, of course, was up to date on the Bag Lady dilemma and had
received her share of calls and letters from district attorneys, judges,
police departments, the ACLU, and citizens at large. She had closely
followed the three women's progress through Reception, and at her

urging they had been placed together in her prison. The social scientist in her reasoned that examples of respectful behavior such as theirs would be beneficial to the prison population. And she had been right. Anyone who dealt with them came away smiling.

She had been watching through the plate glass surveillance window from her office at the foot of the stairs to the visitation units. When they emerged, she rose to greet them.

"Well, folks," she said brightly, "I trust you had a good visit and have come to some conclusions. We have a bit of a problem here, and need your help. Could you step in for a minute, all of you?"

The six of them filed into her small, sparsely furnished office. The men helped seat the ladies in the three available chairs, and they and Paige stood quietly behind them. Warden Sigurdsson took her place behind a desk as solid-looking as she was. Her paperweight read "Lord, grant me patience, and I want it *now!*" She got right to the point.

"I don't know if you're aware, ladies, that Reception has become swamped with geriatric inmates, with more of them coming in every day. All of them acting on your lead. All of them referring to the Bag Ladies."

She leaned forward, arms upon the desk, with her fingers clasped to form a steeple. Her eyes swept over the group, not lingering on any one of them long enough to make them uncomfortable.

"We're going to have to convert the gym to handle the overload. Other prisons are in the same fix. But we don't know what we're going to do if the gyms fill up. Now, I must say these old folks make wonderful inmates. Like you, they're very considerate and don't complain. But the problem is we're not a retirement home. We are a prison, designed to protect the public from the misdeeds of criminals while we try to rehabilitate them. I admit we aren't always successful, but we honestly do try."

The three women sat in silence. They had a great deal of respect for the warden, who they guessed to be about fifty-five, although one could never tell with those age-defying Scandinavians.

She appeared to be casual in her approach to them, but Warden Sigurdsson was keenly attuned to their body language. They looked so pitiful, sitting in a row like naughty children brought before the principal. She understood the plight of the elderly poor. The stories she had heard from some of the old ladies flooding Reception could make the Wicked Witch cry.

"We need to ask a favor of you ladies," she continued. "While we are pleased to find you hold our facility in such high esteem, you can understand our dilemma. We can't condone the killing of anyone, *anyone*, under any circumstances, for any reason whatsoever, especially with the misguided notion that doing so earns the reward of lifetime, all-expenses-paid lodging in our establishment."

Josie stared at her in terror. "Are … are you sending us home?" she stammered.

Her words hung heavy in the air.

"Home? We *have* no home!" cried a horrified Mil.

Mabel seemed to crumple. "Are we going to be punished?" she asked. "Oh, dear! We didn't mean to do anything bad." She was ready to promise anything. Unaware that she had picked up Elsie's habit, she began worriedly twisting a strand of hair that had escaped the bun at the base of her neck.

"You can't turn vicious killers loose," croaked Mil. "We're a threat to society!"

The warden couldn't help laughing at the women's responses.

She doesn't know those old women yet, thought Paige. Heaven help her if they get all worked up and start talking circles around each other. But Warden Sigurdsson was quick to calm them.

"My goodness, ladies," she exclaimed. "No, we're not going to send you home, and we're certainly not going to punish you. You have exemplary records here at Frontera. But we do need your help. As I said, your enthusiasm for prison life has become a problem for us."

"We've agreed to apologize, publicly, if that will help," Mabel quickly offered, remembering Rex's words. "We can tell the other old folks not to do what we did. But I don't want to lie about it and say that prison life is terrible when it isn't."

Behind her, Rex gave her shoulder a warm squeeze of encouragement.

"Andy can help us write a statement," she continued. "Of course, you'd have to approve it before it's published. But then, we promise we'll never again speak of prison life to the press—except for Andy and his book."

"At least Senator Farley should be happy," spouted Josie. Once again, she reminded Paige of an angry little hen, feathers ruffled and ready to do battle. "This just gives him all the more reason for the prisons he wants to build, which means he'll be able to loot the Social Security fund after all. You know, it was his scaring us to death about losing our pensions that started the whole thing in the first place. Maybe you should be talking to *him* about this."

Warden Sigurdsson nodded and jotted a few words on a notepad.

"But if it's an apology you need, we'll certainly apologize," Josie went on, regaining her composure. "With some words of wisdom, as well. But, to tell the truth, it's not the old folks who are the problem. It's those darn hoodlums out there who make life difficult for everyone. If the old folks just had a safe place to live and were sure of their pensions, this problem would go away overnight."

Just as when she had first been struck with the idea of living in prison, the memory of Molly Flannery and the base closures popped into her head. Josie the evangelist started in her chair, inspired by her vision.

"The military bases they're closing," she exclaimed. "The Tustin one and the El Toro one! And there must be others around the country, too. Why, they're self-contained little cities, just waiting to be put to use. The old folks could live there, and then at least *some* of the civilian employees wouldn't have to lose their jobs. And you could build little bungalows, where the ladies could plant flowers, and the men could keep things running …"

Warden Sigurdsson watched as Josie went on with plans of retaining the military to keep out the bad people and of the jobs that could be assigned to seniors to help pay their keep. "Then the old folks wouldn't have to kill people to get in *here*," she said, "or go on hunger strikes. If you can keep the bad people out, the old folks will happily live in peace."

The warden had heard of such ideas before. When the government first opened the doors of its mental institutions, thousands of the mentally incompetent took to the streets. It wasn't long before they fell prey to scammers and illegal drugs. Crime-plagued citizens then suggested this very thing: trading places. Filling the emptied institutions with folks seeking safety from this frightening new class of people. They weren't taken seriously at the time. But no one could deny the crisis that existed now.

Not a bad idea, the warden thought, nor a ridiculous one. She knew that military bases could easily be retrofitted. They had housing, as well as small hospitals and commissaries. And they wouldn't cost nearly as much to run as prisons. But she also knew that land developers were lined up ten deep to get their hands on that choice real estate. And big money talks.

Mil broke into the warden's thoughts. "But *we* wouldn't have to go there, would we? With all those old folks? I really like it here, with the younger women. They're a lot more fun. I mean, it's a good idea for old people, but, well, I like it here."

The warden looked from one to the other. "I must say, you ladies think out of the box. I can't promise you anything, but I'll certainly take your idea to the top. You *will* have to apologize, though, and offer some better advice—publicly and sincerely. The attorney general wants to hear it. Then, I trust I can count on you to keep your word about maintaining silence."

Andy, who by now was feeling much better, spoke up and volunteered to work with them on a statement. "We'll have it on your desk as soon as we can," he said. "I guarantee—and I think the ladies will, too—that when it's published the four of us will just fade into the woodwork. I'll still want to write my book, and I'm sure I can convince my editor of the importance of keeping a lid on it." He paused. "They've already agreed not to be interviewed by anyone else. But their escapades have made good copy, you know."

The warden rose from her desk, dismissing them. "I'll get right on the phone to the DA. I'll need to see what you have to say first, of course, and then if Bennings gets it passed by the attorney general, we have a deal."

Paige, Rex, and Andy walked the women back to the visitor's center, with the women chattering all the way about the splendid idea of making snug little retirement homes out of closed military bases. Andy reminded them to work up a rough draft of their suggestions for him to work on. The women had one last chance to be heard. He wanted it to make a difference.

TWENTY-SEVEN

As the days went by, the trickle of older women pouring into the general population of Frontera became a torrent. Two of the old women, Rosa Regalado and Iris Beauregard, called "Buttercup," were assigned rooms near Josie's and Mil's, and the women immediately befriended them.

Rosa, a tense Hispanic woman, was also from Santa Ana. She kept to herself at first but finally talked to them while waiting for lunch one day. She admitted it was a relief to be rid of her husband, Luis, and her two sons.

"They're all alike," she said of them. "They think women are only here to wait on 'em, and they don't never have to be nice to you."

"Did you ... kill them?" asked Josie, prepared to be shocked. This serious, dark-skinned woman with the single, graying braid worn down her back fascinated her. It was hard not to stare at the ragged purple birthmark that encircled her right eye.

"Oh, no," she cried, aghast at the idea and crossing herself. "That would be a mortal sin. No, I just wann'ed t'make things tough for 'em, an' have a little rest for myself, so I tol' on 'em."

There was a pause in the conversation, filled with the drone of conversations going on around them, while the women waited to hear her story.

"I tol' the mailman they was sellin' drugs at our house," she continued, "an' he told the gover'ment. Next thing you know, we *all* go to prison, an' the gover'ment takes the house."

She smiled a secret smile, proud of her cunning.

"But why would you want to go to prison and lose your home?" asked a mystified Mil. "Why didn't you just divorce Luis and make them all leave? Or leave, yourself?"

"Divorce?" replied Rosa. "You must not be Catholic. The Church don't allow it. But I tried runnin' away. Lotsa times. But Luis and his friends always come after me, bring me back, beat me up. Said I was married in God's house, and God says a woman has to do what her husband says."

They could have cried for this worn-out-looking little woman but only shook their heads and murmured no, they were not Catholic.

"They play cards an' sleep all day while I go cleanin' houses and keep me busy all night bringin' 'em food and beer when those drug people come around. Hit me if I'm not fast enough. Broke my arm one time."

Josie couldn't hide her outrage.

"But, Rosa, couldn't you go to a shelter? Or a sister, or one of your daughters … or your priest? Surely the Catholic Church doesn't approve of men abusing their wives."

Rosa looked at her as though she were from another planet.

"A shelter? I don' know what that is. But when I go to the priest, he says you hafta obey your husband, like it says in the Bible, so he don' have to keep beatin' you up. An' how can my sisters an' daughters help me? They have the same problem. Only I can help myself."

She enjoyed another secret little smile and then went on.

"Mrs. Monson, she keeps the television goin' all day. One day when I clean her house I hear a preacher say God loves a man who is good to his wife. He says it's a sin to be mean to her. But that preacher wasn't Catholic, so I wasn't sure.

"Then I hear about you Bag Ladies sayin' how nice prison is, an' right after that I hear how the gover'ment can put you in prison and take away your house if you sell drugs there. So I put it all together and start thinkin'.

"If that preacher's right, God don't want Luis hittin' me with the broom an' knockin' me around. I figured it out: maybe I could send 'im to prison for sellin' drugs an' beatin' me up. Then him an' the boys can't come after me for a while. But then I figure I can't stay in the house, 'cause Luis's friends would get me for tellin'. So I decide we *all* go to prison and let the gover'ment have that old house. I couldn' make the rent by myself, anyway, without the drug money.

"So I took little bags of that white stuff to Mrs. Monson, an' asked did she want to buy any. A'course she didn', but she did just what I wanna'd 'er to, an' tol' on me. So between her an' the mailman, we all go to prison. An' it gives me a year's vacation before I hafta go where Luis and the boys can't find me. When they get out, they won't have nowhere to live or no one to take care of 'em, so they'll have to go to work."

She was clearly pleased with herself and beginning to relax in her new setting. However, Rosa seldom spoke to the women again. Within the year, she died from a ruptured aortal aneurysm.

Buttercup, an aging but feisty black day-care provider, was another matter. Somewhat like Rosa, she had wanted only to try out a short stay in prison before committing to it, but her plan had gone awry at the last minute.

"It was gettin' harder an' harder to keep body an' soul together on five an' a quarter an hour," she said to the group gathered in the lounge after dinner. "Now, I heard about you ladies sayin' prison was such a good place for old folks, an' I think to myself I'd like to try it out first, do a stickup or somethin', before I get myself put in there for good.

"Maybe I was just goin' crazy from all those screamin' little kids every day, needin' fed an' diapered an' pitchers cut out for 'em to paste, but I decided to try stickin' up Mr. Nguyen. He runs the convenience store around the corner from my 'partment. I knew you hadda use a gun to get put in prison, so I got my son's gun—he always keeps it loaded—an' went in there one night and stuck it right in Mr. Nguyen's face. Tol' him to hand over the money. I didn' tell him the safety was on.

"He says, 'Oh, now, Buttacup, is this a joke?' in his funny accent, an' I say, 'No sir, Mr. Nguyen, I gotta take your money. I wanna try livin' in jail awhile, like the Bag Ladies.'

"Well, he give me the money, and I stuff it in my purse an' start on home. An' he call the police. Now, wouldn' you know, that Lionel who lives over by ol' Mrs. Wilson, he come runnin' up and take my purse right outta my hand and just keep on goin'!

"Now I was mad. He was ruinin' my plan! But before I could figure out what to do, I hear a lotta shoutin', and here come a white boy, who's took the purse away from Lionel, an' he's runnin' like the devil with Lionel right behind 'im. Gits to me and grabs me to put between hisself and Lionel, an' says he'll shoot if Lionel don' go away.

"I tol' you I was already mad. So I just says to myself, 'Okay, honky boy, you askin' for it.' An I shot 'im, deader'n a stump. Lionel, he takes off runnin', an' by the time the police come, why I'm standin' there with a purseful'a Mr. Nguyen's money an' a smokin' gun, an' a dead man who don' have no weapon on 'im.

"So I gotta stay here for three years. If I don' like it, I'll see can I get my job back. But if I *do* like it, they better keep me locked up, 'cause I'll tell 'em I'm doin' it again. An' I would, too."

No one had spoken during the telling of her almost unbelievable story. But the moment she was through, the others besieged her with questions, leaving Josie, Mabel, and Mil to stare at each other, wondering what they had started.

During her stay, Buttercup became an invaluable mentor to the younger inmates, teaching them everything she had learned about preschool parenting.

District Attorney Rupert T. Bennings III couldn't keep up with phone calls from the U.S. attorney general, police departments all over the country, the ACLU, the American Bar Association, the FBI, the

IRS, the AARP, every kind of church, his own people, and the media. With the Bag Ladies as their example, old folks were finding every way they could to get into prison. The FBI, the IRS, and even the CIA had callers backed up on hold, waiting to report one felony or another. The situation was unprecedented; it was hoped that some of the callers would grow tired of waiting and hang up. There simply wasn't the manpower to deal with all of them.

It was the same all over the country: police forces strained beyond their ability to cope and sirens shattering the air at all hours. Old folks either were apprehended at the scene of a crime or simply walked into police stations claiming to have killed someone or committed some felony. And no one knew what to do about it.

NEWS IS THE FIRST DRAFT OF HISTORY read the new, framed sign on Andy's desk. He no longer doubted that history was being made all around him, and that fate had somehow appointed him to chronicle it. He and the women continued to work on what he called their manifesto, although the women weren't so sure about that word. It sounded much too brazen and unladylike. They preferred to consider more refined words like *guidelines* or *affirmation*.

Until their statement was submitted and approved, however, he toned down his updates for the *Orange County Register*, for fear of incurring the wrath of the DA. He knew the DA could refuse the right to publish their statement if he considered Andy a firebrand. His carefully worded articles appeared all over the nation, and were disseminated on TV and radio.

The whole world read and watched incredulously as the news of America's senior uprising reached them. It seemed the war on crime had provided jobs in every community with a jail full of seniors. Townsfolk were hired to prepare food and worked after hours at local laundries. In many cities, armories were hastily converted to hold the overflow in patched-together quarters. And no senior had been known to try to escape. In fact, if threatened with release, they usually vowed to step up their war on crime.

Andy read and clipped press releases from all over the country:

From the Lancaster, Pennsylvania, *Press*: "Police report a rash of activity at the Golden Days low-income senior project north of town. As in cities all over the nation, groups of Golden Days residents have formed what are being called posses and are patrolling the streets of Lancaster, Philadelphia, Harrisburg, and Allentown. The patrolling seniors, who often carry small American flags, have laid claim to the killing of a number of purported gang members and street criminals, as well as the shooting death of a prominent Harrisburg physician, Dr. Alan Hayes. Hayes had practiced medicine in the area for many years, and was recently convicted of running a prescription drug mill and Medicare fraud.

"Although the seniors decline trials, the Pennsylvania State District Attorney feels a trial will be necessary to establish if some of the crimes they lay claim to were indeed committed by them or were ever committed at all. The ACLU is demanding an investigation."

From the *Washington Post*: "Police across the nation have been unable to restrain warring factions of flag-carrying senior citizens and reputed gang members. As a result of their encounters, hospitals and mortuaries in many communities are reporting a severe strain on services. In a reversal of policy, the ACLU has demanded curfews for everyone, as well as immediate gun control laws. They urge the president of the United States to intervene."

From the Sacramento *Bee*: "Groups who feed the homeless in the metropolitan area are reporting a sharp decline in customers. We suspect many who would ordinarily use their services are steering clear of senior citizens, often armed, who patrol the city. Flag-carrying seniors can also be seen near schools and parks, effectively eliminating drug trafficking and loitering. Do we see a faint vision of Camelot emerging through the smoke and tears of our elders' war on crime?"

To round out his collection, Andy added a clipping from the two-page Langdon, North Dakota, *Tattler*. "Looks like we have what no one else has: happy old people. We can't report any of our senior citizens wanting to be in our fine jail. Of course, they know Lars Svensen is the cook, and they'd have to contend with the snoring of Uncle Billy Bodeen most Saturday nights. Guess we have about the best deterrent to crime anywhere."

He also included an earlier article from the *Los Angeles Times* headlined BAFFLED GOVERNMENT SPENDS MORE ON PRISONS THAN ON EDUCATION. That should help get the point across, he thought.

He used a glue stick to paste the newest clippings with all the others in his loose-leaf notebook. This is so easy, he thought. His book was practically being written for him. He couldn't wait for the final, and probably equally unbelievable, last chapter.

Paige had little time to think about Rex McClung in the ensuing days. Her department was overwhelmed, trying to be everywhere at once. Exhausted and out of sorts as she often found herself, the irony of the situation was almost comical. The very search and seizure laws behind which criminals had been accustomed to hiding were the ones now being used by patrolling seniors and questioned by the ACLU.

Search and seizure laws forbade police from stopping patrols of seniors, even those openly waving their little American flags, who, they were certain, carried weapons with the intention of using them. People couldn't be stopped for simply walking in groups and carrying little flags any more than gang members could be stopped for identifying themselves in gang-style attire and colors. However, the seniors made sure to comport themselves properly, giving the police no reason to stop them.

On top of that, easy access to handguns made it possible for seniors to have just as many weapons as their opponents. The older men also had the advantage of prior military training. It took very little to rekindle their Korean Conflict fervor, for within each aging breast beat the ever-young heart of a warrior. As for the senior women, those who didn't have the stomach for war simply joined a hunger strike at their city hall, demanding permanent and safe lodging in prison.

This was the first time Paige had been at her desk in days. And now the ringing of her private line interrupted her train of thought. She had ignored it most of the morning, but something made her pick it up. It was Rex. And he wanted to meet her for dinner at Nieuport 17 in Tustin. Tonight.

Caught off guard, she stammered, "Tonight? Is it open? You know, all the patrols and everything?"

Memories of their ride home from visiting the women in prison washed over her mind. They hadn't said much of anything personal, mostly just discussed Andy and the women, but she had been acutely aware of him. And it seemed he'd lingered over saying good-bye. Now he called her in the middle of a war, not just to go to dinner but to *dine* at Nieuport 17.

He assured her he'd checked it out. Her thoughts tumbled as she listened to him speak. He must be serious. The restaurant named for the one-man, open- cockpit French plane from World War I, was a seriously expensive place, a place she'd been only a few times on very special occasions. She remembered the portrait of the famous plane hanging in the lobby and the ambiance of the warm, wood-paneled interior. War memorabilia adorned the ceilings and walls, everything from a World War I airplane propeller to signed photographs of the astronauts. You couldn't be at a loss for conversation there.

It had seemed a fitting place to meet, he was saying, considering the town was virtually at war. She heard the wail of sirens in the background from wherever he was calling.

"Great," she said, trying to sound casual. She hadn't taken time for an evening out since who knew when. And the past two weeks had been killers—literally.

"I'll have to come just the way I am, though," she said. "Captain's going nuts with this thing and has us in a meeting at five. Meet you there at seven? I have an early morning."

She never thought she'd be tongue-tied, but as much as she wanted to hold on to that voice at the other end of the line, she couldn't think of a thing to say that was worthy of keeping him there. She prayed she wouldn't make a fool of herself tonight.

TWENTY-EIGHT

Like women's prison gym conversions all over the country, remodeling of the gym to living quarters at Frontera was swiftly accomplished. It had required miles of new plumbing and electrical lines, as well as cutting in windows all around the perimeter. The existing forty-foot ceiling would allow for carving out a second story if it should be needed.

Although many of the inmates hated to give up their gym, there was no other immediate solution to the problem. Frontera hadn't been designed to hold so many women. Warden Sigurdsson promised a new gym would be built at the far end of the enclosure. But it would take time and wouldn't be as convenient. The swarm of new residents also meant there were no longer enough jobs to go around. This gave the women a little more free time to do their own thing. The trade-off was well received by all but the athletes. They resented both the old women and the loss of the gym to use in their free time.

Although strained from the overload, the staff was pleased to see many of the younger inmates assisting the oldsters who arrived from Reception. Those whose social skills had kept them on the bottom rung of life's ladder were finding a way to rise above their inadequacies.

All it took was someone to appreciate them. And these someones were non-threatening older women.

The second wave of oldsters from Reception to the newly converted gym brought a radiant Ophelia Jackson. She was ecstatic to be safe, well cared for, and among so many kind women. The three women couldn't believe their eyes when they met her in the lunch line on one of her first days there. The shrieking and hugging that ensued forced the guard who oversaw the lunch line, Sergeant Dawayne, to break it up. "You know the rules, ladies," she told them sternly.

Sergeant Mary Dawayne was a stolid, seven-year veteran of overseeing inmates at Frontera. She could be very pleasant if approached properly but was a brick wall to those who behaved like animals. She'd seen about everything in here and was less sure than the warden about the concept of rehabilitation for some of these women. A lot of them were too badly damaged, with no concept of how to make a better life. She saw these kinds return to prison again and again, until they finally drank or drugged themselves to death or were killed in a confrontation of some sort. Sad as it was, prison was the kindest environment they knew. When she finally got over the pity of it and accepted it as an irrefutable fact, it made her life much easier. So did the addition of all the old ladies, who seemed happy to be here and got along just fine.

Still, she couldn't permit them to hug each other or scream. She had been trained that just such a thing could set off a riot or start a fight or an attack on a guard. They'd had few riots or attacks, but as a precaution, every inmate had to keep her hands to herself and her voice down. Hugging was permitted only with visitors in the secure visitor's area, and loud voices were not tolerated anywhere.

The four women all apologized to Sergeant Dawayne and resumed their proper prison demeanor. But they were bursting to talk to each other.

"What in the world did you do to get in here?" Josie exclaimed, once they were seated for lunch. Ophelia Jackson seemed incapable of anything bad.

Ophelia shook her head, still a bit confused. She said everything had been a blur since the day she had fearfully responded to the pounding on her door, gun in hand as her children had instructed her. They'd known that the Simbas would be back.

"And there stood two of 'em, them Simbas, one of 'em pointin' a gun at me, sayin' it was me blowed up their crack house an' all their frien's. Well, bless me, right on the spot I become one a'them 'Ornery Christian Soldiers, Marchin' as to War,' like the song says. An' I shot 'em. Right there through the screen door. No use arguin' with 'em or I'd be the one is dead.

"Well, that was an awful day, just an awful day. But when I fin' out about *you* bein' the Bag Ladies, I say to the Lord, 'Oh, Lord, Lord, take me to 'em; we have some *talkin'* to do." She laughed her bighearted laugh, looking perfectly natural in her flowing muumuu.

It was nothing the three women were proud of, having left Mrs. Jackson with no explanation and possibly in danger. She could have been the only real victim of their war on crime if there were any Simbas left to retaliate.

"When we regained our senses we realized what a terrible thing we'd done. We abused your hospitality and then abandoned you," declared Josie, with Mabel and Mil nodding an emphatic agreement. Sergeant Dawayne was still keeping an eye on them, so she kept her voice down.

"I hope you can forgive us. Everything just happened too fast. But it was still shameless of us to blow up your whole neighborhood and leave you behind to bear the consequences. Thank goodness you're okay, and it's an honor to have you join us!"

Ophelia acknowledged Josie's apology with a smile of genuine forgiveness. "Well, people has to do what people has to do," she said kindly. "Besides, you doin' that's the thing that got me here, outta that mess I been livin' in. I'd be there yet, if not for you ladies."

She dabbed with her napkin at the perspiration on her brow and then used it to fan herself. "Whew! I thought I'd git outta the heat here.

Thought sure it'd be air-conditioned. But tha's okay. Winter's comin'. An' that'll take care'a the flies, too."

She went on to exclaim over the hearty lentil soup and good bread Josie's crew had baked in culinary the day before. "Now *this* is livin'," she exclaimed. "People so nice. No shootin' an' fightin', an' all this good food."

From that day forward, they ate almost every meal together, and their table continued to be the happiest one in the dining room.

Ophelia was assigned to clerical, where she applied with gusto all her old skills as file clerk for the county of Los Angeles. She was an upbeat influence on everyone around her, and began every day with a prayer of thanks for her new life.

With their newly assigned free time, Josie, Mabel, and Mil set to work in earnest to help the other inmates improve themselves. Ophelia would have loved to join their sessions in the lounge of their cottage. But rules forbade anyone to be anywhere but her own cottage when she was not scheduled for something. So she worked with the inmates of the converted gym where she was housed, placing herself in charge of souls. And no one could have done it better.

The three women joined the joke-telling in the lounge at first but soon found that neither group understood the other's humor. The young ones' jokes dealt with things the old ones couldn't figure out, such as the bird representing true love being the swallow, and the old ones' jokes left the young ones waiting for the punch line, as when Mabel recited her favorite limerick:

"There once was a fellow named Clyde,
Who fell in the outhouse and died.
Then along came his brother and fell in the other,
And now they're interred side by side."

Few of the young women knew about two-holer outhouses or what the word *interred* meant, so the joke and its play on words was lost on them. But they did laugh at hearing the usually prudish Mabel say "in turd side by side."

Mil tried a Polish joke: "Did you hear about the lady who had a wooden baby?" she asked.

"Let me guess," offered her roommate, Betsy. "She got splinters?"

Over the laughter that answer provoked, Mil cried, "No! She married a Pole!" No one seemed to get it. They much preferred Betsy's answer.

Josie, too, got a laugh with one of her jokes. But it was the only one the others found funny.

"This lady went into the butcher shop," she began, "and asked for a pound of kiddlies. The butcher looked at her and said, 'Kiddlies? You mean kidneys, don't you?' Insulted, the lady responded, 'I said kiddlies, diddle I?'"

From then on, "I said kiddlies, diddle I?" became the catchphrase for being confused or making a mistake. However, there were those who simply enjoyed using the word *diddle* in as many rude ways as they could. But their innuendoes went over the heads of most of the older ladies.

They quickly gave up joke-telling in favor of trying to bring something positive to the younger women. They were careful to make their teaching sessions seem spontaneous. They knew the younger women wouldn't have joined in if they thought the old women just wanted to preach and nag at them.

Ordinarily, women talking in large groups were considered suspect, and the corrections officers in charge of each cottage would break them up and move them on. But they had been instructed by Warden Sigurdsson just to watch, if two or more old women were involved, and see what came of it. She had great faith in these wise old women.

Today's gathering in the lounge after dinner included all three of their roommates, Elsie, LaShondra, and Betsy, as well as a handful of other girls. It started off, as it often did, with a rehash of a movie they'd seen on TV, an easy way to set the stage for a good talk. But they had to be sure to keep their voices down so they wouldn't disturb those who were watching television.

"I'm gonna git me a rich one nex' time, like she did," drawled LaShondra, referring to Julia Roberts in the movie *Pretty Woman*. "I'm tellin' ya right now, shit don' happen if ya got money."

Her dull expression showed she thought life was just that simple: nothing required of her, no course of action to be taken between the wanting and the getting. Just saying those words satisfied her simple concept of self-improvement.

"I'm not goin' for no lowlife no more. I don' need none a'that shit no more. When I get the fuck … oops … when I get outta here, get this baby outta me …"

Josie ears always reddened when she heard coarse language. As often as she heard it here at Frontera, she couldn't get used to it. However, LaShondra had grown fond of Josie, and, like many of the other young women who found their language offensive to the older ladies, she really had been trying to clean it up.

"Thank you, LaShondra," Josie said. "But remember, Richard Gere liked Julia Roberts because she *tried* to be a lady. You can't expect a rich man to treat you like a lady if you don't act like one. Those lowlifes you complain about, they're the ones who go for garbage-mouths. They take it as a sign they don't have to treat you right. You'll never get someone with money to respect you until you respect yourself and act like a lady."

"And what do you think you have to offer this man with money?" added Mabel, sensing they had a good topic by the tail. "What reason would he have to choose you over any other woman? Could you balance the checkbook and raise your children to be intelligent and productive? Would he be proud to have you help entertain his friends? Tell us why a man with big bucks would entrust his money to you."

Everyone was silent as LaShondra struggled to think this over. Obviously, she'd never thought of such things as personal assets.

Betsy laughed at her quandary, assuring LaShondra that life was a two-way street. "You're expectin' money outta him, honey, he's got a right to expect somethin' outta you," she said. "So, what? What's it gonna be?"

"Whatchoo think, girl," LaShondra replied with a mischievous smile, certain she had the right answer this time. "He git all the sweet ass—I mean lovin'—he ever need, tha's what he git. S'all any of 'em ever want. They ain't even gonna fool with ya if ya don' give 'em lotsa lovin'. An' a baby or two, so they can prove they's a man. Shit, some'a them home boys got eight, ten kids all over town, so the others gotta treat 'em with respec'. An' we can see I doin' fine in the baby-makin' department, so I don' have to worry none about *that!*" She smiled, patting the small bulge of her tummy. "Excep' this baby goin' to someone else. Someone else gonna git the gover'ment check fer this one."

"And who takes care of these babies!" asked a horrified Mil. By now, a few more women had joined their group, curious at their animated discussion.

LaShondra looked at her blankly. "They mamas do, who else? Or them foster homes. They git 'nuff from the gover'ment; they doin' awright."

"And the men, the fathers of these babies, what do they do?" asked Mil, fearing she wasn't going to like the answer to this question any better than the last one.

LaShondra shrugged, showing that it didn't matter. Their manhood was proved, and that was all that counted.

Josie could sit still no longer.

"You're willing to be used and thrown away, just so these men, these lowlifes, can prove something we all know anyway, that men and women can make babies? LaShondra, that's crazy. If you let them use you and throw you away, then *you're* a lowlife, too. You have *choices*, LaShondra, and the kind of life you make for yourself depends on the *choices* you make. You can start right now. You have a life to live, and you can honor your loved ones by living it well."

Josie met Mabel's eyes. The swift but poignant exchange between them spoke volumes. If their old support group could hear them now! Surely no one had benefited more from that slogan than they.

Josie tried to stifle the urgency in her voice, for fear of driving LaShondra away. She knew she wouldn't get anywhere with her if she became too impatient or judgmental.

"Babies need a home, with a father and a mother, and the dignity to grow into responsible people," she said. "You have to think about them, too. They shouldn't be looked upon as little welfare checks. They should be the joy of your life. The future of our country."

"Just producing babies doesn't make a guy a man, anyway," added Mabel. "*Real* men do important things, like taking care of their families, protecting their country, and using their brains to make the world a better place. Like the people you admire in movies. And *real women* help, too, whether they have babies or not."

She felt it was important to speak up. She thought she was a pretty good example of a childless women who was, nevertheless, a real woman. And certainly Earl was nothing short of a real man.

"This talk reminds me of what my mother told me when I was just getting interested in boys," said Mil, smiling with the memory. "She reminded me that every girl has the same 'equipment' as I had, and that guys weren't very choosy about who they stuck their you-know-whats in. Any girl who'd let them would do. In fact, she said even a knothole would do in a pinch." She laughed along with the others, agreeing that "pinch" described it well, and then continued.

"She said it was a fact that a guy's brains were 'down there,' which naturally made it difficult for him to think of anything else. She swore a guy would tell you anything you wanted to hear just so he wouldn't have to use a knothole."

The group enjoyed a good laugh at her quaint rendition of the birds and the bees.

"But that was another time, before we had AIDS to think about," she went on. "Life was a lot simpler before AIDS and before the pill liberated men."

"You mean before the pill liberated *women*," corrected LaShondra, proud to help educate Mil. "The women takes the pill, 'less they wants the baby."

"No," said Mil. "I meant before the pill liberated *men*. Women were just *told* it was they who were being liberated. Remember, women had to be very careful before the advent of the pill. Having sex, even if you were married or using condoms, was a pretty serious thing because of the consequences. So I guess guys used a lot of knotholes in those days and expected no one with any sense to have sex with them until they were safely married. But once they got the pill, women couldn't risk holding out for marriage anymore. They might lose their man to a more 'liberated' woman. My mother always said, 'Why would a man buy the cow when the milk is free?' So women were reduced to having to prove their love, hoping for marriage, while men were happily freed of both commitments and condoms. Well, that really played havoc with unwanted pregnancies, especially among teenagers, and spread all kinds of diseases. But it did enable men to give up knotholes!"

Everyone laughed, but Mil's twisted interpretation had been lodged in their heads. The idea that things were not always what they seemed, and could be two different things at once, gave them something to think about.

"LaShondra," said Josie, hoping the moment was right, "let's make a real lady out of you. You can show those lowlifes a thing or two and move on to the big leagues, where decent men look for a lady with class. You can do it, LaShondra. You're lovely. You don't want to spend the rest of your life like this, bouncing from one man to another, having to live by your wits. All we have to do is get your GED and work on a new language. I'll help you after lockdown. We can make you an asset in any office."

Josie didn't know what to expect from LaShondra, but some of the other women began to encourage her with, "Right on, LaShondra," and "Don't think they're gonna let you outta here till you get that GED anyway, LaShondra. Better go for it." and "Maybe you could help me, too, Josie."

Elsie had silently taken it all in. She now looked at Josie and Mabel with hope in her eyes. "Do you think you could do me over, too? I mean, you know, help me?"

Mabel acted as though the thought had never occurred to her. "Why, Elsie," she said with feigned surprise, "that would be fun. Just like they do in the movies. We could make a new woman out of you before you ever leave here. You could have a *real* man instead of some nasty old con man. I've seen you typing over in clerical. You'd have no trouble getting a really good job with a new, professional image."

Elsie stood beaming through the flushed blisters on her face, nervously twisting a strand of oily hair around her finger. She loved Mabel. Mabel took the time to talk to her and would always listen. Mabel beamed back at her, hoping visions of Marilyn Monroe weren't flitting through Elsie's head. If so, Elsie was going to be greatly disappointed.

LaShondra was still thinking. She was definitely interested but puzzled.

"A new lang'rage?" she asked. "What lang'rage?"

"English," replied Josie.

Things weren't quite so easy in the men's prisons. The younger ones, who made up most of the prison population, hated the old men for what had brought them here. They were executioners of other young men like themselves. Proof was in the fact there had been few young men entering the prison system in these past weeks but, instead, droves of old ones.

The Department of Corrections knew it would cause a riot to take away the men's gyms, so portable buildings, similar to the ones used in many schools, were brought in and placed in securely fenced-off sections of the prison yards. Each was redesigned to house the older men in small, self-contained rooms. The buildings were not as secure as the main buildings, but that didn't seem to be a problem, because none of the old men wanted out. Most of them just wanted to watch

TV and play cards and were very appreciative of the food and laundry services. They didn't need room to run races or play football, and never at any time, for their own safety, did they cross paths with the general population.

Young men nearing their parole dates grew increasingly nervous about going back out on the streets and meeting up with the patrolling oldsters, although they generally blustered about how they were going to single-handedly wipe all those old farts off the face of the earth. What good were the half-deaf, limp-pricked old has-beens, anyway? The agitation became almost palpable in some prisons, calling for stringent measures to keep the thinly held tension from erupting into fights.

Corrections quickly recognized that these old men had attributes the younger men would benefit from learning. As an experiment, young men who seemed good candidates were sprinkled in among the old men. When that went well, they sprinkled in a few more. The area hummed along efficiently—no fights and few arguments. Instead of congregating in the weight room, the old men gave the library a workout, exposing the young men to it, as well. Among the old men were professionals of all kinds, and they enjoyed helping the young men study for whatever degree or trade they were attempting to learn. It seemed fun for the oldsters to regain what they had forgotten, right along with the younger men.

The old folks' war on crime had earned them great rewards, even as it strained the prison system in every sense. It had also changed the face of corrections forever.

"My fellow citizens," intoned the president of the United States on prime-time TV, "we are at a hard place in our history." With his droopy, sad-dog eyes and heavy jowls, he always looked troubled.

"Our country is at war with itself, generation against generation, household against household, neighborhood against neighborhood. Our prisons are overflowing, and law enforcement is stretched to the breaking point. I fear for all of you who try to go about your business, as you must, in the face of open warfare on our city streets."

Mark Wisneski took a long draw on his Budweiser and said to the TV, "Sure, Prez, that's easy for you to say. You guys in your ivory towers never have to come down and deal with things the average Joe has to deal with. Whatta you know about being raped and robbed and shot on these city streets you speak of? Or having your kid offered drugs on the way to school or your car stolen right out from under you? Huh? You have an army of Secret Service agents around you everywhere you go, and so do your lawmaking cronies."

He shifted positions on the kid-proof Olefin sofa, propping his stockinged feet on Alison's lap. She gazed lovingly at him, stroking his legs with her manicured fingers, and gave his thigh a meaningful squeeze.

It was such a treat for Alison to have him home, if only for one short evening. In anticipation of having him to herself on occasions now grown rare, she kept herself slim and fit, working out at the gym at least four days a week. Her pony-tailed auburn hair made her look much too young to be the mother of two teenagers, who, at the moment, were doing schoolwork in their rooms.

A candle she'd brought back from Hawaii glowed on the coffee table in front of them, scenting the air with the musky fragrance of a warm tropic night. She hoped he could switch gears from the unrelenting stress of these oldsters' uprising long enough to remember how much she loved him.

The president droned on. "... if you can have forbearance with one another, in the great American tradition of 'live and let live,' respecting your neighbor for his differences rather than hating him for them. We are a nation of many races of people and many different cultures, all of them blending together to produce ..."

"Chaos," shouted Mark. "Even our local cultures don't know what the hell the rules are! We're all held hostage by the crap that's clogged up our cities and turned 'em into stinking cesspools. And with your help, sir!"

He took another pull on the can of beer before brandishing it at the screen, still yelling. "Let 'em have guns and medical and just enough to get by on without workin'; then you're back to your ivory tower, and ... presto! They've reproduced more just like 'em." He jerked his feet from Alison's lap and back to the floor, straining over the coffee table to yell at the TV. "Twice as many of 'em, tryin' to make us feel bad if we don't want to give 'em more freebies and entitlements, and now they're busy helping themselves to what their neighbor has, too."

"... terrorizing those less fortunate than we, in this great land of plenty," continued the president. The camera panned in on his sad face, emphasizing the sorrow in his rheumy eyes. "It is so ungrateful of our senior citizens, upon whom fortune has lavished the highest standard of living anywhere in the civilized world ..."

"Yeah? Come down out of the clouds and look around, buddy," shouted Mark. "The prisons you build for your precious 'less fortunate than we' beat the shit out of what a lot of these old-timers have. Why else would they be so desperate to get there? They're old and barely getting by, and they're scared silly of those thieving, murdering 'less fortunate than we'!"

He jumped up and viciously pointed the TV remote at the image of the pontificating president, silencing him in a sputter of light, and then sat muttering to himself in the sudden quiet.

Alison knew when to leave him alone and had retreated to the kitchen during his last outburst. A bologna sandwich—a *big* bologna sandwich—oozing with catsup, mayonnaise, and mustard and dripping with the juice of sliced dill pickles would settle him down again. It always did.

Who in hell's advising the president? Mark wondered. He was sure most congressmen were too busy with their own agendas and big contributors and junkets to want to mess with it. Besides, since the oldsters' rampage had begun, he'd heard that most politicians had buried themselves in more bodyguards than ever and couldn't be reached for comment. The more crooked they were, the more bodyguards.

No one had ever taken old people seriously. He knew enough political science to know that a government watches for conditions that might incite a particular group to riot. The government's job was to keep things from reaching that point. But he bet nowhere in their precious manuals was there any mention of angry old people getting it together to make up one of those identifiable groups.

Well, the worm has turned, he thought. It may not have teeth to bite the hand that fed it, as the president was suggesting, but old folks, like caterpillars within their cocoons, had emerged as angry moths, hungry to excise the national fabric of its moral decay. If the nation were to save itself, it would need to be cleaned up, from top to bottom.

Alison returned with a plate barely able to hold the mountainous sandwich she had put together. Agitated as he was, she knew today was not the day to help him improve his eating habits. The best she could do was to substitute a sectioned apple for his usual potato chips.

"Come on upstairs when you're through," she said, toying with the top button of her blouse. "The kids have turned in. I'll have dessert waiting."

TWENTY-NINE

As LaShondra grew heavier with the baby growing within her, she would find it more difficult to climb to her upper bunk at night. In anticipation of this, six weeks before her due date she was to be transferred to another room where she would have a lower bunk vacated by a parolee. She and Josie would miss each other, for they had developed an easy companionship. But they hoped to be reunited after the birth of the baby.

Neither of them had imagined the fun they would have with their "New LaShondra" program, and LaShondra surprised both herself and Josie with her willingness to work on the basics for her General Equivalency Diploma. But fractions had always stumped her, and she was certain she'd never get beyond multiplying by two, until Josie made it visual for her with a piece of modeling clay.

In the arts room, Josie had LaShondra, and anyone else who wanted to join them, roll out a chunk of clay between the palms of her hands, and then instructed her to break it into specific fractions, all the while writing down the steps she was taking. Then she had her methodically put the pieces back together again, noting how the ratio between them changed.

Josie wrote multiplication factors on separate slips of paper and stuck them on the fixtures of their room, until LaShondra remembered that the toilet was 3 × 3 = 9, and the wall switch was 3 × 9 = 27. It would be a challenge, Josie knew, to find new places to hang her combinations as they worked their way up the multiplication table. But she would worry about that when the time came.

In the evenings, they worked on diction. Holding her finger across LaShondra's lips and forcing her to touch it with her tongue when speaking, LaShondra quickly progressed to the point where the word "with" was no longer "wit" and, using the same principle with the puckering of her lips, "lang'rage" had become "language." Part of her homework was to listen to newscasters speak and try to copy them. It pleased Josie to see LaShondra enjoy her new sense of power. Although LaShondra seemed reluctant to let anyone but Josie know it, she came to look forward to their work sessions.

Mabel reported similar results with Elsie, who took the whole thing very seriously. She scrubbed herself from head to toe every day, with the understanding that she wouldn't be able to experiment with makeup until they could get her skin cleared up. She eagerly practiced proper posture in walking, sitting, and standing. The only part of the program she didn't like was limiting her fat intake: no more potato chips, fewer candy bars, and lots of fruit to replace them. But she complied and even struggled with sit-ups and jogging in place in their room at night, thrilled to see her new image slowly emerge.

"They just needed someone who cared," Josie said to Mabel when they compared notes at dinner. "Someone to work with them. They're really sweet girls at heart. They want to do things right but just never knew what the right thing was."

"It's so rewarding to think we might really be changing their lives for good," agreed Mabel. "If they can just keep it up, they'll be wonderful examples for everyone else. And eventually, we hope, good wives to some deserving young men."

They looked at each other. "Hap and Hali!" they cried in unison.

One afternoon LaShondra didn't appear for her math lesson. And she wasn't in the dining room for the evening meal. A gnawing anxiety overcame Josie and kept her searching among the other diners for that familiar face. After all, it wasn't as though LaShondra could have just stepped out to the market.

Josie was about to approach Sergeant Dawayne for an explanation when Sergeant Dawayne instead approached her, asking her to step over to where they could speak privately. She led Josie to a quiet spot near the food station, marveling at her frailty. It was hard to believe that only months before she had lugged around a loaded .38 and caused unparalleled murder and mayhem. Nevertheless, Josie and the rest of this table of old ladies had become her favorite charges, and it was hard for her not to show it.

"I'm afraid your roommate, LaShondra, had her baby early this afternoon," she said quietly to Josie, who stood in dread of what she was going to hear. She had somehow known it would be news of LaShondra and that the news wouldn't be good.

"She went into labor and didn't know what was happening. She's okay. The baby was small and came easily. But the baby didn't make it. Too early and had too many problems. They'll keep LaShondra for ten days, let her get over it, and then she'll be back."

Josie stood rooted to the floor, her eyes riveted to Officer Dawayne's face. When she could trust her voice, she asked, "Is she all right? And the baby ... was it a boy or a girl?"

"She's okay, and it was a girl," said the guard. "And I hear she named her for you, Josephine Ellen."

The national turmoil peaked but was not over. Many seniors were just hearing of the benefits being enjoyed by the first flush of elders who now resided peacefully in prison. They found that once the long-standing social barriers had successfully been crossed, the rewards were sweet. Better late than never, they reasoned, cleaning their guns and getting in a little practice before hitting the streets. The result was fewer loiterers brave enough to hang out on the streets and become targets for their patrolling elders.

And no laws existed to keep these oldsters from walking the streets in groups or declining a trial before being put in prison. The attorney general and the head of the American Bar Association, with all their resources, did their best to find an obscure law that might force these oldsters to face some kind of trial for the benefit of young lawyers who needed work. But their research produced nothing.

At the same time the oldsters were declining legal services, the numbers of young criminals, who ordinarily provided a need for court-appointed attorneys, became a mere trickle. The Bar Association was in turmoil. If this kept up, there would be a mass exodus from the profession. Already there was chaos among attorneys as they jockeyed for available cases.

The ACLU huddled in many a session, its members still deadlocked in argument over rescinding its historic stand against handgun laws and curfews. And what to do with these oldsters remained a mystery. They had effectively bastardized the prison system, increasingly turning prisons into old folks' homes from which there seemed to be no turning back. It didn't bother the old folks that they were felons, and unrepentant felons at that. They promised more of the same if they were released from their safe havens.

Congress knew it had to do something and do it quickly. Laws must be passed to restrain these old folks if law and order, as currently defined, were to survive. The stickler was that the insurgent old folks had nothing to lose and everything to gain. And they were encouraged by their fellow Americans, who rejoiced that the nation might be brought back to a better place by those who remembered how it used to be.

Senator Farley was able to harangue on the noble senior citizen, "who has earned his Social Security pension as a grateful nation's reward for a life of labor and love of country," without missing a beat. A politician to the core, his doublespeak was meant to ensure that he would go down in history as "the patriot who rescued our great nation from the brink of a certain disaster," obliquely taking credit for instigating "safe housing in converted military bases for those in need."

He went on to extol the virtues of the elderly, "who could depend on their dedicated servant, Edmond Jordan Farley, to see that their pensions not only remained intact but were raised to the level due our revered elders." And he didn't even blush. But he was under strict orders from the attorney general, who had a way of making things happen.

In the midst of all this confusion, Josie, Mabel, and Mil's Declaration of Interdependence was published. At Andy's suggestion, it had been fashioned using the format of the nation's Declaration of Independence, with all its splendid language. But upon seeing his rough draft, the three women voted to modernize it.

"People want to know what we have to say at a glance," said Josie. "They don't want to wade through all that archaic stuff to get to the meat of it, no matter how pretty it sounds."

Mabel agreed. "I'm afraid they'll think we're lecturing them—and there are a lot of people out there who are much smarter than we are."

"All they want is an apology and a few words about why we did it," said Mil. "But I do like the part that says it's our duty, when things get bad, to correct them. That's what we're all about. And it wouldn't hurt to remind them what their *country's* all about."

They worked well together, each giving full weight to the others' ideas. The hardest job for Andy was to keep them from going in all directions at once, but he was happy they let him include a couple of "whereases." He helped them understand that in view of the chaos they had created, they really did need to explain themselves.

Judge S. Carter Thompson sat at his breakfast table, the morning paper spread out before him. He had read their declaration several times, amazed at the clarity of it. He had been right. Those seemingly befuddled old ladies were no dummies.

He looked at his watch, pushed away from the table with the screech of chair legs on wood, and rose, stretching and yawning, to his feet. The docket was full this morning, as usual, with old folks waiting to plead guilty to one thing or another, refusing trials, and wanting their turn at free room and board and the accompanying safety. He knew better than to ask himself when it would end. He feared it never would.

Reaching over to gulp the last of his coffee, he started to fold up the paper and then stopped himself and left it open. Somehow, it seemed wrong to lock the words inside. He hoped people everywhere were reading it.

Declaration of Interdependence
of the People
of the United States of America
By
Mabel Esther Rockwell,
Mildred Edith Steinberger, and Josephine Ellen Winkworth
With
Andrew Joseph Krach

When in the course of human events it becomes necessary for one people to rise above the bonds of subjugation in which another people have placed them, a decent respect to the opinions of mankind requires that they should declare the causes which impel them to action. We were conceived a free nation, united in peacetime and in war, every citizen a part of the greater whole, depended upon to shoulder whatever responsibility may be required of him so that our chosen form of government might prosper. Our collective well-being therefore relies on the goodwill and honorable actions of every citizen.

At issue before our nation are the Constitution's promise of life, liberty, and the pursuit of happiness and the equally important promise of equal protection to all. These lofty principles are balanced by the Declaration of Independence, which grants that should we be reduced to an insufferable state by those who have become destructive to its intent, it is our right, it is our duty, to provide new measures for our future security.

At this time, the abuses of which we speak are perpetrated by a growing number of citizens who exploit the precious rights for which others have fought and died. Not a few among them are the mentally unsound and the drug addicted, whose freedom to remain at large is ensured by the United States government. However, their intolerable actions have brought our nation to a place where our streets are unsafe and citizens live in fear. While this group has had its freedom ensured, there is little assurance of other's protection against their predations. This deplorable situation has made a mockery of the pursuit of life, liberty, and happiness for an untold number of Americans and of their right to equal protection under the law. The result is a groundswell of irresponsibility, encouraged by a government that would placate rather than educate, which threatens to destroy the very freedoms upon which our nation was founded. Those who would in any way abet such abuses should rightfully be considered treasonous, as aiding and giving comfort to those who would bring down our government is defined in the Constitution of the United States of America.

Whereas:

A growing segment of our population shirks its duty to conduct itself in a manner that would ensure a thriving democracy;

Whereas:

A growing segment of our population has found it necessary to give up its freedom in order to seek sanctuary from the lawless ones who prey upon them;

It then follows:

We have arrived at that place provided for in our nation's Declaration of Independence which proclaims it our right, our duty, to throw off these abuses and provide new guards for our future security.

Our nation is in despair. We must address those who would steadily undermine its foundation, all the while enjoying benefits from the very government whose ruin they would bring about. We must renew two concepts to a people greatly in need of them: the concepts of respect and responsibility. It is known to every society that these two principles empower a truly civilized people, whereas the want of them precludes a society of any but the rudest in form.

We submit that it is imperative for each of us, by our deeds, be an example to the nation's children in the tradition of our forefathers, who, at risk of life and liberty, created for us the highest form of civilization on earth, pledging to each other in this end their very lives, fortunes, and sacred honor. We betray this unprecedented selflessness when our actions cannot meet the test of a civilized conscience.

We further submit that to encourage the best in every citizen is not only to educate him to the many rights that are freely his in a democracy but also to instill in him the further truth that every right, every entitlement, bears with it an attendant responsibility. His respectful assumption of these responsibilities honors and ensures these treasured rights not only to himself but to generations of Americans yet unborn. Life in a democracy requires that no child should be devoid of this knowledge.

The time is late, but together we can turn the tide. We must again hold ourselves to the highest standards of civilization. We must once more ensure our forefathers' blessings of a just democracy to ourselves and our children and our children's children. For these blessings, once lost, may never again be found.

We, Mabel Esther Rockwell, Mildred Edith Steinberger, and Josephine Ellen Winkworth, respectfully admit that we did commit the crimes of which we are accused. And while we sought refuge in prison, we did not give up our freedom lightly. We offer our profound apologies to a nation struggling to cope with the chaos we unwittingly set in motion, and humbly rest our case. Our fervent prayer is that fellow citizens not follow our example, but work instead to institute new measures to reclaim the moral nation of our forefathers' dreams.

The following days gave newscasters and preachers plenty to talk about. Josie, Mabel, and Mil were fortunate to be protected by visitation rules and hours, because their new status as patriots produced hordes of those wanting to see them, wanting to be in their presence, wanting to touch them. They were deluged with mail and telegrams, and Frontera's telephone lines were clogged by the throngs who wanted to speak to them or ask about them. Newsmen pleaded for a bend in the no-photography rule, insisting that these ladies were not just famous in the ordinary sense of the word; they belonged to the people.

Nearly the entire prison population stood in applause when the three women entered the dining room the evening after their declaration had aired on TV. Refusing to stand, and jeering instead, were the hard cores, to whom all that fine talk was simply that: just a bunch of fine talk. "How ya gonna eat, with your mouth so fulla shit?" and "Eat shit, Goody Two-shoes!" soon became a steady chant of, "Good-y, good-y, good-y," underscoring the applause. Between the booing and the cheering, it was too much for the three women. They stood in tears, fumbling with their food trays, uncertain how to respond. They were saved by prison guards, who restored order with the threat of using the fire hose.

But their appetites had fled in the commotion. They played with their food for a time, besieged by questions from those around them, looking more distressed all the time. Sergeant Dawayne kept a close watch over them and finally approached, asking if they would like to be excused and escorted back to their rooms. She had a great regard for these ladies. And she certainly didn't want any heart attacks on her shift.

Mil's sons and their wives took the children out of school to visit these women, of whom they were now so proud. Mil was beside herself with the honor of it all; they stayed in a hotel for three days and visited her on every one of those days.

One Sunday, in the visitors' parking lot, a sleek new Lincoln Town Car emptied its odd mix of passengers. Hali had brought the Scheidlers and Betty Jean and Hap. Dressed in a fine black suit and wearing a chauffeur's cap, Hali looked elegant. Familiar with the procedures, they made their way to the visitor's center, where they were scooped up by the three famous inmates. When the commotion of their greetings settled a bit, it started up again when it was revealed that Hali had shared winning lottery numbers with three other lucky people. He was now in the process of buying Gertie and Waldo's place, and Gertie had picked out a three-stage retirement home for herself and Waldo. Now Hap and Hali would be neighbors and could play all the checkers they wanted when they weren't playing their harmonicas. Betty Jean could only dance in circles at his good fortune. Watching her, one would think it was she who had won the lottery. Hali just stood there grinning, not knowing what to say.

Hap had wanted to celebrate the three women's fame by playing his harmonica for them. But his mother made him leave it at home, telling him such things weren't allowed. Besides, they had to bring Waldo along, dressed in his new chinos, and she needed Hap to look after him. Hap dutifully got some candy out of the vending machine and settled in for a futile game of checkers with Waldo.

In the following days, Mark Wisneski relented and came to see them, too. He was overcome with affection for these brave, unassuming little ladies. And when he said his good-byes, he had to steel himself against the tears that welled up and would have spilled freely. The lump in his throat ached all the way home.

Paige, Rex, and Andy also had to wait their turns. On the day of their visit, Warden Sigurdsson again invited all three of them, and Josie, Mabel, and Mil, into her office. They took their usual places, the three women seated in the three chairs, with Rex, Paige, and Andy standing behind them.

The warden couldn't tell the three women she was honored to have them in her prison. They were, after all, felons. However, in her heart she knew these three old women had risen well above the ordinary, and that Josie's attack in the park had been the nudge that unleashed an avalanche of unresolved social problems.

In the preceding weeks, she had been concerned about what they would say in the statement they planned to write. She hoped they would know she couldn't endorse a treasonous or inflammatory statement. But their declaration had moved her deeply. The effect of its appearance in every newspaper in the nation and on radio and TV had been overwhelming.

"I know I've told you this before, ladies," she said, "but I want to commend you again for your Declaration of Interdependence. It was far more than I expected from you. Although I can't in any way condone the actions that brought you to prison, I must admit you've certainly mobilized the nation. Congress has called special sessions, and the judicial system has its back against the wall—both trying to save their professional necks by promising to untangle the sticky web of laws and entitlements that brought us to this.

"You even have educators vowing to restructure the curriculum to include good old-fashioned respect and responsibility with the other three R's," she added. "I guess the ACLU is just going to have to accept the fact that schools need the discipline necessary to create a learning atmosphere."

She picked up the newspaper on her desk and directed their attention to the feature article. "You will want to know the Tustin Marine Base is nearly ready for occupancy by its first 259 senior citizens. Of course, they can't have committed a crime in order to qualify for residency there, which may or may not be fair to the old folks who made the whole thing possible and ended up in prison. We're still not sure how this is going to work. But we're screening the hunger strikers, and we'll bring more living quarters on line as fast as we can, hoping to stop the mayhem and restore order."

Her audience murmured an approval, but no one spoke.

"It seems the situation was simply one of those things no one knew what to do about, until you ladies came along," she continued. "Wasn't it Ayn Rand who said the hardest thing to explain is the glaringly evident, which everyone has decided not to see? You know, the elephant in the living room?"

She didn't expect an answer to her question, although they all looked around, hoping someone among them might be conversant with Ayn Rand.

"Well, anyway, you ladies made it quite clear that we have all become victims of a growing, paralyzing body of laws, many at cross-purposes to their intent, as we tinkered to patch up a system that wasn't working. And all the time, the real building blocks for any successful society, moral and ethical behavior, were being overlooked—too old-fashioned, I guess, in a fast-moving world where money can buy a shortcut to anything.

"Your Declaration has certainly reminded people that, in order to maintain our system of government, we *must* have the best from each other, and self-discipline is the key. Having said all that, I want to tell you it has been my pleasure to work with you, all of you." Her eyes lingered on each of them as she spoke. "Morale has increased dramatically since you ladies have been here, and I applaud your working with the other women to teach them some very useful skills. I understand your impromptu self-improvement classes have been quite successful. I think we're going to see a lot of women leaving here prepared with skills for a better life."

She leaned back in her chair, aware that it was considered a risky thing to do in the presence of inmates. Letting your guard down could get you killed.

"Is there anything I can do for you?" she asked.

Mabel hesitated and then suggested that some quality astringents and face creams would be helpful for her grooming classes. This gave Josie the courage to ask for handheld calculators for her math classes and Mil to request some up-to-date sheet music for the keyboard. They couldn't think of another thing, but each was dying to tell the other they'd seen Officers Turner and McClung brushing hands in the hallway when they thought no one was looking.

The warden then addressed Andy and congratulated him, too, on a job well done.

"You've earned yourself quite a reputation, young man. I want to wish you all the best with the book you're writing. You can be sure everyone will be waiting for it."

Andy murmured a shy thanks for her encouraging words and assured her that he had loved every minute of working with these women. "They taught me about courage under fire, that's for sure. They gave me the opportunity of a lifetime to be in on this thing as it unfolded, and the privilege of writing a book about them." His face reddened at their broad smiles when he also revealed that he and Beverly were doing some "serious family planning."

When it seemed appropriate, the three women excused themselves. Some of the younger inmates would be gathered in the lounge waiting for them. Josie, Mabel, and Mil had work to do.

THE END

Look for the next breakaway satire
by Carol Leonard SeCoy:

LIGHTLY DUSTED CROW

When the justice system is unable to protect abused women from their tormentors, the women must find a way to help each other. Investigators Paige Turner and Mark Wisneski of the Santa Ana Police face the unimaginable: a recipe for murder. Orchestrated by Josie, Mabel, and Mil from their safe havens in prison, every abusive man's worst nightmare will become a serving of lightly dusted crow.

Visit Carol's website, carolsecoy.com. Your questions or comments are welcome there. You will also find a discussion guide for book groups.

6141037R00181

Made in the USA
San Bernardino, CA
02 December 2013